PENGUIN BOOKS

SUCCESSION

'A gripping story . . . Juxtaposing illuminating contemporary accounts of the Wars of the Roses with breathtaking insights into the minds of the principal players, *Succession* puts the conflict into a compelling context whilst exploring the human cost of the bloody, bitter birth of the Tudor dynasty' *Lancashire Evening Post*

'Livi Michael is new to historical fiction and it shows, in a good way. Focused on the earlier years of the Wars of the Roses (about which I knew nothing – and nor did she, by her own admission, before she started), this novel is wonderfully stylistically fresh, making inventive use of contemporary chronicles, which it mimics to blackly comic effect. But it's also a heartfelt account of the eye-opening, hair-raising early life of Margaret Beaufort, mother of Henry VII' Suzannah Dunn, *Waterstones blog*, 'Author's Books of the Year 2014'

'*Succession* is a powerfully written account of the 15th-century Wars of the Roses . . . finely balanced between history and fiction, and a fascinating, riveting read' *Historical Novel Society*

'In *Succession*, Livi Michael engages meticulously with the diverse historical accounts of the Wars of the Roses, but she also invests intimate and poignant humanity into the personal tragedies of an era wrought with conflict and terror' Elizabeth Fremantle, author of *Queen's Gambit*

ABOUT THE AUTHOR

Livi Michael has published four novels for adults: *Under a Thin Moon,* which won the Arthur Welton award in 1992; *Their Angel Reach,* which won the Faber prize in 1995; *All the Dark Air* (1997), which was shortlisted for the Mind Award; and *Inheritance*, which won a Society of Authors award. Livi has two sons and lives in Greater Manchester. She teaches creative writing at the Manchester Metropolitan University and has been a senior lecturer in creative writing at Sheffield Hallam University.

Succession

LIVI MICHAEL

PENGUIN BOOKS

PENGUIN BOOKS

UK | USA | Canada | Ireland | Australia
India | New Zealand | South Africa

Penguin Books is part of the Penguin Random House group of companies whose addresses can be found at global.penguinrandomhouse.com.

Penguin Random House UK

First published by Fig Tree 2014
Published in Penguin Books 2015
001

Typeset in Dante MT Std by Palimpsest Book Production Ltd, Falkirk, Stirlingshire
Printed in Great Britain by Clays Ltd, St Ives plc

A CIP catalogue record for this book is available from the British Library

MIX
Paper from responsible sources
FSC® C018179
FSC www.fsc.org

Penguin Random House is committed to a sustainable future for our business, our readers and our planet. This book is made from Forest Stewardship Council® certified paper.

To Anna Pollard,
a writer's friend

Contents

Lancaster and York
Family Tree

LANCASTER

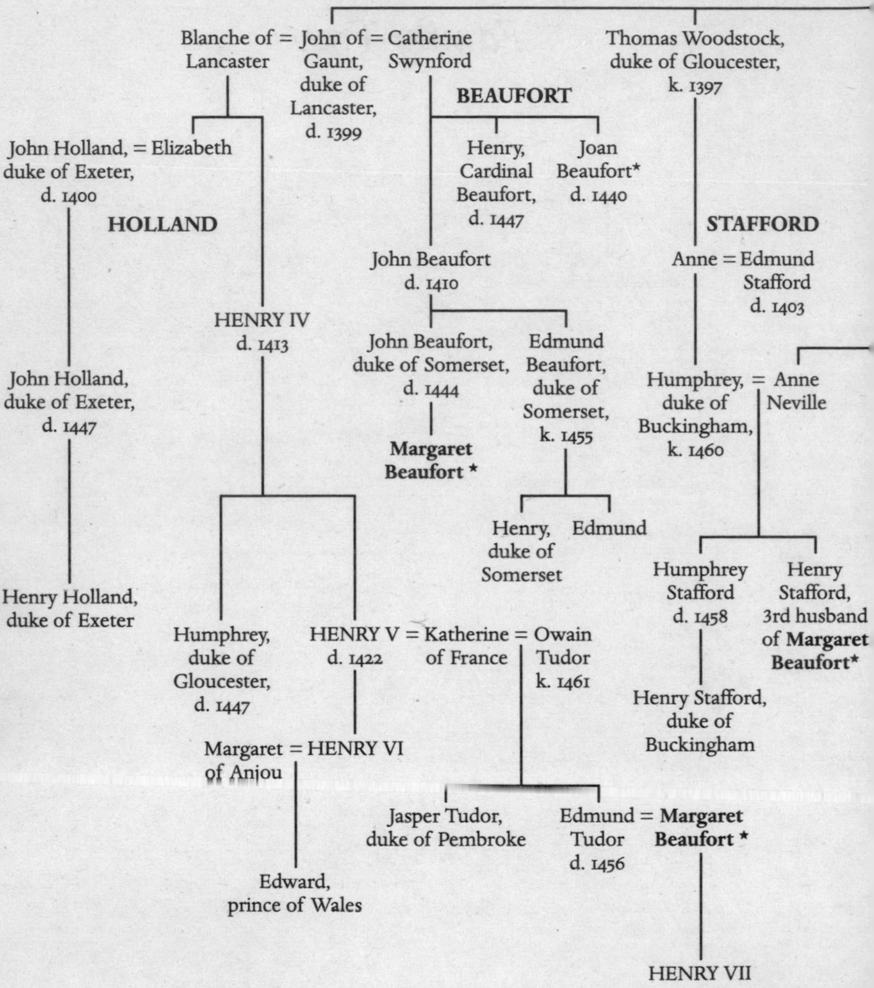

NB children are not necessarily in order of birth
d. = died
k. = killed
*appears more than once

YORK

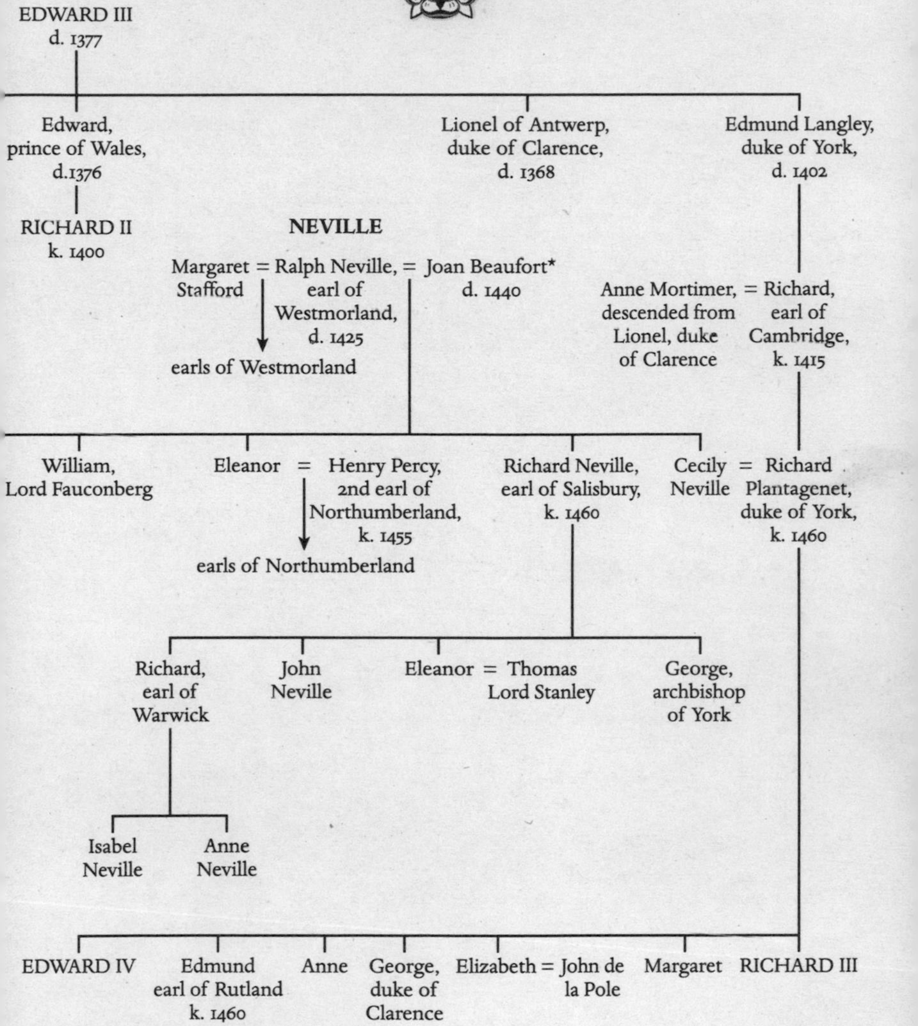

EDWARD III
d. 1377

Edward,
prince of Wales,
d.1376

Lionel of Antwerp,
duke of Clarence,
d. 1368

Edmund Langley,
duke of York,
d. 1402

RICHARD II
k. 1400

NEVILLE

Margaret = Ralph Neville, = Joan Beaufort*
Stafford earl of d. 1440
 Westmorland,
 d. 1425

earls of Westmorland

Anne Mortimer, = Richard,
descended from earl of
Lionel, duke Cambridge,
of Clarence k. 1415

William,
Lord Fauconberg

Eleanor = Henry Percy,
 2nd earl of
 Northumberland,
 k. 1455

earls of Northumberland

Richard Neville,
earl of Salisbury,
k. 1460

Cecily = Richard
Neville Plantagenet,
 duke of York,
 k. 1460

Richard,
earl of
Warwick

John
Neville

Eleanor = Thomas
 Lord Stanley

George,
archbishop
of York

Isabel
Neville

Anne
Neville

EDWARD IV Edmund Anne George, Elizabeth = John de Margaret RICHARD III
 earl of Rutland duke of la Pole
 k. 1460 Clarence

Key Characters

Margaret of Anjou, wife of Henry VI; daughter of René of Anjou and Isabella of Lorraine; niece of Charles VII of France

Edmund Beaufort, Earl, later 2nd Duke of Somerset; brother of John Beaufort, 1st Duke of Somerset; uncle of Margaret Beaufort

Margaret Beaufort, daughter of John Beaufort, 1st Duke of Somerset, and Margaret Beauchamp; great-granddaughter of John of Gaunt, Duke of Lancaster; great-great-granddaughter of Edward III

Elizabeth Carew (**Betsy**), Margaret Beaufort's nurse

Alice Chaucer, wife of William de la Pole, Earl of Suffolk; granddaughter of Geoffrey Chaucer

Edward, Prince of Wales, son of Henry VI and Queen Margaret; also nephew of Margaret Beaufort and Edmund Tudor

Henry VI of England and France; descended from John of Gaunt, who was the third son of King Edward III

Humphrey, Duke of Gloucester, uncle of Henry VI; brother of Henry V

Anne Neville, Duchess of Buckingham; wife of Humphrey Stafford, Duke of Buckingham; sister of Cecily Neville, Duchess of York

Cecily Neville, Duchess of York; wife of Richard, Duke of York

Richard Neville, Earl of Salisbury; brother of Cecily Neville, Duchess of York; father of Richard Neville, Earl of Warwick

Richard Neville, Earl of Warwick; son of the Earl of Salisbury; nephew of Cecily Neville, Duchess of York, and Anne Neville, Duchess of Buckingham

Edward Plantagenet, Earl of March, later King Edward IV; son of Cecily Neville and Richard, Duke of York

Richard Plantagenet, Duke of York; descended on his mother's side from Lionel of Antwerp, second son of King Edward III, and on his father's side from Edmund of Langley, fourth son of King Edward III

John de la Pole, son of William de la Pole and Alice Chaucer; m. (1) Margaret Beaufort, (2) Elizabeth, daughter of Richard of York

William de la Pole, Earl, later Duke of Suffolk; m. Alice Chaucer

Henry Stafford, son of Duke and Duchess of Buckingham; m. Margaret Beaufort

Humphrey Stafford, 1st Duke of Buckingham; m. Anne Neville, sister of Cecily Neville and the Earl of Salisbury

Edmund Tudor, Earl of Richmond; half-brother of King Henry VI; m. Margaret Beaufort

Henry Tudor, son of Edmund Tudor and Margaret Beaufort, later King Henry VII

Jasper Tudor, Earl of Pembroke; half-brother of Henry VI; Edmund Tudor's younger brother

Owen Tudor, father of Edmund and Jasper; m. Katherine of Valois, widow of King Henry V

Prologue

Everything frightened her when she was four years old. A cluster of shadows at the end of the corridor, light winking off a door handle, the open mouth of a hunted stag on the long picture, and her own footsteps tap-tapping eerily, erratically, on the tiled floor.

She had lost her way. She had somehow become detached from her nurse, and all the corridors and doorways looked the same. She was too small to open any of the great doors. Worst of all, right at the end of the hallway and half hidden in shadow, there was an image of the devil, rising out of a crack in the earth, chewing the limbs of the damned.

And she could only totter towards him, because she didn't know where else to go.

If she screamed, and no one heard her, the devil would surely hear.

Her dress was heavy and sticky, chafing her beneath the arms, her breathing hoarse and uneven, coming out in ragged whimpers.

She knew already that it was a terrible disgrace to cry, except in penitence.

Finally she banged the flat of her hands against the carved panel of one of the great doors, and to her surprise it moved smoothly away. She stood in the doorway, light streaming towards her from two immense windows so that she could hardly see.

Then she saw his legs in their silk stockings; the long, pointed shoes.

She had hardly seen the duke since coming to live with him as his ward, yet she knew it was him. There was something spread out on the table in front of him and he was bending over it. She could see more clearly now his thinning grey hair, and the powerful nose with spectacles perched unevenly on the end of it. His lips moved as he read.

Some impulse made her step forward; she didn't know what. She was almost as scared of the duke as of the devil.

He didn't look up until she had nearly reached the table.

Hello, he said, his watery blue eyes clearing. *You must be . . . Margaret?*

And when she didn't answer, he asked if she would like to see a marvellous thing. And when she didn't answer that, he held his hand out and she walked awkwardly over to him, and then he picked her up and stood her on a chair. He brushed the tears from her face with a quick thumb and told her not to touch.

Do you know what this is? he asked, and she shook her head.

It was a great map, he told her, a map of the world.

It curled at the corners and he had pressed it down with weights of various kinds: a small box, an ink stand, a wooden head.

The world was all colours; a mass of colours surrounded by blue. Around the edges the twelve faces of the wind blew the sea in all directions and tossed the little boats upon it. He talked her through the countries.

This is France, see, and this is Brittany, and this – this is England, where you live now.

She listened politely, not believing him. How could England be so small? She waited for him to explain the other features of the map: the fire-breathing dragons and salamanders, great snails and griffins and giants, beasts joined together with heads at both ends, and men with ears trailing along the ground.

In the centre of the world there was Jerusalem, of course, bounded by a circle that was God's holy tower. To the west there was an oval country, where unicorns played. There, he told her, it was possible to find the well of youth, guarded by two-headed geese in the pepper forests of Malabar, where there were trees that grew lambs from giant pods, and wool-bearing hens.

At the top were Adam and Eve in the Garden of Eden. Five rivers spouted from this garden, flowing south and west. If it were possible to sail south on one of these rivers, he said, past the line of the Equator, you would see men who walked upside down on their hands, and rain falling upwards on to the earth.

But she was looking at the margins of the map, which were decorated with feathers and shells, and further up were the sun and moon, representing the firmament, and beyond that, of course, the glory of God. Which some men maintained you could sail to, he said, following her gaze.

She listened carefully, not liking to say that his fingers were digging into her as he held her on the chair. Sunlight shifted into cloud, and there was a spatter of rain at the windows.

He had sailed to some of the countries himself, he told her, and knew for a fact that Ireland was not near Spain. *And yet*, he said, half smiling into her serious face, *there is the world we live in, and the world of the imagination, and who is to say which is the more real?*

And now he was smiling not so much at her as at some inward vision.

He released her then, so that she tottered slightly, and he put out one hand to steady her, then began to roll the map up, methodically and swiftly rolling up the known world. She had a sudden dizzying sense of scale: England a small, brown corner of the world and herself a tiny speck on it.

He spoke about his time abroad, especially in France, where he had been captured by a woman wearing armour.

Do not underestimate the strangeness of the world, he told her. And then he said that this woman, who was known as Jeanne d'Arc, was the bravest woman that ever lived.

And then her nurse had appeared, flustered, anxious, and the duke had lifted her down from the chair, and she had hurried towards her in a stumbling run, back to the known world.

Later, much later, she learned that the world had changed from the flatness of a map into a globe, that it was not bounded by dragons and giants but by a sea of ice at both poles, that Jerusalem was no longer the centre of the world, and that there was a new land to the west, which was bigger than anyone had realized.

She learned also that her guardian had been accused of treason, that he had lost much of the nation's land in France, and that he had plotted to take the throne by marrying her to his son. For which crimes he had been sent to the Tower. And upon his release from the Tower he had been murdered on a ship. And the sword that killed him was rusty: it had taken six blows to sever his head. After which his headless body had been thrown upon a beach.

Still, when she thought of him, she remembered that afternoon in his study, the hiss of rain at the windows. He had spoken of a brave woman with deference, she remembered that. And he had unravelled the world for her, bigger, more colourful and stranger than she had ever known.

PART I: 1444–50

I

1444: The Earl of Suffolk Stands Proxy for the King

In this time by means of the forenamed Earl of Suffolk a marriage was concluded between the king and Dame Margaret, the king's daughter of Sicily and Jerusalem, a woman of exemplary birth and chargeable to this land, for . . . it was agreed by the king . . . that he should give over all his right and title in the duchy of Anjou and the earldom of Maine, the which two lordships were in the keep of Normandy. The which conclusion of marriage was the beginning of the loss of France and of much heaviness and sorrow in this land.

Great Chronicle of London

She was not beautiful in the English sense, being small and dark, but there was a vivid quality to her, an intense attentiveness. She walked like a dancer; her ribs were lifted, her collar bones open so that her neck seemed long. It took most people some time to realize she was not tall. Her father had given her no dowry, so she walked taller than ever. Seed pearls glistened like tiny teeth in her hair.

The Earl of Suffolk adjusted his body to an attitude of admiration and deference. She was fourteen years old, but it seemed to him that she would require a great deal of deference. As she drew closer he could see the minute contractions and dilations of her pupils, a nerve quivering in the soft upper lip.

'They will not love me, I think,' she had said to him once, with that air of certainty that left no room for doubt or hesitation. He had said that of course the people would love her, just as the king had loved her, from the first. Though, privately, he considered that *love* was an accommodating word, like *beauty.*

It was true that the king had felt *a passion fix't and unconquerable* from first seeing her portrait. The dim miniature which to everyone else had seemed unclear, slightly damaged by its journey, had in the king's eyes resolved into a composite of everything he yearned for, for himself and the nation. He had attached himself to this vision with that fixity of which he was unexpectedly capable. Amenable to most things, he would from time to time grow obdurate as a stone; there was no reasoning with him, no persuasion. That was why the earl had accepted, on his behalf, this young girl who brought with her no dowry, who had to be bought at the great cost of the territories of Maine and Anjou.

It had been part of his mission to win her confidence, and he had won it. In any company she looked first to him before speaking or taking a decision. Now he smiled encouragingly as she took her place beside him, and although she did not smile back he could see a certain release in the set of her shoulders, the tilt of her head. They stood together while the choirs sang in a soft curtain of light that came through the great windows, and the earl had the sense of being as insubstantial as one of the motes of dust that danced about in its rays.

Then there was the journey to England.

After several hours at sea the clouds gathered out of nowhere; the sky began to brood and churn, and the sea to broil and foam. It twisted like the coils of some monstrous intestine, spewing out extraneous matter from its depths.

The crew, fleetingly illuminated by flashes of light, battled frantically with the sails. Soon the air was nine parts water and it was difficult to breathe. All the passengers were ordered below, where they clung to one another and prayed.

Some said they saw armies marching from the battlements of the sea, while others saw the faces of devils in the waves, and yet others the faces of their saints, to whom they cried out for aid. The first ship was dashed against hidden rocks but remained afloat, lurching dangerously, with part of its belly gone and some of the crew swept overboard.

One man swore he saw the Son of God walking towards him. In His hand He held a shining cross and His face was smiling. This smiling Jesus came towards him on a wave, and the man tried to cry out to Him, but his mouth was full of the storming sea, and so the Son of God walked past.

Yet he was saved, this man, by the beam of timber from the broken ship to which he clung, though afterwards he always said he had been saved by the smiling Jesus. In later years, when he told this tale, some laughed, while others grew sober and joined in with fantastic tales of their own, and others asked, half mocking, what the Son of God had been smiling about, which was hard to say. Also it was hard to describe the nature of the smile. 'Was it pitiful?' they asked him. No. 'Was it joyous, for He was bringing His flock home?' No. Nor was it triumphant, nor sad. When they doubted him, because he could not describe the face of his Lord, nor say how he knew for certain that it was Him, he remembered how in childhood he had walked across the rafters of a burnt-out house for a dare. And in a burst of inspiration he said that it was just as if He was right pleased at being able to walk on water again.

And at this several members of his audience withdrew, shaking their heads, and saying that his wits had been addled by the sea.

But the Earl of Suffolk had been charged with the duty of bringing the king's new wife back to him. Somehow he got her into a tiny boat together with his own wife, Lady Alice, and a boatman who rowed them strenuously towards the shore.

Several people had assembled on the sands, startled by the news that their new queen was landing. No one had expected her to land there, at that point. But the mayor of that town, Porchester, was a man who considered himself equal to any task that the Lord should throw at him, and he ordered carpets to be laid across the beach, and hastily summoned a small band of musicians to play the royal party in. They waited for more than an hour in the rain and wind, while the little boats bobbed restlessly back and forth and the bigger ships lurched on the horizon. As soon as they drew near enough the mayor commanded his men to run into the water and haul them in.

So the earl at length emerged on to the shore, carrying the crumpled princess, though his legs were unsteady, surprised by the feel of land. His soaked clothes clung to him, his hair was plastered to his head, and he was only recognizable as the earl because of the insignia he wore. He stumbled drunkenly across the carpets, holding what looked like a bundle of rags, so that the mayor and all who stood with him doubted what they saw, and the musicians began to play uncertainly, out of time.

Suffolk could think only of how he had begged the king not to give him this mission. His right arm hurt where he had been battered against the side of the ship, and his ribs felt bruised, so that he carried the princess with some difficulty, but she was too sick to walk and he would not entrust her to anyone else. He concentrated on putting one foot in front of the other, and on not dropping his royal charge as he trod unevenly over the carpets. By the time he reached the mayor he had hardly enough breath left to request that they should be taken to a shelter where the princess could lie down. He saw doubt in the eyes of the mayor, so he spoke sharply, and they were conducted to a tiny cottage where the startled occupants offered them what they could. And he carried the princess all the way, though his right arm grew numb in the process. He was too old for this, he thought; he felt every day of his forty-eight years.

When at last he set her down on a wooden pallet with a straw mattress, her face was as white as death and she could only whisper at him in French. He knelt down heavily to hear what she was saying, and found she was enquiring about the other ships, and her attendants, and the storm. He assured her that they were not lost; it was entirely possible that some would be swept up later that day or the next, or further along the coast.

He thought she must have misheard him, for despite his assurances she turned her face away and wept. Gradually he understood that she was weeping for a greater loss.

2

The King Prepares to Meet His New Bride

Our dear and best beloved wife the queen is yet sick of the labour and indisposition of the seas, by occasion of which the pox has been broken out upon her.

Letter from Henry VI to the Lord Chancellor

As soon as Suffolk was admitted to his presence, the king broke away from his attendants and went straight to him. The earl sank clumsily to his knees, but the king raised him up and kissed him on both cheeks and clung to him in a long embrace.

Suffolk, still suffering from his ribs, and unused to the awkward weight of a king in his arms, winced, and the king drew back at once in concern.

'You are injured!'

'It is nothing, your grace.'

The king immediately embraced him again, more carefully, and Suffolk noticed that he was quivering with excitement or relief.

'She is really here?' he said, finally releasing the earl.

'She is, your grace.'

The king's face was luminous with joy. He could look, in such moments, like a handsome man.

'And – she is well?'

'She is recovering marvellously, my lord.'

In fact, the princess was far from well. She had been taken to a convent to recuperate, but was showing no signs of improvement as yet. But Suffolk assured the king that it was nothing serious, she merely wanted to look her best, as women do, when she met her new husband for the first time. As soon as she was well enough she would be taken in state to Southampton, and the king could meet her there.

Actually, the delay had allowed Suffolk to hire a dressmaker from London to create a new trousseau for the princess. When her cases and trunks had been recovered, and the contents inspected, the earl had been appalled by the state of her wardrobe: old dresses visibly made over and mended, some of them threadbare. He had felt a spasm of rage towards René, who had sent his daughter off so shoddily to be England's queen. Then his wife had suggested that they should contact her dressmaker in London. There was nothing for it but to pay for this himself. The princess had no money; she had already begun to pawn her plate. To spare her feelings he had told her that the rest of her clothes had been lost in the storm.

But his majesty was still talking.

'I hardly slept all night for fear, when I heard,' he said, 'but that is nothing now – God heard my prayers.'

You should have prayed harder, Suffolk thought, *then maybe there would not have been a storm.*

'He heard my prayers,' the king repeated, 'and she is here at last, safe and well. The people will see this as a sign of God's blessing on our union.'

The people, as the earl well knew, would see nothing of the kind.

'It is all thanks to you – you have saved her from the teeth of the storm!'

Suffolk bowed and said words to the effect that he had done his duty to the best of his ability. Not even a storm at sea could part two people who were destined to be together. The king nodded emphatically.

'Does she speak of me?' he asked eagerly.

'All the time, your grace.'

In fact, she hadn't mentioned him at all; she seemed to have fallen into a state of melancholy, from which Suffolk hoped the new clothes would rouse her.

But the king was restless. Some perfunctory questions followed, about the health of Suffolk's wife, then he said to his attendants, 'I would speak with my Lord of Suffolk alone,' and ushered him into a tiny room.

Suffolk anticipated, with some anxiety, that awkward questions might follow about the deal he had brokered with the French, about the loss of lands and money. The cost of transporting the queen had exceeded the sum allotted, and some of the fifty-six ships were as yet unaccounted for, but as soon as the king turned to him he could see that he was full of suppressed excitement.

'I have a great plan,' he said, 'for when we meet.'

He outlined his plan to the earl, who allowed his gaze to rest on the soft squares of sunset on the wall. Each square was alive with the nodding shadows of leaves, stirred now by a much gentler wind. He was thinking that the king, who had not yet seen his bride, had never once asked the question that any other king might have asked: whether she was as beautiful as her portrait had suggested. And this was because in his mind she was beautiful, fixed and eternally so; Suffolk might have presented him with an old washerwoman and he would have greeted her with the same delight. Suffolk thought of what the king's tutor had said when he had begged to be released from his duty of instructing the king: that either he was a natural fool or a holy innocent, and he did not know which was more dangerous to the nation.

But the king was looking at him now with anticipation. He had pressed his fingers to his mouth in the kind of unkingly gesture that his tutor had always tried to train out of him, and Suffolk realized that he was expected to speak.

'It is a marvellous plan, your grace,' he said, and the king at once expanded upon it in greater detail, while Suffolk again contemplated the light from the windows, how beautifully it fell upon the wall. A few days ago he thought he had seen his death in the rearing waves, but now there was only this soft beauty. And the king's voice, outlining his marvellous plan, with which he was expected to collude.

I am so tired, he thought, *so tired*.

3

The New Queen is Deceived

When the queen landed in England the king dressed himself as a squire, the [Earl] of Suffolk doing the same, and took her a letter which he said the King of England had written. While the queen read the letter the king took stock of her, saying that a woman may be seen very well when she reads a letter, and the queen never found out it was the king because she was engrossed in reading, and she never looked at the king in his squire's dress, who remained on his knees all the time.

Milanese ambassador

She had hated it, of course; who wouldn't?

They had knelt before her for some time while she read the letter with the utmost concentration. And several times over, or so it seemed to Suffolk, who knelt behind the king with his head lowered, and thought about his complaining knees. It was not a complicated letter, nor overly effusive; the king had read it to him for his approval. It bade her cordial welcome and assured her of the king's affections.

Suffolk hoped that, whatever the king thought he might see in her preoccupied face, it would not change his mind or his heart. And that the princess would not keep them waiting too much longer or, worse still, lose her temper with them for bringing her a letter rather than the king. As it was, when she had finally finished, she turned to her chamberlain and said, 'But why does he not come here in person?'

Suffolk thought then that the king might give them both away; he could see suppressed laughter in his majesty's shoulders. It might have been the moment for him to declare himself, but the princess turned away in evident disappointment and, after a pause, the king rose somewhat clumsily and left the room, and Suffolk followed.

Outside, the king put back his hood from his thinning hair, and Suffolk was relieved to see that he was smiling. But he said nothing, only with a series of gestures and nods conveyed that Suffolk should go back in. Then he mounted his horse and rode away.

Resisting the urge to sigh, Suffolk took off the cloak and hood identifying him as squire and went back into the room. The princess looked up at him with a face full of eager uncertainty, and the earl said, 'Most serene highness, what do you think of the squire who brought you the letter?'

The princess's eyes moved fractionally from left to right as she scanned Suffolk's eyes. She was disconcerted, but not yet suspicious of a trick.

'I did not think anything of him,' she said. 'I was reading the letter.'

But realization dawned on her with that quick apprehension that often caused her to respond to what people said before they had finished speaking.

'Ah!' she cried. 'Why did he not tell me?'

And Suffolk, who had every sympathy for the princess in that moment, said, 'It was a whim, your highness – it pleased his majesty to see you unawares.'

She turned away from him, biting her lip, and said, 'But I kept him on his knees all that time!'

The earl assured her that she had done nothing wrong.

'But why? Did he want to see what he thought of me? What did he think of me?'

'He thought you were delightful – his most gracious beloved, soon to be queen.'

'But what did he *say*?'

The king had said nothing, but she would not believe that, and so for the next few minutes Suffolk had a hard time of it, until he promised to go and escort the king back to her in proper guise that evening.

And when they returned with the king looking almost regal, tallish and slender in his royal clothes, she was waiting for him in a new gown created for her by the dressmaker. She had been sitting, but rose, of course, at the king's entry, then sank into the deepest curtsy with admirable grace. He raised her and said nothing, seemingly overcome, and she looked at him earnestly, and Suffolk wondered what she saw. The king had a boyish face, overly sensitive, almost raw, as if he had never grown that extra skin that all courtiers necessarily developed. Then he smiled at her, that unique smile of great kindness, and Suffolk was startled to see that her eyes filled with tears. She stood blinking rapidly, momentarily unable to speak. The king said a few words, extended his hand and led her to the table. And Suffolk saw that it was all right between them, and he felt a vast relief – he had not realized until that moment how oppressed he had felt by the whole business. But the king's ideal passion was undimmed, and she had responded, not to the way he looked, but to his kindness, which was what she needed, after all.

And if the king and queen were all right with one another, he thought, surely the nation would follow.

4

The Wheel of Fortune

The next time Suffolk saw the king he was restless, and inclined to talk about the things that vexed him. The Duke of Gloucester, his uncle, was speaking out of turn again. He still assumed an authority over the king that was no longer his, and had spoken openly against his nephew's marriage. Then there were all the demands for money from his cousin the Duke of York, in Normandy, and the trouble in Brittany caused by another cousin, the recently deceased Duke of Somerset.

Suffolk and his wife, Lady Alice, sat to one side of the king, making commiserating noises when necessary. To Suffolk's relief, he did not mention the loss of Maine and Anjou (it had been decided that it would be best not to break this news generally just yet); the fact that Suffolk had only brokered a truce rather than peace with France; the excessive cost of transporting the princess. He returned several times to the subject of the Duke of York, whose overweening pride made him ever more demanding, and to the tragic Duke of Somerset – who had driven a much harder bargain than York, it had to be said, because he had never wanted the commission in Gascony in the first place.

The king's voice was becoming somewhat querulous. He was not like his father, whose rage was to be averted at all cost; he was an injured boy, complaining that it wasn't *fair*. Also, he was distressed by his cousin's death. However aggravating Somerset had been, and incompetent – failing to settle the war in Gascony and almost causing war in Brittany in the process – his death was something of a calamity for the king, who had so few relatives to rely on. Every attempt had been made to suppress the rumours of suicide, but rumour, like the tide, could not be suppressed.

'How is my lady, the duchess?' Lady Alice said, her large blue eyes raised sympathetically to the king, who shook his head.

'How can she be?' he murmured. For Somerset's wife was beside herself, it was said. She had taken to her rooms and would not come out.

'I have visited her, of course,' Lady Alice said, and the king looked at her in some surprise.

'She is accepting few visitors,' Suffolk added, 'but my lady wife is always welcome.'

'I took gifts for the little girl,' said Lady Alice. 'She is such a bright little creature – you should have heard her prattling to our son, John – they played together so sweetly. It was good for them both to have a playmate.'

Suffolk gave her an appreciative glance. He had often had cause to be grateful that he had married, late in life, a clever woman.

'They are of an age, are they not?' said the king.

'Just a few months apart,' his wife said. 'And they took to one another right away.'

Suffolk could almost hear the king thinking. Somerset's daughter, Margaret Beaufort, was heiress to a great fortune and everyone at court was competing to be her guardian. It was known that Somerset had stipulated that custody of his only child should remain with his wife, but then, the king could not afford to pay Suffolk directly for his services in France.

'I believe that both mother and daughter would benefit from a little time apart,' his wife was saying, 'while the duchess recovers from her illness.'

But the king's restless mind had shifted back to York, whose latest bill for his expenses was almost forty thousand pounds.

'So much money!' he said, bewildered. 'How can he have exceeded his budget by such an amount? He has not even accomplished his project.'

'I hear that rumours of his efficiency are greatly exaggerated,' Suffolk said.

'Forty thousand pounds!'

Suffolk said that bills, like rumours, were also often exaggerated. 'Your majesty has no way of knowing how he is spending his money,' he said.

'I am his *king*,' the king said, as if this should settle the matter.

'He has the mind of a market trader,' Suffolk said. 'He should know that your majesty has better things to spend his money on at this time. Your loyal subjects would not dream of asking you for money.'

Suffolk thought the king looked at him sharply at this point, before returning to his theme. The Duke of York and the Duke of Gloucester were in league together, he did not doubt it – they conspired against him at every turn.

'There should be more dukes,' the king said suddenly. It was not good for one or two men to be so elevated above other nobles – it was time to rock the bastion of their pride. Suffolk dared not look at him. He glanced instead at his wife, who had dropped her own gaze downwards.

But the king was looking at Suffolk with luminous eyes; he would have to make some response.

'His majesty giveth, and his majesty taketh away,' he ventured, and the king's eyes registered uncertainty for a moment, then understanding.

'You have asked for nothing, for all your services,' he said, in a voice full of suppressed emotion, and Suffolk hastily assured him that he wished for nothing – service to his king was his best reward – and Lady Alice said, with apparent inconsequence, that if it were the king's wish, she would ask the Duke of Somerset's widow to stay with them for a while.

'With little Margaret, because she would be such an excellent companion for our son.'

'She would be like a sister to him,' Suffolk added, and the Lady Alice said that she would treat Margaret as her own daughter, placing one hand on her stomach in a poignant reminder that she was unlikely to have any more children.

'I am sure she would benefit from the company,' said the king after a pause.

Suffolk's wife leaned forward earnestly. 'I would instruct her myself, to the best of my ability. It would be my great pleasure to do so.'

The king nodded slowly. 'She would have much to gain from the care and instruction of the most cultivated woman in the realm,' he said.

He was referring, of course, to the fact that Lady Alice was the granddaughter of the great poet Chaucer, and was herself the patron of poets and scholars. 'She should come to you,' he said, then, remembering that he had promised the duke that his only child should remain with her mother, added, 'Perhaps not to stay – but she should visit you often. I will write to my lady the duchess, and to the archbishop – the matter should be settled.'

Lady Alice was overwhelmed, and Suffolk's gestures indicated that he was lost for words. 'Your majesty is more than gracious,' he said.

On the way home they did not discuss it further, for their marriage had reached the stage where there was an understanding between them about all important matters, and the smile in his wife's eyes said it all. Suffolk sat with more ease than he had in months: the set of his shoulders, the tilt of his head, proclaimed a sense of well-being. The mission which so far had brought nothing but disaster now seemed set to yield a greater benefit than he had thought. For little Margaret Beaufort, Somerset's daughter, brought with her the Beaufort fortune, and the advantageous alliance with her uncle, Edmund Beaufort. Who was currently the Earl of Somerset, but might soon be the new duke. All because of the fortuitous demise of little Margaret's father, the late Duke of Somerset.

The noble heart of a man of such high rank . . . was moved to extreme indignation; and being unable to bear the stain of so great a disgrace, he accelerated his death by putting an end to his existence, it is generally said; preferring thus to cut short his sorrow rather than pass a life of misery, labouring under so disgraceful a charge.

Crowland Chronicle

5

1445: The Coronation

On that Friday the mayor of London with the aldermen, sheriffs and commons of the city, rode to Blackheath in Kent, where they remained on horseback until the queen's coming. Then they accompanied her to the Tower of London, where she rested all night. The king, in honour of the queen and her first coming, made forty-six new Knights of the Bath. On the morrow, in the afternoon, the queen came from the Tower in a horse-bier with two steeds decorated all in white damask powdered with gold, as was the clothing she had on; her hair was combed down around her shoulders with a coronel of gold, rich pearls and precious stones and there were nineteen chariots of ladies and gentlewomen as well as all the crafts of the city of London, who proceeded on foot in their best array to St Paul's.

Brut Chronicle

Suffolk's men rode among the crowds, ushering those who were cheering to the front, rounding up and harrying those who expressed dissent, who shouted that their new queen had beggared the country and 'was not worth ten marks'. They saw to it that the conduits ran with red and white wine for the full three hours of the procession, that the streets were hung with silver and gold silks, that no one should tear down or make off with the valuable hangings, and that everyone was supplied with bunches of daisies, or marguerites, the new queen's emblem, to throw in her path. Suffolk himself rode ahead of the queen, carrying a sceptre of ivory with a golden dove on its head. The procession stopped in several places, where musicians played and children sang, and verses by the court poet, John Lydgate, were recited. An array of gods and goddesses, lowered on harnesses from the heavens, reminded the new queen that her main duty was procreation, to bring forth an heir to the throne, and the figures of Peace and Plenty blessed the fruit of her womb. Three days of feasting, tournaments and miracle plays followed, and in all that time Suffolk sat at the king's side while his wife tended the new queen.

It was enough time to ponder his changing fortunes; the fact that he was descended not from the nobility but from wool merchants in Hull who had grown wealthy enough to bail kings out of their debts. After his older brother had died at the Battle of Agincourt he had inherited the title of Earl of Suffolk. Now he might soon be duke, though the king had not mentioned this again. At any rate, his pedigree was now held to be unimpeachable.

The same could not be said for the Duke of York, whose father had been executed for plotting to kill Henry V – and whose mother came from the Mortimer line; from that Mortimer, in fact, who had deposed the second King Edward and, it was commonly believed, had arranged to have him killed. Yet this man had his ardent supporters, men who said that his claim to the throne was better than the king's. He had money and influence and a growing brood of children.

It was, of course, fervently to be hoped that the king would have children. If there were no heir, either the Duke of Gloucester or the Duke of York would be in line for the throne. Neither of them was a supporter of Suffolk, nor of his policy in France. It could be said, however, that little Margaret Beaufort, who had already been to stay at Suffolk's home, would have her own claim. For the king had been an only child, and his family was not extensive. There were his half brothers, of course, though they were the sons of a Welsh steward; Suffolk did not think anyone would take them seriously.

At the end of the first feast, after all the ladies had danced together, Suffolk rose to dance with the queen. His wife handed her to him with her dazzling smile. He could feel the tension in the queen's young body, lithe and bristling. Her face was flushed with open affection for him, and it seemed to the earl, as he whirled her around on his arm, that they were natural partners.

6

The Earl of Somerset

At the time we are talking about there were in the kingdom of England two parties contending for the government and administration of the king and his people. In one of these parties there was Humphrey Duke of Gloucester, King Henry's uncle, and Richard Duke of York . . . the other was an alliance between [the earls of] Somerset and Suffolk.

Jean de Waurin

While it was obviously unfortunate that all three of his older brothers were now dead, the Earl of Somerset could not help but see it as significant. Who would have thought that he, the fourth son, would have inherited all those lands and titles? Was it any coincidence that he was the only brother to have a large family of his own, and the only one to enjoy the special favour of the king? Not to mention the queen, who was, even now, waiting breathlessly for him to defeat his opponent.

It had to be said that he cut a better figure than any of his brothers, especially poor John, who might have been mistaken for a clerk of law rather than a courtier or general. No one would make that mistake about Edmund Beaufort. Sunlight glinted on his helmet and the tip of his lance as he paraded round the field; he wore a whole garland of marguerites in the queen's honour, and a silk ribbon as her token.

The king and queen sat in the gallery, with Suffolk at their side: Suffolk, who was descended from a family of wool-pedlars but was richer than Midas, people said. He had been granted wardship of Somerset's niece, little Margaret Beaufort, and was assiduously cultivating an alliance with Somerset – who had not discouraged this, because it seemed to him that something was necessary to offset the influence of the Dukes of Gloucester and York.

The king had already said that there should be more dukes in the land.

And Somerset, like York, was cousin to the king. His great-grandfather was Edward III, but the Beaufort line was illegitimate, and had been debarred by the fourth King Henry from any claim to the throne.

Still, it was not beyond one king to correct what another had done.

It seemed to the Earl of Somerset, as the crowds cheered for him, that while the mind of God might be impenetrable to some, to him it was transparently evident. He, the fourth son, had been chosen to restore the family fortunes, its honour, its greatness, as he had done once before in France. He had already suggested to the king that he would do a better job there than the Duke of York. York, who had referred to the Beauforts as 'that bastard clan'.

The bugle sounded and the earl took his place to one side of the wooden fence. He could feel the tension in his horse; a coil of power. As he lifted his lance and prepared to charge, all he could see was not his opponent in the field, but his absent enemy, the Duke of York.

7

The Duke of York

As Governor-General of the duchy of Normandy, Richard of York's duty was to protect this country from the French our enemies, and during this time in office he governed admirably and had many honourable and notable successes. Nevertheless envy reared its head among the princes and barons of the kingdom of England and was directed against the Duke of York. Above all envy prompted Somerset, who found a way to harm him so that the Duke of York was recalled from France to England. There he was totally stripped of his authority to govern Normandy . . . *Jean de Waurin*

He left the council meeting feeling a rage such as he had never felt before, so that once he was outside he had to stand for a moment against a tree and close his eyes.

Few people had ever seen Richard of York really angry. But now he was sweating and his heart was banging unevenly, as though it might burst out of his ribs. For the first time he understood what it must be to suffer 'an attack of the heart'. In the meeting his face had congested with blood; he hadn't been able to help it. For they had all been there: Somerset, Suffolk and that smiling fox Moleyns, Suffolk's lapdog, who had dared to accuse him of financial malpractice.

'Your majesty is pleased to believe many things of me without evidence,' York had said. And that was all he had said before leaving. He could not have trusted himself to say anything else.

He had spent almost forty thousand pounds of his own money in the service of the king; he had pawned his most prized possession, a gold collar enamelled with the roses of York and adorned by a great diamond. The king had repeatedly ignored his requests for money and troops. And Edmund Beaufort, Earl of Somerset, had stood there smiling while false charges were made against him.

What was it Beaufort had said to Moleyns?

'My dear bishop, it is not fair to reproach the duke with miscalculation, when it is not at all clear that he can count.'

And this, of course, had raised a general laugh.

Even with his eyes closed he could see Beaufort's smiling face as though it were printed against his eyelids.

It was not hard to imagine stamping that smile out.

When he opened his eyes he was surprised to feel the fine rain on his face, cooling his heated skin. He got on to his horse and rode hard, without giving any orders to his men, who followed him wondering whether they were being pursued, or in pursuit. Then, gradually, his anger congealed into something more brooding and sullen. He settled to a slow trot, and then a walk, soothed as ever by the motion of his horse, that rhythmic movement of muscle and bone. He could feel his horse's ribs moving against his knees.

He had learned in childhood to suppress his rage. Shortly after his father had been executed he had been sent to stay in the noisy and burgeoning household of the Earl of Westmorland. It was the first of several visits to the castle of Raby, before he went to live there. No one had spoken of his father's disgrace, though he had always been a little set apart. Solid and taciturn, he had made few friends, though some of the earl's children had been roughly his own age. He had recoiled from kindness, endured cruelty with a stoic silence and learned to be alert and more observant than he seemed.

On that first visit, he had seen, by chance, the earl's new baby daughter. He had somehow evaded his nurse, the other children and their tutor, and was trying to find his room, when a door opened very softly. He saw a maid leaving a chamber, carrying a small bundle. He hung back, but she smiled at him. 'Would you like to see?' she said, and sat on a stool to one side of the door.

Cautiously, he approached the linen bundle, which might

almost have been laundry, apart from a tiny fist that waved defiantly in the air.

'Her name is Cecily,' the maid said, and when he didn't respond she said, 'What do you think?' But he didn't know what he thought. The baby's face was somewhat blotchy, its eyes tightly closed and its mouth a small bud, continuously working, now puckered and pursed, now stretched as if to cry, then folded in on itself so that the lips entirely disappeared. The little arm waved erratically as though summoning aid. The maid touched the baby's fist and it opened promptly, grasping, the fingers splayed wide like the rays of a star. Richard's own fingers moved and he touched the baby's palm, which was so soft, like wrinkled silk. At once, the baby's fingers curled round his own, and in that moment something changed. He had the sudden, keen sense of being her one connection in this alien and shifting world. He smiled, astonished, and the baby clung on as though she had no intention of ever letting go.

That was thirty years ago, of course, but the little girl had not outgrown her attachment to him. On subsequent visits she had toddled after him where possible, so that he was forced to discourage her at times, though secretly he looked for her when she wasn't there. At the age of three she had loudly declared her intention of marrying him, and everyone had laughed. By the time she was nine, however, most of his titles and estates had been restored to him, and they were betrothed.

Now he was riding back to her as though drawn by an invisible rope, seeking restoration in her eyes, so that his heart could begin to heal. She would come to meet him, and her eyes would seek his and he would not need to explain anything, not at first. In her eyes he would find a sense of connection in this alien and shifting world.

8

The Queen Speaks Unwisely

This King Henry was chaste and pure from the beginning of his days. He eschewed all licentiousness in word or deed . . . and neither when he espoused the most noble Lady Margaret . . . did he use his wife unseemly, but with all honesty and gravity . . . this prince made a covenant with his eyes that they should never look unchastely upon any woman. Hence it happened once, that at Christmas time a certain great lord brought before him a dance or show of young ladies with bared bosoms who were to dance in that guise before the king, perhaps to prove him, or to entice his youthful mind. But the king . . . angrily averted his eyes, turned his back upon them, and went out to his chamber saying:

Fy, fy, for shame, forsothe ye be to blame.

John Blacman

The queen had told no one about the problem that had come to preoccupy her excessively. No one, that is, until one of her ladies, an older woman who had come with her from France, had come across her one day when she was vexed almost to tears, and had persuaded the young queen to tell her what the matter was. Scarlet with mortification, the queen had eventually conveyed her belief that she would never have a child. Her lady's shaved eyebrows shot upwards.

'But why not?' she said.

This was harder.

'Because the king – seems not to – desire me in that way.'

There was a moment's startled silence, then the lady asked whether the king had performed his duty.

'– Yes,' the queen said hesitantly. On her wedding night she had produced a small amount of blood.

'And he still comes to you . . .' It was not a question. All her ladies knew when the king came to her.

'He – prefers us to pray,' the queen said.

'To pray? Does he pray for a son?'

The young queen nodded miserably.

'Does he think an angel will appear?'

The queen was sorry she had started this.

'I . . . think he believes . . . that if a child comes . . . it will be by divine grace.' Her lady's silence spoke louder than words, so she added, 'He thinks it is different for kings.'

'I can assure him it is not.'

The young queen looked at her sharply. She had often had cause to wonder about this lady and her father, King René.

'Have you not spoken to him? Have you not told him that God's grace works in particular ways?'

'The king is fully conversant with God,' said the queen, and there was hardly any bitterness in her tone.

Then the advice began. She was to ensure that the king came to her more often – 'Tell him you must pray together every night, if possible' – and when she was with him she must not be contentious.

'Contentious – how?'

The lady paused, then suggested that, lately, on certain subjects, her majesty's voice had become a little – shrill.

'You mean because he has not kept his promise to my father and my uncle? But he must keep it!' The queen rose and began to pace. 'There will be war, I know it – war between my father and my husband – between my two nations. And the king promised to hand over Maine and Anjou – he signed the treaty. They will not wait much longer. And what will I do then – what will I do?'

Her voice had risen again, and her face was flushed.

The lady waited for this outburst to finish, then said merely that no man likes to be told that he is in the wrong, and the queen sank down again, as though collapsing into her chair.

'Is it my fault then?' she said.

The lady doubted that, given what she knew of the king. She

assured the queen that it was not a question of *fault*, as such, but she must talk to him sweetly, always look her best, have music playing where possible, take scented baths . . . She clapped her hands suddenly. 'I can arrange it so that the king comes to you when you are *in* your bath!' she said.

'No,' said the queen, very definitely. She would never forget the look of horror on the king's face when she had pushed back the bedclothes suddenly and revealed herself without her chemise. What was that quote he was so fond of? 'The nakedness of a beast is in man unpleasing.' At any rate, for the next few days he had avoided her, and had seemed to be in the grip of an excessive melancholy.

But her lady was thinking. And when she had finished thinking she ventured to say that it was possible to arrange . . . certain entertainments . . . of the kind favoured by the goddess of love, featuring certain young ladies, perhaps . . . or, perhaps, young men.

At this the queen turned to her with an intensity of expression that would have cowed another woman. She spoke in a low voice, but quite vehemently.

'Listen to me,' she said. 'The king, my husband, is a good man – you do not know him if you think such vulgar tricks will work on him. I forbid you to talk about him in this way – I forbid you to talk about any of this – to anyone at all.'

Her lady looked as if she would say something, regardless, then thought better of it and inclined her head. 'I will not speak of it, my lady,' she said. 'Of course I will not. You may count on my discretion – I will not tell a soul.'

And she had told everyone, of course. Or at least the queen noticed a change in the attitude of those around her. Her other ladies attempted to dress her hair in different ways, to suggest propitious dates for the fostering of love, when the moon was in certain signs or Venus made an angle to Mars. Elizabeth Butler suggested a potion that she herself had used in order to get her husband through a period of difficulty. The queen had vented her wrath upon her French lady, but she had merely said that it was no secret that the queen wanted to produce an heir: all the court was hoping for it.

And, indeed, though it might have been the queen's imagination, it seemed to her that even the minstrels were looking at her with a certain speculative pity, and the other lords at court with a different kind of speculation. For she was beautiful – everyone said so. Only recently, she had been called 'the most beautiful woman in the world'. But none of that was real to her. It was as if she could not know her own beauty without her husband's touch; she needed to see herself through his hands.

And still when he visited her rooms it was in order that they should pray. Whenever she was with him, she could sense the subtle turning away from her if she stood too near. Even when he got into her bed he kept his distance, and despite her inexperience she knew that nothing could happen like this, while there was enough space for another body to lie between them.

9

February 1447: The Duke of Gloucester is Summoned to a Parliament

The king held his high court of parliament at Saint Edmunds Bury in the county of Suffolk . . . during which parliament the Viscount Beaumont, then constable of England, with the assistance of the Duke of Buckingham and other nobles of the realm, at the king's commandment arrested the famous and noble Duke of Gloucester, uncle to the king. *Great Chronicle of London*

The Duke of Gloucester had ridden to the parliament in good faith, through the bitter weather, though he was troubled by gout and by an unnamed complaint of the bowels. And even though the parliament was held in Suffolk's county, he was not unduly apprehensive.

Everywhere was deserted; the few cows and sheep they passed stood motionless, as if frozen to the earth. The sky was white, like a helmet of bone; each blade of grass had whitened and stiffened, and where sky and earth met there was only mist like the vapour that rose from his horse's nostrils. He wondered if his eyes were failing, along with the rest of him, for it was hard to tell where the earth ended and the sky began, and from time to time the mist seemed to form misleading shapes. At one point he could have sworn he saw his brother the warrior king riding towards him, as he used to ride towards his generals before a battle. Then the mist shifted and the image disappeared and, mentally, the duke shook himself. His brother was not the king. His nephew, his brother's witless, ill-starred son, was king and was even now waiting for him in the abbey of Bury St Edmunds. The duke was one day late, but they could not expect him to travel so far quickly, in such weather, and so he did not hurry his men or their horses over the frozen ground. Though he was well wrapped in furs, the cold scalded his cheeks and the inside of his nose. He rode on steadily through this landscape that was like a ghost of itself, thinking of fires and wine and other bodily comforts.

But his reception was not warm. At his lodgings there was a message to say that the king expected him immediately. He was irritated by this, but since relations between them had deteriorated recently and he had been refused an audience on more than one occasion, he left his men to see to their horses and went on with only a few attendants.

As soon as he entered he saw an unsmiling king, and the queen, who would not normally have been present at such an assembly, together with a group of those lords who were most hostile to him: his old enemy the Cardinal Beaufort and his puppet nephew, the Earl of Somerset; Suffolk and his lackey Moleyns (recently made Bishop of Chichester); Salisbury and others who fawned upon the queen. He looked at their faces and began to understand.

Still he was not daunted. He, the brother of the warrior king, veteran of so many victories against the French, would not keep quiet in the face of their ruinous counsels – he would speak the truth as he saw it, before them all.

Before he could say anything, however, Suffolk rose and accused him of plotting against the king.

He was outraged, of course, that this son of merchants and traitors should stand before him at all. He would not speak to him; he spoke directly to his nephew.

'What nonsense is this?'

And the Earl of Salisbury rebuked him: 'Do not speak out of turn to his majesty!'

'Your dog is barking, my lord,' the duke said to the king. 'I find it difficult to hear your reply.'

At once it seemed that everyone was shouting, including the queen, that yapping French bitch who should not even be there. But it was not for nothing that he had bellowed orders to thousands of men on French soil, and he raised his voice above them all.

'I will not speak before this pack of wolves!' he shouted. 'Where are the other lords?'

And into the sudden silence Suffolk said, 'Do you say you will not answer to your king?'

'I will answer,' he said, 'if the king will speak.'

'Make no conditions before the king,' Suffolk began, but the king had risen and was walking towards the duke. Gloucester found himself looking at his nephew as though he had never seen him before: that vestigial resemblance to his dead brother was wrongly assembled somehow – it was hardly possible for a son to be less like his father. There was stubbornness in the face rather than conviction or assertion, and that injured look, that deep uncertainty in his walk, though he did not take his gaze from his uncle's face, and did not stop until he was within several paces of the duke.

'My uncle,' he said, 'you have betrayed my trust.'

'Traitor!' someone shouted, and there was another outburst of accusations. The duke had spoken against the king's marriage, he had made public the loss of Anjou and Maine without the king's consent, he had spread malicious rumours about the queen.

'What rumours?' the duke demanded, but the king simply turned his back on him and walked away. The duke could see the look of triumph on the queen's face. Furiously, he shouted after the king, 'You are listening to traitors now – to the counsel of traitors – and women!' but his voice could hardly be heard. And the king merely continued to walk away from his uncle, towards the back of the room, where the duke could hardly see him. But the duke had only made public that which the public ought to know – that Suffolk had bought the queen so dear. And the people hated him for it, as the duke had known they would. Then Suffolk said loudly that he had made vile insinuations against the queen's honour.

He had said, in fact, that the queen kept her bedfellows close. People could make of that what they wished.

'Ask him about his own wife,' someone called, and suddenly he knew, or part of his mind knew, that it was over.

He could have defended himself, for though his wife had been condemned for treason, for using witchcraft against the king, he had been cleared of all complicity. But he had lost battles as well as won them, and could detect those changes of fortune against which no man's efforts stand. He could see the eager savagery in their faces, the cardinal's vulpine smile. He raised his voice once more, addressing the king he could hardly see.

'I will not speak here, where I cannot be heard. Your majesty knows I am no traitor – I have acted for the common good. What else would your majesty have me do?'

And into the sudden silence the queen – not the king – spoke.

'The king knows your merits, my lord.'

And there was a rousing chorus of assent.

The duke would not even look at her. He looked instead to where he believed the king sat, partially obscured by the other lords. 'Why do you let others speak for you?' he called.

And the king heard. He rose unsteadily; Gloucester almost felt sorry for him. So many talons, he thought. 'Let the king speak,' he said, and another silence fell. 'What is it your majesty wishes?' he continued in a conciliatory tone, though he could not keep the contempt from his stare. He wondered if here and now the king would pass sentence on him for treason, but somehow he doubted it. And he was right. The king spoke unevenly.

'You may go – to your lodgings – and await our pleasure there.'

Gloucester bowed and immediately turned to leave.

Only as he left did his thoughts start to race and he began to speculate. Would the king go so far as to have his own uncle executed? Surely there would be a trial?

He could already see the probable outcome of events. Yet, oddly, he felt more alive than he had done for months. Lately, he had begun to feel a little displaced from his life, as though only on the battlefield had he felt truly alive. He spurred on his horse and rode swiftly through the streets to his lodgings. He would not dishonour himself by attempting to flee; he would make no admission of guilt.

As he rode he had a powerful memory of the king as a little boy: foolish, affectionate, usually cheerful but very prone to tears. Disinclined, from the first, to take any part in military sports. He had promised his brother he would be a father to his son; he had failed, entirely, to love him.

Then another memory surfaced. He was a child with his brothers, all three of them, in the orchard of some castle's grounds. And Henry, the eldest, had suggested that they should have a race to see who could gather up the most fallen apples. Henry had won, of course, and he, the youngest, had gathered up the least. He had tried to smile, and failed, then Henry had generously tipped his share of apples into Humphrey's basket. 'You will always receive your portion from me,' he had said. In the duke's memory there had been a halo of light around him; he had looked up at him through a blaze of sun. Even then, he had hated himself for smiling up at this brother, whom he had hated and admired and loved.

That was irrelevant now that all three of his brothers were dead. His parents had had six children, and he was the only one left. It was a strange thing to be the only one to have survived. He felt as though he were a relic of a bygone age in which honour and glory, not flattery and acumen, ruled.

Still, he was alive, and they were dead.

Even before he entered the street where his lodgings were, he could see them waiting for him. A group of lords on horseback: Stanley, Stourton, Somerset and the queen's own steward, Viscount Beaumont, Lord High Constable of England, who rode forward to meet him, closely followed by Buckingham. He reined in his own horse and waited until they were close enough to hear, then said, 'Gentlemen, what can I do for you?'

And the Lord High Constable of England rode forward and formally charged him with treason.

10

The Good Duke Humphrey

And this foresaid noble duke . . . was found dead in his inn, of whose death many tales were blown about the land . . . and when he was found dead his corpse was carried into the abbey church that all might see him, but on his corpse might no wound be seen or found. *Great Chronicle of London*

Some said he had been strangled or suffocated in his bed, between two mattresses, or else 'thrust into the bowel with a hot burning spit', while others, more inventively, said he had been drowned in wine and dried again. Whatever they imagined, almost all were agreed that he had been foully murdered, and no viewing of the body changed their minds. Those few who reminded them that the duke was old and fat and drank to excess were shouted down, though some were prepared to concede that he could have died from shock and grief because of the nature of the accusations levelled against him.

There was no doubt in anyone's mind, however, that Suffolk was to blame: Suffolk, who was giving away their lands in France piece-meal, and enriching himself in the process, so it was said; Suffolk, who had brokered a dishonourable deal with the French, and brought them a worthless queen.

Within days of the Good Duke's death, the mysterious alchemy of public opinion was turning supposition into truth: Gloucester had been murdered and Suffolk had arranged it. The king, who was famously pious, could never have done such a thing. Suffolk had taken it upon himself to rule the king and country both, and was even now bedding their worthless queen.

Gloucester himself, bellicose, degenerate and profligate, was remembered for his kindness, his many deeds of patronage, his willingness to stand and fight – not for marrying a witch who had conspired to put him on the throne.

For who now would stand between them and those wolves and jackals surrounding the king? Who would defend them against the French?

Many people turned out to mourn Gloucester, or to touch his shroud, for it was already said that miracles might occur, and the people needed a miracle to save them from the disorder and lack of governance in the land, for the country stood on the brink of ruin and disgrace.

And anon after the death of the Duke of Gloucester there were arrested many of the said duke's servants, to the number of twenty-eight squires, beside other servants that never imagined the falseness of which they were accused. And on Friday the 9th day of July next following, by judgement at Westminster, five persons were damned to be drawn, hanged and their bowels burned before them, and then their heads to be smitten off, and then to be quartered, and every part to be sent unto divers places by assignment of the judges . . . [and] on the said day [they] were drawn from St George's throughout Southwark and on London Bridge, and so through the City of London to Tyburn, and there they were hanged, and the ropes smitten asunder, they being still living, and then, before any more marks of execution were done, the [Earl] of Suffolk brought them all a general pardon and grace from our lord and sovereign, King Harry the VI.

Gregory's Chronicle

And all the commons of the realm began to murmur and were not content.

Brut Chronicle

II

The Duke of York Accepts a Commission

And in that same year the Duke of York, Richard Plantagenet, was exiled into Ireland for rebellion . . . fully and falsely as it was afterwards known.

Gregory's Chronicle

He had already pulled off his boots, sent for wine and was sitting in front of a roaring fire when his wife came in. She walked towards him eagerly, then stopped at the look on his face.

'Well?' she said.

'Ireland,' he said, looking into the fire.

'Ireland? Not France?'

There was only a slight alteration in his face; his eyelids flickered downwards. Then he leaned forward and poked one of the logs back on to the fire.

'So who is Lieutenant of France?' she said.

'Somerset.'

She made a small sound that might have been a snort of disgust. He poured wine for them both.

'The king looks forward to me subduing his land of Ireland,' he said.

'I'm sure he does,' she said. 'And he will provide you with much money, and many ships.'

The duke only glanced at her sideways. Everyone knew that the king had no money. It was said that he had pawned the crown jewels for his wedding.

'How much?' she asked, meaning the annuity.

'Four thousand marks.'

She closed her eyes briefly. He was grateful there was no outburst. He did not mention that Somerset would be given twenty thousand pounds a year. In all probability, neither of them would see either amount.

'So generous,' she said. 'Or is that what you have to pay him?'

There was a gleam of humour in the duke's eyes, but he did not respond.

'When?' she said.

'As soon as may be arranged.'

'I imagine,' she said, 'that will take some time.'

The duke merely said that it was Ireland, not the North Pole.

'Did he not think to send you to the North Pole? That was remiss of him.'

The duke said that he would be sure to remind the king, next time. But the duchess was pacing the room, frowning.

'Or to one of the circles of hell,' she said.

The duke said that he would not compare Ireland to hell.

'Your uncle might have,' she said, and the duke said nothing. His uncle, his uncle's father and his father before him had all died in Ireland. It was partly to retrieve the lands left to him there that he had agreed to go.

A gift of land in Ireland is a gift of blood, it was said.

'I will not be sailing in winter, at any rate,' he said. 'It will take me until spring at least to muster some men. And the ships. It will be summer before I can sail.'

The duchess stopped behind his chair and put one hand on the back of it, near his shoulder.

'*We*,' she said. 'Before *we* sail.'

The duke turned to look at her; there was the beginning of a smile in his eyes. The Rose of Raby they called her, after the castle in which she was born. As she was growing up, everyone petted her because she was so pretty; she had the kind of prettiness that even now led people to think she must be sweet.

They did not think it twice.

'You believe that you can subdue the Irish?' he asked.

'I will not be left behind,' she said.

The duke's smile broadened. She did not like to travel, but she accompanied him everywhere. Three of their children had been born in Normandy. Now she leaned forward so that her face was almost – not quite – touching his, and spoke softly.

'You did not think that you were leaving me behind?'

'*We* will sail,' he corrected himself, looking up at her. And, almost imperceptibly, the look changed between them: hers softened; his became more intent.

12

The New Duke of Somerset

And in the year 1448 on the day of St George, the earl [of Somerset] was made Duke of Somerset and about Pentecost the Earl of Suffolk was made Duke of Suffolk.

John Benet's Chronicle

The queen had asked to see him in private.

There was nothing unusual in this, given the recent crisis. These days, the new Duke of Somerset was almost permanently in the company of the queen. The king had finally ordered the governor of Maine and Anjou to evacuate those territories, but he had refused, saying that he did not think the letters were valid. There had been scenes of rejoicing in Maine, and riots in London, where the king's unpopularity was such that his council had decided to send him around the country. The king himself had suggested that he should go to France, but they did not trust him there. All the preparations had been made for him to tour the north of England, but then he had suffered a reactive melancholy. His face was sunken, his eyes haunted. He had taken to spending even more hours in his chapel, or playing with a staff, to one end of which a bird had been tethered. He was mesmerized, apparently, by its struggling upwards dance.

The Duke of Somerset had been made Lieutenant of France, but he had not sailed yet, because of the difficulty with that country and because the queen needed him. The king had not yet set off on his tour, no agreement could be reached with the French and the queen was in despair.

And York had not sailed to Ireland. He had petitioned the king many times for money, and rumour had it that he was preparing to mortgage his lands and would soon be bankrupt. So there were many reasons for the new duke to be cheerful as he went, wearing his ducal robes, to keep his appointment with the queen. It had even occurred to him that she might want to discuss the question of the succession.

No one else had been named heir since Gloucester had been gone. York was the obvious choice, but the king and queen did not like York. They liked him, Somerset.

However different they were, and they *were* different – he retreating into sanctity, she like a caged beast – this much could be said: there was no disagreement about the people they liked, who were beloved by them, for they loved like children do, with that same terrifying openness and disregard. There was no limit to their affection, or to their generosity.

And even though it was a sensitive issue, it was not the worst time to broach this subject with the queen, because the king would agree with her. In his present state, it could be taken for granted that he would agree to most things.

So the new duke entered the queen's privy chamber with confidence, but was disconcerted to find her with her hair unbound, wearing only a simple gown over her chemise, which parted as she moved. She stood a few paces away from him, her eyes anxious, her face taut.

'My husband the king is unwell,' she said when he did not speak.

The duke made a movement as if to leave. 'I must go to him,' he said. 'I will see what I can do. He should be here, with you.'

'No, wait,' she said, stepping closer, so that her gown parted again. 'He does not want company – he cannot bear it. He – does not want to be touched.'

Ah, thought the duke. All the rumours he had heard were true. And he had thought of it before, of course he had. She had made her preference for him quite plain.

Now she was standing very close and, without looking at him directly, she touched him, her hands moving awkwardly to his chest, his face, his lips.

Unexpectedly, he felt a terrible pity for her, because her touch told him what she had not said, that she did not know how to touch a man; that she was a young, beautiful woman in a hostile land and her husband could not permit himself to desire her; that in the cold, pure air of his chastity she would know neither the heat of love nor motherhood.

It confused him, this compassion, for he was not easily moved to sympathy. In a fleeting moment he could see it all: unclothing her, she raising her hips to his, then bearing his child, his son, who would be heir to the throne.

Also he could see himself, hanged, drawn and quartered for treason. The king was not vengeful, but the duke had many enemies at court.

So much time can pass in a single moment!

He lowered his face to her scented hair, knowing as he did so that this was the single most dangerous moment of his career. Briefly, he wondered whether it was more dangerous to offend a queen or a king. Beneath the scent he could detect another odour, sharp and sour. He enclosed her hands in his, removing them gently from his face. Then he murmured, 'My lady, you are afraid.'

She stood absolutely still for a moment, and neither of them spoke. Then, subtly, he could feel her withdraw.

'Why should you not be afraid?' he continued. 'The king is sick, and the nation also, and you are their queen. All you want is to heal them. But you do not know how.'

She was pulling away from him, mortified by his presence. Nothing would ever be the same again between them. Greatly daring, he moved her hair from her face, as a lover might.

'This is your country, and you are its queen.'

She was listening to him, and she didn't move. But he had absolutely no idea what he was going to say next.

'Our lives are not our own,' he said, somewhat desperately. 'They are not ours to give – you have already given yours to this country.'

It was true. By sheer accident of fortune, he had hit upon a truth. There had been a moment, in all the hours of the coronation, when she had known it, a moment of piercing knowledge: this was her country, she was its queen.

She had learned its language, studied its history and its laws. She had travelled the length of it, with her husband the king. It was not her fault that its people hated her.

There it was again, this strange wringing of his heart. Somerset fell to his knees and clasped her, then looked up at her, his face brimming with emotion.

'I cannot take what is not yours to give –'

She looked at him, then away. She spoke slowly. 'This country,' she said, 'hates me, and would be well rid of me.'

'No,' he said. 'The people need you. They need your courage and your dignity and –' he hesitated only for a moment – 'your loyalty. The king needs you. And I need you,' he added. 'I need you.'

Again, it was true. He was quite unaccustomed to this discovery of unfamiliar truths. But there it was. He needed her.

For several moments he felt as though she were seeing right through him with her piercing stare. But for once he had nothing to hide. And her shame had shifted, he could sense that. He released her as she made a movement away.

'According to the people,' she said, 'I am leading a most interesting life.'

'No one who knows you would think such a thing.'

'But they think it. And they think I am in collusion with my father and my uncle against them. They think that I cannot give them an heir. My husband . . . prefers to sleep on his chapel floor. Do you know that?'

Somerset could only hang his head. 'My lady –' he said, but could think of nothing else to say. He had ruined everything, he thought, he had destroyed the relationship between them. But he knew better than to beg her forgiveness.

She was speaking again, as though to herself, or to the wall.

'The king . . . is preparing to leave,' she said, as if rehearsing lines. 'I must go to him.'

Still looking towards the floor, Somerset shook his head. 'My lady –' he said, but she interrupted him.

'Come, my lord,' she said. 'You must not wear out your knees.'

He looked up at her, hardly daring to hope, but she extended her hand to him with a resigned smile. He got up clumsily, with none of his usual elegance, and looked at her earnestly. 'Your majesty –' he said, but she made a small sound, a gesture, to silence him.

'"Our lives are not our own,"' she said, quoting him.

It was over then. He left her rooms without knowing how much damage he had or had not done, knowing that he had made a choice, of sorts, though it had not felt like a choice. Later, he would look on it as a choice of good over evil, which is to say that he regretted it deeply in some part of his mind. In that moment he could only walk a little way along the corridor, and then rest against the wall, profoundly shaken by what had happened, and by his response. Especially by his response, because it had revealed something about himself that he had not previously known.

And after that the Duke of Somerset went to Normandy with 2,000 men.

Chronicles of London

Around the Feast of the Assumption of the Virgin, almost thirty towns with their castles were lost . . . on the 29th October [1449] Rouen was taken in an assault by the King of France, who captured the Earl of Shrewsbury and others while the Duke of Somerset fled to Caen. Besides this the said king took the town of Harfleur and the land of Anjou in Maine, and all the land in Normandy across the river Seine.

John Benet's Chronicle

In this year, despite the truce prevailing between England and France, an English knight, Francis de Surienne, took a town in Normandy called Fougères; and this was the occasion for the French to take the whole of Normandy.

Brut Chronicle

The clerk of the Privy Seal [Adam Moleyns] was killed at Portsmouth by soldiers and sailors, whom the king pardoned because the said bishop before his death accused himself and the Duke of Suffolk and others of being traitors to the crown.

John Benet's Chronicle

13

The Duchess Alice Looks to the Future

Her first thought was for her son, of course.

When her husband turned to her for reassurance, as was his custom, she made all the expected responses. He said that he would be blamed for the losses in Normandy, and she asked in what sense, exactly, was he to blame? It would not happen; he should not think such a thing. How could he possibly be accused of treason, when he had never been anything other than faithful to the king?

Privately, she considered it more than likely.

Accordingly, without mentioning it to her husband, she had already written to one or two of her cousins on her mother's side. Relations between her husband and the Burghersh family had cooled considerably in recent months, so she wrote a conciliatory letter, saying little, testing the ground. She had expressed the hope that one of their younger sons would soon be presented at court for preferment.

When there was no reply, her suspicions were confirmed. The Burghersh family were connected to the Nevilles, as she was, and through them to the Duke of York. They did not wish, now, to be associated with the Duke of Suffolk.

She had gone on to consider their other connections like pieces on a chessboard. It seemed to her that none of them would stand in the current situation; they were all drawing away from the duke.

However, it also seemed to her that, should certain conditions change, she could write again to her Burghersh cousins. If she were alone, for instance, they might be relied upon to take her and her son, because she still had all her own estates.

The duke was now enumerating all those lords who stood against him, who would like to see him fall. His face was quite contorted; Lady Alice could not help but consider how fear makes men ugly.

Also, she remembered her father, son of the greatest poet in the land. He was no poet himself, but he was fond of his similes and metaphors.

'Warfare,' he used to say, 'exposes what is hidden in a man's soul. Much as hanging, drawing and quartering exposes his guts.'

But she should not be thinking about warfare. Surely it would not come to that.

'My lord,' she said, 'you distress yourself. You must remember that you have only ever acted on behalf of the king.'

The Duke of Suffolk stopped pacing and wiped his sweating face. 'They say,' he said, 'that I have acted *instead* of the king.'

'That is nonsense,' she said. 'What has happened is due entirely to the incompetence of the Duke of Somerset. You cannot be blamed for that. Such situations pass,' she added. 'The important thing is to consider what might happen then.'

'Then –?'

'There will be a great shaking up of things,' she said, just as if she could see the outcome precisely. 'We have to consider the possibilities.'

She was speaking more to herself now. 'One is that they will turn against the king.'

He was watching her closely.

'Another is that the king will save his position by making certain radical changes in his government.'

'And then we lose everything,' he said. 'All lands and manors, titles –'

'I shall keep my father's estates,' she said. 'And my mother's.'

He looked at her, fascinated. 'Are there any further options?' he asked, with only a touch of irony.

She glanced at him quickly. Both of them knew the third option was that the duke would not survive. But she could tell from the look on his face that he had not expected her to know this.

'In either case,' she said decisively, 'we need to consider what happens afterwards.'

That word, 'afterwards', seemed suddenly the wrong word to use. She did not look at the duke, but she could sense his horror deepening into outrage. He said nothing for several moments while she chided herself for her uncharacteristic clumsiness.

'My lady's foresight is impressive,' he said at length. 'I have often had reason to be grateful for it.'

She would not dignify this with a response. None of this mess was her doing.

'Tell me your plans for "afterwards".'

She turned to him then. 'I am talking about your *son*,' she said, and he made a gesture to indicate that she should carry on.

She said that now was the time to consider his marriage – to their little ward, Margaret Beaufort. It would tie them more closely to the king, and although (as she did not say) the king's future was by no means certain, if he survived this crisis in his reign, their son's position would be strengthened.

'It would be different if the king had an heir,' she said, and let the sentence hang. For little Margaret was second cousin to the king. And the Duke of Somerset, who in theory had a greater claim, was now in an unsafe position because of the disasters in France.

The Duke of Suffolk listened to her without changing the expression on his face. It was as though he were listening to something else, beneath the surface of her words. She turned away from him uneasily.

They had discussed this plan before; she had raised the issue several times. He had always found some reason to delay – until their son was older, or until he had been granted this or that title. Or until the king had a daughter, though he did not say this. But, now, he had to see that the time of waiting was over. Their son would need the best connections they could make for him. And if the king did not survive this crisis, the marriage would add significantly to his estates and wealth. It was time to assert their rights of wardship – before anything else was lost.

When she looked back at the duke he was gathering his papers and putting on his spectacles.

'My lord?' she said. He did not look up.

'You must do as you think best,' he said.

'So I have your permission to write to her mother?' she said.

'My permission?' he replied, gazing at her over his spectacles. 'I'm sure you can manage without that.'

'So – you do not agree.'

She had never before seen such hostility in his eyes.

'I think it is the best possible plan, given the circumstances,' he said in low, even tones. 'And you must make your plans, my dear. For *afterwards*.'

There it was. The naked revelation between them.

She turned away. If she had spoken, she might have started blaming him. She herself was not going to take any blame for looking ahead, to her son's future. One of them had to retain the ability to think.

She turned back to him, willing to appease, but he had already gone. And she had said just one wrong word: 'afterwards'. After all these years of saying only the right words! She was sick of saying the right words. Like a courtier. How many wives could teach their husbands how to speak at court?

A little discomposed, she sat at her desk. Her heart was beating faster than usual, but it was not her custom to pay attention to her heart.

She selected a pair of the spectacles she had only recently acquired to correct her vision. Recently, she had found she could see clearly only from a distance – anything close to her was somewhat blurred. There was a metaphor for you, she thought, sharpening her quill. For even as a child she had tended to think in the long term rather than the present, as if the present were vague and only future possibilities seemed real. It was a trait that had carried her through most of the crises in her life: the deaths of two husbands, and (she did not add to herself) what might be the imminent loss of a third.

Distance vision was an appropriate metaphor for her perspective on life; she had often thought that she, rather than her father, might have inherited her grandfather's abilities. In other circumstances, perhaps, she might have been a poet, like him; she was sure he would have approved. Instead of which, she was the patron of poets.

Still, she could write a good letter. Dipping her quill, she began to write to the mother of her ward, in order to arrange the future of her son.

On the day of St Vincent the Martyr, a parliament began in which everybody complained to the king about the Duke of Suffolk, hearing which the iniquitous duke came into parliament before the commons, excusing himself of many charges. And on the same day the iniquitous duke sought permission from the king to retire to his estate of Wallingford which he kept in the best manner, but all the commons complained to the king, saying that if the iniquitous duke was allowed to go, the whole of England would be destroyed by his evil plans and deceptions, because he was a traitor to the crown . . . And so on the 29th day of January the evil duke was arrested and taken to the Tower of London.

John Benet's Chronicle

14

The Duke of Suffolk Suffers a Premonition

She bent over him with her blackened, smoking eyes, saying, 'Do you think you are Duke of France?'

Or was it Normandy?

Small flames flickered from her lips and helmet as she raised her fiery sword then brought it down.

And he woke, sweating. It was not the first time he had dreamed of the Maid of Orléans, whose execution he had, in fact, witnessed. What disturbed him was the vivid quality of his dreams. There was nothing to occupy him in his cell, relatively little light and air, and his dreams had begun to seem more real to him than his waking moments. Indeed there were times when both his present condition and much of his previous life seemed like a dream.

It was as though the substance of time itself had become distorted, so drawn out that it almost stood still, then gushing faster than a flooding stream as memories and images of his past life returned to him. He remembered playing with his sister, who had died, the tutor who had mocked him in private, the first prostitute he ever slept with.

Then he was walking with his wife in her herb garden, or holding his son.

Very often the smiling face of Adam Moleyns came back to him. They were discussing policy together in the duke's house at St Giles. Then the bishop's head, still smiling, addressed him from a pole. 'Soon it will be your turn,' he said.

Thoughts and images and memories swirled into whirlpools or drove him through mazes, and he lost all ability to concentrate. He tried, for example, to remember lines of poetry – his own, that he had composed for the queen – but could remember only fragments:

> *My heart is set and all mine whole intent*
> *To serve this flower in my most humble wise . . .*

The queen had been so pleased by his verses, she had received them with a childlike pleasure; but now he could not remember them.

Both the king and queen had written to him several times, assuring him of their love, and that he would be released. By contrast, his wife had written only once, to tell him that she was going ahead with the arrangements for the marriage of their son. The little Margaret Beaufort was staying with her all the time now, so that the wedding could be arranged quickly before any objections might arise.

Alone in his cell, the duke could imagine her making those arrangements, with the same efficiency and assurance that had first drawn him to her.

There were moments when he could not remember her face.

What he could remember were the faces of those in parliament who had stood against him. All the commons, of course, and several lords. He had tried to speak in his own defence:

In the matter of ceding Maine, he had said, other lords were as privy thereto as he.

It would have been impossible, he told them, for him to have done such great things without the cooperation of other men.

And they had shouted him down.

With terrifying lucidity he recalled their distorted faces, pulled and contorted by the sheer weight of their malice. He had not known before that men's faces would change as he fell from grace, becoming animal, unclean.

For this reason the horror of this imprisonment exceeded that of his imprisonment in France. Then, he had been a prisoner of war, fighting for his country; now, his country had turned on him. And there was no place for him, none, despite his many manors, apart from this narrow cell and the hostile territory of his mind. He slept and woke, slept and woke, always with the horror of his situation covering him like a pall, a sheen of sweat. He lay stinking in its fetor, amid all the phantasms of his brain.

Accordingly, when the king finally sent for him to say that he was taking him into his own custody in Westminster Palace, he had to read the message several times over, then he pressed it to his face to smell it. Later, he sat in the boat sent for him, blinking in gratitude at the night sky, which was stippled with stars. Never had he seen anything more miraculous or wonderful. The air he breathed, though it reeked of the city, had never seemed sweeter.

As they approached the king's chambers, the king himself came out to greet him. The duke fell clumsily to his knees, acutely conscious of his clothes, which he had been unable to change, of his straggling beard and weeping eye. But the king, who was himself dressed like a monk, had no interest in appearances. He raised him up at once and embraced him.

'My dearest friend,' he said, 'how you have suffered.'

And at once the duke began to feel restored to himself, for how could he be traitor if he was the king's dearest friend? He had never acted against his king.

'It is nothing,' he managed to say, 'now that I am here – with you.'

And the king embraced him again. Then he led him into his privy chamber, and from there into his private chapel, a small, bare room containing only a wooden bench and crucifix and a tapestry of St Sebastian. The king sat with him on the bench and looked earnestly at him. His own face was drawn in lines of tragedy and suffering, but he said, 'My friend, you are not well.'

The duke thought of saying that he had not been visiting a spa, but it did not seem the right time for irony.

'A little fever, perhaps, your grace.'

His left eye was evidently infected; it would not stop weeping.

'I will send for my own physician – you must rest and recuperate.'

The duke thought of saying that he had rested enough, but again he suppressed the thought. The king stood suddenly and gazed out of the chapel window. 'But you cannot stay in London – the city is not safe. The people . . . rise against me.'

The duke thought he had heard the sounds of rioting from his cell.

'A man has been sentenced to death for speaking against me.' The king turned his bewildered face towards the duke. 'I did not require it – my council required it: not I.'

The duke bowed his head, wondering who had taken his place on the king's council.

'I have been praying for days,' said the king.

Ah, thought the duke.

'Only to know what I have done wrong – if I have done wrong. But there is no answer.'

No, thought the duke.

'I have loved my people, but they do not love me.'

It is better to be feared rather than loved, thought the duke, but he could not remember where the quote came from.

'I have been a merciful king. I have sought to rule by Christ's law.'

They both knew that if he had been a tyrant, the people would have loved him more. But the king was looking at the wooden cross in some perplexity. 'I have begged for the answer in prayer – how is it that I, who seek only to live in charity with all men, have brought about such evil?'

He turned to the duke with troubled eyes, but the duke, for once, was at a loss for words.

'The only answer I receive is this,' he continued. 'I am doing penance for the nation – for the land. Like a blood offering.'

'Your majesty –'

'If the people require my blood, they may have it. But they will not have yours.'

His eyes were fervent, like the eyes of a martyr. He had the courage of a martyr, not a warrior. But the people required a warrior.

'I will not let them execute you, my friend.'

The king's words began to echo strangely in the duke's head. He looked at the king with that fractured vision that had come to him in his cell. He could see that if he, the Duke of Suffolk, were to advise his king truly, he would have himself executed; if he had been king, he would have signed the death warrant by now. But he did not say this, of course. Despite the circumstances, he could feel in himself a surprisingly strong desire to live.

'I will stand between you and your enemies,' said the king.

He sat down beside the duke again and took his hands in a characteristically inappropriate gesture. The duke could not look at the simple belief in his face. He stared instead at his own hands in the king's. He could feel, almost like a physical force, or a current at sea, the compelling power of the king's goodness. But the king was speaking again.

'As soon as you have recovered you must leave London secretly – you must decide where to go.'

The duke thought. He would not return to his wife (who had written to him only once) because to return to her would be to endanger her and his son. He could go, perhaps, to one of his lesser manors.

'I would keep you with me,' the king said, 'but I would rather keep you safe.'

The duke smiled. 'I have too many enemies for that.'

'But I am their king!'

He spoke as if kings could not be deposed; as if his own grandfather had not deposed a king. But the duke felt suddenly too weary to argue. He swayed in his seat, and the king caught and held him with surprising strength.

'You must rest,' he said. 'But first we must pray together – pray for the fortunes of this land, that we may bring good to it and lay all the evil to rest.'

The duke was a little wary of prayer. He thought of all those prayers, throughout time, that had risen like flies from the lips of the dying and the desperate, apparently unheard. But the king was pressing him forward, into a kneeling position, and began to pray for mercy and wisdom and the power of goodness. The duke knelt beside him, with the king's arm still supporting his shoulders, and knew suddenly, with a penetrating clarity, that the king's goodness would be the nation's doom.

And after St Hilary's Day the parliament was removed to Leicester . . . and the king brought with him to that parliament the Duke of Suffolk, and when the commons understood that he was out of the Tower and brought thither they desired to have execution upon him for the deliverance of Normandy and also for the death of that noble prince the Duke of Gloucester. And to appease the commons the Duke of Suffolk was exiled out of England.

Gregory's Chronicle

15

The Duke of Suffolk Writes a Letter

Something had happened to him while he prayed with the king, something extraordinary, but he could not say what it was. It was almost as though a skin had been lifted from him. And although it had been painless, this spiritual flaying, it had left him feeling raw. Ever since, he had been affected by a profound melancholy.

Of course, the circumstances were not good. He had been lucky to escape from his house in London when a mob had attacked it. And now here he was in his manor of Easthorpe, making arrangements to leave the country. But he was not under sentence of death; the king, as promised, had 'stood between him and his enemies'.

It was a beautiful day, but even the clear light – watery, pristine – could not lift his melancholy; he could feel no renaissance in his flesh. Birds were calling, hares darting about the field, but they merely increased his sense of hopeless sorrow. He turned away from the window and made an attempt to gather his failing resources. He had decided, that day, that he would write a letter to his son, John. Paper and quills were set out for him on the table, but he did not know what to say.

He sat down, in any case, because his legs were trembling. He looked down at his hands, resting on the polished wood; how they had aged. They were elegant hands, with tapering fingers: a poet's hands, or an artist's – not a general's. That was what his wife had said to him once, in the early days of their courtship. His wife, who had not written to him here, who had gone ahead with the marriage of his son.

An image of his little boy came vividly to his mind. The small, pointed features which had lengthened until they resembled his wife's features. He had not expected to have a son after so many years of marriage. Yet he remembered, as though it were happening now, the sensation of holding the small, crumpled body for the first time, that trembling rush of love. He hadn't expected that either. He was not aware that his own father had felt anything at his birth other than a certain grim pleasure at having another son.

The duke was fifty-three years old, and had already lived longer than many men, but his son, John, was only seven. He could remember himself at that age; how vividly things had affected him. His mood could be entirely transported by shifts in the weather or the light. He had begun each day with a sense of excitement and possibility, because it was new, and anything might happen. He remembered the first time someone had lifted him on to a horse, the dizzying sensation of terror. The horse had seemed huge and the ground so far away.

Was that what he wanted to write to his son? 'Do not be afraid when you sit on a horse'?

'Do not be afraid,' perhaps. And he could say that he was sorry. Sorry he had to leave, that he would not see his son grow up, that he had not been a better father. And sorry for any disgrace that would follow; any blows of fortune.

But he did not want to alarm him. And anything he wrote would be read to John by his mother; he could hear her crisp, editorial tones. He could say that he hoped, as far as hope was left in him, for John's future. For his marriage to the little heiress, Margaret Beaufort.

Who was six years old, as John was seven.

His thoughts were too scattered, that was the trouble. Blown about as chaff in the wind. And he could not see the future, that was his wife's gift; his own vision seemed oddly foreshortened.

But he had to start somewhere.

The Duke of Suffolk, as he remained, adjusted his spectacles and the piece of paper in front of him and lifted his quill. Then he gazed ahead of him at the map of Jerusalem on the wall. Maps, he had always loved them, and had a great collection, which would pass to John. He wondered if his son would love them also.

He should not give the impression that he would never return, though in fact his grandfather had died in exile. Perhaps that had been the beginning. His son had so few and such insecure connections that the duke had striven, at least partly for him, to secure land and titles.

He was sorry that John had no more family, no better connections. God knew that, when the world turned on you, you needed support.

I wish I could be there with you, my son.

The outlines of the map seemed to shift and blur as he looked at it and waited for a sense of focus, the words that would not come.

And last of all, as heartily and lovingly as father ever blessed his child on earth I give you the blessing of our Lord and me; which of His infinite mercy increase you in all virtue and good living. And that your blood may by His grace from kindred to kindred multiply on this earth to His service, in such wise as after the departing from this wretched world here, you and they may glorify Him eternally among His angels in heaven.

Letter from the Duke of Suffolk to his son, John de la Pole, 1450

PART II: 1450–55

16

The Wedding

When Margaret closed her eyes she could still see the colours of the stained-glass windows, scarlet, indigo and gold. It was another world, behind her eyelids, with its own patterns of light and shade, its own depths and shallows. It was where, she believed, God was hiding. God, whose presence was immanent in the world, which meant that you couldn't see Him. But if you waited without ever giving up hope, and paid attention to the spaces between words or the pause between one breath and the next, God, like a shy deer, might emerge from the hidden, shadowy places.

God was also in Heaven, of course, which was part of the mystery. The chapel ceiling had been painted a deep blue to represent the cerulean of Paradise. This she could not see through her eyelids, but if she pressed the balls of her eyes surreptitiously, contrary to the warnings of her nurse, she could see swirling lines, blocks of colour and dots which spiralled away from each other and re-formed differently. If she kept up the pressure long enough, it seemed to her that these patterns might resolve into a different world; one that was ordinarily too dazzling for human eyes.

This was what she thought about while the priest intoned the mass in Latin, and further along the pew her guardian's son, John, fidgeted and twisted in his seat and kicked the bench in front. They had been separated because he kept trying to pull her hair from its cap, then tie it to the pew behind. Even now he was trying to attract her attention – she could see him from the corner of her eye. Which was another reason for keeping her eyes closed.

She had been told that she must play with him like a good little girl; he was her brother now.

Which was a little confusing because her mother had married again and had a little boy who was also her brother, and also named John.

At first there had been other children to play with in this household, and then just Margaret and John. The other children were never mentioned again; she did not know if they had died, or been sent away. But she understood that she was in some way special. 'This is your second home,' she had been told. And her nurse had said she was lucky – 'a lucky little chick' – to have such a grand home in addition to her own.

She knew she was lucky, though she sometimes wished she could play with someone else. When she glanced secretly at her foster-brother he was pulling faces at her, as if he knew, all the time, that she would look. She leaned forward in her seat and pressed her fingertips still more firmly into her eyelids, waiting for the revelation of God.

When it didn't happen, and the service ended, they were taken to John's rooms to play, because they played together so well.

They played together well, she had discovered, as long as she let him win. If not, she had been astonished to find that he cried louder and harder than she, and his nurse would come running to comfort him, while her nurse chided her gently: it was only natural that a boy would want to win.

'But he always wants to win,' she had objected on more than one occasion, and her nurse would say 'Well!' As if it were of so little consequence that she shouldn't make a fuss. And then she would make one of the comments that even from a young age had outraged Margaret's logic, such as 'Losing is the way little ladies win', or 'The ball that would rise, must fall.'

'Not if you catch it,' Margaret would say, but her nurse would never engage in arguments of this kind. She would only press her lips together over her toothless gums and tell her that she had lost one tooth every time her little ward argued; every time she was good she stood a chance of growing one back. 'But look,' she said, opening her lips and exposing her shrunken gums; Little Peg had obviously not been very good yet. If she went back to play, like a good little lady, she could come back later to see whether her old Betsy had grown a tooth back.

Her nurse's name was Elizabeth, but Margaret had always called her Betsy, to distinguish her from all the other Elizabeths in the household. And because it was all she could manage to say when she was very young. That or Bet-bet. In return, Betsy called her Little Peg, for there were almost as many Margarets in the household as Elizabeths. Her own mother was called Margaret, as was the queen.

For as long as she could remember, Little Peg had slept between Betsy's heavy breasts and rounded stomach. Before sleep, Betsy would let her play with the folds and creases of her face. Her tiny fingers pried into the dimples of her nurse's cheeks and chin and even into her mouth, when she would pretend to bite. Betsy's face was softly furred with downy lines and when she laughed she was like an infant, revealing crinkled gums. She had large eyes full of greenish lights and heavy eyebrows that seemed at odds with the wispy tendrils of her hair, the darkish strands on her upper lip.

And she was full of stories, for her mother was a Cornishwoman, and it was a different world down there, she said, magical, disappearing at night. People told stories all night long to make the land come back each morning. And it was a different land each time, for nobody could tell the same story twice.

If you cut your finger at the new moon you were bound for ever to the goblin king unless you turned round quickly three times and said your own name backwards. If you were using salt you had to throw some over your left shoulder, or the devil would appear.

As she got older, Margaret would question her nurse or argue until Betsy would throw her arms up in mock horror, and call her Little Miss Plato, and tell her she was far too clever for her old nurse, now that she was being tutored by the Lady Alice.

It was Betsy who had taken her on her first visit to the new household, where she had clung fiercely to her nurse or followed her around like a tiny planet orbiting her sun. It was Betsy who had lost her that fateful day when her guardian had shown her the world in all its strangeness and colour, and Betsy whose footsteps had come pounding along the corridor to find her. Coming on them finally, breathless and distracted, she had sunk into a curtsy so low that she could not get up again, and the duke himself had helped her to her feet.

And it was Betsy who told her that she must play nicely with her new brother – 'like a good little girl' – and let him win.

Once he was breeched this was easy for him, because he could run about in his new trousers and she could only stumble after him in her long skirts. She could not climb trees or ford streams anywhere near as well as he. Also she was several months younger than he was, and small for her age, all of which made him well disposed towards her. Once, he had carried her across the stones in the stream like St Christopher, though she did not much like being carried and had clung to his neck for all she was worth, convinced he would drop her by accident or on purpose. She had worked out quite quickly, however, that he was not supposed to treat her 'with any discourtesy', and so she always made sure that if she was about to do anything to enrage him, such as winning at hide and seek, they were within earshot of his mother or his nurse.

And if he annoyed her by insisting on winning at indoor games he would sometimes find that his carved geese or horsemen, or his finest marbles, would mysteriously disappear. His nurse said that if he didn't leave them scattered around they would not be lost, but she would question the servants; in all probability they had simply been put away.

And so they had: in Margaret's room, in her private box.

On this particular Sunday it was very cold, and they had to play inside. So John took out his castle and his carved wooden knights and horses and they each had a mounted knight which they pushed down a ramp until they collided and the one that fell over lost. And since John pushed harder, Margaret's knight always lost. And then they played Siege, and her knights waited in the castle to be captured.

After that, since it wasn't snowing, they were allowed outside briefly, well wrapped in furs. It was a still, brown day with strands of pale light in the sky. They made their way to the pond to see if there was any life beneath its frozen surface and crouched down. John said he could see a fish, but though he pointed with a stick she couldn't see anything beneath the opaque patterns of ice. She wondered if the fish in its shadowy world was dreaming of the sky, or whether it thought that the surface of the pool was the sky, glinting above it in shards of light.

'We will be married soon,' John said suddenly. She looked up at him sharply but he was still studying the pond and his face was sober.

'I'm not getting married,' she said, and he cleared some withered stalks from the surface with his stick.

'You are,' he said.

'I'm not.'

He looked at her. 'You have to. Girls have to.'

She got up, shaking her skirts. 'Who says so?'

'My father. And my mother.'

'I'm not getting married to *you*,' she said. She hurried away from him then and only stopped when she heard a noise from behind. He was crying loudly, his mouth wide open. But she hesitated only for a moment, and then ran all the way to her nurse.

'I'm not getting married,' she panted.

Betsy sat back in dismay.

'Of course you are, my poppet,' she said.

Margaret was outraged. 'But – he is my brother – you said so!'

Betsy gathered her up on to her knee in the way she used to when Margaret was very small. 'He is not your real brother, poppet – he is your brother in spirit. Which is the best thing that a husband can be. Don't you want to be married to your very best friend?'

Margaret started to protest that she didn't want to be married at all, but Betsy swept this aside. Of course she wanted to be married. All good little girls got married, it was God's blessing on them for being good. Because God knew how good she was, he wanted to bless the earth with more little girls and boys who would be as good as she was.

Margaret looked at her, appalled, but her nurse said she would be a fine lady, like Lady Alice, and have her own household. She would be a duchess and her husband a duke. Didn't she want to be a duchess?

At the mention of Lady Alice she tried to wriggle off her nurse's knee. 'I will ask her,' she said, but her nurse clasped her more tightly and said she mustn't, she was not to bother Lady Alice when she was so busy making arrangements. It was going to be the best wedding in the world, she said: the Faerie Queen herself had said so.

Betsy told her that the Lady Alice had spent a week or more on her knees praying to Our Lady in Heaven to know who would be the perfect wife for her son. And at the end of that week the Queen of the Faeries had come to her in a dream. Her hair was as wild as bracken and her eyes were like the night sky. She had taken a garland of daisies from her hair and given them to Lady Alice. And in each daisy, instead of droplets of dew, there had been a shining pearl.

Pearls and daisies were the symbols of her name, Margaret.

Betsy's voice had grown hushed and her eyes luminous, but Margaret's forehead contracted into a frown. 'Why would Our Lady send the Faerie Queen?' she asked.

Betsy said that God's mother could choose her own messengers if anyone could. And, anyway, if she didn't believe her old Betsy, she could believe the dress that was being made for her. It was being embroidered with seed pearls in the shape of daisies. Betsy herself had seen it. 'You will look like a little angel from heaven,' she said, her eyes misting over.

Margaret finally wriggled free. 'I'm going to ask Lady Alice,' she said, and set off at a run so that her old nurse couldn't follow.

Lady Alice was not in the schoolroom where she taught Margaret, and she was not in the little chapel, listening to her choir of poor boys. Nor was she in the hospital where she cared for paupers, or for her own servants who had fallen ill. In the end Margaret had to ask one of the servants, who said she was in her private room, and reluctantly agreed to disturb her. And Lady Alice said she could be shown in.

She stood facing the window, with her back to Margaret, but as soon as the servant left she turned, then stood entirely still, with her face partially obscured by the light that was shining from behind.

'Well,' she said softly. 'What is it?'

But Margaret was suddenly overcome by the sense that she had done a monstrous thing, demanding to see the duchess in her room. She looked down at the floor and mumbled something to the effect that she had heard, Betsy had said, that she was to be married.

'Do you not wish to be married?' Lady Alice said.

When Margaret did not answer she came towards her, then unexpectedly crouched down on a little stool so that her face was more or less level with Margaret's own.

'You are so young,' she said. Margaret looked at her in growing dismay. It was not possible that Lady Alice had been crying.

There was no one Margaret admired so much as Lady Alice; she loved nothing better than to be taught by her, while John was learning to ride, and wear armour, and manage a sword. Lady Alice would read poems to her in French and make her repeat them. Even when she didn't understand the words she understood that Lady Alice loved reading them aloud and Margaret loved being read to; they were bound together by this love. Lady Alice praised her constantly for doing well in her studies and had insisted that she should be called Margaret, not Little Peg. When she grew up, Margaret wanted to be just like Lady Alice: elegant and learned, healing the afflicted by the soothing power of her presence. But it was not possible to love the Lady Alice in the same way as she did her nurse; there was always something inaccessible about her – she was as remote and serene as the moon.

But now she had been crying, and Margaret was shocked into silence.

Lady Alice touched her face and moved a strand of her hair, which had escaped from its cap.

'I was not much older than you when I was first married,' she said, and there was a catch in her voice. She tried to smile, but her eyes filled with tears again. Then she rested her hands on Margaret's bony shoulders. 'You are like a little bird,' she said, and she went on to say that she had her whole life in front of her, but life was often difficult, and marriage – marriage was difficult also.

Margaret was hardly listening, transfixed by the Lady Alice's unnatural smile, which did not reach her eyes.

'I would have liked a little daughter,' she said, nodding. 'I would like you to be a daughter to me. I would like you to marry my son.'

All the protests died away on Margaret's lips. There was no question in her mind that she would be a daughter to Lady Alice if that was what Lady Alice wanted.

Lady Alice said a few more words: that she hoped Margaret would be a companion for her son, that they would be companions for one another, throughout all life's difficulties. Together they would face any adversity that life had to offer, and they would never be alone.

'That is the great beauty of marrying young,' she said. Then, unexpectedly, she let her head fall on to Margaret's thin shoulders.

Margaret did not know what to do or say. She wondered if she should hold her tightly, as Betsy held her, or pat her shoulder. But Lady Alice rose swiftly, dabbing at her eyes, and went to the door where the servant was waiting outside. And Margaret understood that the interview was over.

Outside, the light seemed suddenly dazzling, though it was quite a dull day. John was waiting for her, scuffing one heel on the frozen earth. He looked up as she approached, and she looked at him as though she didn't recognize him.

'I told you we were going to be married,' he said. When she didn't answer he said, 'And you will love me for ever. Wives do.'

She said nothing, but went to stand beside him. He looked at her uncertainly. 'Will you marry me then?' he asked, and she nodded. And hesitantly, awkwardly, he took her hand.

Soon she was standing with him in the little chapel, wearing the white silk dress with seed pearls in the shape of daisies, while the little choir of poor boys sang. Their voices floated upwards to the ceiling which had been painted blue in imitation of the infinite sky. Then the priest told Margaret and John that marriage was a sacred sacrament, and they were joined together in an eternal bond.

Eternal was one of those words, like *infinite*, that was hard to imagine. But she promised to marry John and to stay with him for ever, and to love him, as wives do.

17

Lady Alice Receives News of Her Husband

And on the Sabbath day at about the tenth hour they beheaded him in a small boat and left his body with the head on the sea shore near Dover. And the body lay unburied for a month.
John Benet's Chronicle

Lo! What availed him now all his deliverance of Normandy? And here you may learn how he was rewarded for the death of the Duke of Gloucester.
Brut Chronicle

After the messenger told her what had happened she said nothing for several moments. Then she said, 'When?'

The messenger, a sharp-eyed man in rough clothing who had given his name simply as Watkin, pulled the corners of his mouth down. Then he advanced the opinion that it was probably three weeks ago now.

'Three weeks?'

The man shrugged. He said that they had not discovered the body for a day or so, and at first they hadn't known who it was. It had been stripped of its outer clothing and the head was . . . somewhat battered about. Once they had identified it as the duke they had sent a messenger straight away, but he had been attacked by robbers. He had been found not six miles away, so badly beaten it was unlikely that he would ever walk again. After that no one had wanted to make the journey, until Watkin had said that he was travelling north in any case.

She turned away from him then. She would not be sick.

'The roads are bad, ma'am – very bad. It has taken me the best part of a week to get here.'

She knew he was hinting at payment. But he had not told her enough yet; or nothing she could comprehend. Her husband had been killed on a beach.

'Where is my husband's body?'

Watkin said that he was sure they would have moved the body by now. Into the church, most likely.

'He must not be buried there,' she said.

'No, ma'am.'

'You will take back my instructions to the monks.'

'No, ma'am.'

She turned back to him.

'I am travelling north,' he said sturdily. 'To Coventry. I am six days late already. I will not risk my life again on those roads.'

She stared at him. 'What roads?' And he began a long, rambling tale, about the soldiers coming back from Normandy in such great misery and poverty that all they could do was to rob poor people on the roads or in their own homes. No one was safe, he said. And the people of the countryside had grown unquiet.

She hardly heard him. Her husband's body, with its severed head, had lain rotting on a beach. If she closed her eyes briefly she could see his face. *William*, she said, and he smiled at her.

'So even if I did go back,' the man was saying, 'there's no telling how long it'd take. And no saying I'd get there, either.'

She looked at him. He seemed like a man who could take care of himself. But she wasn't going to argue. All she said was, 'It doesn't matter. I will send my own men to bring the bod– the duke back here.'

Watkin pulled his mouth again. Then he said that they should be well armed, and that if it were him, he would not travel in anything bearing the duke's insignia.

She stared at him. 'You may go,' she said.

He bowed his head. 'My lady –'

'You may eat in the kitchens,' she said, and he bowed his head once more and left.

Lady Alice made her way to a chair and sat on it. She wondered if she was trembling, but she was not trembling. Then she wondered again whether she would be sick, but she was not sick. She stared ahead without seeing anything. For the first time in her life, it seemed, she did not know what to do. When she closed her eyes she could see her husband's face again, still smiling.

'Tell me what to do,' she said. She did not say it aloud but her lips moved as though she were praying. Her husband merely pointed out that she had always told him what to do. Then, superimposed over the image of his smiling face, came the image of his severed head, *somewhat battered about.*

She opened her eyes again quickly. There were many things to do; many arrangements to make. The whole household had to be in mourning. She would send men for her husband's body. And she would have to prepare for the funeral.

Still she did not move, but sat in her chair trying to comprehend this thing that had come to her; what it might mean. Her husband of nearly twenty years was gone, his body left on a beach in Dover. And there was her son.

At the thought of her son a low moan escaped her and she let her face fall briefly into her hands. Then she stood up, because there was so much to do.

The next morning her steward set off for Kent in an entirely plain carriage bearing no insignia, with a small company of armed men. But within three days he returned. The roads were impassable, he said. They had tried more than one way of getting through but had been turned back by great numbers of armed men. There was an insurrection in Kent.

[In June 1450] the commons of Kent arose with great power and came to Blackheath where they remained for seven days, surrounded by stakes and ditches.

London Chronicle

Lady Alice Receives News of Her Husband

Fifty thousand men of Kent rose in rebellion choosing as their captain a most impudent and clever man calling himself John Mortimer.

John Benet's Chronicle

The said captain and the Kentishmen came unto Blackheath, and there kept the field a month or more, pillaging all the country about . . .

An English Chronicle

18

Lady Alice Visits the Queen

It grew on her slowly, the horror of this thing, until some days after her steward returned she could no longer eat or sleep. At last she decided that she herself would go to visit the queen.

She travelled the next day at dawn so that she could make the whole journey in daylight, in an unmarked carriage. The queen received her at once, and the Lady Alice sank into a curtsy, then lifted her sorrowing face so that the queen could see. But all she said was that she begged permission to retrieve her husband's body for burial.

The queen gripped her arms tightly, so tightly she would surely bruise them, and said, 'It is true then?'

Lady Alice said nothing and the queen said, 'It cannot be true!'

And she turned away from Lady Alice and burst into a storm of passionate weeping.

Lady Alice remained where she was, since she had not been given permission to rise, but after a few moments, when the queen's frenzied weeping showed no signs of abating, she raised herself stiffly, holding on to the edge of the table, and took a few steps forward.

'Your majesty –' she said.

The queen turned towards her; her red, contorted face was almost unrecognizable.

'How can it happen? How can it happen?' she cried, her voice rising to a shriek. And she clutched handfuls of her hair as though she would tear it out.

Lady Alice felt calmer in the face of the queen's distress. Now that another person was giving voice to her own fear and incredulity, they both faded. It could happen, and it had.

'Your majesty, you must not distress yourself,' she said.

'No!' shrieked the queen. 'No! No!' and she pounded the wall at her side.

Lady Alice thought briefly of sending for the physician, but then the queen stood still, clutching her hair again, as though by a vast, inhuman effort, she was containing her emotion. Then she began to make a high, keening sound, and Lady Alice put her arms round her. She was much taller than the queen, who collapsed against her, weeping into her shoulder.

Lady Alice felt quite assured in this role. Had she not, many times, offered comfort to the people on her estates? She was able to lead the queen over to a low seat and make her lie down. Then she summoned the queen's ladies and the physician.

For the next few days she was constantly with the queen: holding her hands, insisting that she rested, making her eat. She gave orders for her own herbal remedies to be made up and fed them to the queen herself, on a spoon. She got little sense out of the queen in all that time. Sometimes she seemed calm, and would try to speak, but the sentence would end in another storm of tears.

It occurred to Lady Alice, from time to time, to wonder where all this grief was coming from. *Who is bereaved here?* she wondered. But she did not dwell on this. She did not believe the rumours about the queen and her husband, and if she had believed them, she did not know that she would have cared.

He would have done what he could to secure their position.

Besides, she came to see that the queen was not weeping for one single cause. It was as though the fragile shell of her world had fractured, and everything was spilling out.

'They will destroy us,' she moaned into her pillow, and Lady Alice did not know whether she meant the French, or the men of Kent, or the murderers of her husband.

So she comforted the queen in general terms, as though she were a child.

'Ssh-sssh,' she said to her. 'Ssssh.'

And she felt better as she did so; or at least as if she was able to step to one side, observing herself in this tragedy. All her life she had stood a little to one side, observing herself in this role or that, as though she were a player on a stage.

She felt safe in the palace for now, though she did begin to wonder when she might return.

Then, on the fourth day, the queen sat up and said, 'He must be buried.' Which was the point that Lady Alice had been making all along. But the queen was finally calm. She insisted on getting up and dressed. Then, on hearing that her husband was travelling from the parliament in Leicester back to London, she said, 'I will go to meet him.'

She would not listen to any arguments; Lady Alice had done enough, she said. There were no words to express what she had gone through. She must go home now and attend to her affairs; the queen would make sure that her husband's body was returned to her if she had to collect him herself. And Lady Alice was to worry about nothing; she would take care of her for the rest of her life. 'You are my family now,' she said.

And Lady Alice, curtsying deeply, wondered whether that was not the very thing she had to worry about.

The king sent unto the captain at Blackheath divers lords both spiritual and temporal to learn why such a great gathering of that misadvised fellowship had occurred . . . *Gregory's Chronicle*

The captain showed them the articles of his petition concerning the mischiefs and misgovernments of the realm . . . *An English Chronicle*

We believe that the king our sovereign lord is betrayed by the insatiable covetousness and malicious purpose of certain false and unsuitable persons who are around his highness day and night . . .

The king's false council has lost his law, his merchandise is lost, his common people are destroyed, the sea is lost, France is lost, the king himself is so placed that he may not pay for his meat and drink . . .

The king should take about his noble person men of his true blood from his royal realm, that is to say the high and mighty prince, the Duke of York, exiled from our sovereign lord's person by the suggestions of those false traitors the Duke of Suffolk and his affinity.

Proclamation of Jack Cade, June 1450

19

The King's True Commons

Because the queen had insisted that she would go to London to meet with the king, her chief of guards had sent scouts ahead of them, as though before battle, to an enemy army.

He had sent out three scouts, and only two had returned, one of them almost insensible with fear. The man they called Jack Cade, or John Mortimer, he said, had somehow obtained the keys to the city.

Cade's men had taken to robbery and plunder. They had emptied the prisons and thrown the rich into them, holding them until they paid their own ransoms. The Captain, as Cade was called, rode about the city like a lord in gilded armour and a blue velvet cloak, bearing a naked sword in his hand, while all the rioting and looting spread.

There was worse news. The Bishop of Salisbury had been dragged from the altar after saying mass and had been killed by his own parishioners. They had torn his clothing to pieces and gone about waving the bloody shreds like rags.

The mob had cried for more of the king's 'false councillors' to be handed over to them, so King Henry had shut certain of his lords in the Tower for safekeeping. Then he had sent his men against the mob, but the rebels had fought these men and won. And many of the king's men had said they would rather assist the rebels, and were daily deserting the king.

Then Jack Cade, or John Mortimer, had demanded that Lord Say be brought out of the Tower, and had executed him at once, without trial. He had tied Lord Say's feet to his own saddle and dragged him naked through the streets to London Bridge. There he had circled a great stone, beating it with his sword, before putting Lord

Say's head on the bridge and dragging the headless body over it to Southwark, where it was hacked into quarters.

At the same time, William Crowmer, Sheriff of Kent, who had married Lord Say's daughter, was dragged out of the Fleet prison, 'for many crimes against the commons', and his head stricken off. The two heads, of Lord Say and his son-in-law, were placed on long poles and carried through the streets and made to kiss several times at different places, for the entertainment of the mob.

Now it was said that the Londoners themselves had risen up against the rebels and were trying to drive them back. There was a great battle on London Bridge but 'many a man had been slain and cast in the Thames', and the water was bobbing with bodies.

And nobody knew where the king was. Still, the queen wished to go to him, through the streets of the city.

'She'll get us all killed,' said the chief of guards' second in command. 'I'm not going on and neither will they.' He jerked his head to indicate his men.

The chief of guards, a sallow, wary man, whose face was pulled into a permanent grimace, could read quite plainly the mood of his men. There would be mutiny if he ordered them forward, and his second in command would not back him up. But he could not think how to communicate this to the queen, who sat impatiently in her carriage, waiting to know the source of the delay.

'Tell her she can go on her own,' his second in command said. 'They won't be looking for an unaccompanied queen.'

The chief of guards looked at him. He was a short, squarish man. The kind of man, the chief of guards reflected, who would always take a grim pleasure in making unhelpful suggestions. He looked away from him and gazed instead towards the smoke rising from within the city walls.

After several moments, however, the queen called out sharply. When no one responded immediately, she was forced to call out again.

'Good luck,' said his second in command, as the chief of guards turned round slowly.

'What is it?' she asked before he even reached her. 'What is this delay?'

The chief of guards paused eloquently, so that she could take in the muffled roar from beyond the gates of the city that was like the roar of the sea, punctuated by distant explosions; the dull orange glow of the sky; the smell of smoke.

'I do not think that we can pass through the city, my lady,' he said.

'Of course we can,' she said. 'How else are we to reach the king?'

'The disturbances,' he said, as though she had not spoken. 'The reports – are not good.'

'What reports?'

He lifted his left shoulder in what was not quite a shrug. 'My lady, there is warfare on the streets. The rebels have assailed the Tower – it is said they have fired the bridge.'

'Who says this?' she demanded, then when he did not reply she said, 'You are armed men, are you not?'

'Yes, but –'

'You are on horseback – you can ride them down, trample them back into the dirt from which they came. That, in fact,' she said, 'is what you do, is it not?'

The chief of guards turned his face slightly away from her and paused again, weighing his words carefully.

'No one knows how many of them there are . . . Some say there are many thousands.'

'And?'

'My men – are reluctant to go ahead – in the circumstances.'

She looked at him as if she could not believe what she was hearing.

'They will not go to help their king?'

The chief of guards shook his head slightly, still without looking at her.

'I do not think that his majesty would want me to risk so many lives – especially not yours, my lady.'

'Do I have to go on alone?'

'My lady,' the chief of guards said, turning towards her, 'that would not be wise.'

She stood with a sudden, violent movement. The chief of guards did not move. He knew that he could not lay hands on the queen or manhandle her back into the carriage, but he spoke rapidly and with urgency.

'Your majesty – you will not get so far as the gates. And if anyone sees you – anything could happen. The king would not wish it, my lady.'

He was standing in front of her as though he would obstruct her, and staring very directly into her eyes. The queen was forced to pause, but she still looked as though she would climb down from the carriage.

'Warfare is won by the wise,' he said. 'It is not wisdom to approach a blood-crazed mob – how will I tell the king if anything happens to you? He needs to know you are safe. This is not helping the king, my lady,' he added as she moved forward. 'How will it help his majesty if you risk your life in this way? It will only help his enemies.'

She stopped then, glaring at him.

'Think of his majesty,' he said. 'It would break his heart.'

She closed her eyes for a moment, then released a stream of impassioned French, so rapid that the chief of guards could only pick out certain words – *traitors, cowards, scum* – that he chose to believe were referring to the rebels.

'My lady, I will find lodgings for you – just for the night. In the morning, all this –' he gestured towards the city – 'may have died down and we can try again.'

For a long moment she did not move, then all at once she collapsed backwards into her seat. He could feel the fury and disbelief bristling from her. She spoke in a low, shaking voice. 'What do they imagine is their grievance, these – traitors?'

The chief of guards hardly knew where to begin: the loss of all the towns and castles of Normandy; the return of soldiers in such great misery and poverty that all they could do was steal and attack the poor people of the countryside; the corruption of all those officers who dealt with the law; extortion and rapine.

Fortunately, the queen did not seem to require an answer.

'In my other country,' she said, 'they would be strung up and whipped in the marketplaces, and then have their limbs struck off one by one.'

The chief of guards inclined his head. He did not doubt it.

'There is nothing to be gained by pressing forward now,' he said. 'I will find you lodgings for the night. And in the morning we will try again.'

Then, reluctant or unable to pursue the discussion further, he returned to his horse, mounted it and rode back towards his men. If she got out of the carriage while he was not looking there was nothing he could do. *I will resign my command*, he thought.

He reissued his orders to his men as though he had not lost command of them, as though they had not refused outright to enter the city. He told them that they would ride to a place six miles away, where they would find lodgings for the queen and where they could set up camp. His second in command pulled his own horse up alongside him.

'And she has agreed to this, has she?' he said.

'She would have gone on alone.'

'And you stopped her? That would have saved us all some trouble.'

The chief of guards said nothing to this, only spurring his horse forward so he could check that the queen was still in the carriage. His second in command eyed his retreating back resentfully. 'French bitch,' he said, and spat.

But he marshalled his men together and they followed the carriage away from the heat and clamour of the city.

After the wooden bridge was set on fire the men of Kent withdrew, little by little. Their captain put all his pillage and the goods that he had robbed into a barge and sent it to Rochester by water, and he went by land and would have gone to the castle of Queenborough with the few men that were left with him, but he failed in his purpose. And so he fled into the countryside near Lewes . . .

An English Chronicle

And that day was that false traitor the Captain of Kent taken and slain in the county of Sussex, and upon the morrow he was brought in a cart all naked and at the White Hart in Southwark the cart drew to a halt so that the wife of that house might see if it was the same man that was named the Captain of Kent who had lodged there. And from there he was taken to the King's Bench and there he lay from Monday evening to the Thursday following, and within the King's Bench the said captain was beheaded and quartered, and the same day drawn upon a hurdle in pieces, with the head between his chest, from the King's Bench throughout Southwark and then over London Bridge, and then through London unto Newgate, and then his head was taken and set upon London Bridge . . .

And the same year the king was at Canterbury, and with him was the Duke of Exeter, the Duke of Somerset, my Lord of Shrewsbury with many more lords and many justices and they held sessions for four days and condemned many of the Captain's men for the uprising and for talking against the king and for favouring the Duke of York over the king. And the condemned men were drawn, hanged and beheaded . . . and at Rochester nine men were beheaded and their heads were sent to London by the king's commandment and set upon London Bridge all at one time, and twelve more heads were brought at another time . . . and at other times more. Men called it in Kent the harvest of heads . . .

Gregory's Chronicle

And about the feast of the Assumption of the Blessed Mary [August 1450] the town of Cherbourg surrendered to the King of France and so the whole of Normandy was lost; which was an irreparable disaster for England. And the Duke of Somerset came back to England when he had ruined the whole of Normandy . . .

John Benet's Chronicle

20

Richard and Cecily

She recognized the seal at once on the letter he was reading: it had been sent by the abbot of Gloucester.

'Your old friend,' the Duchess of York said, sitting beside her husband.

'He would be my friend now if he could.'

'It's a little late for that.'

Nothing. She looked more searchingly at his face.

'What does he want?'

Again he did not reply. It worried her that he did not reply.

'I do not suppose he is sending you any of the money that the king owes you . . .'

Silence.

'. . . nor enquiring after your health. Perhaps his own coffers are so depleted that he wants you to send money to him? No? Well then, let me see.'

She leaned forward. 'He wants you to return to England to help him and the king out of some godforsaken mess – yes – I can see that is it.'

The duke did not like his wife's mood. He moved the letter away from her.

'Should I disappoint him?'

'You are not serious.'

The duke didn't smile.

'Richard – you cannot go.'

'Somerset is back.'

'All the more reason to stay away.'

He picked up the letter and read: *'They are saying that from the time that Jack Cade or Mortimer, called Captain of Kent, raised a rebellion in Kent, all disturbances are at the will of York, who is descended from the Mortimers.'*

She did not flinch. 'It is not safe for you to go.'

'Somerset will not rest until I am indicted for treason.'

'You are needed here.'

'He drips poison in the king's ear.'

'Listen to me,' she said. 'You have served the king loyally and well. No other lieutenant in Ireland has done so much – and all without one penny from the royal coffers. Somerset has lost all of Normandy – he is the one who should be impeached. But if you leave this country now the king will think you are breaking the terms of your commission –'

'My exile, you mean.'

'– and if you enter England with all your men he will think you are declaring war.'

He closed his eyes briefly. 'I could go without my men.'

'You cannot! Richard – you will not!'

'If I stay I am condemned behind my back.'

'If you go you will be condemned in court – to death. Or just killed. That would suit them.'

He shook his head. 'It is not often said that an Englishman is safer in Ireland.'

'But you have friends here. And your family.'

He did have friends. Even among the Irish lords. The parliament in Dublin had been advancing him funds in the absence of any money from the king. Cecily had made her home here; their son George had been born in Dublin less than a year ago. Still, it was not safe enough to leave her here. Anyway, she would not be left. And he would not take her with him, into a death trap.

'Ireland needs you,' she was saying. 'Your children need you. And I need you. You cannot go – I will not allow it.'

'You will not allow it?'

'I will go first.'

Despite himself, he almost laughed. 'You will go? How will that help?'

'I will not stay here and let you walk to your death.' She put an imploring hand on his arm. 'Richard, you owe this abbot nothing. You cannot just go – at least write to the king first.'

He had written many times without response. His last letter had been written to his brother-in-law, the Earl of Salisbury, instructing him to read it aloud in parliament. That would have annoyed the king still further, he thought.

'At least ask for the king's permission to leave your post. Assure him of your allegiance – your goodwill. Offer to help. He may not respond, but he cannot ignore it. I will write it, if you like.'

'You will not write it.'

'Then I will read it. Yes, Richard, there is a time for wrath and a time for conciliation. Do not vex the king at the moment. He is like a fox trapped in a hole.'

He gave her a long, considering look, then said, 'I will write to him. But you need not read it.'

The duchess raised her eyes briefly to heaven. They both knew that the duke was not good with words. Then she said, 'Do not mention the Duke of Somerset for now.'

There was only a hint of irony in the look the duke gave her as he took some paper from a drawer.

'You may leave me to write the letter,' he said.

21

Margaret and Henry

'How dare he?' she said.

She had snatched the letter from him when she had seen the seal. Now she was white and her head was shaking. 'How dare he?' she repeated. The king looked at her in some alarm.

'My love –'

'He is dictating to you!'

'Margaret –'

'He writes as if he were king!'

'He wants to clear his name.'

'By transferring all the blame on to our cousin.'

He did not point out that the Duke of York was also his cousin.

'*The Duke of Somerset should be brought to trial* . . . Why do you not summon York to trial?'

The king ventured the opinion that he had done nothing wrong.

'Nothing? Except incite your people to rebellion against you!'

'There is no proof –'

'An Irishman called Mortimer leads an insurrection against you – and you say there is no proof!'

'Jack Cade –'

'Mortimer! His name was John Mortimer.' She scanned the letter again. Her head was still shaking. 'He asks for money – hah! *I will pursue this matter to completion* – how dare he speak so!'

'Give it back to me. Please.'

'It was another Irishman who murdered the Duke of Suffolk,' she said in low, shaking tones. 'Our dearest friend.'

The king was worried about his wife. She had not been the same since the murder of the Duke of Suffolk. At his funeral, which had finally been arranged, she had wept inconsolably, without caring what people might think. She was so passionate; it was one of the things he had always loved about her. But since that day she had seemed . . . fragile.

'Will you let him murder another dear friend?'

The king remonstrated with her. She was too extreme. There was nothing to implicate the Duke of York in the murder of their friend. He was not even in the country at the time.

'Exactly! He was in Ireland. And while he has been in Ireland two Irishmen have inflicted untold damage on this land.'

'He cannot be held to blame for the actions of all Irishmen.'

'Then let him stand trial. Let him prove his innocence.'

'The people would never stand for it. They are on his side –'

'Yes! That was always his plan – to gather the people around him. He thinks you will not dare to stand against him while he has their support. We will show him otherwise.'

The king closed his eyes. 'The situation is too . . . difficult,' he said.

'That's what he thinks.'

'And he is right. If anything, we need him on our side.'

'So we give in to him? We let him dictate his terms?'

'For now, perhaps –'

But the queen turned on him furiously. He had already lost France, she said. Was he preparing to lose England also?

She meant to wound him, but inexplicably the king was filled with tenderness for her. He was reminded piercingly of the first time they had talked together, when he had seen that same combination of trepidation and courage, or defiance. Since then she had suffered one blow after another, and he had wished, many times, that he could make it better, but he could not. He wished he could hold her, but he knew her in this mood and she would not be held.

'I will stand between you and your enemies,' he had said to Suffolk. Unexpectedly, his eyes filled with tears. She registered this at once.

'See how he distresses you,' she said. 'But you must show him your strength, not your weakness. He wants to bring your dearest friend down – you must raise him up.'

The king released a long, shaking sigh.

'And if he comes into this country, my lord, you must arrest him.'

The king stared at her.

'You *must*! Or he will destroy everyone around us! He will lead all the people in a coup and overthrow you.'

There was a note of hysteria in her voice. It took little, these days, to induce it. People thought she ruled him with her strength; sometimes he thought he was the only one who could see her weakness. He was not afraid of her, but *for* her. He stretched out his hands towards her; she regarded them warily, without moving.

Once, at communion, the king thought he had seen a tiny figure of Christ in each of his cupped palms, shining with the promise of peace. When he had pressed his hands together the light had streamed upwards from his fingertips. He wished now, as the queen somewhat reluctantly came towards him, that light from God would pour towards her through his hands and bring her peace. He wanted to bless her as he placed his hands on her hair. She stood unresisting, but did not yield either.

'Do not let him destroy us,' she said, somewhat feverishly. 'You must act at once.'

The king closed his eyes and lowered his face to her hair.

'I will see what I can do,' he said.

11th September 1450: appointment of Edmund Duke of Somerset as Constable of England. *Calendar of Patent Rolls*

22

Richard and Henry

And about the Feast of the Nativity of the Blessed Mary [8th September] the Duke of York came back from Ireland and landed in Wales.

John Benet's Chronicle

He had taken a circuitous route from Wales to avoid the agents of the king who had tried to intercept him at Beaumaris, Chester and Shrewsbury. He had travelled mainly by night, skirting the great forests, though it was hardly possible to hide the progress of so large an army, and he had known, on more than one occasion, that they were being followed. Then, on reaching London, he had been appalled by the unrest in the city. All through the streets men were rioting and looting. The warden of Newgate had released all the prisoners from their cells; they were throwing stones and injuring as many as they could. But as the duke progressed through the city many of these people cried out to him for blessings or aid, and several, including the prisoners, fell in behind him, chanting, 'Hail to the Duke of York; true lord of this land!' The duke neither encouraged nor prevented them, but rode ahead of them with a set face. More and more of them joined his ranks, so that it was a great army that approached Westminster Palace.

The king's expression was serious as the duke knelt before him. Then, with a sudden smile, he said, 'Welcome, dearest cousin. We thank you for your assistance.'

The duke did not look up. 'I and my sword, and everything I have, are always at your service, my lord,' he said distinctly.

He lodged that night at the house of the Bishop of Salisbury, but when he learned of the promotion of the Duke of Somerset he returned at once to the palace. He demanded to speak to the king, but was told that the king was at prayer and did not wish to be disturbed.

'He will be disturbed,' said the duke. 'I will disturb him.'

He strode past the guards along the corridor and rapped sharply on the door of the king's privy chamber. And when there was no answer he hammered on the door.

It finally opened and the king himself stood there, clutching the front of his gown.

'What – what is it?' he said.

He was wearing a rough shirt, open at the neck, that hung below his knees. Some cloth was bound around his legs and feet, from which his yellowing toenails protruded. The duke took in his appearance at once, and registered it with an absolute dislike.

'There are some matters I must discuss with you,' he said, quietly enough.

'I was praying,' the king said, and the duke almost told him that God could wait, but instead said that the business was urgent.

The king looked left and right along the corridor where the guards gathered anxiously, but then he retreated into his room, indicating with the slightest motion of his head that the duke might follow.

Only two candles were burning beneath a crucifix. The king took some time to light a third, then he turned to the duke and lifted his hands and let them fall.

'You see I am alone.'

He *was* alone. It was not usual for any king to be entirely alone, but this king spent so much time in prayer that he regularly insisted upon solitude. And suddenly it was the duke who was uncomfortable with the situation: he had grown used to ensuring that there were witnesses to any interaction between him and the king.

'Do you want to send for – someone?'

'Am I not safe?'

The duke gave the king a searching look, but all he said was, 'Your majesty has nothing to fear from me.'

He saw that the king was, in fact, afraid. His hands shook as he lit a fourth candle. The duke hesitated for a moment, then knelt.

'I am your servant and I will always be obedient to your command.'

'Then there is nothing to fear,' said the king.

'But there are things I have to say.'

The king said nothing, so the duke remained on his knees.

'Your majesty must see that there is a great sickness in this country – it is being brought to ruin. Certain reforms must be made. And they will never be made while the country is run by a coven of corrupt councillors!'

He stood up suddenly, without waiting for permission.

'What is this that I have heard about the Duke of Somerset?' he demanded. 'He has lost all Normandy and been promoted? To Lord High Constable of England?'

Moments earlier the king had been praying, following a thread of light through the inner reaches of his consciousness. He had felt, briefly, the sensation of hands on his head. Now the duke's short sentences fell like hammer blows on the same place. Fortunately, York was not waiting for an answer.

'All the people cry out against it – you have heard them! If they cannot have justice, they will have blood.'

'Do you threaten me with the people?'

'I do not threaten you at *all*. But the people are crying out to you and you must listen – you must be *seen* to be listening. You must dismiss your current advisors and bring as many as possible to trial. I advise you, my lord, to summon a parliament immediately. Make it known that you are dealing with the abuses in government.'

'Is that all?'

'No,' York said. 'It is not all. You have excluded me from your council for long enough. I am your cousin, and the first magnate of this land.'

This, they both knew, was the crux of the matter. Behind York's words were other, unspoken words, concerning his ancestry, and the king's. For it was not clear by lineage who had the greater right to the throne.

'You have not been excluded,' the king said faintly. 'You have been made Lieutenant of Ireland.'

'And now that I am back from Ireland,' York said, equally quietly, 'you may consult with me on matters of state.'

Each could hear the other breathing. Then Henry said, 'I am your king.'

And before the duke could reply to this, Henry continued, 'I have always been king. I was a few months old when my father died, and suddenly I was king of both England and France. I did not choose it – how could I have chosen it when I could neither walk nor talk? God chose it for me. Yes,' the king said, nodding as the duke began to speak. 'God chose for me and I accepted it – as I will always accept God's will. If He wills it, I will stop being king. But I will never, of my own volition, give up the task that God has given me.'

The duke was silent. He understood, of course. To any other man the fact that he had not chosen his high office might mean that he could give it up. But not to the king. If it had been of his own choosing he might have given up the crown. But it was not his choice; it was God's will.

From time to time, it seemed, God did choose entirely unsuitable men to be king, but that was the mystery of His will, and His divine right. Only God had the right to determine who was king.

Both men understood this, and so neither spoke nor moved, impaled upon their concept of kingship. In the last century two unsuitable kings had been deposed; the king's grandfather and the duke's ancestor had been the deposers. But neither man wanted to speak of deposition, aware of the tragedy involved and the immensity of the crisis that would follow.

In the shadows thrown by the candlelight they were two men facing each other, stripped to their naked intent. But one of them was king.

It was York who spoke first, breathing so heavily that all the candle flames guttered.

'No one is asking you to give it up,' he said. 'I ask only that I am allowed to serve you as is my right. I should not be excluded any more, and I will not be treated as a criminal!'

His voice was rising again, but it was no longer clear who he was angry at. 'I will not stand by and watch the Duke of Somerset ruin all England as well as France – he must be brought to trial!'

The king started to protest, but the duke cut him short.

'Summon a parliament,' he said. 'I will present my petitions there.'

Sometimes, lately, the king thought he could see a white light from the corner of his vision, surrounding people or objects. Such a light had now formed around the Duke of York, but it did not appear beneficent. It was livid and oppressive, and the king turned away from it.

'I will see what I can do,' he said, and without waiting for dismissal York left the room, passing the grooms and guards and courtiers who had now gathered outside. Some looked outraged and others terrified, but he strode past them all, ignoring the apprehension on their faces.

All the king's household was and is afraid right sore, and my lord has desired many things which are after the desire of the common people, and all is upon justice and to put all those who are indicted under arrest . . . to be tried by law.

Paston Letters

The Duke of York stayed in London at the lodging of the Bishop of Salisbury until the feast of Dionysus [9th October]. And about that time the King of France launched an assault against Gascony. *John Benet's Chronicle*

On 6th November parliament began at Westminster and the commons chose Sir William Oldhall, knight with the Duke of York, as Speaker . . . at the same time it was ordained in various parts of the city that chains should be drawn across the ways to keep the city safe, for people stood in great fear and doubt on account of the discord between lords . . .

On the 23rd day of November the Duke of York, with 3,000 men and more, came riding through the city, his sword borne before him, and rode to parliament and to the king. And on the following morning came riding through the city the Duke of Norfolk with a great crowd of men in full armour and six trumpets blowing before him. Then on the following morning the Earl of Warwick came through the city with a great company arrayed for war.

Bale's Chronicle

On St Andrew's Day, when they realized that neither the king nor his counsellors were punishing those who had so scandalized the whole nation by their treason, and chiefly the Duke of Somerset who had so negligently and shamefully lost Normandy, the men who had come with their lords to parliament made a huge uproar in the Hall of Westminster and called upon the king three times to provide justice against the traitors and punish them, and the king and his lords were seriously terrified . . .

The following afternoon almost 1,000 well-armed men attacked the Duke of Somerset without warning and would have slain him. But at the request of the Duke of York, the Earl of Devon calmed them and prudently seized the duke and led him secretly from Blackfriars to the Thames and thence to the Tower of London.

John Benet's Chronicle

And on the 18th of December parliament was prorogued until the 20th of January. And the king and queen spent Christmas at Westminster . . .

John Benet's Chronicle

23

So Pore a Kyng was Never Sene

For ye have made the king so poor
That now he begs from door to door
Alas so it be.

contemporary ballad

The steward did not get up when told to rise, but remained kneeling in a crouching position so that his voice was somewhat indistinct and they had to ask him to repeat his message.

There was no food, he said, no food for the feast.

The queen glanced quickly at the king.

'Of course there is food,' she said. 'Has it not arrived?'

'No, your majesty – your royal highness – there is no food to arrive.'

'I do not understand you,' she said.

Still kneeling, the steward stammered out that the usual tradesmen had not supplied the meat, because they had not been paid for the last feast. Or the one before.

'What is he talking about?' the queen demanded from the king.

The king replied merely that if there was no meat, then perhaps they should fast. It was a religious festival, after all.

The queen could hardly believe what she was hearing. 'We do not *fast* at epiphany,' she said.

Eleanor Beauchamp, wife of the Duke of Somerset, ventured to say that they were welcome to celebrate the feast at her house – she had more than enough food.

'That will not be necessary,' said the queen. 'Tell him that if the usual suppliers have failed, he must try other ones.'

But the steward said there was not a tradesman to be found anywhere in the city who would supply the royal household.

The queen looked as though she would have him executed on the spot.

'This is nonsense!' she cried, but the king was already telling the steward that he could go.

'See what you can find in the markets,' he said, and the steward, vastly relieved, almost ran from the hall.

The king turned to face his guests.

'It seems there will be no feast today,' he said.

'Henry!' said the queen.

'You must go and break bread in your own homes,' he continued, with hardly a quaver in his voice. 'In commemoration of this day – when, after so long a journey in sorrow and doubt, the wise men, guided by Our Lord, found the infant Christ and His blessed Mother in a poor place – not for Him were the riches of this world. So keep this day,' he said, nodding, 'in remembrance of His sacred poverty.'

No one uttered a sound in the hall; not even the queen made any comment or contradiction. Then in ones and twos the guests left, until only the king and queen remained, he standing, she sitting, facing one another. A breeze stirred through the hall so that the hangings shifted and settled again, which was the only sound to break the silence.

After Christmas the Duke of Somerset [released from the Tower] became Captain of Calais, and most familiar with the king, so that he controlled everything, both within the royal household and outside it . . . Also in May [1451] Thomas Young of Bristol, apprentice in law, moved that, because the king had as yet no offspring, it would promote the security of the kingdom if he openly established who was his heir apparent. And he nominated the Duke of York. For which reason he was committed to the Tower of London.

Annales Rerum Anglicarum

In May the King of France . . . ordered the Count of Dunois, his commander in chief . . . to go and conquer Guyenne. On 2nd June, the Count of Dunois sent men to lay siege by land and sea to the castle at a place called Fronsac. This was the strongest in the whole region of Guyenne and had always been guarded by English troops . . .

In spite of this though . . . the invading army was too strong . . . The besieged in Bordeaux were confident of eventual help . . . but on sunset [of 23rd June] the beleaguered English, seeing that help had failed them, had a herald cry out in anguish for the help which had never arrived . . .

Jean de Waurin

And the king appointed Lord Rivers with four thousand men to fight against the King of France at Bordeaux, which lay at Plymouth for a year for lack of wages and so nothing progressed. And on the 3rd day of July the city of Bordeaux was lost and afterwards the whole of Gascony was lost . . .

John Benet's Chronicle

After Candlemas [February 1452] the king ordered Richard, Duke of York, to join him in Coventry, but the duke refused to come and marched vigorously towards London.

Chronicon Angliae

On 1st March the king, with 24,000 men, rode to Blackheath and then to Welling. The bishops of Winchester and Ely, the Earls of Salisbury and Warwick and others, meanwhile sought to negotiate a settlement between the king and the duke . . .

John Benet's Chronicle

24

March 1452: Dartford

They had urged him, in the king's name, to take no action that might be construed as rebellion. He had responded, of course, that he had no such intention: he would never take up arms against his king, his actions were for the good of the country and directed against those who had betrayed the king.

However, here he was, with a large army drawn up for battle, a great number of cannon positioned to confront the royal army if it advanced (as it must) along Watling Street, pits and fortifications dug all round, and seven ships on the south shore of the Thames laden with supplies.

It would be difficult to convince anyone that he was not planning a rebellion. Certainly the king was not convinced; he had ordered London to close its gates against him.

Still, he had sent a delegation to ask York to return to his allegiance. And York had replied that he would willingly do so if Somerset was punished for his crimes against the state. He would have the Duke of Somerset or die therefore, he had said, and then he'd said that he wished to be acknowledged as the king's heir.

At this, he thought he saw the light of hope die in their eyes, but he would not retract his statement. He could not see the crown go to Somerset.

And so they had left him, promising they would do their best. And the duke stayed in his tent for a while, then rode around his camp, surveying his men, their equipment, their supplies, their horses. He was always meticulous about the horses. He went to the shore of the Thames and there were the great ships waiting with supplies, or so that they could make an escape if they needed to.

Everything was prepared: he had never been more prepared for war.

But his heart was not glad.

He could feel a band of absolute tension round his shoulders; they were curved like a bow, as though the clavicles were fused together. He watched the water lap and suck at the sides of the great boats.

He squatted suddenly, a soft breath huffing out of him, and looked down at the water, his hands hanging between his knees. Directly beneath him it lurched and swayed in a contradictory motion reflecting miscellaneous lights. Close up, it was green, covered with a thin slurry; further away, it was a stippled silver, except in the brown shadows of the great boats, and the underside of waves, which were brown. A seabird bobbed randomly on its surface.

He watched another bird dive into the water and emerge with a fish flapping in its beak. In nature there was no decision to take. Only man was blinded by choice.

Behind him on the field were thousands of men, cleaning their armour, leading the horses to drink, preparing food. That night some would lie awake crying and praying while others would fall quickly and suddenly asleep. He was leading them all against their king.

What he was doing was treason, there was no doubt about that. The penalty for treason was a traitor's death – it would be better, far better, to die in battle.

Then there would be reprisals: against his family, against everyone who had supported him.

If the king would listen to reason . . . but the king would not listen. They would have to kill the queen, or knock her unconscious, because she would surely intervene.

He looked at his hands, as if he would find the answer there. They were short, squarish, fleshy at the base of the thumbs, with strong, deep lines on the palms. The hands of a practical man, a soldier, calloused from wielding a sword. When he had not been able to trust his mind, he had trusted his hands.

Were they a traitor's hands?

They were a killer's hands; he had often killed.

Once he had seen a horse, blinded in battle, remain by its wounded rider to the end.

It had given its heart.

Once the heart was given there was a certain freedom, because everything else followed. But his heart was torn; he could almost feel it bleeding in his chest.

He missed his wife.

If Cecily were here, what would she say to him?

She would say, *Stay alive if you can.*

The Duke of York turned his hands over, as though examining the stubby, wrinkled fingers, greyish in the fading light.

Everything would depend on what they said to him on their return.

If they returned.

The feeling of doom intensified in him, so that when in fact they *did* return, he felt only a dull surprise throbbing at the back of his skull. The king, they said, would accede to his demands provided that he disbanded his army and came to him, and made a full submission on his knees.

He did not ask for the details of how they had managed this, of what they had done with the queen. For a long moment he said nothing at all. Then he said that he would dismiss his men, though Lord Cobham said he should be wary of a trap. There was something they were not telling him, he said. The duke only nodded.

'We will dismiss the men,' he said.

When they had mustered on Blackheath, certain lords were sent to the duke to negotiate terms with him . . . They concluded that the Duke of Somerset should be required to answer such charges as the Duke of York should put to him, and that the Duke of York should break his field and come to the king . . . But when he was come, contrary to the promises before made, the Duke of Somerset was present, awaiting and chief about the king, and made the Duke of York ride as a prisoner through London, and after they would have put him in prison. But a rumour arose that the Earl of March, his son, was coming with 20,000 men towards London, whereof the king and his council were afraid. And they concluded that the Duke of York should depart [into protective custody] . . .

Brut Chronicle

Later the Duke of York swore an oath before the king at the high altar of St Paul's, declaring that he had never rebelled against the king and promising never to take up arms against him in future. *John Benet's Chronicle*

After 29th September [1452] the Earl of Shrewsbury put to sea with a hundred ships, heading for Aquitaine. He sailed up the river Garonne where he overcame and captured 33 ships. On 21st October he took the town of Bordeaux by storm and went on to take 32 villages and towns in Aquitaine.

John Benet's Chronicle

[Later that year] the king, complying with the counsel of the Duke of Somerset, rode to several of the Duke of York's townships where the tenants were compelled to come naked with choking cords around their necks in the direst frost and snow, because previously they had supported their lord against the Duke of Somerset . . . Moreover, although the king himself pardoned them, the Duke of Somerset ordered them to be hanged. *London Chronicle*

25

The Queen Consults Lady Alice

She had travelled to the shrine of Our Lady in Walsingham to make an offering of a tablet of gold in the hope that she would conceive, and also to light a candle for her mother, Queen Isabella, who was mortally ill. On the way back she called at the house of her friend, Lady Alice, because there were certain matters she wished to discuss.

The duchess was looking older – she noticed that at once – and thinner; there were signs of permanent strain on her face. But she greeted the queen warmly, and they spoke of how affairs in Gascony were going so well, and how the king's half-brothers, Edmund and Jasper Tudor, who had been newly knighted, had accompanied him for the first time to the parliament in Reading.

'The king's mind is much upon his family,' the queen said. She could not smile as she said this, because she was so estranged from her own family in France – from her mother who was dying – and because here she had no family of her own.

This, in fact, was the main reason she had come to consult Lady Alice, who was well known for her medical expertise.

Lady Alice said merely that she hoped the king's family would be a comfort to him, as family ought to be. The queen gave her a sideways glance.

'Sometimes I dream that I have a child – a little boy,' she said. 'Last week I dreamed that when they gave him to me he was already arrayed as a knight, and I took him and put him directly on a horse.' She laughed a little.

'Your majesty must not give up hope,' Lady Alice said, but the queen sighed.

'Sometimes I think it will never happen,' she said.

But Lady Alice was full of reassurance. Many couples took a long time to conceive. Lady Alice herself had no children by either of her first two husbands and she had been married to the duke for eleven years before she had produced a son. And the queen was still young, in her twenty-third year – Lady Alice had been much older.

The queen was hesitant. 'I wanted to ask you,' she said, 'whether there was anything else we could do.'

The duchess looked down. She was a little wary of discussing this matter. No one spoke openly of the possible impotence of the king, It was widely said that the king had too much of the watery or phlegmatic humour, while the queen was all heat; which was the worst possible combination for producing a child.

But the queen, from listening to her ladies when they thought she wasn't listening, had come across the notion of the *emission and exchange of fluids*, which had caused her to wonder, because in all her experiences with the king – the secret fumblings to avoid exposure of flesh, the hesitant thrustings while mumbling prayers – she was not aware that there had ever been an exchange or emission of fluids.

Lady Alice was not entirely surprised by this information. After a short silence she explained that there was indeed a fluid, produced by the male, which was responsible for procreation. In order for conception to occur it had to be deposited as near to the neck of the womb as possible.

When the queen said nothing she went on to explain the origin of this fluid and the means by which it was produced.

'But what if it is not produced?' the queen said. 'Is there a potion?'

Lady Alice replied that there were indeed potions, mainly for the woman to take, but she believed there was also an ointment. She hesitated. 'Personally, I believe its effectiveness is at least partly due to the action of applying it,' she said, and went on to explain how it should be applied.

Neither of them looked at one another during the course of this conversation. The queen was finding it hard to imagine how her husband would respond to her 'encouraging the organ with her fingers'. She looked at her fingers. 'But I do love you,' he had said to her the last time they had tried and failed. 'I have always loved only you.'

'Can you make this ointment?' she asked.

'I can try,' Lady Alice said cautiously, for it was dangerous to prescribe anything for the king without the knowledge of his physicians. But it seemed to her that she could put together a general lubricant. To be applied before the act, she said.

There was another short, concentrated silence, then the queen thanked her and said that she was greatly indebted to her, but the duchess waved this aside.

'I trust that your majesty will soon have a son,' she said. 'My own son is such a comfort to me,' she added. 'And the thought that he is already married is also a comfort. I pray that he and his little wife, being so young, will have many children with no trouble at all,' she said.

The queen stirred in her seat, for this was the second matter she wanted to raise with the duchess, and it was at least as awkward as the first. But since there was no avoiding it, and the queen believed in taking the most direct approach, she turned to face her friend.

'About that,' she said.

26

Margaret Beaufort Comes to Court

It was Betsy who told her she was to marry again.

'But I am married,' she said.

They were in the gardens of Maxey Castle, her mother's home. She had been taken there only a short time after her marriage to her guardian's son.

John had not spoken to her, not even to say goodbye. As her carriage pulled away she had looked up and seen his pale, pointed face looking down from a window. Only later did she hear that his father had been killed.

But now Betsy was telling her she was to have a different husband.

'The king himself has chosen this fine gentleman for you,' she said, and she showed Margaret a portrait of Edmund, sternly handsome, with golden hair curling to his shoulders. Betsy put her whiskery face close to Margaret's and said, 'What do you think, my angel? He is the king's own brother!'

But Margaret, young as she was, still had a sense of the fixed and permanent state of marriage. Had she not taken vows? And told her little husband that she would always love him?

'I already have a husband,' she said, turning away from the portrait of the young knight.

But Betsy put her on her knee. The king would decide on that, she said. Promises made in childhood were not always binding, thank heaven. It would be a cruel thing for children if all the words they uttered, in spite or rage or on the impulse of the moment, bound them for ever. Why, already her so-called 'husband' would be choosing himself another wife.

Margaret was startled by this, but she recovered, remembering John's painfully hopeful face when they had stood together by the pond.

'I don't believe you,' she said.

Betsy's alarming eyebrows flew up. 'Well, if you don't believe me,' she said, 'you must believe the king.'

But Margaret was unconvinced. 'I made my vows before God,' she said.

Her nurse said that the king was God's representative on earth. He had the power to make or break marriages, to decide on 'vows'.

When Margaret remained stubborn, her nurse's face took on a cunning look. There were ways to tell for certain, she said. They could peel all the skin off an apple and throw it over Margaret's left shoulder, to see what letter it formed as it fell on the ground. Or she could look in a basin of water by the light of the full moon to see the reflection of her husband's face. But it would be best to do this in a graveyard, where a fetch of him would appear.

Margaret was a little shaken by this. 'Will you come with me?' she asked, but her nurse said no, the magic would only work if she went alone. Margaret shuddered, and Betsy said they would try the apple peel first.

So they went into the kitchens where a great basket of apples stood by the door. She chose one that was less spotted than the others and held it out to her nurse, and they went into the yard away from the kitchen staff. Then carefully, so carefully, Betsy cut the skin from the pale flesh in a curling ribbon that almost, but not quite, broke. When she had finished Margaret realized she had been holding her breath, and Betsy laughed.

'Now you must stand with your back to the sun,' she said, 'and throw it over your shoulder and say, "So fall the peel, true love reveal."'

And Margaret threw the peel and whirled round instantly, and they both peered at it.

It was a 'T' for Tudor, Betsy said, though Margaret thought it looked more like a 'J'. Disappointed as ever by the inconclusive nature of her nurse's evidence, she still refused to wait in a graveyard at full moon, which was, in any case, more than a week away.

Then Betsy told her there was a third way. If she prayed to St Nicholas on his own eve, he would bring her husband to her in a dream.

Margaret would not commit herself to this. St Nicholas's Eve was even further away than the full moon. But her nurse talked of no one but Edmund Tudor, who was the king's own brother: how handsome he was, how brave. So on the eve of St Nicholas, Margaret lay awake praying after all. And she did have a dream.

She dreamed that a bishop stood with a red mitre in his hand, holding out his other hand towards a knight. She could not see the knight's face, but it must have been Edmund rather than John, who was not a knight. And by the time she told her nurse, it already seemed more like a vision than a dream.

And so it was decided, as she thought. It did not occur to her that it had already been decided.

Time passed quickly at Maxey, because Christmas was coming and there was plenty to do. Margaret was shy of her mother and hung back a little whenever she was present. She did not often come into the same room as Margaret, or address her directly, unless she was not sitting correctly, or her appearance was unkempt. She had a way of not looking at her when she said this, so that Margaret was forced to wonder how she could tell. Her eyes seemed to be supernaturally keen.

'The hem of that dress needs sewing,' she would say to Betsy, or, 'Is that a smudge on my daughter's face?'

But her stepfather was kindly, and let her look through his eyeglass at the winter stars. Two of her mother's older children from her first marriage came to stay, Oliver and Mary St John. Oliver was still happy to run and play in the gardens, and Mary was sweet-natured and taught her to sew; and Margaret's little brother, John, from her mother's third marriage, toddled after her everywhere, in much the same way as she had once toddled after Betsy. And soon it was possible to forget her small husband with his worried eyes.

Then, shortly after Christmas, came the summons to court.

Suddenly the whole household was in a fever of preparation, and her mother was everywhere, issuing instructions in her brittle voice. Margaret was to have a new set of furs, she said, and a new dress. Her hair would never do.

Betsy said, surely they would not travel in the depths of winter? They would all catch their deaths of cold. But Margaret's mother said that the summons was urgent and the stay would be prolonged. She herself was ordering a whole new wardrobe. And several jewels. They had been invited to the Ceremony of the Garter.

Margaret had only the faintest idea of what this might mean. She had never been to London or seen a real tournament. She had only played with John de la Pole's toy castle and wooden knights (some of which were still in her box). She imagined a scene that was something like Paradise, painted in brilliant colours like the chapel at Ewelme.

'Will we see the queen?' she asked, but Betsy would only say that it was madness to travel in February – the roads were flooded and they would all drown.

There was rain, but not enough to drown them, and by the time they approached London fitful sunlight illuminated the walls. Already they could hear a muffled roar from the city, and they passed through the gates into what seemed like a wall of noise. Everywhere there was building: building up and tearing down, scaffolding, ladders and carts. And more carts unloading barrels, and more people than Margaret had ever seen, crying out their wares or shouting orders. Bells rang, hammers struck stone and pigs ran squealing from an alley. And the smells! Of beer and roast meat and rotted vegetables and gutted fish; and such filth in the streets that the carriage skidded more than once and the driver had to get out. Her nurse clamped her hands over her ears, and her mother held a cloth to her nose and told Margaret not to look, but Margaret could not stop looking. Wedges of pale, water-sharp sunlight alternated with blocks of deepest shade. Shop fronts were bleached pale but their sides and the alleys between were absolutely dark and mysterious. The light made everything sharper and more intense, and yet at the same time somehow transitory and unreal. People were briefly illuminated before disappearing into the darkness: the man with a red headscarf; the woman with a basket on her head; another woman pulling her child along; a dog running on three legs; a man sitting in a doorway, his face lifted, his mouth open for no reason that she would ever know.

There were cages of live birds in the marketplace; three women laughing next to a basket of struggling doves. Geese waddled between the stalls, and all these things seemed permanently imprinted on Margaret's senses, yet fleeting, because she would never see the city in quite this way again. It was as if someone had upended the glass of time and exposed everything in it momentarily to the light. Yet even as they passed through the city the light faded to a soft, yellowish-grey. And then they reached the lodgings where they were to stay that night.

Her nurse said that she would never sleep, and then fell asleep promptly, snoring raucously all night, so that only Margaret lay awake, listening to the sounds of the river: boats bumping into harbour, barrels unloading. The next morning her mother said she looked very pale and pinched her cheeks, for they were going to meet the queen that day. They were going to travel by barge to the palace.

Even the stench of the river was exciting. White birds dipped and flashed and great boats left a deep 'v' in their wake. And the castle looked exactly like her picture of Camelot, in her book about King Arthur; it had turrets and flying banners. Liveried men met them as they left the barge and conducted them through a great hall. They were to see the queen right away.

They passed swiftly along a corridor, Margaret trotting after her mother to keep up. A squire announced them, and her mother instructed her not to look at the queen, and Margaret did not know what she meant. But she kept her eyes lowered as she entered the room and sank into the deepest curtsy she could manage, almost disappearing into the skirts of her new dress. And the queen spoke to her in English, which surprised Margaret, who all morning had been practising her French.

'Welcome, little cousin.'

She wore dark blue, which was all Margaret could see without looking up; a dark blue mourning robe for her mother who had recently died. (Betsy had told her this and warned her to be very solemn.) As Margaret rose from her curtsy, her heart beating like a panicking bird in case she stumbled or did anything else wrong, she could see that the gown was trimmed with white fur.

'Your name is Margaret, is it not?' asked the queen, but still she did not dare to look up.

'Yes, my lady,' she ventured in English, aware of her mother's watchful eyes.

'It is a good name,' said the queen, and at last Margaret raised her eyes.

She was surprised to find that the queen was quite short; no taller than her own mother, who was not tall. She had always thought that a queen would be very tall, like Lady Alice. Also, she had been told that the queen was 'the most beautiful woman in the world'.

Wings of hair were swept up on either side of her face; Margaret could see there was a lot of it – it was very full and thick. Her upper lip was full and her eyes were sorrowful and dark; two smudges in the dull cream of her face.

'We are so sorry for your majesty's loss,' her mother said, and the queen said that such a loss, when it came, was terrible indeed.

'You are so lucky to have one another,' she said to both of them. Margaret could not think what to say to this, but her mother said something appropriate in reply.

Then the queen spoke directly to her once more, and Margaret almost curtsied again before remembering that she didn't need to.

'I understand that you will be marrying our brother,' she said.

Margaret looked to her mother for help.

'It has pleased his most gracious majesty to release my daughter from her previous agreement,' she said.

'So we shall be closer family than ever,' the queen said, and her upper lip quivered for a moment. 'That is the important thing,' she said, and Margaret's mother agreed with her heartily. Then the queen said that unfortunately she might not meet her future husband as he had gone with the king to Reading. But the contract would be drawn up for them while they were in London.

'I hope you are not too disappointed, to see only me,' she said.

Margaret did not know whether she was disappointed or not, but her mother laughed excessively and said it was the greatest honour for both of them. Then the queen said to Margaret, 'I have something for you.'

Again Margaret glanced at her mother, but received only a prodding look in reply. So she followed the queen to a table and the queen picked up a small casket that was inlaid with pearl.

'For your name, and mine,' the queen said. She took a small book from it, wrapped in silk. It was a book of hours.

'Keep it with you always,' she said. 'And when you write in it, think of me.'

Margaret was a little disappointed, for the casket had looked as though it might contain jewels. But her mother said that it was a priceless gift, and she would treasure it always. And she glared meaningfully at Margaret, who remembered, just in time, to thank the queen.

Then they were free to go, and her mother said that she had not thought Margaret would be so tongue-tied after all her lessons with Lady Alice.

'But at least you did not say anything foolish,' she conceded as they returned to the barge.

Betsy, of course, wanted to hear all about it, and she exclaimed many times over the little book. 'You must write in it every day,' she said. 'There will be so much to see and do.'

And, in fact, there was a great deal to see and do, though she did not see the queen again until the Ceremony of the Garter at Windsor, where she led the procession to St George's Chapel with the king. The king did not look very splendid, but the queen was transformed, in robes of crimson with glittering, exultant eyes. For it had just been announced that she was at last expecting a child. And the Earl of Shrewsbury's victories continued in Gascony, and so the ceremonies were celebrated with great splendour, with many fanfares of trumpets. The blue robes of the Garter knights and the scarlet mantles of the poor knights stood out against the green field, and all of them were contained in a soft glove of light. For a short time at least it was the gayest court on earth.

27

A Sudden and Thoughtless Fright

After Easter the king sent a thousand men to Gascony and they besieged the town of Fronsac and seized control of it, but in August John Talbot, Earl of Shrewsbury, and his son Lord de Lisle were killed at Castillon, and in September the town of Bordeaux was again lost. *Jean de Waurin*

Around the first day of August the king declined into a great sickness at his house of Clarendon, which lasted for a long time . . . *John Benet's Chronicle*

A disease and disorder of such a sort overcame the king that he lost his wits and memory for a time, and nearly all his body was so uncoordinated and out of control that he could neither walk, nor hold his head upright, nor easily move from where he sat . . .

Whethamsted's Register

When he held his hands up to bless the feast as usual, it suddenly seemed to him that blood was streaming from his palms. He shifted his feet and knew that blood was streaming from them also. When he opened his mouth to speak, no words came. And the lines on his palms seemed to have turned into the rivers of France, which were streaming blood.

As though from a great distance he could hear the queen say, 'My lord the king is not well,' and several people got up. He wondered, as they helped him to his room, why they made no attempt to staunch the flow of blood that streamed from his side now as well.

But they took no notice of it as they made him lie in his bed, and covered him with sheets that he would surely stain.

And they left him there, to sleep, they said, though he thought that he would bleed to death. He tried to tell them this, but he was suddenly tired, so tired that he couldn't lift his head. He heard the doors swing shut behind them, and some more doors after that, and then it seemed that all the doors were swinging shut against him, in the corridors of his mind.

It is necessary for lethargics that people talk loudly in their presence. Tie their extremities lightly and rub their palms and soles hard . . . let their feet be put in salt water up to the middle of their shins and pull their hair and nose . . . open the vein of their head or nose or forehead and draw blood from the nose with the bristles of a boar . . . and let a feather be put down his throat to cause vomiting . . .

Rosa Anglica

28
Alone

They tried to persuade her to leave; she was distressing herself, they said, and the baby. But she was convinced that only she could penetrate the wall of her husband's silence, that something she could say or do would reach him, that he would give some sign or in some way acknowledge the bond between them.

But I do love you, he had said. *I have always loved only you.*

So she continued to kneel before him, holding his hands and chafing them.

'Henri,' she murmured, 'come back to me.'

'It is Marguerite,' she told him. 'Your Marguerite.'

Because in private they were always Henri and Marguerite. *La petite*, he called her. His daisy-flower.

She would not give up, not while there was any chance at all that she might provoke him out of his torpor. She gathered up his hands and kissed them; before all of his attendants she kissed his face and his poor, shaved head. She pressed his hand to her stomach so that he could feel their baby moving in his own turbulent little world. But when she released his hand, it fell lifeless and dangling to his knee.

She clasped his face, searching it for even a flicker of recognition, but there was nothing.

It was his eyes that frightened her, that terrible emptiness. In them she could see the depth of his absence; the vast distance between them. It was as though she had been removed from his eyes. Or as though he were lost in some unending labyrinth and there was no thread connecting them – nothing that would lead her to him at all.

It made her palms sweat, her heart race and pound.

They made him sit up, but he sagged forward, as though he might fall.

Once, in fact, he had fallen, and was only prevented from toppling on to her by the quick movement of his physician, who had raised him up with some difficulty and, with the assistance of his steward, had made him walk backwards and forwards across the room.

She could not bear the sight of his feet dragging across the floor; their yellow, crinkled soles.

Then, of course, they had insisted on returning to his regime: the cuppings and bleedings, the pinching and burning and slapping, and all the other indignities to which he was hourly subjected.

She had raged at them, his attendants, while they ministered to him.

'Leave him alone!' she had shouted. 'Can you not see that he needs to be alone? It is you – it is people like you – who are doing this to him!'

Because in her mind they were becoming confused with his enemies and persecutors: the French, the House of York, all the rebels and dissenters in the land.

She realized that she must have seemed like a madwoman, spit flying from her mouth. The king's physician, a small man with a drooping eye, had turned towards her and addressed her firmly.

'This is not helping, my lady,' he had said. 'You are not helping either his majesty or yourself. I must insist that you get some rest, or you will damage the baby.'

And so she had allowed herself to be led away, and made to lie down, *for the baby.*

But the next day she insisted on feeding Henry herself.

She sat next to him on the bed and prised the thin soup between his lips, scooping it up as it dribbled out again.

'Like this, your majesty,' his servant said, tilting her husband's head backwards as she spooned the gruel in, so that it slipped down his throat and she could see the muscles of his throat contract.

When she could coax no more in, she set the bowl aside and knelt before him again.

'There,' she said to him, 'that is better, is it not? It will do you good. You must keep your strength up, for me, and for our baby. And then, Henry – you can return to being king.'

Just for a moment she thought that he had heard, had understood. His mouth worked and she thought he was trying to say something. He opened his lips.

And it all spilled out, the soup and his saliva, spilling on to her face.

She put up her hand to wipe her face, and suddenly her breath seemed caught up in her throat.

She couldn't breathe.

It was one of her ladies who saw her, who saw that she couldn't breathe.

They rushed forward then; together with his attendants they manoeuvred her on to the couch, wiped her face for her, loosened her gown, gave her strong wine to drink.

'Oh, your majesty,' her lady cried. 'You must not distress yourself! You are distressing the baby – your little prince!'

And so she allowed herself to be taken away from her husband, to Westminster Palace, so that her confinement could begin.

She had never felt so alone, though she had often been lonely since coming to this hostile land; this land that had received her warmth with coldness. But what she felt now was like the purest distillation of loneliness.

Her mother had died. Her father no longer responded to her letters, deciding, no doubt, that his best chance was with the French, not the English, king.

And her husband had left her. There was no other way of putting it.

An image came to her, unbidden, of a lone tree on a barren heath; its branches stood out starkly against the sky.

But she was not alone, not while she had her baby.

She began to talk to him in French. At nights, when he was most wakeful, she crooned to him all the songs her nurse had sung to her, all the ones she could remember, in her small, fractured voice.

She told him of his ancestry, of the line of kings from which he came. She told him what it would be like for him to be prince of both nations, English and French, and then king. It did not even occur to her that he might be a girl.

She made herself eat every day – small, regular amounts – despite the fact her stomach was so compressed that all food caused a burning pain to spread from her stomach to her chest. But she would keep herself strong for her baby because she was all he had; it seemed to her that he had only his mother, not his father.

Everything would change, she told herself, when her son was born.

In the days before the birth the October light changed to a lucid gold. A cold breeze blew through the palace gardens so that all the trees trembled with light. She insisted on sitting by the window so that she could look out. Her fingers had swollen so that she could no longer wear her rings. Her toes were like small sausages stuffed with meat – she couldn't feel them at all – and her face was strange to her so she had stopped looking at it. In the pearl-grey dawns her ladies helped her to walk, to ease the aching of her back.

When she closed her eyes, the image of the solitary, blighted tree came back to her; now it was clinging to a precipice, over a dizzying fall.

But she was not barren and blighted – she had her son.

One night she dreamed she was taking a warm bath to ease the pain in her back, but she couldn't get comfortable – there was something like a metallic ridge or pipe digging into her. And then as she shifted it must have pierced the side of the tub, and the water was gushing out, red with her blood.

Then she woke, and all the bed was wet.

And she screamed.

All her ladies came running.

They made her lie down on a mattress while her bed was changed. They begged her to pray, to think about the Holy Mother, who had suffered all the tortures of childbirth in a virgin body without once crying out.

But it was hard, hard. The pain in her back increased. It was as though something were gripping it like pincers. The pain spread out to her hips and down her thighs.

The noises were coming out of her of their own accord, or as though they were being tugged out by a rope.

Her ladies bathed her face and stomach and spread her legs. The pain spread upwards, to her ribs. One breath shunted out after another. One hour passed after another.

She rolled over, clutching the mattress, her nightgown twisted round her chest. She bore down with all the strength she had in the world.

And then again.

'That's it, your majesty – that's it!' they cried.

But it wasn't it, and she was splitting right down the middle – splitting in two.

'PUSH!' they screamed at her, and she did push – she would do anything at all to be rid of it. She bore down from her divided chest and felt the great muscle of her womb contract –

And something giving way between her legs –

Something slithering and warm as though all her insides were spilling on to the bed.

There was a buzzing sound in her ears.

'Your majesty! Your majesty!' they cried. 'He is here! You have a son!'

And upon St Edward's day [Saturday the 13th day of October, 1453] the queen being at Westminster had a prince, on account of which bells rang in every church and 'Te Deum' was solemnly sung, and he was christened at Westminster . . .

Bale's Chronicle

On St Edward's day a son was born at Westminster and baptized in the Abbey with the greatest solemnity, and the royal council, seeing that the king was not recovering, put the kingdom under the governance of the Duke of Somerset.

John Benet's Chronicle

29

Duchess Cecily Speaks Her Mind

'You must go to London,' she said. 'Summon all the lords to you there.'

Somerset had called a council, and had not invited the Duke of York. But at the last moment he had received a letter telling him that he could go 'peaceably, and measurably accompanied'.

'I will go straight to the meeting,' he said.

'Take care,' she said. 'You do not know who will stand against you.'

'No one will stand against me.'

'The last time you spoke against Somerset you were arrested.'

'I will not speak against Somerset,' he said. 'The Duke of Norfolk will.'

'You know that, do you?'

'I do.'

'Somerset is powerful.'

'I Ic is nothing without the king.'

'He still has the queen. If he is madc regent you will be in great danger.'

'He will not be made regent.'

'Richard –'

'Gascony has surrendered to France. He has no credit left.'

'How many men will you take with you?'

'I am not anticipating a battle.'

Cecily started to protest but her husband interrupted.

'The men at this council will stand by me. Norfolk for one. Your brother, the Earl of Salisbury, for another. And your nephew, the Earl of Warwick.'

'You do not know how long the king will be ill –'

'But while he is, someone must govern the land. And that someone will not be Somerset.'

'He is the prince's godfather.'

'But until the king recognizes his son, he cannot be made heir.'

'I have heard that the king cannot recognize anyone.'

'He remains in his stupor.'

'He will have a shock when he comes out of it.'

'It is said that he thought the pregnancy was a gift of the Holy Spirit.'

His wife snorted. 'In the form of the Duke of Somerset,' she said.

Richard of York sat back. His wife had a bad mind. He had always liked that about her.

'So you see, Richard,' she said, 'the duke may have more power than you think.'

'He will have no power when I have finished with him. After this council his career will be over. And he will be out of the queen's reach.'

'You frighten me, Richard.'

He glanced at her. 'I do not frighten you.'

'No,' she said. 'You do not.'

They were smiling at one another. For it seemed that now, finally, the duke's hour had come.

When the royal council realized that the king's health was not improving, and fearing the ruin of the realm under the Duke of Somerset's governance was imminent, the magnates of the kingdom sent for the Duke of York who arrived in London with a small retinue and entered the council. And in the council the Duke of Norfolk accused the Duke of Somerset of treason on many counts. And on 23rd November [1453] the iniquitous Duke of Somerset was arrested . . .

John Benet's Chronicle

30

The Earl of Warwick Makes a Speech

He was not overly tall, but he was handsome, although his appearance was full of contradictions. He had a Roman profile with white-blond hair; a stern nose with a rosebud mouth. One of his eyes had a slight cast, as though his attention might be elsewhere, but his focus was absolute. He was an earl with the manner of a duke – or, some said, a king. The people loved him for his grand gestures: the six oxen roasting in his kitchens that any man could cut meat from; the fountains of ale and wine where any man could drink; the unexpected benevolence to a sick tenant. He went everywhere accompanied by a large retinue of men in scarlet livery, wearing the white badge of the muzzled bear.

He arrived in London soon after the prince's birth. The sky was grey with frills of white. White sunlight blew across the sky and disappeared again. As he climbed the steps to Paul's Cross, where a crowd of magnates had assembled to hear him speak, it seemed to him that sky and river and crowd were all in motion.

But as he held up his hands, silence fell.

'Unto us a child is born,' he cried. 'Unto us a prince is given. But I say to you – what kind of prince is not recognized by his own father?'

He waited for the wave of protest and assent to die down.

'She would have you believe that she has given you a prince. She would have you believe that this prince is son to your king and true heir to this realm. But the king has not acknowledged him and never will.'

Once again he waited.

'Ask yourselves – whence came this child? I say to you that this is no prince, but a foundling – no true heir, but a changeling bought from a French witch – and for proof I offer the spell cast over our beloved king!'

A roar of approval and rage surged towards him.

'What is more likely: that the queen, after eight years of fruitless marriage, has given the king a son – or that she has perpetrated a foul trick upon us all?'

There were cries of 'Shame!' but it was not clear whether they were directed at the queen or at Warwick.

'The queen has tricked you,' he continued, raising his voice above them all. 'She has played you false and the king false. She has offered to you, as your lawful prince, either a changeling or a bastard. Good citizens – high and worthy lords – true liegemen – can you be so deluded as to accept this changeling as heir to the throne when the king will not? Will you pledge allegiance to him – lay down your lives and give up the kingdom – when you do not even know that he is your prince? When – for all you know – he is nothing more than the bastard son and heir of the Duke of Somerset?'

And now he had to get down hastily from his platform as the crowd surged forward and fighting broke out. His men surrounded him and cleared his way as he left, with a smile of satisfaction and without a backwards glance.

[The Earl of Warwick] had in great measure the voice of the people because he knew how to persuade them with beautiful soft speeches. He was conversible and talked familiarly with them – subtle as it were, in order to gain his ends. He gave them to understand that he would promote the prosperity of the kingdom and defend the interests of the people with all his power, and that as long as he lived he would never do otherwise. Thus he acquired the goodwill of the people of England to such an extent that he was the prince whom they held in the highest esteem and on whom they placed the greatest faith and reliance.

Jean de Waurin

31

The Queen Makes a Resolution

She knew, of course, what Warwick was saying about her. That same day she had retrieved her son from his nurse; insisted on holding him alone.

He had been washed and was wrapped in blankets. His eyes were closed.

He looked unbearably cross.

That was the first thing she had thought about him: how angry he seemed to be. Angry at her, she thought, for bringing him into the misery and cruelty of this world.

Her second thought was that he was much darker than his father; he had a tuft of blackish hair, on a head that was substantially bald. On closer inspection she could see that his face was a blotchy, yellowish red, his lips already full. He did not resemble his father.

It was unfortunate, perhaps, given what the serpent Warwick was saying, yet secretly she was glad.

He was like her.

He was hers.

He would have all her fighting spirit. Which he would need, because it seemed that he would have to fight – for two nations.

Now, as she held him, he pulled his full lips apart into a resentful, straining cry. His fingers peeked out of his blanket, splayed and closed again. They were so wrinkled, like the fingers of a tiny, ancient man. She felt a sudden fierce compassion for this child who in his infancy had inherited the full weight of the crowns of England and France.

But he would never be alone, not while he had her. She would keep him with her, always by her side. She did not like to give him back to his nurse, even while he fed.

The Duke of Somerset was in the Tower. Her father had still not replied to the letters she had sent to him, to the news that he had a grandson. And her husband – her husband had not responded either.

But she had her son.

Everything had changed now, with his birth.

She folded his wrinkled fingers back into the blankets.

'As soon as I am churched,' she said, 'we will visit my lord the king. He will recover,' she said, 'when he sees his son.'

At the prince's coming to Windsor the Duke of Buckingham took him in his arms and presented him to the king in goodly wise, beseeching the king to bless him, and the king gave no manner answer. Nevertheless the duke abode still with the prince by the king, and when he could no answer have, the queen came in and took the prince in her arms and presented him in like form as the duke had done, desiring that he should bless [the child] but all their labour was in vain, for they departed thence without any answer or countenance, saying only that once he looked on the prince and cast down his eyes again without any more.

Paston Letters

She knelt before him as if in prayer. 'Henry,' she said. 'This is your son – your beautiful son.'

She could not for the moment say anything else, but then she continued in a lower voice.

'If you ever loved me – if you ever loved God – you must come out of this. Please.'

His eyes were entirely opaque to her. He had many small scars around his head, which was still shaved, and there were traces of blood beneath his nose. He was so, so thin. But his eyes were still the most troubling thing to her; it was as if he had been removed from his eyes.

She did not know where he might have gone. She wondered briefly whether it was better for him there.

She couldn't seem to stop her own mind racing. Or her heart.

She put out her hand and touched his, which was cold and limp.

O my husband.

For the first time it came to her that he might die, without ever acknowledging his son.

If the king *did* die they would never accept an infant prince.

The prince burbled, and a small thread of milk spilled from the corner of his mouth. She wiped it quickly with the edge of her sleeve.

'Henry,' she said, 'you must come back to us. You must.'

Nothing.

It occurred to her that she had been a long time on her knees, and had achieved nothing. She gave her husband's hand a final squeeze, which was not returned, then stood up and faced the Duke of Buckingham.

'When does parliament begin?' she said.

The Duke of Buckingham said it would be in the next month. All the lords had been summoned, he said; he did not know how many would attend.

'You will present a bill for me there,' she said.

'A bill?'

'I wish to be made regent,' she said. 'I will look after the interests of my son.'

The Duke of Buckingham looked as unhappy as a man could.

'It is usually the king's council who elect a regent,' he said.

'But I will save them the trouble,' she said. 'You must put it to them that my son the prince must be provided for. He must receive his titles – he must be made Prince of Wales and Earl of Chester – and acknowledged heir to the throne.'

The duke's long face looked even longer. 'There are those,' he said, with extreme caution, 'who say that the king must recognize him first.'

She looked up at him then, stung.

'My son –' she said, then stopped and corrected herself. 'The *king's son* is heir to this realm, and the king would know that if he were well. Do you think for one moment that he would doubt it?'

The duke hastened to assure her that he thought no such thing.

'Then you must act in the king's name,' she said, and she left the room without looking back at her husband, still carrying the prince in her arms.

The queen hath made a bill of five articles, desiring these articles to be granted. The first is that she desireth to have the whole rule of this land, the second is that she may appoint the Chancellor, the Treasurer, the Privy Seal and all other officers of this land, the third is that she may give all the bishoprics of this land and all other benefices belonging to the king's gift, the fourth is that she may have sufficient livelihood assigned her for the king, the prince and herself. As for the fifth article I cannot yet find out what it is.

Paston Letters

. . . it is a right great perversion
For a woman of this land to be regent –
Queen Margaret, I mean, that ever has meant
To govern all England with might and power,
And to destroy the right line was her intent

Yorkist ballad

32

The Queen Receives a Message

Through all the furore that followed her bill, the queen remained in her rooms. She received messages from the outside world: that a great fight had broken out in parliament, that she had brought the city to warfare; that Cardinal Kemp had hired an army and paid every man, so they could arm themselves with all the weapons of war and patrol the streets of London; that the Duke of York's own army was approaching the city, with the Earls of Salisbury and Warwick supporting him; that the Duke of Somerset, from prison, had sent out spies to discover the movements of his enemies and warned his own men to be ready to meet them when they came.

In February she heard that her bill had been utterly rejected by parliament. Power had been granted to Richard, Duke of York, to hold parliament in the king's name. In March she was told that yet another delegation had gone to the king to plead with him on their knees, and exhort him to speak, because without him the Duke of York would be made governor of the country. When they had failed to provoke any response, the Duke of York had indeed been declared Protector and Defender of the Realm 'during the king's infirmity'.

In April the duke had made great changes to the king's council and government. That same month, he sent a message to the queen instructing her that she would take no further part in the affairs of the realm, but remain in her rooms at Windsor with her husband and her son. She would not be allowed to leave the palace until her husband recovered.

That summer the duke successfully repressed all rebellions against him and for the queen. He imprisoned the Duke of Exeter in Pontefract Castle; the Duke of Somerset was still in the Tower and was discharged from all his offices.

Through all this the queen remained in her rooms, watching her son grow into the kind of prince he would need to be.

The king was in the same palace, but in different quarters, sequestered with his physicians. She visited him less frequently these days, relying on regular medical reports. She had stopped presenting the prince to him because she did not want to expose her son to the terrifying emptiness of his father's gaze.

Every day the little prince grew more wonderful in her eyes. He was so alert – all her ladies agreed that they had never seen an infant so young noticing so much. He responded equally to all things: laughter, a rustle of skirts, the bright flags flickering in the wind, an insect on the window – all were treated to the same questing stare, the same rapid, birdlike movements of his head.

And he had such determination. By the time he was seven months old he was attempting to pull himself upwards using a table leg or his nurse's skirts.

He couldn't quite manage it, of course. His little face would turn pink with the effort, then his legs would buckle and he would give vent to his frustration with his straining cry. But even as he struck the floor again he would do his best not to topple over completely. His head would wobble and she could see all the muscles in his back working to keep him upright before his nurse scooped him up to prevent a further fall. Then immediately he would struggle to be set free.

And his nurse, a round-cheeked, beaming woman, would say, 'He is a fighter, my lady,' and the queen would correct her, 'He is a warrior,' and hold out her hands to take him and feel how, even in her arms, he seemed to hold himself erect. She could not help thinking how well he would look on a horse.

Also, he was astonishingly handsome, with dark, intent eyes, a small, pointed chin and strong dark hair that curled round his ears.

He looked nothing like his father – Warwick was right in that respect. It was as though he had no father; he was wholly hers, as if she had willed him into being.

She had not missed a single stage of his development: his first tooth, the moment he could grasp and point, the first time he successfully hauled himself to a standing position, took his first step, said his first word. Which was not 'mama' or 'nurse' and certainly not 'papa'. It sounded like 'gnu', but his nurse swore later that he had pointed to the bible and said 'book'.

Her ladies compared him to his grandfather, Henry V, the warrior king. They rarely mentioned his father.

Most of the time it was easier not to think about the king, who had still not recognized his son, or taken any part in the affairs of the nation for more than a year.

Who had let the would-be usurper, Richard of York, take his place, and confine her, the queen, in this castle.

With each day that passed the king seemed further away. Which was why, when the messenger came, her first response was not pleasant; she felt a kind of sickening jolt.

He knelt before her, spreading his arms wide, an expression of theatrical joy on his face.

'The Lord be praised,' he said.

And she half turned away from him; she could hardly hear the rest of what he said for the rushing noise in her ears.

Her ladies made little gasps and cries of delight. Elizabeth Butler stepped forward and took hold of her hands, smiling.

'It is a miracle,' she said, but the queen felt something inside her closing.

Then, rapidly, her mind began to work. There was so much to do, so much that could be done. York could be dismissed, imprisoned – preferably executed, along with that lying whelp Warwick. The Duke of Somerset could be released at once.

So many thoughts, vying for ascendancy in her mind. She touched her hair, her face, then spoke a little breathlessly.

'We must prepare ourselves,' she said. 'We must dress the prince. We must go to the king.'

Blessed be God, the king is well amended, and has been since Christmas Day, and on St John's Day commanded his almoner to ride to Canterbury with his offering and commanded his secretary to offer at St Edward's shrine. On Monday afternoon the queen came to him and brought my lord prince with her . . .

Paston Letters

Her ladies walked ahead of her, carrying the prince, but as they reached the doors they parted seamlessly to allow her to pass before them.

She had drawn her hood up, partly because it was cold in the palace, and partly because she did not want them to see her face. A kind of numbness had spread down one side of it to her lips, and her vision was slightly blurred, though not with tears.

What if? she couldn't help thinking.

What if the madness has done permanent damage? What if he refuses to recognize the prince?

'Wait,' she said. She had not walked far, but she felt as though there was a stitch in her side.

They will all be watching, she thought. All the king's attendants, and her own, to see how the king responded to his son. If he did not recognize the prince, her son could not be named heir to the throne.

She could not do it, she thought. She could not walk through the doors.

And then they opened.

And so she walked in, blinking rapidly.

She saw him at once, despite the blurring of her vision: his shaved head propped up by pillows; the long gown, from which his legs protruded like yellow sticks.

She hesitated only a moment, then hurried forward, putting her hood back, sinking into a curtsy just moments before she reached him, so that he could not see her face and she did not have to look at his.

'My lord,' she said.

'You have come to me,' he said in a voice that was strained and creaking from disuse. *But at least he recognized me*, she thought. And still she dared not look at him for fear that she would weep uncontrollably at what she saw.

'I have come,' she said unsteadily and now at last she was able to look up. Past the skull-like contours of his face to his eyes. Which were filled with an ethereal light as though his soul shone out of them. Because for so long he had been so near death.

He was trying to speak again. His mouth worked strangely to frame the words. The muscles were wasted, she realized; all those muscles in the face and throat that we do not even know we have. But at last he said, 'It has been a long time.'

'Yes, my lord,' she said, and now the blurring of her eyes was due to tears. 'It has been a very long time.'

'More than a year,' his physician said.

'But you have come back to me,' he said, as though it were she who had left. But she didn't contradict him. He extended his wasted fingers and she pressed them to her lips.

And at that moment the prince, tired of being held in his nurse's arms, gave a strained, impatient cry.

'Who is this – a child?' the king said.

'Yes, my lord,' the queen said, and she rose and took the prince from his nurse, then sat with him on the couch beside the king.

She had never been so aware of the gaze of so many people.

Nervously, she took the prince's cloak off and stroked his fine curls. The king watched as though mesmerized, and the little prince, who seemed at first as though he would cry, gazed solemnly into his father's face. For a moment she thought that the muscles of her own throat would not work, but then she managed to say, 'He is your son.'

'My – son?' said the king wonderingly, and she nodded emphatically.

'Yes, Henri – your son. I was with child when you – fell ill – if you remember.'

'I do not remember,' said the king, and a soundless ripple passed around the room.

Her chest felt tight, as though there were a band round it.

But the king had extended a finger to the prince.

'What is his name?' he asked, and he touched the prince's petal-soft face, and the prince did not shy away or cry but gazed wonderingly at his father with eyes as dark as his father's were light.

'His name is Edward – after your patron saint. He was born on St Edward's Day.'

'In October,' the king said at once.

'On the thirteenth of October,' said the queen.

'Why, then,' he said, looking around the room. 'I have a son!'

His face was lit by an unearthly smile.

It was as though the whole room exhaled.

Awkwardly, the queen put the prince on his father's knee, and the king placed his hands on the child's head as he squirmed.

'It is a miracle,' he said. 'We must give thanks for so great a miracle.'

The queen wished that he would not use that word; there had been nothing unnatural in the birth of the prince. But she bowed her head and prayed with him.

Then he asked who the godparents were and she told him and he seemed pleased.

'My – son,' he said, 'is very handsome,' and the queen felt almost that she could have loved her husband again, in that moment.

They wept together a little, for joy, but the queen's mind was already working furiously.

'Henri,' she said, wiping her eyes, 'there is so much to do.'

She told him briefly about the many changes that had been made, that the Duke of York was still ruling the country and must be dismissed. And the Duke of Somerset was still in prison and must be released.

But the physician was stepping forward, and telling her not to overtire the king. He said it with a kindly smile, so that she knew he had registered the king's acceptance of his son.

'There will be time enough for all that very soon,' he said, 'once the king is well.'

[And in December] by the grace of God, King Henry was restored to full health at Greenwich. And on the 6th day of February the Duke of Somerset was liberated from the Tower of London . . . *John Benet's Chronicle*

Edmund, Duke of Somerset, who during the king's illness, was imprisoned in the Tower of London for more than a year and ten weeks . . . has been set free.
Calendar of Patent Rolls

. . .and immediately afterwards the Duke of York resigned his office to the king at Greenwich . . . who had governed the whole kingdom of England in the best and most noble way, and had wonderfully pacified all rebels and malefactors according to his oath but without undue harshness . . . And the Duke of Somerset again resumed the role of the principal governor under the king, when he had previously through his bad regime, almost destroyed the whole of England.
John Benet's Chronicle

Once the king recovered his physical and mental health, and resumed the government of the kingdom, he immediately released the Dukes of Somerset and Exeter and the Earl of Devon from prison [as a result of which] Richard Earl of Salisbury resigned the chancellorship. The king, on impulse, created Thomas Bourchier Archbishop of Canterbury chancellor of England. The Duke of York, and the Earls of Warwick and Salisbury, finding these changes unacceptable, left the royal household and council . . . *Chronicon Angliae*

This same year in the month of May the king would have rode to Leicester for to have held a council there, and he rode by the town of Watford abiding there all night . . . *An English Chronicle*

Because of [this] . . . the Duke of York and with him the Earls of Salisbury and Warwick approached London with 7,000 well-armed men. When the Duke of Somerset heard this news he suggested to the king that York had come to usurp the throne.
John Benet's Chronicle

[The duke and earls] realizing that they might not prevail against or withstand the malice of Duke Edmund, who daily provoked the king to their final destruction, gathered secretly a power of people and kept them covertly in villages near the town of St Albans. When the king was there they encircled the town and sent to the king, beseeching him to send out to them their mortal enemy and enemy to all the realm, Edmund Duke of Somerset; if he would not they would seize him by strength and violence. The king, by the advice of his council, answered that he would not deliver him.

An English Chronicle

I, King Harry, charge and command that no manner of person abide not, but void the field and not be so hard to make any resistance against me in mine own realm; for I shall know what traitor dare be so bold to raise a people in mine own land, wherethrough I am in great disease and heaviness. And by the faith that I owe to St Edward and the crown of England, I shall destroy them, every mother's son, and they be hanged drawn and quartered that may be taken afterward, of them to have example to all such traitors to beware to make any such rising of people within my land, and so traitorly to abide their King and Governor. And for a conclusion, rather than they shall have any lord here with me at this time, I shall this day for their sake, and in this quarrel, myself live and die.

Rotuli Parliamentorum

The Duke of York

'Now we must do what we can,' he said, and pulled on his helmet. He ordered his trumpeter to sound the alarm, and then made a speech to his men. Together, he said, they would overcome Somerset. He referred to himself as Joab, and King Henry as King David, but he did not dwell on this, because he was not good with words, and because there was no need; his men were keen for the fray. And, besides, he had already spoken to some of them, instructing them about the real purpose of this battle. Then he took up his position and reined in his horse.

He could feel the tension in his horse, an alertness, a readiness or acceptance of this mission, which until the last few days the duke had hoped to avert. His horse knew; he had always believed that a horse knew in advance whether a battle would be won or lost, and now he could sense a quiver of eagerness, not fear, in its flanks. He spoke to it reassuringly.

High above, in the blue air, a hawk wheeled then hovered. It was a good sign, he thought, because his own symbol was the falcon and the fetterlock. He pulled his visor down.

The Duke of Somerset

From this distance he could not see what kind of hawk it was, which was a pity, for he was always interested in birds. As a child he had been fascinated by their flight; by the way their wings lifted and spread. He had watched them, feeling his own shoulder blades arch in sympathy.

Once he had come across a dead bird, and had opened out its wings. He thought he had seen nothing so beautiful as the arrangement of feathers spreading out from the spine to the tip. He had gathered leaves together, arranging them in the same pattern, thinking to make wings for himself. But then his brothers had come upon him and mocked him. His older brothers, who were now dead.

With an effort he brought his mind back into focus; now was not the time to be distracted. He put on his helmet – there was nothing like a helmet for making you sweat – and pulled the visor down. In his mind's eye he could still see an image of the bird, wheeling in the still air. It was a good sign, he thought, because he had always been fascinated by birds.

The First Battle of St Albans: 22 May 1455

The alarm bell was rung and every man went to harness . . .

John Benet's Chronicle

The battle started on the stroke of 10 o'clock, but because the ways were narrow few combatants could fight there . . . *Dijon Relation*

The Duke of York

The narrowness of the lanes meant that only a few men could engage in fighting at any time, and they presented an easy target for the king's archers. Time after time his men were driven back by a hail of arrows so thick it was hardly possible to see.

It seemed to Duke Richard that his battle was lost before it had started, that he would never even get to fight; he would be executed as a traitor without striking a single blow.

It was Warwick, of course, who changed the course of things; Warwick who led his men through the gardens at the back of Holywell Street and instructed them to break down the doors of the houses and then their walls. And his men set to with their pickaxes and rams until a great section of the street collapsed in a pile of smoking rubble.

For it was Warwick's great virtue as a fighter that he knew no limits.

Through the noise and confusion the trumpets sounded, and all of Warwick's army burst through the barriers and poured into the marketplace, taking the king's army entirely by surprise.

[The Earl of Warwick] took and gathered his men together and furiously broke into the town by the garden sides between the [inns] of the Key and the Checker in Holywell Street. His trumpet sounded and his men cried out with a great voice 'A Warwick! A Warwick!' *Paston Letters*

The fighting was furious . . . *John Benet's Chronicle*

I saw a man fall with his brains beaten out, another with a broken arm, a third with his throat cut and a fourth with a stab wound in his chest, while the whole street was strewn with corpses . . . *Whethamsted's Register*

Four of the king's bodyguard were killed by arrows in his presence, and the king himself was wounded in the shoulder by an arrow . . . At last when they had fought for three hours the king's party, seeing they had the worst of it, broke away on one wing and began to flee. The Duke of Somerset retreated into a house to save himself by hiding but he was seen by the Duke of York's men who at once surrounded the house . . . York's men at once began to fight Somerset and his men who were within the house and defended themselves valiantly. In the end, after the doors were broken down, Somerset saw he had no option but to come out . . .

Dijon Relation

The Duke of Somerset

He came out fighting, flinging the door open and instantly impaling the man who rushed through it on his sword. All that mattered to him was that his son should escape by the back way, while he kept his enemies occupied at the front.

He struck out blindly at first, but a grimness overtook him, and he fought with greater focus, feeling the cut and thrust, the sensation of death when someone dies so close to you that their blood spurts across you and might as well be your own.

It was as if he knew there was a reason his heir would need to survive. He fought harder and with more concentration than he could usually summon.

And the second man fell, then the third.

He could feel the pumping of his arteries; all the force and will of life itself concentrated in the muscles of his arm. There is nothing like such force and concentration, and nothing like the suddenness with which it leaves.

The first blow of the axe.

It did not fell him, but it made him miss his mark, and a second blow hacked into his shoulder and a third split his face. Still he struck out blindly, until a fourth blow severed the tendons of his knee.

Then the fall, and the world upending itself around him. No sky, just faces contorted above him, then blood in the eyes so that he couldn't see at all, and the violent quivering of his legs.

Blades piercing downwards like the beaks of so many birds.

Thus all who were on the side of the Duke of Somerset were killed, wounded, or at the very least, despoiled. The king, who was left on his own, fled into the house of a tanner to hide. And to this house came the Duke of York, the Earl of Salisbury and the Earl of Warwick, declaring themselves to be the king's humble servants.

John Benet's Chronicle

[The Yorkist lords] fell on their knees and besought him for grace and forgiveness of that they had done in the king's presence, and besought him, of his highness, to take them as his true liegemen, saying that they never intended to hurt his own person . . .

Paston Letters

The Duke of York

He had thought to deliver the death blow himself; he had envisaged it often enough, thrusting into Somerset's stomach then winding out the intestines like the traitor he was. But in the end he had decided that it would not be a good thing for him to kill the duke personally, considering what he hoped to achieve afterwards. Anyway, there was no time, for someone was shouting that they had found the king.

He was in a tanner's house, propped up on a bench, having a wound between his neck and shoulder tended. His eyes were closed and he did not look up at first as the duke approached.

Behind him the door opened again, and Salisbury came in, followed by Warwick. Richard of York got on his knees, clumsily, for one of them was hurting. And he was sweating, and streaked with blood and dust.

One by one they spoke, saying that they had never intended any wrong to the king; that they wished only to serve him, as his true liegemen. No one was more grieved than they that matters should have come to this pass.

Warwick said also that if they had gone to Leicester as summoned, they would have been taken prisoner and suffered a shameful death as traitors, losing their livelihood and goods, and their heirs shamed for ever.

Silence.

The king opened his eyes and closed them again. The silence extended itself while they all remained kneeling on the dusty floor.

Richard of York's thoughts were cramped; his mind over-stuffed with them. If the king did not accept their obeisance, they would have to take him as their prisoner to London. Also, he would have to tell the king about the Duke of Somerset, before the rumours started; before people could blacken his name further.

There was no precedent that he knew of for this situation.

The king cleared his throat.

'You must cease your people,' he said. York glanced up. 'You must stop the fighting,' he said, 'and then no more harm will be done.'

Warwick, in particular, was profuse in his thanks. They all proffered their loyalty and their devoted service once again. But Duke Richard still had to tell the king that his favourite cousin and dearest friend was dead. He did not want to be seen to be responsible for any harm coming to the king; he certainly didn't want the king to fall into another attack of grief, or dementia, or whatever it was. He considered one way of breaking the news, then another, but when he finally raised his eyes, the king was already looking at him with a mixture of fear and revulsion on his face.

'Where is my Lord of Somerset?' he asked.

The Duke of York shifted uncomfortably on his wounded knee. 'Your majesty –' he started, but Warwick interrupted: 'Alas, my lord the duke has fallen,' he said smoothly. 'He died nobly, I believe. None of us here were present.'

The king's face turned very pale. He lifted his eyes as if to heaven, then they rolled back as though he might faint. The three lords got up at once.

'Look to the king,' Salisbury said, and York said that he should be taken to the abbey, for safekeeping, where the monks would tend him. Then, as if this brief interview had been more than he could bear, he left the cottage and went back on to the street; back into the clamour and stink of battle, to stop his men looting, and call them from the fray.

On 23rd the king and York and all returned to London. On 24th they made the solemn procession and now peace reigns. The king has forbidden anyone to speak about it upon pain of death. The Duke of York has the government and the people are very pleased at this.

Milanese State Papers: newsletter from Bruges, June 1455

PARDON FOR THE YORKISTS AND THEIR RENEWAL OF ALLEGIANCE, 24TH JULY 1455

We [Henry VI] declare that none of our cousins, the Duke of York and the Earls of Warwick and Salisbury, nor any of the persons who came with them in their fellowship to St Albans on 22nd May, be impeached, sued, vexed, grieved, hurt or molested for anything supposed or claimed to have been done against our person, crown or dignity.

The First Battle of St Albans: 22 May 1455

In the great council chamber, in the time of parliament, in the presence of our sovereign lord, every lord spiritual and temporal freely swore: I promise unto your highness that I shall truly and faithfully keep the allegiance that I owe unto you and do all that may be to the welfare, honour and safeguard of your most noble person, and at no time consent to anything to the hurt and prejudice of your most noble person, dignity, crown or estate . . .

Rotuli Parliamentorum

PART III: 1455–58

Margaret Beaufort Travels to Wales

They travelled first in a boat, then a carriage. Betsy clung to her most of the way, convinced that at any moment they would be killed and eaten, for the men of Wales were all cannibals, she said. Or shape-shifters, turning into wolves at night and howling at the moon. And there were some, she said, as they passed through a dark ravine overhung by rock, that didn't change shape at all, but always had the bodies of men and the heads of dogs, and lived in little villages where the houses were like kennels, clustered together in a pack. And all day long they went about their work, scything and brewing and herding sheep, just like humans, only when you got up close you could see the fearful fangs and bristles, the long, lolloping tongues.

They passed through a forest, which stirred and moaned as the wind blew. Leaves rustled and black branches dripped overhead. When a fox barked, her nurse cried, 'Save us!', and at the call of the screech owl she clasped her hands round Margaret's ears, and Margaret felt at once the thrill of fear and the assurance of God's protection, for at that time she thought that the amount of time she spent in prayer bore a direct relationship to the amount of protection God would give. And so she took Betsy's hands from her ears – they were very cold, and trembling – and told her not to worry, they would say their prayers together. And Jesus would protect them both.

On the other side of the forest there was a landscape of black slate, spindly trees made ghostly by cloud, and scraggy sheep perched on the crags. Then came the first settlements, a few huts clinging to the base of the mountains, and Betsy clapped her hands over Margaret's eyes this time for fear that she would see the dog-headed men. But when she prised her nurse's fingers open Margaret could see only a muddy old woman bent almost double to the earth, and a younger man, bent forward similarly, carrying sticks.

The road was bumpy and uneven, and her nurse complained that all their bones would be broken. But even she stopped complaining when they saw the sea.

As soon as she laid eyes on it, Margaret understood how the land was haunted by the sea; a silent grey expanse, dissolving into sky. Between earth and sky there was a no-land of mist where the sun and moon glowed palely, exactly similar in size and luminosity. As they drew closer, she saw that the sea was not still, but like a great grey muscle, swelling and contracting around the earth, glistening and sleek. Then that it wasn't grey, but shifting rapidly between one colour and another. As they veered off the coastal road, she twisted round in her seat as far as she could, trying to keep the sea in her eyes.

Now the landscape was windswept and treeless, with scattered farmsteads and strange black cattle, then there were trees once more, and a grey town spilling from the trees, and finally, jutting into an estuary, a tower of grey stone. It reared above the town and cast its shadow like a spine along the straggling streets. Trees clustered round the walls and great circular towers surmounted them.

Pembroke Castle. Here she would meet Edmund at last, and they would stay a little while until a new home was prepared.

It was no home, but a fortress. She knew immediately that she would not want to live here. Their carriage rose up a steep path to a massive gatehouse. A steward met them, and then the great gates opened, and there, beyond them, was an immense line of servants.

But it was Jasper who came out to greet them, stern, sallow-faced and gaunt. He welcomed them stiffly; Edmund wasn't there, he said, but he would be back soon.

He was quelling riots in the surrounding hills and valleys. Some of the local people had organized themselves into armed gangs who lived in the hills, raiding cattle, setting fire to the lands of the English lords. But she was not to worry, he told her, seeing a shade of anxiety cross her face. The Welsh people loved Edmund and were loyal to him. They looked to him to bring peace to their divided nation. Many sought his lordship and had flocked to his affinity. He was their one great hope, because Edmund's father was Welsh, yet he was half-brother to the English king. And Jasper, too, of course. But already the bards were composing songs to Edmund; their golden-haired warrior, radiant as a shining shield, fleet as a stag or the wind's breath.

Jasper smiled stiffly. His own hair was thinning and brown.

He had a note for her, from Edmund.

My own swete Lady Margrete, it said. *Of your grete curteyse forgyve me my absence. I will cherish the moment that we may mete, by the grace of God . . .*

She folded up the note, suppressing her feelings of dismay. Did she really have to stay here with Jasper?

Jasper was watching her with a quizzical expression on his face.

Was that when she first decided she did not like him?

She had to walk past the long line of servants, who looked at her with curiosity, pity or amusement. She was so small, their new mistress, looking younger, even, than her twelve years. She walked as tall as she could and stared into each of their faces until, in some cases at least, the amusement or pity disappeared.

There was food in the great hall – salmon stuffed with wild berries, a plate of eels – though Margaret hardly ate at all. And then they were shown to their rooms. Betsy had a separate, small room, with a truckle bed, though she soon abandoned it. 'Not for my old bones,' she said, and Margaret was glad not to be left alone. So she slept with her nurse, in the large oak bed.

And in the morning Jasper showed them round the castle. Spray blew up almost to the castle walls and the seagulls circled and cried against a sulphurous sky.

The great keep was five storeys high; you could see the whole county from its dome.

'This tower and the walls make the castle impregnable,' Jasper said. 'We could withstand any siege for more than a year. Because of the keep and this other thing – I will show you.'

He took them down the stairs again to a vast cavern set deep in the rock beneath the castle, a shelter for cave-dwellers since the dawn of time.

'No other fortress has this,' he said, looking almost happy, or as happy as Jasper ever looked. 'People say that on the eighth day, God's finger pressed into the earth at this point, forming the cavern, and at the same time a great voice spoke, saying where the fortress of Pembroke was to be.'

Bones had been found there, and tools from ancient men, yet now it was used mainly for storage.

'This is where we would take refuge under siege,' he said, but Margaret shuddered at the thought of hiding in this dank and dripping place.

The steward of the castle lived in the gatehouse with his family, Jasper in his private mansion to one side. In the inner ward there was the chancery with its justices and clerks, and also a chapel and kitchens, workshops for carpenters and masons. There were stables and pens full of livestock, and a dovecote containing pigeons for winter meat. And a dungeon tower. Until recently there had been a man, John Whithorne, who was imprisoned in the dungeon at the bottom of the tower for seven years and more. He had lost the sight of both eyes and suffered other incurable ills. They could see the dungeon room through a grille, which would have been the only access of light to that prisoner. All those years he would have been close enough to the kitchens and halls to hear the noises of the castle, feasting and toil, and at the thought of it Margaret was stricken with a piercing sorrow, for she had not yet become hardened to the misery of the world.

They stayed in the castle for several days, waiting for Edmund. Each day Margaret and Betsy walked the walls, which were patrolled by guards, but there was little to do. It was not her own household and she could not give orders, or even familiarize herself with the working of it, though as they passed through the kitchens she watched people pounding herbs, or making soap from fat and lye, or scouring dishes with sand.

All the time she was building up a vision of Edmund in her mind: handsome, heroic, the subject of epic lays. He would take her from the castle, and her whole life would be transformed, though she did not know when, or how. But the consciousness of him followed her around; in her mind he was following her with his gaze.

Then one day she was reading her copy of Aesop's fables in the garden, when a shadow fell across her, and she looked up and there was a tall man bending forward.

She could not see him properly because of the sun, yet she knew who he was. He dropped on to one knee before her, and her heart quickened. She looked round automatically for her nurse, who was beaming and making gestures that signalled to Margaret she should curtsy.

But she could not move. Edmund kissed her hand and there was a fluttering in her stomach.

'My Lady of Richmond,' he said. He was not exactly smiling, but there was a hint of a smile in his eyes. And still she couldn't speak.

She didn't know if he was as handsome or more handsome than she had imagined him. His features were thinner than she had imagined, his cheekbones higher, his hair not so much golden as light brown. He sat down beside her on the rock, stretching out one leg with a casual elegance.

'Is that a good book?' he asked her, and she stared down at it, disconcerted, then finally managed to speak.

'It is a very good book,' she said, 'though not so good as *Tristan and Isolde*.'

He raised his eyebrows. 'Is that a better book?'

She was comically earnest. 'I think it is better in its composition,' she said, 'though it does not have the same philosophy.'

'I see I shall marry a scholar,' he said. Instantly, she felt a complicated pride, as though she had said the wrong thing. But he extended his hand and she rose and walked with him, and her nurse dropped into the deepest curtsy as they passed.

He asked her about her studies, and about the garden, and how she was adapting to the weather. Her answers were so constrained;

she could not believe that she could not remember all the conversations she had prepared for him, which were witty and fluent. She did not know how to ask him what he had been doing, or whether he would think that proper. She was conscious all the time of the great difference in their heights, but he acted, at least, as though he were oblivious of this.

In the great hall she sat at his right hand and Jasper at his left, and he behaved towards her as though she were his lady, presenting all the food to her from his own plate first, and sharing the goblet of wine.

Later, she thought that might have been the moment she fell in love with him: for his courtesy, for treating her as if she were truly his sweetheart, his lady-love.

But all his conversation was with Jasper. She listened to him telling his brother that some of the local lords were feuding and stealing one another's cattle, that there were many tenancy disputes. She did not know whether she could say anything, or interrupt him while he talked.

After the meal everyone rose while he led her out of the hall. She was conscious all over again, now that everyone was watching, that she barely reached above his elbow, and she tried to walk taller. Then he kissed her hand and left her to her nurse once more, while he accompanied Jasper to his own suite of rooms in Jasper's mansion.

Betsy could hardly contain her excitement as she helped her to undress: he was so tall, so handsome and so . . . *knightly* there was not a better knight in all of Christendom. She, too, did not like Jasper – taking up all of Edmund's time in that tedious way.

'He is just jealous that he can't have you, my poppet,' she said, brushing her hair, and went on to say how impressed Edmund was at her scholarship and learning. But Margaret frowned at herself in the bronze plate that was her mirror.

'I wish –' she said, and stopped.

'What, my duckling?'

'I wish I might be pretty.'

And Betsy exclaimed and clucked over her. She *was* pretty – what did she mean? She had pretty hazel eyes and fine bones. But Margaret looked with dissatisfaction at her hair, which was neither thick nor shiny, and would not grow, like Isolde's, to cover her naked hips, but straggled to a halt just below her shoulders; and at her mouth, which was a thin line.

'I am too small,' she burst out eventually.

'Oh, my pretty – my pretty sweet!' cried Betsy, clasping her. 'There is so much time left for growing! One day, my precious, one day you will be beautiful and tall – so beautiful that none of the bards will sing of Nesta any more. *You* will be the Helen of Wales!'

They were married at Lamphey Palace, where they were to live. Once again she wore a white satin dress stitched with seed pearls as token of her purity. Her nurse combed out her hair and dressed it as well as she could, threading into it a pearl net, and told her how pretty she was: no bride had ever been prettier. And Margaret looked, disbelieving, at her yellowish skin and indeterminate eyes.

But she would be beautiful one day.

She and Edmund stood together, Jasper on one side and Betsy on the other. Edmund looked very handsome in his doublet of peacock blue. They repeated the vows she had said once already, in a different chapel, to a little boy, and Edmund held her fingers lightly, and she shivered in the sun.

Afterwards there was a banquet for her new household, eel pie and a roasted kid with quail stuffed into its belly, and carrots carved into the shape of a swan. They sat in the gardens of their new home, which, with its big windows and its orchards, was as unlike Pembroke Castle as it was possible to be. And she danced three times with Edmund and once with Jasper, and her nurse said she danced very prettily. And this went on until late in the evening until she was tired and Edmund kissed the top of her head and told her she could go to bed. So she left with her nurse, and did not see who Edmund left with.

And in the morning, Edmund had gone again.

That was the pattern of their life together: long absences and sudden reappearance. She would wake up in her own room, the anticipation of seeing him lighting her whole day to a luminous sheen, then gradually the day would grow dull again as she realized he wasn't there. Even when he was there she didn't always see him, but sometimes she came on him unexpectedly, and then something in her unfurled and she walked taller. He would be in conversation with Jasper or his steward, but he was unfailingly good-humoured and courteous.

'My Lady of Richmond,' he would say, bowing.

Only sometimes would she catch a look of something like resignation in his eyes, passing swiftly.

If they were outdoors he would say, 'How does your garden grow?'

She was always very serious, she couldn't even smile.

'It is growing well, thank you,' she said.

'Have you checked the new flowers?'

'I am going to.'

'They won't grow unless you check them.'

She was silent then, recognizing the tone as one you would use to a much younger child. His smile broadened, then he turned to her nurse.

'And you, Mistress Carew, how are you settling in to your rooms?'

And Betsy, bashful as a young maiden, would curtsy deeply, though she had already curtsied once, and say, 'We are getting used to them, my lord, only they are rather draughty.'

And he would declare that he would send for more tapestries immediately.

Then he would turn to Margaret and bow, or kiss her hand, and say that he would see her later. But he rarely did.

The same pattern resumed, for this new household ran itself – no one needed her to give instructions and, besides, she was too small. She had no say in the management of the kitchens or gardens, the dairy or brewery, or the wash house. There was no point noticing where a wall needed mending, or a field had flooded; she could only practise her needlework and pursue her reading. She started work on a history of the Tudor family in silk, pausing from time to time to look out of the window at the sheep as they gathered and dispersed themselves under a changing sky.

Edmund was rallying support for the king's cause, suppressing a rebellion here, settling a dispute there, and negotiating with the Welsh leaders and bards. And sometimes when he returned he went straight to Jasper at Pembroke, and did not visit Lamphey at all.

She was lonely, that was the trouble. She had never been lonely before, not at Bletsoe with her half-brothers and -sisters, nor at Ewelme with her young husband, and Alice Chaucer teaching her French. Sometimes the memory of her first husband's stricken face as she rode away came back to her. He had been abandoned, she could see that now.

When Edmund came back he was always with Jasper, and would remain closeted with him in one of the upstairs rooms. She could not demand more time with him, and she could never interrupt him. Edmund's face, his blue-grey eyes, could turn steel cold if interrupted. And he could never tell her what business took him away from her and kept him locked in furious consultation with his brother.

So she took to listening at doors, which was easier here, because there were no guards patrolling the windy corridors. Yet she rarely understood what was said. Names such as the Duke of Buckingham and those of her own Beaufort cousins passed in and out of the conversation, then the unintelligible names of bards.

But she understood that the Duke of York was ruling once more, and the whole country was divided and might at any time rise against the king.

Soon Edmund had to leave again, but he would be back, he told her, for Christmas, and they would spend it at Pembroke Castle, because his father would visit.

'You will like my father,' he said. And Margaret wanted to say that she would rather spend their first Christmas in their own home, but she could only nod solemnly. She did not say that she did not want to visit Jasper, and that she did not want him to leave. She curtsied and he kissed her lightly on both cheeks in the French way, then on the mouth in the English way, then he patted her hair in its net, and she could only watch him as he left through the snow that was already falling, and rising in little flurries around the horses, and settling again.

She did not want to go to Pembroke Castle for the Christmas season.

In fact it was the most extraordinary Christmas of her life. She travelled to the castle with her nurse, and once again Betsy was full of fear. They were being followed, she said, by Welsh warlords, who were accompanying them silently in the form of hunting birds. They would summon the little people to fly at their horses' eyes and madden them. But they mustn't look at them, no, for if they glanced out of the windows of their carriage, they would find no driver but an owl, guiding them straight into the underworld, where white and red hounds bayed, and licked the bloody feet of humans, and none of them should ever return.

Betsy worked herself into a still greater terror with her stories ('Oh, if it wasn't for you, my own precious duckling, Old Betsy would stay in her bed and never come out more!') so that Margaret had to hold her trembling hands again, and tell her that everything was all right, God was looking after them, and nothing bad would happen.

They could hear music and shouts of laughter even before they reached the great hall, and as they entered, flanked by pages, they looked in on a mass of people. Then one of the pages blew a horn, and called, 'The Lady Margaret,' and the sea of faces all turned towards her so that her heart started hammering. She did not want to see the expressions of curiosity, amusement or pity, so after scanning the room for Edmund, but failing to find him, she lowered her eyes.

Then the sea parted before her and she was guided towards a seat. And finally she saw Edmund at the top end of the longest table, and at the head of the table Jasper, looking quite different now in his scarlet silk. And to the right of Jasper, almost facing her, was a grey, grizzled man with red and broken veins on his cheeks and narrow, puffy eyes. His green jerkin was shabby and stained, and he seemed too rough to sit at the head of so great a table, but as she approached them all three men rose, and Edmund told her, 'This is my father, Owen Tudor.'

Suddenly, to her great surprise, he was no longer at Edmund's side. He disappeared, and she had no time to think where, for his head bobbed up between Edmund's place and her own, and she saw that he had dived beneath the table and was kneeling before her, his head almost level with her own. And he cried in a great voice, 'A daughter-in-law at last! Praise be to God – someone to civilize these savage sons of mine, eh?'

And he seized her hand and kissed it, then her wrist, then when the pale green sleeve fell open, revealing the kirtle beneath, he kissed her arm almost to the elbow, then looked up again at her and kissed her full on the mouth.

'Forgive my father,' Edmund said, smiling at her startled look. 'He is part troll.'

'Part troll, am I?' Owen Tudor shouted. 'Well, a troll may kiss a lady! But you should come and kiss her for yourself – some lusty bridegroom you!'

And Edmund filled his mouth with wine and leaned across his father, and pressed his mouth to hers. She felt the warm liquid flowing past her teeth and had to gulp quickly before it all spilled down her chin.

When she opened her eyes the three of them were laughing – even Jasper was smiling and relaxed – so that for the first time she could see the likeness between them, though the two sons were so courtly and the father so grizzled and wild. Yet beneath the courtliness there was some similar element, which would be more at home in the forests or the hills than in castles or at court, and she had never seen this before.

'Now, mistress,' said Owen Tudor, 'I trust you will dance with me after dinner,' and he took her hand again, quite gently.

'Thank you,' she said, very formal, 'I shall be delighted,' and

Owen in his turn was delighted with her, and he proposed a toast immediately, and everyone raised their glasses and she sat there smiling and blushing and shyly proud.

Then the food arrived, dish after dish of hare and boar and peacock – its beak and claws replaced by vegetable sticks and almonds – and a wild boar's head surrounded by meatballs fried in batter and coloured green to resemble apples, and a swan with outstretched wings. There were more than forty courses, and she could manage hardly any of them, but Owen managed all. Minstrels came and played around their table, and the mummers acted a farce about the wild men of the woods, and a great green man strode through the hall followed by live pigs running and squealing. And Owen Tudor chased after one and managed to ride it for almost a minute, and all the women laughed and the men cheered.

Then the dancing began, and Owen Tudor lifted her and whirled her round, and she tried not to notice that Edmund was dancing with a tall girl with breasts, for it was all she could do to keep up with Owen and not stumble against him as he steered her past rows of clapping people.

And the dancing got wilder as the wine flowed and the pigs returned and everyone gave chase, and Edmund leaped from table to chair, and then to the back of the largest pig, while all the women clapped and screamed.

'He is so handsome, your husband,' the tall girl with the breasts said, and Margaret felt pain and pride burning through her like a torch. For this girl, who was younger than she had thought, maybe just two or three years older than herself, would never have him fully; she would have to return to her own wrinkled, red-nosed husband, who had just collapsed, sweating, in his chair, and Edmund would have to return to her.

And one day she would be tall, with breasts.

So she kept her head high as the tall girl, whose name was Alice, danced with Edmund again and again. And she did not protest when Edmund came over to bid her goodnight, because it was time for her to leave the great hall with her nurse.

But the next day he came to her room unexpectedly. She had been getting dressed for another feast when he came in, and her heart lurched as usual; and, as usual, she could think of nothing to say. But he sat on the edge of her bed and asked her what she thought of his father.

'I like him,' she said at once, and he said he had told her she would. And then he started talking to her, but not in his usual manner: telling her about his father, who had been persecuted by the Duke of Gloucester for marrying his mother, Queen Katherine of Valois, who was the widow of King Henry V.

This same year [1438] one Owen, no man of birth, brake out of Newgate one night with the help of his priest and went his way hurting foul his keeper, but at the last, blessed be God, he was taken again. The which Owen had secretly wedded Queen Katherine and had three or four children by her, though people knew nothing of this until she was dead and buried.

Great Chronicle of London

Queen Katherine had been lonely, Edmund said, living in a great castle without either husband or son, for her young son was now king and was looked after by his uncles. It was said that Owen had charmed her by falling into her lap drunk at a ball. Later, Margaret heard another version of this story – that she had followed him to a river secretly to watch him bathing; that she was 'unable to curb her carnal lusts' – but this was not the version Edmund told and she was happy to listen to him; happy that he was speaking to her at all.

He told her that after his mother's death his father had been arrested, and waited for her to ask him why, but it was obvious to her that only the most reckless commoner would marry a queen. And only the most reckless queen would dare to marry a commoner.

'No,' Edmund said. 'It was because he was Welsh.'

He told her then of all the laws enacted against the Welsh, that they should not marry out of Wales, or own land, or be given any office, or bear arms, or have guests in their own houses without special licence. His father had fallen foul not only of these laws, but of a special statute devised by the Duke of Gloucester and the king's council that made it possible to imprison and even execute a man who married a queen. Only the king could give permission for his mother to marry, and only when he came of age. So Owen and Katherine had lived together secretly, outside London. But after Katherine's death, when Edmund was six or seven years old, the Duke of Gloucester had Owen thrown into prison, and the marriage declared unlawful, and their children bastards.

She could not read the expression on his face, but a muscle on the side of his jaw was twitching. She said, 'But you do not fight for the Welsh.'

'I fight for my brother, the king,' he said. But he was hardly English at all, Margaret thought. His father was Welsh and his mother French. Yet he was half-brother to the English king, who had eventually rescued Owen Tudor, taking him into his own household and exempting him from the laws against the Welsh. Also King Henry had treated Edmund and Jasper well, according to his mother's wishes. They had been looked after by Katherine de la Pole, sister of the Duke of Suffolk, and then taken to court. Now the king had given Edmund the job of negotiating with the rebel chiefs, because of his Welsh father. And because he would not betray his brother, the king.

She could see this contradiction in him. And she saw also that, when all the bells of the nation had rung for the birth of a son and heir to the king after eight long years of marriage, certain of his hopes, his unspoken desires, had been blighted. It would be that much harder to be the hope of Wales when it would one day be handed over to the little prince.

Yet he would guard the prince, his nephew, with his life.

She admired him for this. She would have liked to tell him that she admired him for his complicated loyalty. Yet she knew instinctively that he would not want to discuss the subject. His face had already changed; the conversation seemed to be over. He said he would leave her to prepare for the feast.

The Christmas season passed, after many more festivities, and at last all the guests left, and Owen Tudor with them. Margaret saw the look on the tall girl's face when Edmund came to bid everyone farewell. He was polite enough, of course, and formal, given that her husband was there. But the look that Lady Alice cast after him was stricken, full of regret, and Margaret was suddenly and meanly glad.

Then Edmund said that he was leaving too, but she was to stay in Pembroke Castle because of the snow, which was banked up high on all the paths. And before she could prevent herself, Margaret cried 'No!' and he looked at her with mild surprise, until she said, 'Why do you have to go?'

She knew from his expression that this was the wrong thing to say. But he began to tell her anyway, that he had to go to the queen. He and Jasper were to leave the next day, to meet up with her cousin, Henry Beaufort, who was the new Duke of Somerset. There were many things to arrange and he would have to spend the rest of that day in consultation with his brother.

She was silent then, but it was a mutinous silence.

'You are always talking to Jasper –' she said at last, sounding petulant even to her own ears.

'Listen to me,' Edmund said, interrupting her. 'The king is ill again – not so badly as last time, thank God, but the queen has taken affairs into her own hands. She has moved the court to Coventry, and is setting up her own council around the prince.'

Henry Duke of Somerset and Humphrey Duke of Buckingham, with many other noblemen who held and stood with King Henry, lamenting his adversity . . . went secretly to Queen Margaret, privately offered her their counsel and declared that the Duke of York sought to deceive the king . . . [or to] kill him unawares . . . The queen, much moved by this warning and afraid both for herself and her husband, took occasion to persuade him to withdraw to Coventry . . .

Polydore Vergil

Margaret said nothing as he spoke to her. The prince was Edmund's nephew, and therefore her own, and the new council would look after him. The woman in her could see this, but the child knew only that she never saw Edmund, that he was never available to her. And now he was explaining that both he and Jasper would spend the winter season at court; he did not know when he would return. She herself could leave as soon as the weather changed, to return to Lamphey.

At this, in one awful moment, the child won.

'Don't go,' she begged him, but his face became cold and still, and she learned the most important lesson of her married life: never to complain.

And he left anyway, of course. She could only bow her head as he went out of the room, feeling a stark and terrifying hollowness inside. Edmund was leaving, and she had shown herself up to him as an ungrateful child.

She watched as he set out the next day, his colours bright against a leaden sky, a freezing rain turning the snow to slush and churning all the roads to an impassable mud.

'It is the life of women,' her nurse said behind her, putting her hands on her shoulders. She could feel the warmth of Betsy's flesh on hers, but it didn't reach her, for she was freezing inside. She would not know if the ice cracked, or his horse slipped, or he was lost in a whirling storm. All she could do for him was pray.

It was part of her bargain with God that she stopped eating. She took to offering up a portion of food each day as part of her prayer. She would no longer eat breakfast, or any mid-morning meal. Frequently she did not eat at all until partway through the afternoon; and then only some dried wafers or biscuits and figs, until the evening meal.

By supper she was nearly fainting with hunger, light-headed, yet strangely calm, almost exhilarated, for God and all his angels could surely see she was keeping her part of the deal. And if St Bridget could exist off only communion wine and wafers, then so could she.

Betsy grew suspicious, but she was clever at concealing her fasts.

It was easy to hide some food in her long sleeves, then throw it to the birds. Sometimes she held the food she was not eating in her mouth until her nurse left the room. But if Betsy caught her she would not hear the end of it.

'You must eat, my precious duckling – how else are you going to grow tall? Your bosom will not grow [Margaret had taken to checking this every day] unless you eat. Come now, eat a little something, my poppet, just for Betsy.'

Ever more dainty dishes were prepared for her, and still she would not eat. But on the fifth day she had a headache, and could not move, and her nurse stayed by her side.

'What would your husband say?' she asked.

She tried and failed to spoon-feed Margaret herself, small portions of pigeon pie, pigs' trotters broiled into a soup, all the time admonishing her with unlikely warnings.

'I know a girl who would not eat and she did not grow into a lovely young woman. She grew spindly and black with hunger, until at length she turned into a spider and crawled away into a crack in the wall.'

Margaret didn't answer; she was too old for Betsy's stories now. But her nurse did not give up.

'I thought you wanted to be beautiful,' she said. She could even change by the time Edmund returned: her hair would grow long and glossy, her cheeks pink, her bosom develop. She might be two or three inches taller.

Margaret kept her face turned away, but she was listening. It would not be a good thing, her nurse went on, if she were to meet him in a shrunken and scrawny state, with her hair falling out and her skin yellow, no. Did she not think there were too many pretty girls around him for that?

Margaret's throat constricted suddenly. How could she tell her nurse that if she ate, Edmund might never return to her at all?

A clever wife, a sensible one, her nurse continued, might give up *something* in order to bring her husband back, but not those things that made her beautiful, oh no.

Slowly, Margaret sat up. She looked at the dish her nurse was holding – a little soup and bread. Her throat constricted again. 'I will eat a pear,' she said.

It was not the season for pears, of course, yet a dried one was found, and boiled in cider, so that it took on the appearance again of the golden, rounded fruit. And she ate almost half of it before lying down.

The weather did not improve, and they stayed in the great granite fortress till it was almost spring. Until Margaret insisted, against all the wishes of her nurse, on returning to Lamphey.

She began to take more interest in the household and estate; to notice when a stream had overflowed its banks, or when a sheep was in trouble, lying on its side and watching the world of the hill with grudging, resentful eyes. She began to have some say in the food that was ordered, and in the ordering of cloth. All the time she was performing these tasks for Edmund, though he was never there; she was conscious of his approving gaze on everything she did.

And still Edmund stayed away at court, looking after his little nephew, the prince.

Then at last they heard from him. They could meet him, he said, at Caldicot, near Chepstow, some hundred miles east of Pembroke Castle. They made the long journey to visit him, but he was hardly there. And when he was, he wouldn't tell her what business kept him away from her, closeted so many hours with his brother in his own suite of rooms.

So she returned to listening at doors.

Much of the time she didn't understand what she was hearing, but on one occasion she heard him say, 'She's a little girl – a child.'

'It's not unheard of,' Jasper said, and Edmund said, 'She's a child, Jasper. Twelve years old – she looks eight. I am twenty-six – married to an infant. Do you not see how that looks?'

'She is an infant with the Beaufort fortune,' Jasper said. 'And you are in need of an heir.'

She had heard enough. She walked away quickly, unsteadily, and without direction. Her heart was pumping painfully, irregularly, and her face felt as though it might burst. What she felt most clearly was the need to avoid her nurse. She went to sit on her own in the garden.

The long winter had continued through April, and now the streams ran high with melted snow. The air was shrill with birds and the sky a sharp, precise blue.

Normally she felt the spring as a quickening of the blood. At Ewelme she and John de la Pole would have run and shouted through the gardens; at Bletsoe her half-brothers would have taught her to fish. But here, when her nurse had suggested they should go out into the fresh air and see all the new lambs, she had said, 'I'm not a child any more.'

She sat on a large stone near a pond. There was a mass of spawn like a green cloud in the water. She sat hunched over it in a thoughtful study, solitude wrapped round her like a cloak, and when she heard his footstep she did not even look up. She did not wish to see his face rearrange itself, for her benefit, into a mask of pleasure.

His steps paused, as they had to; he could not simply pass her by. 'Are you counting the tadpoles?' he said.

Something about the way she sat, hunched and concentrated, must have intrigued him, for he squatted beside her. Normally the nearness of him would make her mouth too dry to speak, and quicken her heart. Now it only thumped painfully once, twice, before settling above her stomach like a lead weight.

'Are you sure there are enough?'

She looked at him then, with eyes turned suddenly old. His expression changed – she had piqued him – then he began to smile.

'Are you looking for fairies?'

'No.'

He tilted his head so that he was gazing directly into her eyes. His face was filled with a tender enquiry, so tender she had to look quickly away.

He touched her cheek, returning her gaze to his.

'Something ails my lady wife,' he said, and his expression was all concern. She couldn't bear it. But she couldn't look away. She could see her own reflection in each of his eyes; they were blue now, not grey, reflecting the clear sky, and she saw something else in them – a flicker of alarm.

'What is it?' he started to say, but he didn't finish, because in a sudden movement she had leaned forward and kissed him.

It was no more than a butting of her mouth into his. He drew back, laughing a little in astonishment.

'What –?'

But before he could withdraw or stand up, she flung her arms round his neck and butted his mouth again; her teeth banged on his. Then she looked at him.

The expression on his face changed from surprise to wariness to speculation. And understanding. He understood her perfectly, she could tell.

'Well,' he said, and she waited, breathless with terror. He put his hands on her shoulders, holding her away from him. 'What's this?' he said softly, and she could not stop looking at him; she could not take her eyes away, willing him to see.

He looked at her consideringly, then away. He made a small sound that was almost, but not quite, a laugh.

Then he looked back, and she could see something had changed in him. The tender amusement had gone, replaced by something she couldn't read.

'I'm afraid . . .' he said solemnly, and the whole of her stomach and throat contracted in terror. 'I'm afraid you are in need of a little instruction in kissing.'

She couldn't move or take her eyes from him as he touched her face, turning it slightly one way then the other.

'You have all the right equipment,' he said, teasing her again, but not quite in the old way. 'One mouth, two lips.' He brushed his thumb over them lightly and a prickling sensation shot along her spine. 'A tongue,' he said, and she wondered dizzily what a tongue had to do with it. 'I have heard you are a clever student,' he said, and he kissed her then, gently, without opening his mouth. Blood rushed to her head and her stomach felt weak.

'Do you wish to learn?' he asked her. She had closed her eyes and could not open them, but she nodded. 'Well, then. Open your mouth. Just a little.'

He kissed her again. She felt his tongue against her teeth.

'You mustn't keep me out,' he said.

All the time she couldn't believe it; she couldn't believe it was happening to her.

She sucked on his tongue gently, doubtfully, just as he told her to, but when he undid the lace ribbon at the neck of her chemise, she stiffened suddenly, knowing what he would see there: the ridges of her breast bone and the ribs attached to it – a flat expanse. He slipped one finger into the neck of her gown and over one nipple, then the other. She kept her eyes shut, but all he said was, 'It is chilly. Shall we go inside?'

And she nodded vigorously, finally opening her eyes.

He helped her to her feet and she hurried beside him, almost running, because he was striding now, quick and decisive. They passed her nurse, and Margaret saw the look of surprise, shock even, on Betsy's face as she remembered just in time to drop a deep curtsy, that yet had a scandalized air as though she *knew*, and Margaret felt the urge to laugh – shrill, improbable laughter was brimming up inside her.

Edmund held the door of his room open for her, and she walked past him. He was looking at her now as from a great distance; his eyes had gone narrow and cold, unfathomable, and all her laughter turned to terror again. She walked past him anyway, to the centre of the room, towards his bed on which there was a splendid coverlet of fur-lined silk.

And there she faltered, not knowing what to do.

She felt him come up behind her, and put his hands on her, and somewhere inside she started to pray, *Holy Mary, Mother of God . . .* but Mary was a virgin, she thought wildly, how could she help? And she cast around in her mind for an appropriate saint, finding none. And he was lifting her, then, placing her on the bed. He stripped off her gown, so that she was in her kirtle and chemise. Then he lifted her chemise.

No one had ever seen her naked, apart from her nurse. She shrank from seeing herself through his eyes: scrawny, unformed. She had prayed so hard for breasts.

But he did not take her undergarments off, he merely lifted them to her thighs, then began stripping off her hose gently, holding each foot in his hand as he did so, then pushing her kirtle and chemise up higher, exposing her.

All this time she lay paralysed between shame and desire; then he touched her softly, and sensations she had never dreamed of flowered in her belly.

Later, the pain came and it was very bad. He stopped, withdrew himself, and started again; she clung to him, sweating, and gripped him with her knees. Sharp splinters of pain drove upwards into her abdomen. Stars burst behind her eyes, her lungs seemed stuck together and she could not breathe, but she would not cry or beg him to stop. Four or five times he tried, his member covered with her blood, then at last he gasped and lay forward on her and she lay beneath him like a crumpled rag, trying to grasp the fact that it was over, and the pain had stopped.

It was over. She was a wife now, fully, and a child no longer.

She looked at Edmund, who was falling asleep, strands of light brown hair across his face.

It had really happened. He was her husband. She touched his hair, moving it from his face, his beautiful face, and a feeling overcame her then, a feeling she had never known before, welling from her stomach: a deep, shining joy.

She loved him, she loved him absolutely: the planes and shadows of his face, the ridges of his sternum, the slope of his hip, the fine hair on his chest, the pale stalk between his legs in its nest of hair.

She spent more time with him now, walking with him in the gardens, sharing his rooms. He was more inclined to talk to her, and to listen to what she had to say. Subtly, but distinctly, her status within the household had changed.

Betsy had taken to calling her 'My lady'. Even the servants seemed to know.

And Margaret was proud; she had never been so proud, of her altered status, her tall, handsome husband. She wanted to be with him all the time.

But in early May he was called away again, to subdue the Welsh rebel, Gruffydd ap Nicholas, who had encroached on lands belonging to the Marcher lords. He had taken control of several castles: Conway, Cardigan, Kidwelly, Aberystwyth, the great and almost impregnable fortress of Carreg Cennen, and then the northern fortress of Carmarthen. So Edmund had to go to Pembrokeshire and Cardiganshire where Gruffydd's two sons, Thomas and Owain, were stirring up the people to rebellion.

'But when will you come back?' she said, before she could stop herself, and then she had to watch his face closing again, becoming cold and still.

She watched him leaving her, his colours bright in the May sunshine, and wept like a child in Betsy's arms. At the last moment he turned and lifted a hand towards her, and she could feel rather than see his flashing smile. And together they watched him leave, the dust rising from the horses' hooves, the company of men at first solid and then, in the heat shimmer, insubstantial and unreal.

Soon she heard that he was 'greatly at war' with Gruffydd ap Nicholas, and might not be back for some time. Margaret and her nurse returned to Lamphey.

Later that month, around the time of her thirteenth birthday, she noticed that her breasts were finally beginning to bud and swell. The trees were bowed with thick white blossom and from a distance they looked like giant sheep. Fat bumblebees probed into flowers and each morning the sky was pristine. When Edmund returned she would finally have breasts, like ripe plums.

They were tender, especially at night, but she rejoiced in this tenderness, prodding them surreptitiously throughout the day. They didn't seem to be growing very fast, but they were increasingly painful.

On the morning of her birthday, she asked her nurse, 'Do – female parts – hurt before they grow?'

She indicated with her hands, and Betsy looked at her.

'Sometimes they do,' she said. Then she said, 'Sometimes they hurt before your monthly courses.'

She had never started her monthly courses. So her nurse explained that the womb was like a holy chalice that weeps if disappointed of the seed. And at the expression on Margaret's face, she said, 'It means you are becoming a woman, my sweet.'

Margaret said nothing to this, but hugged the information privately to herself. She was becoming a woman. She would be a woman when Edmund returned.

There was no bleeding, and she was grateful for this. But over the next few days she wondered, did breasts make you feel sick as well, when they started to grow? Because she could no longer stand the thought of food in the morning, Betsy sighed and clucked over her as she sent her breakfast back.

Then one morning she was actually sick, into her chamber pot, and her nurse hurried to empty it.

'Why are they so much trouble, growing?' she fretted aloud.

Her nurse said nothing, but when she was sick again the next morning, Betsy wiped her face, then clasped it between her hands.

'Oh, my precious,' she said, with a catch in her voice. 'Praise be to God. Bless you, my angel, my sweetest child,' and she hugged her hard.

'What?' said Margaret, squirming uncomfortably, and already feeling sick again. 'What is it?'

And that was how she learned she was with child.

'You must eat,' Betsy said to her, over and again. For Margaret was fasting once more. Her lips had taken on a bluish tinge, and the flesh of them was dry and cracked.

'You think he will want to kiss them when he comes back?' Betsy said. But this time her rejection of food had less to do with prayer than with the fierce nausea that gripped her during the early weeks of pregnancy.

She woke each morning with a tremulous consciousness: *what if she should fail, what if she should fail?* Women did fail their babies, she knew. Her own mother, after hearing of the death of her father, had miscarried a son.

'It will be safe soon,' her nurse said. But Margaret did not know if she would ever feel safe again. She would never forgive herself if something she did made her lose this baby. Already in her mind it was a boy, and looked like Edmund.

When Edmund returned, she would say to him, 'I hope you will be back this winter – I would not like you to miss the birth of your son.'

Between fits of nausea she tried to eat, for the baby, but often the mere thought of food made her feel ill. Betsy resorted to her old bullying tactics. She instructed all the servants to watch the Lady Margaret, because her own eyes were failing, and she understood that she was being cheated over the question of food. She sat with her at every meal and refused to leave until Margaret had been persuaded to eat a little watered-down pottage. And Margaret accepted this mainly because she was too weak to remain kneeling for long when she prayed, then too weak to rise again once she had knelt. And if she could not pray, then Edmund might never return.

The weeks passed and Edmund did not return. The weather grew hot and the land lay baking under a weight of sun. The grass was the same colour as the corn and the blue hills shimmered in the distance. Margaret stayed in much of the time, reading Boccaccio or embroidering, taking a little wine and bread, or praying.

Sometimes she had the sensation of light streaming upwards from the palms of her hands, or even her forehead, and wondered, dizzily, if she would fly up to heaven. But automatically she resisted this: she was not ready – her place was here, with Edmund.

Yet after such moments she always felt an uncanny peace; an inner certainty that Edmund would be returned to her, and all would be well.

'I don't believe you,' she said.

Jasper knelt before her, hot and dusty from travelling.

But it wasn't supposed to be Jasper, it should have been Edmund.

Someone had spotted the Tudor colours approaching from the distance, and a great cry had been set up: 'He is coming, he is coming!'

Margaret had been sitting by the pool in the orchard. She barely had time to hurry to the gateway before she heard him riding up the path.

Her hand flew to her hair; she could remember nothing she had meant to say.

And then he rounded the bend, and it was not Edmund at all, it was Jasper.

She saw him dismount, hand his horse over to one man and give instructions to another. All this without looking her way. He took off his helmet and his hair was plastered to his head with sweat. He looked grim, exhausted. Then he fell into some consultation with his captain at arms.

There was no sign of Edmund.

She stood for a moment, her cheeks alternately burning then pale. Then abruptly she turned and went into the house, walking swiftly past the line of servants who had assembled to greet their master.

He could say whatever he had to say to her inside.

She waited for him there, with her nurse and her steward, two lady attendants and two grooms. And Jasper finally appeared with two or three of his own men, and he walked towards her, then dropped clumsily on to one knee.

Her stomach shifted and something fluttered in her throat. He had never done that before.

Then he told her that Edmund had been taken prisoner at Carmarthen Castle. Not by the Welsh, but by William Herbert, who was an ally of the Duke of York.

She replied quickly, automatically, that she didn't believe him.

He had been looking not at her, but at a mosaic pattern of tiles on the floor. Now he glanced up at her swiftly. She had spoken in a low voice, and he chose not to hear her. He went on telling her what had happened.

At the end of July, Edmund had won a great victory, wresting Carmarthen Castle from Gruffydd ap Nicholas and his two sons. Messages were sent to the king. But it was York who was Constable of Carmarthen Castle, and he was less pleased about this boost to the king's authority, this victory in the king's name. On 10 August, some 2,000 men from Herefordshire and the neighbouring Welsh lordships had set out for west Wales by order of the duke. They were under the command of Sir William Herbert, the duke's chief retainer. They went straight to Carmarthen and seized the castle. They had taken Edmund's garrison by surprise – no one had expected to fight the English rather than the Welsh. And they had imprisoned Edmund in the castle itself.

The king would, of course, do everything in his power to secure Edmund's release. Jasper planned to go to the king, who was still at Coventry. York was no longer the chief power in the land now that the king had resumed his role – he would have to obey his king. Jasper was sure this was all some kind of misunderstanding that could be sorted out. But, in the meantime, Edmund was still held prisoner, and Jasper had broken his journey to Pembroke Castle, because he had thought that the Lady Margaret would want to know.

There was a silence in which Jasper continued to gaze at the floor.

Margaret said, more distinctly than before, 'I don't believe you.'

Jasper's face changed, and a stir passed around the room. She could hear the way she sounded – childish, rude – but she couldn't help it. She averted her gaze from the look he gave her, which was like Edmund's at its most stern.

'Edmund would never let himself be taken,' she said.

She should have said, *My Lord of Richmond.*

'My lady,' Jasper said in even tones, 'he was taken by surprise. He thought that Herbert's forces had come to relieve him, to reward him, even, for his victory. He rode out to greet them. And suddenly, with no warning, he was surrounded and pulled from his horse. But he was taken alive – Sir Roger swears he was still alive. There were several witnesses –'

'No! It isn't possible!' she cried. She was blatantly rude now, and shrill. Her nurse remonstrated with her.

It was impossible – brave, laughing Edmund, taken prisoner at Carmarthen Castle, by that notorious earl, William Herbert – what was it they said about him? *A cruel man and prepared for any crime.*

But she mustn't think about that, she must try to focus on what Jasper was saying. For he was speaking again, he had spoken, and was looking at her in grave reproof; then, when she failed to respond, he looked at her nurse with a mixture of impatience and uncertainty.

Margaret had always hated Jasper, his long, crooked nose, his sweating face.

'Why are you here?' she said suddenly, and Betsy said, 'My lady has not been well.'

'Why are you here if he has been taken?' she demanded.

Jasper looked stricken. He stood up abruptly and swept the dust from his knees. He was angry, more angry than she had ever seen him, but so was she. She felt an unprecedented rage.

'You should not be here,' she said, and someone gasped.

'My lady is overwrought,' said her nurse. 'It is the heat.'

'I am not overwrought,' she said, and her voice rose. 'I don't believe he would be taken – he would rather die! And if he has been taken you should not be here – you should be trying to rescue him! Why are you not trying to save him?'

There was a clamour of voices and it seemed that everyone was speaking at once, explaining, remonstrating, apologizing. Only Jasper did not speak. He looked down at her with glittering eyes. And she too said nothing; there was nothing left to say. Her throat felt wounded, she could speak no more. Abruptly, she rose, without ceremony, and turned her back on Jasper and left the room, her nurse running after her in dismay.

'Oh, my lady, what have you done?'

She had violated all the codes of conduct, all the rules of hospitality and homage due to a kinsman and an earl. But all she could think about was Edmund, trapped in a stinking cell when he loved to ride and to be free. How he had looked when he set off that May morning, the sun glinting on his armour. How he had turned and waved at her, unusually, and she had felt rather than seen him smiling.

Betsy clucked and fussed over her, loosening her gown at the throat, dabbing at her face with a damp napkin. She would have to beg the Lord Jasper's forgiveness, she said.

'I will not,' said Margaret.

The next moment she was clasped to Betsy's ample chest while her nurse broke into weeping, all the time trying to reassure her.

'At least he is only taken, not killed,' she sobbed. They would not dare to kill Edmund, who was brother to the king. As soon as the king heard, they would have to release him. And Jasper had sent messengers to the king and was going to him himself, to plead Edmund's cause.

Still clasping Margaret, she sank on to the window seat, out of breath from her outburst, and from the stairs.

Margaret turned suddenly, pressing her face into Betsy's bosom. She sobbed three or four times, harsh, dry sobs. Then she pulled back, pushing a strand of hair from her eyes.

'We need to take care of this little one now,' her nurse said, laying a hand over her barely swollen stomach.

She hadn't even told Edmund about the baby.

And Margaret rose and stood, distracted, in the middle of the room. *Edmund*, she thought. How had she not known, not been able to sense what was happening? He had not written to her, but he was not good at writing.

She could have written to him, of course, but she was never entirely sure where he was, or that the messenger would find him. And she had wanted to tell him about the baby herself, when he returned. He might return quickly, she hung on to that thought. She would let him rest a little, and then go to him. He would look at her blankly at first, and then his face would light up with joy, and he would catch her in his arms. He would be overwhelmed that she, who was so tiny and unformed that he still thought of her as a child, had done this thing for him; that he would be a father at last.

Betsy caressed her face and said she was hot, she was sweating; she needed some cooling water and chamomile to refresh her before the evening meal. She would have some sent up for them at once.

Somehow, as always, Betsy wore her down. She allowed herself to be placated, and dressed with special care.

When she went down to table, and sat at Jasper's side, there was no further mention of her discourtesy. Jasper paid her special attention, pouring her wine himself, and explaining to her in great detail what would happen next. He would not be returning to Carmarthen, partly because plague had broken out in the villages surrounding the castle – but she was not to worry, he said quickly, as a look of horror passed across her face. The castle itself was safe, and getting its supplies by river to avoid contamination. He would go to the Duke of York personally, and to the king – King Henry's forces would liberate Edmund, and he would be awarded great honour, of that he was sure.

Margaret smiled and nodded as he poured her wine. She knew that Betsy must have told him about the baby, because he was so attentive, so prepared to overlook her rudeness. She felt aggrieved in her heart, and resentful of her nurse. Because now Jasper knew and Edmund didn't. And Jasper would tell Edmund, of course, all that would be taken from her. But how else could her nurse have explained Margaret's insulting behaviour?

Jasper didn't mention the baby, and for that she was grateful. He wanted to soothe her, and she allowed him to think that she was soothed. She allowed herself to be persuaded that it had all been some terrible mistake. The king did not even know about Edmund, and as soon as he did, Edmund would be set free, and York rebuked – even sent back to Ireland, which was the best thing for him.

She was not to worry, Jasper said again. While he was in the castle, Edmund was safe – safer, even as prisoner, than fighting in the field. Or in the plague-ridden villages.

She listened to him attentively and consciously removed the worried frown from her eyes. Her nurse watched her approvingly, but she would not meet Betsy's gaze. When she retired early no one objected, because of course everyone knew about the baby. But she held her head high and left the room smiling. Betsy followed her, as usual, so that even in her room she could not vent the rage and sense of injury that was burning in her heart.

As August drew its last, laboured breath, Jasper set out once more, to meet the king. Before he left, he came to her room. He stood in front of her for a moment, ponderously, the whole of his face pulled into a frown.

'If I had known,' he said eventually, 'I would not have told you.'

And Margaret, who had meant to say only courteous and pleasant things, looked at him sullenly.

'Yes,' she said, 'it would be like you not to tell me.'

Betsy started to protest, but Margaret shot her a look of such venom that her words died away. Jasper looked taken aback.

'I did not mean –' he said, then seemed to bite his words back. He looked thoughtfully at the floor. 'I mean I would not for anything put the baby at risk. You might have – the shock –'

She would not help him. He had not saved Edmund. She looked at him with sunken, dark-ringed eyes.

He carried on talking.

Already the Welsh were banding together in support of Edmund. Their father, Owen Tudor, was raising a great force of men who were even now crossing the Menai Straits. And soon they would be joined by the king's men.

He waited for her to speak, but it was her nurse who thanked him and wished him God speed; Margaret said nothing. She had not eaten that morning, despite Betsy's remonstrations. She had gone straight to her chapel, and lain on the floor and tried to pray. But the only image in her mind was of Edmund in a cell, languishing in darkness, like that unfortunate prisoner in Pembroke Castle.

After Jasper left the heat grew worse. Crops withered in the field. In the church of St David's masses were said and sung continuously for Edmund. In the north there was famine as first Herbert's soldiers then Gruffydd ap Nicholas's men took what was left of the harvest. In the south the plague was spreading. It was said that it always spread in times of heat, as though borne on waves of sun. Lamphey was safe, because of its isolated position, but Betsy said she should certainly not go to St David's. It was too far, and apart from the plague the land was at war. Everywhere the rebels were coming down from their hiding places in the mountains and setting fire to English property; the bards were once more singing their prophetic songs. There was no news of Jasper.

But one of the Tudors was always present in the church of St David's at harvest time, because the family represented both England and Wales. It was more important than ever now in this time of war, and so she insisted she would go.

She arrived late, due to a wheel falling from her carriage and having to be repaired on the road, so that when she got there the congregation was already standing in the nave. She proceeded along the main aisle of the church past many villagers, farmers, tenants and labourers, to the seat she would normally occupy with Edmund. With every step she was aware of them staring at her, of mingling currents of hostility, pity, resentment and curiosity emanating from them. She was sweating, but could not wipe her face in front of all these people. She pressed one hand to her stomach as she took her seat. She did not think the baby was showing yet; she did not think anyone outside her household knew.

The service proceeded as usual, the priest reciting the liturgy in Latin, until the point where he began to sing, chanting lines of the mass alternately with the choir of men and boys.

Then unexpectedly, powerfully, the congregation broke in.

Their voices rose like a broken wave, becoming higher and louder, the stones and pillars of the church vibrating with the noise. It took her several moments to realize they were singing their own song, in Welsh.

And another moment to realize there was a small quivering in the pit of her stomach. She did not know what it was – if anything, it might have been anxiety or surprise. But when it happened again she knew. She knew it was her baby moving, quick and live.

Much later she would tell him that he was truly a Welshman, for he had come to life to the tune of the Welsh anthem as it soared inside the great church.

Every time the priest began to chant in Latin the congregation sang, and the voice of their singing was at first unwieldy and inharmonious, but then came together in a powerful harmony as it gathered force.

Lady Margaret and the priest looked at one another, and she saw her own fear and uncertainty reflected in his eyes; she knew he did not know what to do.

He could not do anything, it seemed, only wait, while the voices sang on, rising and falling and breaking into a chorus that was like the broken heart of Wales itself.

And when they had finished they all stood, looking at the priest, who looked back at them and said nothing.

Then he managed to say the final prayer in a shaken voice, dismissing them, and Margaret rose. She walked back down the aisle, past them all, keeping her gaze carefully lowered, praying all the time that she would not be molested. It was a long walk, but no one moved, no one stood in her way. She arrived safely at her carriage.

But that was the last time she went to the great church; she would not put her baby at risk again. She confined herself to Lamphey, where she was safe, and returned to her private prayers, to fasting and waiting for news.

In October the great heat was replaced at last by heavy rain, too late for the harvest. And still there was no news of Edmund. Or rather, there was contradictory news – news of his escape, then news that he was back under lock and key, or that he had never escaped at all. News that Owen Tudor was captured with him, then that he had never left Anglesey. The Duke of Buckingham's men were obstructed by unexpected floods. The king had not the means to muster an army, but Jasper had gone directly to complain to the Duke of York. The Archbishop of Canterbury, together with several bishops, had already written expressing outrage at Edmund's imprisonment. And so the Duke of York had finally given the order for Edmund's release.

This news came towards the end of October, that month of storms. There was rejoicing at Lamphey. Margaret gave the day to fasting and prayer and thanksgiving in her chapel. Yet Edmund was still in Carmarthen Castle, the next messenger told them. He was waiting for the flooding to subside, before Jasper's men could reach him to escort him home. Or perhaps he was still wary of the plague.

He was in the castle, but he was free. She could imagine him strolling about the walls and the palace gardens, thinking of her, perhaps, as she was thinking of him coming home. At night she dreamed of him, and woke feeling his touch, the imprint of his body on hers. And increasingly she felt the movement of her baby, daily now, but of this she said nothing. This much at least was hers. She got up before daylight, roused by its movements, and leaving Betsy still asleep and snorting like a war horse, she went straight to her chapel. And she remained there all morning, fasting and praying until she knew, finally, that God had entered into her bargain. Edmund was safe.

He would return to her.

Which was why, when the messenger came, she could not hear him. There seemed to be a buzzing noise inside her skull.

He knelt before her, repeating the words she could not hear, then there was a commotion in the hall and Owen Tudor arrived. He entered, walking uncertainly, not like Owen Tudor at all. His shirt was stained and undone; she could see the grey hairs sprouting from the open neck. *He should fasten it properly*, she thought.

He came towards her with reddened eyes, and a collapsed face, and she could not speak. He had ridden ahead of Jasper, who was delayed, he told her, but he was following close behind.

Already there was the sound of sobbing in the room. Owen

Tudor made a tottering movement towards her, then he grasped her knees and buried his face in her lap and sobbed.

It was mid November, but suddenly it seemed too hot. Her clothes were suffocating her. She could hardly breathe.

She got up too suddenly and the room lurched around her. She could see Betsy moving towards her, her stricken face. But she didn't want Betsy. Or her father-in-law. She pushed Betsy away from her violently and hurried out of the room.

Faster and faster she went, despite the shortness of breath, the heaviness of her stomach, along one passageway after another, not knowing where she was going. She struck the walls as she passed them, and felt no pain in her hands. Then up a narrow stair, until finally she was alone on the roof, looking over a parapet in the direction in which Edmund had gone.

The sky was a billowing grey, and all the earth was in motion, the trees and the grass in a great wave-like motion, like the sea.

She could not see Edmund.

If she leaned forward and fell into the wind the currents of air would take her to him.

She would be able to breathe.

She could hear someone calling her name, but she wouldn't look round. She leaned forward, over the parapet, and felt her lungs expanding gently in the moving air.

Then her nurse was there, panting from her exertions, her face pink and terrified. She came to Margaret in a stumbling run, and folded her in her arms.

That was no good, she was obstructed, she couldn't breathe. She struggled a little, but her nurse held on.

'Oh, my lady, my lady,' she moaned into her hair.

Then she heard another noise, a different moaning, a deep, bellowing moan that sounded like a lost calf. She felt herself sagging in her nurse's arms.

Other people followed, bearing her away, and she had no resistance to them. She allowed herself to be led away from the roof.

Somehow she was back in her room and many hands were

helping, to lay her on the bed, to unfasten her clothing, to bring her cinnamon tea. Her nurse was chafing her hands and talking all the time: she had to be strong, because of the baby – Edmund's baby – she was carrying his son – the only heir to the house of Tudor – that was what was important now – Edmund would be looking after her, day and night, until the baby was born – and for the rest of its life . . .

None of her words made sense. Margaret turned away from them, into the pillow.

Usually with her eyes closed she could feel him around her, enfolding her, always as though he were about to laugh. But this time when she shut her eyes, her mind lurched dizzyingly over a void; she had to cling to the bed to prevent herself from falling. She was trembling, she realized, from the sheer strain of trying not to fall in. She hung over it, suspended, but with the weight of the thing she could not bear to know pressing her down.

Edmund was dead of the plague.

She was carrying his child.

Brother of King Henry, nephew of the dauphin, son of Owen – [Wales without Edmund] is a land without water, a house without feasting, a church without a priest, a castle without soldiers, a hearth without smoke.

Lewis Glyn Cothi

Each night after hearing of his death she dreamed of him, and when she woke, feeling his touch, she believed for one precious moment that he was there. Then came the more terrible awakening, the crushing realization, so that soon she came to dread going to sleep.

'You must eat,' her nurse said, over and over. 'Do you think your husband would want his son to starve?'

She allowed herself to be spoon-fed a little milk and honey mixed with oatmeal, held it in her mouth and deposited it into her sleeve or her bedclothes when no one was watching.

A doctor was sent for, and he said that bed rest was allowable; he recommended building up the fire to sweat out the evil humours of grief. He sat on her bed and explained to her that too much grieving would harm the baby; she must begin to look forward to the birth.

Margaret looked at him and saw death hovering behind his eyes.

Jasper came and she turned away from him. *You do not belong here*, she thought, meaning, *with the living.* Why should he be alive, grey and pale as he was, when her Edmund, laughing and golden, lay rotting in some grave?

Everything had changed, but he had not changed. A little more stern and sallow, maybe, his dark hair flecked with grey and the lines running down from his mouth cut deeper so that he looked far older than his years. But he had always been old.

It should have been you, she thought.

He sat on the edge of her bed, then unexpectedly he reached out and touched the mound of her belly, through the bedclothes.

'Is the baby quick?' he said.

She flinched away from him and pulled her knees up as far as they would go beneath her swollen stomach. He looked at her for a moment, then left the room. She could hear him talking with her nurse outside. It seemed that they were always talking together these days, but she did not care and did not try to hear. All she could really hear was the silence and emptiness in her skull.

But that night she dreamed that the child in her belly was covered in plague spots, and woke screaming. And her nurse crushed her to her breast, and then she cried loudly, in a high-pitched tone, and her nurse rocked her saying 'shusha, shusha', but she could not stop crying.

'My baby, my baby,' she cried.

Her nurse climbed into the bed with her and stroked her hair and asked her, what about her baby? And Margaret could hardly speak, hardly bring herself to say it, but in the end, moaning and babbling, she spilled it out: that her baby had the plague.

In vain did her nurse point out that no baby had ever been *born* with plague. Margaret cried hard and would not be comforted, convinced that infected humours had passed from Edmund's blood to her child's.

Betsy stopped trying to reason with her and only clasped her tightly, rocking her.

'Oh, my baby, my flower-pod, my little chick,' she murmured, and Margaret had to listen, for she did not raise her voice, but murmured on, and gradually she realized that she was telling her a story, the story of Nesta. That one day she would be like Nesta, and have a long neck like a swan and a mass of hair down to her knees. None of the bards would sing of Nesta any more; *she* would be the Helen of Wales.

Her nurse talked on, combing her fingers through the snags in Margaret's raggedy brown hair, and Margaret listened as she had listened many times before, though now there was no Edmund, of course, and no reason to be beautiful any more.

They said that she had given up the will to live, but that was not quite true. She was terrified of death; it was vividly real to her, a huge darkness in the depths of her mind. If she truly loved Edmund she would want to be with him, but she didn't want to, the blank darkness was terrifying to her. Everyone told her that he still existed, he was looking over her from heaven, with God, but she was shocked at the thoughts that spoke so clearly in her head, without permission: *he does not exist, he is nowhere.*

It was as though God had died in her heart, and death squatted there instead.

She had known death before, of course: her father (when she was an infant); the Duke of Suffolk, her guardian (though she had not known him well); her cousin, the Duke of Somerset, though he was little more than a stranger. All these deaths were distant from her, though she had often imagined them. Lying awake at night, staring into the darkness, she had imagined what it would be like to lie in a tomb.

This death was different. She could smell it in her nostrils and feel its horny wings unfolding in her soul. She had said goodbye to her childhood as surely as if a line had been ruled through it. Losing her virginity, becoming pregnant, had had no such effect.

Only now did she know in the most intimate way that she could die.

Jasper came to see her again. He was trying to raise an army, he told her. The king and queen had sent out many summonses to Herbert, who had not responded. And if Herbert summoned his allies there could be war.

She responded dully to this. There was always war. It was as though they had all fallen into some dark, terrible dream of war.

But the next thing he said woke her up immediately.

'That is why I have decided,' he said, 'that you should go at once to Pembroke Castle.'

'No!' she said quickly.

'You will be safe there,' he said, moving his hands awkwardly in the way he did when he was distressed. 'Herbert's allies will attack soon. They may already know about Edmund's heir. It would be a great advantage to have you hostage.'

He had frightened her. William Herbert reared in her imagination as a monstrous figure, almost supernatural, *a cruel man prepared for any crime.* She was more terrified of him than of the plague. Yet she did not want to go.

'You must be safe – for the birth,' Jasper said. She would not look at him. She was amazed that he could not feel her hatred radiating towards him. Then suddenly she knew that he did feel it; she hated him and he knew it, but he did not know why. At least she had that.

'My child will be born here,' she said, 'in my home . . . My husband –' she could not say Edmund's name – 'he wouldn't want it.'

She waited for Jasper's wrath to break over her, but when he spoke his voice was soft.

'He would want me to look after you.'

She shook her head, mutinous, but he went on. 'And that is what I intend to do. Pembroke is better fortified against attack and against the plague. We have enough food for the whole winter if needs be. I have already made the necessary arrangements – we will set off tomorrow.'

Margaret could hear her heart hammering. It would be no use to fling herself at the feet of this man and beg, or to burst into stormy tears – nothing moved him. Yet it seemed to her vitally important that she win this point. For the first time she stared into his eyes, directing the full force of her hostility into his gaze.

'I am not going to Pembroke Castle,' she said.

Pembroke Castle rose like a cliff of grey stone out of the estuary. Margaret looked at it once and turned away. She had cried silently most of the way, and her nurse had tried to comfort her.

'You will be safe there, my poppet – we will all be safe – it is what Edmund would have wanted – it is the best place for the baby –'

Later she would wonder why her nurse had come out with all the same arguments as Jasper, and why she had seemed unsurprised by the move in the first place. But for now all she could do was to permit her face to be crushed into Betsy's shoulder and to be rocked like a little child.

As the carriage juddered to a halt she dried her eyes but wouldn't look at the fortress as the great gates opened, because it still seemed like a prison to her.

Jasper himself greeted them and took them into his living quarters beside the gatehouse. She did not reply to his greeting.

Inside it was unexpectedly bright; there were torches burning and tapestries on the wall, an Arabic carpet across the table. The portrait of Edmund and Jasper had been moved to the dining hall. She could not look at it – it wrung her heart with a piercing sorrow.

And she could eat very little of the food. She crumbled some bread in her hands and chewed a little but could not swallow. Her nurse remonstrated, but Jasper shook his head, indicating that she should be left alone. He talked of the changes he was making: a new window was being put in, a section of the outer wall was being repaired and the roof of the great tower too. So she and Betsy were being lodged in a tower to the other side of the gatehouse – he had thought they would not want to be disturbed by so much banging and hammering.

'Is that not thoughtful?' Betsy said as Margaret maintained her stony silence. If they were near the gatehouse they would be near Jasper; he would have access to them at all times.

'We will be able to dine together in the evenings,' he said.

Also, there was a fine view of the town – he thought it would be more interesting for her to see what was going on in the town than to overlook the estuary, with its flat grey expanse of water and sky.

'But it is well guarded,' he said. Guards patrolled the adjacent walls and there were lookouts on the roof of the tower itself.

'My lord has thought of everything,' Betsy said. Margaret did not say that she had no wish to watch all the comings and goings of the town while she herself was kept prisoner. She merely stared at her plate and toyed with her food as her nurse made her exclamations of gratitude. She had discovered that there was a power in silence, that she could free herself entirely from the impulse to speak when spoken to, and Jasper was mystified by this: he did not know what to do.

The tower had simple furniture and impressive views. There was a serving maid called Ceri, and an older lady called Joan who would help with the baby when the time came. She was calm and capable, with large hands and reddish cheeks. There was a short passage from the bedroom to a tiny chapel, which was for Margaret's own use; she was free to use it whenever she liked, and here at least she could be alone.

As soon as she could she sent Joan away, and the other servants, and retired as before to her bed. *We will not stay here*, she whispered to her baby when they were alone, but she knew that there was no choice. So she stayed in her bed and ignored Jasper when he came.

'He is grieving too, you know,' Betsy said, but Margaret did not care. Only here, in her bed, could she retain the sensation of Edmund, the scent of him which remained behind the bridge of her nose. She could sense him in the darkness behind her eyes, and still feel his touch as she awoke.

The festive season approached, but there would be no festivities, no mummers or bards this year; the castle was in mourning. Jasper went away again and Betsy became increasingly anxious for

Margaret. She was so thin her belly looked like a seed that was about to burst. Her navel had popped out and blue veins ran like a map over the mound. When the baby moved it was possible to see which part of him pressed against the skin: his head, his foot – even, her nurse said, his nose.

'I'll send for your mother,' Betsy warned, and Margaret tried to force down a further mouthful of meat. She did not want her mother to come. But the food choked her on the way down, then burned her in her gut as though there were no room for anything inside her but the baby.

'You'll need your strength, for when the baby comes,' Betsy told her at least once every day.

Both Joan and Betsy insisted on feeling her stomach each morning to check that the baby was quick. She lay beneath their fingers, beneath this alien, quivering mound. Because she would not speak, they spoke to one another, over her head. Betsy rubbed goose fat into her stomach, and the smell was foul.

When the baby prevented her from sleeping, she made the short walk from her room to the little chapel, holding on to the wall. Ceri brought her a special stool to sit on at prayer; kneeling was bad for the baby, she said.

It was cold in the chapel, they all said, which was true, since there was no glass in the window. Joan suggested covering it with a tapestry.

'No,' Margaret said. She liked the breath of knife-cold air, the tang of the sea, even if she could not see it. She liked to see the gulls wheeling and calling. She liked the simplicity of the little chapel. It was a tiny room yet in it she had a sense of space and light that she did not have in any other part of the castle. She leaned forward on her stool and felt the damp air on her cheeks and listened to the roar and pound of waves and the seagulls' plaintive cries.

Her attendants didn't know that she could not pray.

Afterwards she would make her way back to her room, climb into her bed and lie watching the slit of grey sky that she could see from this angle, or sink back into the darkness of Edmund.

At Christmas, Owen Tudor arrived. He came straight to her room, sending Betsy and Joan and Ceri away.

She was shocked at the change in him. His hair and face were greyer, his eyes sunken.

He knelt by the bed, and took her hands and kissed them, then instead of releasing them he buried his face in them and groaned aloud. When he did look up, his eyes were wet and helpless as a babe's.

'Look at me,' he said, in his hoarse, musical voice. 'I keep asking myself why it is that I should still be alive. I'm past fifty. Most of the bones in my body have been broken at one time or another, and knit back together like a badly hewn frame. I have lost the sight of one eye and my liver is damaged beyond repair. Yet he – who was beautiful and young –'

But he could not go on. He twisted the sheets of the bed in his fists, then suddenly clasped her to him, sheets and all, crushing her face to his chest and roaring in agony.

He was as strong as a bear and she could not breathe. He rocked her and his own body was rocked in a passion of grief. He buried his face in her shoulder and sobbed aloud, and there was a note of incredulity in the sobbing.

She did not know what to do. She could feel the heat of his breath through her hair.

They stayed like that for a while, until his sobbing died away into silence.

And at length Owen Tudor shifted on his broken knees and said, 'Edmund loved you, you know.'

She recoiled a little, a pang of pure pain passing through her. But all she said was, 'He did not love me.'

It was the first time she had allowed herself even to think it, let alone say it out loud. But she found she could say it, and feel nothing; she was cold and still. He had never loved her, and now he never could.

Owen Tudor shook his head and crushed her fingers.

'You think there is only one kind of love?' he said, lifting his head and looking at her. 'He was always talking about you, how fine and dignified you were, how lucky he was. He was so proud of your learning – Edmund was never one for books himself. "Our children will be scholars," he said.'

There it was: the raw, bloody pain. Her throat tightened and tears spilled down her cheeks. Owen Tudor did not take his eyes from her, he kept on talking.

'He knew he had found the right wife,' he said, nodding at her. 'Despite the difference in age, despite everything. He knew you would have the rest of your lives, you see – he wanted children with you – he knew you would be the best mother in the world –'

He pressed her stomach through the sheets, to feel the baby moving. 'My grandson,' he said. Then he said, 'It is a huge burden you carry. You are so young for it, so small –'

She was shaken, speechless. No one else had acknowledged the burden of what she carried. He grasped her hands again and kissed the tips of her fingers.

'I will serve you, and your baby, for the rest of my days,' he said. And she understood then that the baby linked them both, that he (for it never entered her head that it would not be a son) was now all that mattered. That they both had something to live for.

Later, Owen Tudor claimed credit for the fact that she sat up in her bed and allowed herself to be washed and her hair dressed, and said that she would take some soup.

At the end of January her waters broke.

She was alone in the little chapel, leaning forward on her stool, her head bent, thinking of Edmund as usual until her mind was overtaken by blankness. Then there was a gushing flow between her legs.

She felt a moment of horrified shame, thinking she must have pissed herself. Scarlet with horror, she struggled to rise, then felt a cramping pain in her side, travelling round the side of her belly, taking her breath away.

And suddenly, sharply, she knew what it was.

No one was with her; she had insisted on being alone in her chapel. She got up awkwardly, ungainly, and the movement made her dizzy. She felt her way down the stairs and along the little corridor that led back to her room, but no one was there either; they must all have been preparing or serving food. And suddenly she was stopped by another cramping pain.

The bed. She knew she had to get to the bed, but she didn't want to lie in it in her wet clothes. Ever since she'd been small she'd had a horror of making a mess. She pulled and tugged at her soaking gown, but it wouldn't come off. She couldn't get it over the girdle she was wearing, a birthing girdle which had been sent for specially. She had been told it had belonged to the Virgin.

When her nurse returned finally she found Margaret on her bed with her knees drawn up and her wet skirts bunched up around her hips, in her eyes an animal fear. And Betsy had run to her and held her hot face in her hands that smelled of eggs and honey.

'Everything will be all right, my lovely, my precious sweet,' she said, and those words were the last coherent memory Margaret had.

Of the subsequent rending and tearing and splitting of her small frame, she remembered little.

She had promised herself and her saints – St Margaret, St Petronilla – that she would not scream while her son was born. St Cecilia had not screamed when they had attempted to smother her with steam; she had sung in her heart to the Lord. St Hadrian of Nicodemia had not screamed when they had struck off each of his limbs on an anvil, and she would not scream now. But she made low, guttural grunting noises that lengthened slowly to the baying of a farmyard animal, as though the pain were turning her inside out. She couldn't prevent them any more than she could prevent her nurse pressing a sponge to her lips, which she said was full of the Virgin's breast milk, or the midwife pressing down on her stomach until the tendons of her hips were stretched and tearing. Prayers were written on scraps of parchment and pushed into her mouth; her body was no more her own.

She was dimly aware of daylight fading, then coming, then fading again.

Then at last came a moment when it all seemed suddenly to stop. The scene around her was snuffed out like a candle. And there was no light, no comforting presence, no sign or vision. It was as though her senses were opening on to silence and darkness.

That was the moment, she later discovered, when they all thought she had died. ('You went all waxy and pale, my cherub, all those terrible noises died away.')

At some point, as from a great distance, she was aware that a crucifix was before her eyes, and either before this or after, Jasper himself was there, gripping the doctor's shoulder (somehow now both a priest and a doctor were there) and she distinctly heard him order the doctor to cut the baby out if necessary.

But even as the doctor lifted the knife, her stomach muscles heaved and shifted of their own accord, and she was forced back into herself, away from the infinite peace, back into the narrow contortions of her body, that of itself, it seemed, was forcing the baby out.

Blurred light – an oblong, hazy, shifting, fading into darkness, then returning.

Window.

Daylight.

But she did not want to get up, or move.

It was very cold.

She closed her eyes.

The blurred light shifted and faded into a shadowy darkness, in which there were voices and movements.

She tried to sit up, pushing feebly at the covers, trying to make her legs work. But they were like wool and she soon sank back again.

Somewhere she could hear a baby crying.

*

There was the sound of sobbing around her bed, and the stench of blood. And a new scent came to her that was sweetish, and also sour. She felt the weight of something on her pillow, and opened her eyes slowly on to her baby's face.

It was yellowish, crumpled, and blotched with red.

'He is a fine, healthy boy,' Betsy said, her voice catching and breaking, 'and very like to live,' and Margaret wondered why her nurse was crying, but not for long, because her mind folded once more into darkness.

The next time, keeping her eyes on the light, and the shape of the light, she pushed the sheets back and pulled her legs from under them.

The soles of her feet shrank from the freezing floor, but she pressed down on them, rising slowly, bent almost double, clinging to the wall for support.

The room swung dangerously around her. The muscles between her ribs, down her sternum, all the way to her thighs, felt intolerably bruised as though she had been beaten; the lower part of her stomach felt as if it had been ripped away. She kept her eyes focussed on the light as though it were the most important thing in the world, a luminous pale grey.

Then somehow she was there, at the window, smelling the scent of rain. She could see the roofs of Pembroke, curtains of rain falling over them and all the way out to sea. That was the noise she could hear, all that rain falling from the sky to the sea. She could imagine the moment when the individual drop became one with the vastness – she closed her eyes and imagined it, all the turmoil of the water contained as though by an invisible skin.

She was interrupted by the shriek of her nurse.

She was hustled back into bed, her legs folding feebly under her, her nurse scolding her all the time. A maid sponged her face, tugged her chemise from her and somehow got her into a new one; she looked with dull surprise at the gouts of blood on the old one. She seemed to have no resistance to any of this, her voice had no strength.

Betsy clasped her face in her hands and asked if there was anything she wanted, food or drink. She had to repeat the question twice.

Margaret stared up at her. Her lips moved but the words wouldn't come out. Betsy bent her damp, whiskery face close to Margaret's mouth and Margaret summoned her reserves of strength.

'My baby,' she said. 'I want my baby.'

Everyone vanished then, but Margaret closed her eyes, confident that they would return.

They brought him to her, swaddled in the arms of a youngish woman, with red, broken veins on her face.

'This is Jane, wife of Philip ap Hywel,' Betsy told her. 'She has been feeding him.'

But Margaret could only look at the small, bound bundle Betsy placed on the pillow beside her. His mouth puckered to a tiny 'o', and then it stretched again, opening as though he might cry, but he didn't cry, he only yawned, and she could see the little ridges of his gums, that were like the wrinkles on the sea.

And, just for a moment, his eyelids fluttered and opened, and she saw those eyes in that wrinkled face, a deep underwater blue. They were so dark and filmy, as though not yet fully part of the world. She had a sensation of fall. Ill and exhausted as she was, she registered suddenly the journey he had made, all the way from non-existence into being.

She made an involuntary sound, and her nurse hurried to take him from her.

She was being supported, propped up from behind, so that her baby could be laid in her lap. His eyes were tightly shut. He did not look like Edmund, or like anyone other than himself.

'He is the prettiest babe that ever lived,' her nurse said.

She freed his hands so that Margaret could look at them; long yellowish fingers opening and closing slowly.

'He is a fine, healthy boy,' his nurse said. The baby opened his mouth to cry. 'It's time for his feed,' she said, and lifted him once more.

Margaret didn't protest at the sudden emptiness of her lap, but sank back, watching him all the time. His face puckered again and he made a sharp, mewling sound, and the wet nurse opened her gown. Her breast was heavy and blue-veined, almost the same size as the baby. Involuntarily, Margaret's fingers moved towards her own breast, which was still flat, though very sore. She watched with a kind of hunger as her baby's mouth found the nipple, which seemed enormous, then, puckered face to puckered nipple, he began to suck.

Betsy's arms were round her; she could feel herself slipping down. But she managed to frame a question: 'What day is it?'

'It is the last day of January,' her nurse replied. 'He is three days old.'

Three days had gone from her. She had lost three days.

She lay, semi-conscious, in the small chamber, while Jasper and the doctor discussed her, assuming she could not hear, their voices above her bed.

'She has lost a great deal of blood,' the doctor said.

'Yet she is young,' said Jasper, 'she may survive.'

'Oh, certainly,' the doctor hastened to agree. 'But there is something else.'

He explained that her internal organs had been greatly damaged by the birth, specifically by the hooks he had been obliged to use to haul the baby out. He thought that more than the afterbirth had come away.

'It might mean,' he said, ever more hesitantly, 'that she will have great trouble conceiving again. It is not likely, in fact.'

She could imagine, rather than see, Jasper's face as he took this in.

'Still, she is young,' he repeated. 'It is possible that she will recover.'

The doctor made a doubtful noise. 'It would take a miracle,' he said. 'The womb itself –'

'Are you saying that a miracle cannot happen?' Jasper interrupted him.

'Of course not,' the doctor said at once.

'Well then,' said Jasper. 'If it takes a miracle, then we must hope for one.'

She did not fully understand the significance of this conversation. Did they think she *wanted* to go through that again? Besides, Edmund, her Edmund, was dead.

Only later did she understand that her fertility, her youth, was Jasper's bargaining point. She was too tired to understand anything then.

'My Lord Jasper has named him Owen, after his father,' Betsy's voice said.

'No,' said Margaret distinctly. Until this moment she had thought she would name him Edmund. She looked at the fine bones and veins of his skull, the already darkening hair. He was not like his father at all.

There was no question of calling him Jasper.

The king was his next relative, and the king would be his patron. Since Edmund's death she'd hoped and prayed that the king would deliver them from this war-torn country. There was no reason for them to stay, with Edmund gone. It was dangerous, in fact, because he could no longer protect them from their enemies. If she named her baby after the king the king would surely send for them, and they could leave this country which had become her prison, and her husband's tomb.

'Henry,' she said, adding defensively, 'Edmund wanted to name him for the king,' and her nurse did not argue with her, though it was the first she had heard of it.

'So should I tell my Lord Jasper –' she said, and Margaret looked at her fully.

'Tell him he is called Henry,' she said. 'After the king.'

So he was christened Henry, quickly, on Candlemas Day, in case he should not survive.

Yet he did survive, and thrived.

She grew stronger and was allowed to sit up with him. As soon as she could she took him to the window, because she wanted him to have a view. She sat by the window with him as if offering him to the sky and sea.

Jasper came to see her and did not interrupt but watched her with his speculative gaze. A variable sky cast patches of light and shade over the town. Her baby's face crumpled and uncrumpled; his tiny fists, unbound, flailed jerkily.

Then Jasper came towards them and touched the baby's hand, letting the tiny fingers curl round his own. His mournful features set into something resembling a smile.

'So young, and heir to so much,' he murmured.

It was true. In his ancestry were the kings of England and France. Owen Tudor's family were descended from the royal house of Wales. Still, she did not like to be reminded of this. It was as though some burden had already fallen on his fragile shoulders. Yet she did not mind Jasper so much now that the baby was a common source of interest. It was a miracle that this small, fierce life had come to her and stayed; everything, even his father's death, paled into insignificance besides.

'I have a letter from the king,' Jasper told her, and she did not look at him, but her heart began to pound. At last he had sent for her; she would return to court with her baby. There was a short pause then Jasper began to read.

The king sent his heartfelt condolences to his beloved kinswoman in the hour of her grief. He felt the loss of his brother as a blow to his body and his soul. Such a loss was beyond measure of words, beyond all hope of redress. He could only pray for his enemies as Our Saviour Jesus Christ had prayed for His. He hoped that in the fullness of time they would all find forgiveness in their hearts and live in peace.

Now she did look at Jasper, as he finished reading.

'Is that all?' she said.

'He thanks you for naming Edmund's son after him,' said Jasper.

No hint of rage, or retribution, or even the hope of bringing Edmund's murderers to justice?

'Let me see the letter,' she said.

After a pause Jasper handed it to her.

She read it through twice, scanning the words as if she might have missed some hidden message that would tell her that the king was going to pursue his brother's killers, and take care of his widow. But there was nothing, and nothing about sending for her, to take her away from Wales and into his own protection.

She let the letter droop in her hand.

Jasper was looking at her ironically. 'We should prepare for a journey,' he said.

She didn't hear him at first, so he said it again.

'A journey?' she said. 'Where to?' thinking he meant to take her to the king.

'To Newport, in Gwent,' said Jasper, and she stared at him. 'The Duke of Buckingham has invited us to stay in his household.'

'Why?' she asked, then, realizing this was not very polite, she added, 'Perhaps later in the year. When the weather improves.'

'We have not been invited later in the year,' Jasper said. 'We have been invited this week.'

'This week?' She laughed a little. 'But the roads . . .'

The roads were still flooded; she had heard the servants talking about it.

'Difficult,' Jasper said, 'not impossible.'

'But – there might be snow. And the plague – the plague is still in the villages.'

'We can bypass the villages.'

'But where will we stay for the night? I will not put my baby at risk of plague.'

Jasper wasn't angry. He appeared to be considering what she said. He reached over and touched the silken curls in the soft folds of her baby's neck.

'It will not be for long,' he said. 'A month, maybe two. No more than that.'

She stood up then, unsteadily, clutching her baby. 'I am not going anywhere,' she said. 'He is too young to travel.' Unexpectedly, tears were threatening, and she was furious with herself.

Jasper nodded, without looking at her.

'Listen to me,' he said. 'The Duke of Buckingham is the most powerful magnate and the greatest landowner in all of Wales. He will offer protection to your son. How long do you think it will be before Lord Herbert turns his attention to Edmund's heir?'

Margaret said nothing, but her grip on her baby tightened. The name of William Herbert filled her with horror.

'He would not try to attack in winter,' Jasper went on, looking at her now. 'But the spring is coming.'

Margaret sat down again. Her knees felt weak and a sense of helplessness overtook her. The king had deserted them. He had left them to their enemies.

'Can the duke not – come here?' she said.

'He has invited us to stay with him there,' said Jasper. 'It is a most gracious invitation. Do you wish to offend him?'

She would not look at Jasper, but all her protests died away. As usual she felt outmanoeuvred, and as though there was something he wasn't telling her.

'I will make all the necessary arrangements,' Jasper said, and she looked at him with reddened eyes.

'I do not want to go,' she said.

It was a long journey, over rough terrain. She travelled in a carriage with her nurse, Betsy, and the wet nurse, Jane, who held her baby, swaddled, on her knee. The carriage shook and rattled so much she feared it would damage him, but in fact he seemed to like the motion and remained sleeping, except when he fed.

Jasper rode alongside the carriage, pointing out views or objects of interest from time to time, or feeding them information about the duke.

'He is the greatest landowner in England as well as Wales,' he said, and her nurse clucked and said, 'Fancy.'

'The manor at Greenfield is not his largest, but still it is impressive – more than a hundred rooms, I'm told.'

'A hundred!' her nurse said in amazement. 'Did you hear that, my lady? And not his biggest house, either.'

Margaret turned her face away. She wanted to tell her nurse to stop parroting what Jasper said, that maybe he would go away and leave them alone if she did. But she would not give him the satisfaction of acknowledging him and her silence had resulted in this pantomime.

The duke's eldest son had been dreadfully wounded at the Battle of St Albans, Jasper told them, and had been ill ever since. Her nurse said, 'Oh, what a pity,' but Margaret only thought of Edmund with a piercing pain.

His wife was Margaret's cousin, Jasper told them, daughter of the Duke of Somerset who had been killed in that same battle. Her son was also called Henry.

'Did you hear that?' said Betsy in amazement.

'I am not deaf,' Margaret said.

She would also be staying at the manor at Greenfield, so the two of them would have plenty to talk about, Jasper said, and then, to Margaret's vast relief, he spurred on his horse and rode ahead.

They had come to a particularly rough stretch, where a stream had burst its banks and flowed over the road. The horses slipped and stumbled, and everyone in the carriage was flung from side to side. All conversation stopped for a while as Jasper struggled with the horses and her nurse exclaimed that all the bones in her body would be quite broke. Slowly they forded the stream and the road levelled out again, and Jasper joined them once more. And he resumed talking just as though he had never left off.

'The duke has other children, of course – it is quite a large family,' he said, and Betsy commented that that must be a comfort.

'The second son is also called Henry.'

'I hear he is a very fine young man,' her nurse said.

Margaret stopped listening, for now they had turned a bend in the mountain road and the land fell away from them into clear blue air. Blue-green woodland clustered up the valley sides, curlews called and the clouds were tinged with fire.

It was a beautiful land, God's own country, as all the poets said, blown out on His breath and shaped by His fiery fingers. But it was an oppressive beauty – the towering mountains like a fortress, the sea an impassable barrier. And Edmund could no longer see it, all the beauty and magnificence; Edmund would see nothing any more.

'Whoever marries the younger son, of course,' Jasper was saying, 'will inherit many of the Stafford estates. Which are considerable.'

'How fortunate they would be!' said Betsy, and just for a moment a dark suspicion flickered in Margaret's mind, but she dismissed it as unfeasible, too horrible even for Jasper. Who was nothing if not loyal to his brother.

They had to stay overnight at an inn. It was an out-of-the-way place, built for travellers and near no villages, since Margaret was still haunted by fear of the plague. She was to share a room with her nurse, while Henry's nurse took him into an adjacent room, and Jasper took a room on the next floor. His men camped outside.

While they were settling in, Jasper knocked on their door. He had come to see how they were recovering from their journey, and to assure them that the next part would not be as rough. Then he sent Betsy away, to order wine and ale, and sat down in the chair, crossing his long legs, watching Margaret. She could feel his gaze upon her, though she did not look at him.

'The duke is most anxious to see you,' he said. He told her how important it was to be on good terms with him, how hard he had worked for it. It was their only chance of suppressing the rebels in Wales. As she listened to him a growing dread crept over her. Finally she turned to face him.

'Why am I here?' she said.

If Jasper was surprised, he did not show it.

'I have told you,' he said. 'We have been invited.'

'But why?' she persisted. 'Why have I been invited?'

Jasper stood up then and stared out of the window, and her stomach contracted.

'The duke – wants to be gracious to Edmund's widow,' he said. 'You are his kinswoman, after all.'

'Tell me,' she said.

Jasper turned slowly and looked at her. It was one of the occasions when she wished she was taller. She stood very straight and stared back at him.

'The duke thinks – we both think – that it would be best for you, and for your baby, if an alliance were made –'

'No,' she said.

'– and for the king,' Jasper continued as if she hadn't spoken. 'The king wishes it. To create a stronger link between the Duke of Buckingham and the crown.'

'No,' she said again. She could not believe that he was even considering it.

'I understand,' he said, looking at her, but she wouldn't have this.

'I am not a child,' she said. She could hardly get the words out, they were so important to her. 'I am – Edmund's widow.'

And once again she was almost crying. She hated herself; she hated him. Why did he always have this effect on her?

Jasper let out his breath. He turned back to the window, then shook his head, started to speak, then stopped. She carried on, her voice so choked with emotion she could hardly wring the words out.

'You treat me as a child – but I am not a child. I am Edmund's widow. And the mother of his son. It is just four months since he . . .'

Jasper nodded. Then he sat in the chair again, pressing the tips of his fingers together, watching her face.

'Edmund – is gone,' he said, then he carried on quickly before she could interrupt him. 'What is the most important thing now that he is not here?'

She knew the answer to that, of course, but she would not answer him. He leaned forward.

'What is the best way of securing the interests of your son?'

She shook her head and Jasper spoke again.

'What happens if I am not here to protect him? What happens if I die? You are surrounded by your enemies.'

Even her breath hurt, catching at her ribs.

'It is – too soon,' she said.

Jasper stood now, and started to pace.

'It is not too soon for your enemies to attack,' he said. 'Do you not know that the vultures are already gathering? Even now Lord Herbert is rallying his forces in the north. Your baby – Edmund's son – needs all the alliances we can make. And the Staffords are most powerful: if they stand behind him he has a chance – the best chance . . .'

She could hear him, but through a barrier of noise that was the blood rushing to her head. This was what they had planned together – Jasper and her nurse – in all those hidden conferences, behind her back.

'No,' she said faintly, but he didn't hear.

'Now that his heir is so ill the duke is anxious to secure the interests of his younger son. Nothing matters to him so much – he will act and act soon. That is why I went to stay with him after Christmas. Because if he does not look to you, my sister-in-law, he will look elsewhere. He wants his son married before the end of the year. And he is well aware of your value.'

He sat down again, facing her.

After Christmas? she thought. *So soon after Edmund's death? Before the birth of his son? Had it all been settled even then?*

When she didn't speak, Jasper went on, somewhat awkwardly. 'I wasn't going to tell you any of this. I was going to let you settle in there and enjoy their hospitality – which is famous, you know – and to meet the younger son, Henry, for yourself – to see for yourself what a pleasant fellow he is –'

'But you did not tell me.' Her voice sounded distant and strange.

'Of course there would be no question of marriage if you did not agree – no question at all. I am simply trying to secure the interests of your son.'

What about my interests? she could have said, but this was the man who would have had her cut open to save Edmund's child. And he was still speaking.

'You cannot remain a widow for long, you know – your estates are too vast for that. It is my duty as your brother to look after you and my nephew.'

She started to speak, to say that it was too soon; her husband had been dead for just four months, his child was one month old. She would have liked a year, one year at least – one year of mourning, to be with her son – was that too much to ask? And to have been consulted, of course, but then that would never have entered into it. Not with Jasper.

'You do not have to marry straight away,' he said. 'But we need to seal the alliance.'

Somewhere inside she felt a white-hot spoke of rage. Jasper was still talking, but she cut right through him.

'I won't do it.'

He stopped talking then. There was a complete and deadly silence. Then he said, 'You would rather be taken by your enemies, and forced into marriage with the Herberts or the Fitzwalters? Your husband's murderers?'

She blanched a little at this, but he went on.

'You do not seem to realize the danger you are in. You can stay with me, of course, but that is the first place they will attack.'

He paused, and into that pause she forced her words: 'I love Edmund.' Her voice was unnaturally tight. Jasper did not respond to it.

'You could return to your mother. But the king will expect your marriage to be arranged – and arranged by me.'

'I love him,' she said.

Jasper sighed. 'You will love again,' he said.

'No!' she said, still in that high, unnatural voice. 'I loved him – I still love him – I think about him all the time. Every morning I wake up and feel him next to me – the touch of his breath here – on my neck – I can still smell him . . .'

Jasper looked shaken by this outburst, but he recovered.

'You loved him as a child loves – yes – but that is soon forgotten. You will marry again and learn to love as a woman loves a man.'

'NO!' she shouted, at the same time furiously aware that she sounded like a child.

He started to tell her to behave herself, but he got no further because she took several steps towards him, towards the chair in which he sat.

'Did the Duke of Buckingham outbid William Herbert for your brother's son?' she whispered. 'Do you think my affections can be so easily bought?'

She had barely time to register the terrible shock on his face. In a lightning movement he grabbed her wrist and rose, jerking her arm upwards. The bones in her wrist grated against one another.

She would not cry, she would not cry out, even if he snapped her wrist.

'Do you think you are the only one who grieves for Edmund?' he said in tones so low she could hardly hear him. 'I miss him as I would miss my right arm, my lungs, my heart. His son is my son now, and my heir. Do not think that I will neglect any aspect of his future, or allow anyone, even his mother, to stand in his way.'

He released her then, and she stumbled back, almost falling. Her face was burning and she could hardly see. All her breath seemed to be caught up in her throat. She would not look at her wrist or rub it, she would not give him that satisfaction. She could feel the weight of his contempt bearing down on her, but she would not cry. Above all, she would not cry.

'Now,' he said, in the old, impersonal tone, 'I do not imagine that you would choose to turn back alone and walk all the way to Pembroke, so what I suggest is this. In the morning you will feel better and we will continue on our way. We will take advantage of the good duke's hospitality, for one week at least, and if you truly do not enjoy any aspect of your visit, we will leave. Otherwise we will extend our stay for as long as they extend their hospitality. Does that seem fair to you?'

What choice did she have? With Jasper, what choice did she ever have? She managed to nod.

'Good,' he said. 'Now I will leave you to your toilette.'

She sat down on the bed as he left, because her legs were trembling. He had brought her to this. Jasper and her nurse had colluded together to betray her. All her visions of herself, her life that was to be dedicated to chastity and prayer, were collapsing around her. She would be given to another man. He would touch her as Edmund had. She felt a kind of nausea at the thought – she might actually be sick.

'There you are, my sweeting,' Betsy said with a slightly forced heartiness as she entered the room. 'I've had such trouble getting a simple bowl of water and a jug of wine –' She paused, placing them on the chest beside the bed, then changed her tone. 'What is it, my little dove?' she said.

And the next moment she was enfolded in Betsy's arms.

Everything about her was so familiar – the smell of her, which was slightly stale and spicy, the whiskery face, the rolls and folds of the body she had turned to for comfort most of the days of her life, but now never would ever again. Betsy lowered her considerable weight on to the mattress, necessarily taking Margaret with her, and rocked her as she had done since her infancy. When Margaret neither resisted nor responded, she released her slightly and looked into her face with those luminous greenish eyes.

'What is it, cherub?' she said again, quietly, and the words and her face tugged at Margaret's heart as if trying to break it, though it was already broken.

But she only turned her face away.

'I am tired,' she said, her voice muffled by Betsy's sleeve. 'I must sleep.'

'Of course you must,' said Betsy heartily, already manoeuvring her into position, and tucking herself in beside her as she always did, her knees bent into the crook of Margaret's knees.

Margaret lay beside her, staring into the night, into the darkness that surrounded them both, feeling the intolerable weight of Betsy's body on her own.

If he had been anything like Edmund, in looks or manner, she could not have borne it, but he wasn't. He was older, with thinning hair. Also he was plumpish, with scars on his skin. And he didn't seem to know what to say. Margaret glanced up at Jasper, but he was staring straight ahead. The duchess was beaming vaguely at them both, but she and her servants had withdrawn a little way from them, and Jane and Betsy had taken her baby to his room.

A painful silence extended itself until the duchess called her away to introduce her to the rest of the household.

After the introductions, which went on for some time, the duchess said she wished to talk to Margaret, and as they left together she nodded at the young woman who was Margaret's cousin, and perhaps closest to her in age. Margaret's cousin followed them into a little room and the duchess ordered a tray of cakes. Then she sat down and Margaret's cousin sat down, and the duchess said, 'Well,' to no one in particular, and apparently did not require a reply.

The duchess wore a green and silver silk, and Margaret's cousin wore a gown of palest rose. Margaret sat with them, painfully conscious of her own, weathered state.

Like the duchess, Margaret's cousin wore her hair shaved back from her forehead, so that her face appeared egg-like and pale beneath her pointed wimple, and her eyebrows were shaved too as a sign of piety, though this was also high fashion. Her long sleeves covered her hands and her gown was slashed at the neck to reveal her kirtle and chemise. She was the grandest young lady that Margaret had ever seen, better dressed than the queen, it was said, and certainly better dressed than Margaret herself, but she did not think her pretty. Her face was too pointed and her eyes too close together for that.

The duchess was saying how pleasant it was to have company so early in the season, and Margaret murmured something in reply. Then the duchess said she had planned several feasts, to brighten up the dark days at the end of winter, and much dancing.

'There will be a special one to celebrate the betrothal,' she said, beaming, and Margaret did not say that there was no betrothal yet. She was thinking instead of a problem that had not previously occurred to her.

Since Edmund's death she had given no thought to clothes. The supply of money sent by the king for her wardrobe had long since run out, and no one had had time, since the birth of her baby, to order her anything new. She had only two gowns that fitted and neither one was suitable for a banquet.

Ordinarily she would have asked Betsy, who could have passed this on to one of the duchess's servants, but Betsy wasn't there.

They were waiting for her to speak. Finally she said that she had not brought many clothes with her – she had not been sure how long she would be staying.

The duchess said there was no question at all of them returning while the weather was so unpredictable.

'We will send for the rest of your wardrobe,' she said.

Margaret stared at the floor. Then she managed to explain that since her baby nothing had fitted her properly, and nothing new had been sent for yet.

'But of course!' cried the duchess, clasping her hand to her escaping hair. 'You poor child – it is all those men, is it not? You have been surrounded by men – you poor, poor child!'

Margaret's cousin was staring at her as though she were some curiosity from a travelling fair, then she said, 'You may have one of my old gowns if you like, I will have it made down for you.'

'But we will send for materials!' the duchess said, and they began to talk together as if Margaret wasn't there.

Margaret's face burned with humiliation. She couldn't bring herself to ask how long it might take for the new clothes to arrive, or how much they would cost. She wanted to go home.

'The first feast is tonight,' the duchess said. 'But I believe I have just the thing.'

They ate in the great hall, course after course of meat – hare, pheasant and boar – served on silver platters and swimming in sauce. There was a whole pig, stuffed with swallows, and a swan shaped into a dragon, coloured green and gold and breathing actual smoke. A deer was brought in, roasted on a spit, but Margaret sat stricken in a blue velvet gown, unable to eat. The duchess leaned forward and asked if the food was not to her liking, and she protested that it was. Then the duke said that she needed some meat on her bones, like her cousin, and he turned to the older girl and slid his moist fingers round her neck, and kissed her fully on the lips, while the duchess smiled brightly in a different direction, and Margaret glanced down quickly at her plate, on which there was a pigeon breast, sinewy and veined; her throat closed as she looked at it and she knew she could never eat. The duke, releasing her cousin, said that what she needed was some ox-blood with her breakfast, and Margaret felt as though she might faint.

Then the duke, reddened by pork and wine, insisted on dancing with her, and after the first dance he bore down on her, leaning on her shoulders as though he would crush her, and leading her a little way away from the guests. Then he asked how she thought she would like her new husband, and without warning he wept and begged her to provide him with more grandchildren.

Margaret wondered what would happen if she pushed him away from her, hard.

To her relief, someone interrupted them. It was Henry Stafford.

'My Lady Margaret has said that she will show me her son,' he said.

The duke said he knew what they were up to, he had been just the same at their age, but she took Henry's arm gratefully and he led her from the room.

A sliver of moonlight shone on her baby, on the tiny fists curled either side of his head, his pale face even whiter around the lips. He was a still, small, concentrated world on his own. She had to touch him – his cheek and the reddish down on his head – then she leaned over the cradle and lifted him out.

He stirred and his face creased, and he gave a little sigh but did not cry – he hardly ever cried. She held him close to her heart and wondered if he could hear it beating, and thought that so recently he had heard it beating inside her.

Henry stood close beside her, frowning into her baby's face.

'I wonder what it is like to be born,' he said softly. 'To be suddenly in a strange world – cold and bright.'

She didn't answer, but adjusted her baby's blanket.

'It must be a fearful thing,' he said, 'and sad also, to be suddenly separate.'

She glanced up at him quickly, at his frowning face, at his eyes that looked as though they were working out some inscrutable problem. She understood, suddenly, that she was not a child to this man she would marry, as she had been to Edmund, an insignificant child, to be humoured or tolerated. She had been through the mystery of birth and he regarded her with a kind of awe, as if she were older, and very wise.

She showed him how to hold her baby, supporting his head. They sat together on the wooden seat, wondering at his tiny fingers and the little pulse beneath his hair. Slowly the feeling of unreality she'd had since coming to this household began to ebb. The man who would be her new husband did not touch her, but she could feel the heat of him through her dress, a plump, comforting presence. She felt the tension in her shoulders and her lips and the back of her neck begin to ease. She had not known there had been such tightness there.

The following week the materials arrived: pearly silks, spun lace, finest cotton for her chemise, a green silk for dancing in, a new woollen robe for travel. Margaret watched them being cut and shaped, almost as her new life was being cut and shaped before her, and the duchess and her cousin personally supervised her transformation. Her hairline and eyebrows were shaved so that her forehead stood out in a huge dome, then her hair was braided and pulled tightly back from her face, pulling the flesh of her forehead back even further so that she looked permanently, fashionably, surprised. Finally she was given a tall headdress, to add to her height, and then she stood in front of a bronze mirror, staring at someone she did not know.

She was not, nor ever would be, pretty. But that did not matter here, apparently. It did not matter to the duchess, or to her son – the man she had agreed to marry. She looked again at her new face. She would get used to it, as she would get used to her new life. It was like a mask, for a part she had to play.

Their stay was extended for several weeks. She learned to avoid the duke, who seemed permanently eager to bear down on her, but fortunately he was often out hunting or showing off his grandson. Her cousin's son was a handsome little boy with brown-gold curls who was petted and made much of by the entire household. The duke had given him a tiny sword and loved to see him brandish it and swagger about, but Margaret considered him to be a bad-mannered and disagreeable infant, and she took care to keep her own son away from him.

She did not share a room with Betsy any more; she had requested a room of her own as soon as she had agreed to the betrothal. At mealtimes Betsy sat at the other end of the great table with the other servants, trying and failing to catch Margaret's eye.

In April they travelled with the duke and duchess and a small household to the duke's favourite residence of Maxstoke in Warwickshire. There, the Bishop of Coventry and Lichfield granted a dispensation for the marriage between the Lady Margaret, Countess of Richmond, and Henry Stafford, second son of the Duke of Buckingham. This was important because Margaret's grandfather and Henry's grandmother were brother and sister.

And after that she returned with Jasper to Pembroke, for it had been agreed that they would not marry immediately; she would have her year of mourning.

By the end of that year the duke's eldest son had died, and the whole household was in mourning. Against all expectations, William Herbert had been pardoned by the king. And Jasper had made peace with Gruffydd ap Nicholas, who had sworn loyalty to the crown. She heard also that John de la Pole had married one of the daughters of the Duke of York, and wondered what that meant for Lady Alice. But she had little time to wonder; she was preoccupied with other news.

She had inherited Bourne Castle from her grandmother Margaret Holland. The property was technically part of her mother's estate in Lincolnshire, and close to her castle of Maxey. Margaret had not seen her mother for several years, but now it seemed she was anxious to accommodate the new couple and set them up in a household of their own, as her wedding present to them both.

Margaret did not look at Jasper when he delivered this news, she didn't want to. When she looked at him she could only remember the pressure of his fingers on her wrist.

So she looked instead out of the window, where the sky was a blank grey yet the fields were filled with a damp yellow light. Her heart began beating faster, as though it might burst out of the cage of her chest.

'It is not a large establishment,' Jasper said, 'there are only thirty servants. You can take your own attendants also, of course.' He paused. 'I hope you will still come and stay with me at Pembroke,' he said, and Margaret knew he was thinking about his nephew. But she would be mistress, finally, of her own household. She would not have to live with Jasper. And she would leave Wales. She never wanted to come back.

'Perhaps you will visit us,' she said to Jasper, and felt rather than saw the expression of anxiety deepen in his eyes. But this was the first time she had real reason to be grateful to her mother, and to God, who had finally answered her prayers.

In the next few days she made up her mind.

She sent for Betsy and received her in her room, waiting with a peculiar tension between her shoulders, a feeling that was almost, though not quite, fear.

Betsy hurried in and would have embraced Margaret immediately had she not stood up, moving swiftly away from her nurse.

'I am to have my own household,' she said.

'I know it!' said Betsy. 'Oh, my precious, it's a grand day for us.' And she made a move again as though she would kiss her, and Margaret drew back.

Betsy hardly paused.

'You will soon be as fine as your cousin – finer even – who knows when she will marry again – and you, my sweet pea, will have more heirs –'

'That is not what the doctor said,' Margaret interrupted, and her nurse faltered at the look on her face. She had not known that Margaret had heard what the doctor had said. Yet Betsy knew – Margaret could tell from her nurse's reaction that she knew. Jasper had told her, no doubt.

But Betsy rallied. She told Margaret that she should pay no heed to what the doctor had said, none at all – did she not know someone herself who had lost her entire womb due to a curse, but then she had prayed at the tomb of St Margaret and the next year she had given birth to triplets.

Margaret nodded. 'I will not be giving birth to triplets,' she said. 'We will have to hope that my husband does not mind too much having no heirs of his own.' Her smile was bright and cold. Her nurse looked as though she would speak, then suddenly sat down on the bed.

'Oh, my lady,' she said, pressing one hand to her breast, 'you can't blame poor Betsy for wanting the best for her little Peg.'

There were tears in her eyes. Margaret turned away from her, but her heart was beating faster. 'You did not consult me,' she said. 'You went behind my back . . .'

'Oh, now what would you have said if I had consulted you?' cried Betsy. 'You were all for going into a convent. But Lord Jasper – he had other plans.'

'And you helped him.'

Betsy wrung her hands. 'What was I supposed to do? Neither of us knew what to do for the best, you being so ill, and surrounded by your enemies; your husband dead, your babe so new and feeble – he had to find a new husband for you. Either that or marry you himself.'

Margaret looked at her in horror.

'Or let your enemies get their hands on you. The Duke of York – he could have had you for one of his own sons, or you could have been given straight to Lord Herbert – and then what? Would you have liked that any better?'

Margaret turned away again. All her life she had been persuaded by Betsy's arguments.

'So, you see, he had to act, lambkin, in your own best interests – and you were so sad and ill – he had to ask your old Betsy.'

Margaret shook her head. *I will not listen*, she told herself. And yet she did.

'And it has all turned out for the best,' Betsy said pleadingly, 'hasn't it, my chicken? You will have a new husband who loves you and loves your son, and we will all move together to a fine new house –'

'Not all of us,' Margaret said distantly.

'Yes, all of us together. And I will help to look after your babe just as I looked after you when you were a tiny scrap.'

'He has his nurse,' Margaret said. 'And I do not need one any more.'

'Oh,' Betsy said, 'you will always need your Betsy.'

Margaret looked at her fully. 'I am about to be married for the third time,' she said. 'I do not need a nurse.'

She could see then, and always, the look on Betsy's face.

'You will receive a generous pension,' she said, and her voice, even to her own ears, sounded uneven. 'I am sure that my Lord Jasper will take you wherever you wish to go.'

'But I don't wish to go anywhere,' Betsy said, 'except with you.'

'You had better make the necessary arrangements.'

'But, poppet,' Betsy said, getting up, 'you mustn't send me away. What have I done other than take care of you? What have I done that was so wrong?'

Margaret moved her head impatiently, but her nurse appeared to misunderstand her and stepped forward in hope.

'You can't do without old Betsy,' she said. 'And I can't do without you. All I want is to live with you and look after your baby, and love you both with all my heart!'

Margaret let out a long breath. 'I have already told my Lord Jasper that you will be leaving my service. He will help to place you elsewhere if you wish. But if you want to retire he will help you to find a cottage.' Her voice rose as her nurse made another movement towards her. 'Our time together is done.'

And at last she saw that Betsy understood.

She expected noisy tears, but Betsy only looked at her with stricken eyes, then dropped a curtsy, but stumbled in the execution of it and almost fell. And Margaret, from long habit, held out her hand, and her nurse steadied herself and rose. She looked at Margaret's hand in hers, then at her face, and said, 'Oh, my lady – I hope you find others to love you as I have done – all your life –' but she couldn't go on. She left the room, weeping and bowed over like an old, old woman, and Margaret sank down on to the bed.

Treacherously, her body remembered the embrace of her nurse, the warm comfort of it, the stale and spicy smell.

Since infancy the world had come to her through Betsy's eyes, magical and fearful, but now she was no longer a child. She had a child of her own, and would have her own household; she needed to see the world through her own eyes.

Even then she knew it was not likely that others would love her as Betsy had.

Two days later she set out for Maxstoke, leaving Betsy to make her own arrangements. She did not say goodbye to her nor look back, afraid of seeing another face at the window, watching her as she left.

The night before her wedding she could not stop crying over Edmund, great sobs that threatened to tear her apart. It was incredible to her that he should be dead, that he who had been so vivid, so alive, could be dead and gone. She sat up in bed finally, pressing the heels of her hands to her eyes. When she took them away she would see him. He would be looking at her from the shadows of the room with that half-smile on his face; as though it had been just another of his protracted absences or an elaborate joke.

What, marrying so soon? he would say.

The sense of unreality deepened as she walked into the church that morning wearing his presence around her like a veil or a shroud. She stood next to her new husband hardly seeing him. The words she had to say echoed strangely in her mind. This was, after all, the third time she had made her vows. And she was still only fourteen.

She reminded herself that he was a kind man, her new husband. He would not treat her as a child. He would not touch her if she didn't want to be touched. And she was to have her own household, where she and her husband and her son would live.

But later, at Bourne Castle, she learned, to her great grief and distress, that Jasper had been awarded custody of her son.

PART IV: 1456–62

33

The Hanged Man

Now the government of the realm stood most by the queen and her council.

Brut Chronicle

[In 1456] John Helton, an apprentice at court and formerly of Gray's Inn, was drawn, hanged and quartered for producing bills asserting that Prince Edward was not the queen's son; however, before his death, he retracted all his statements.

John Benet's Chronicle

It was at the queen's insistence that the extreme penalty was applied – 'It is treason, is it not?' – and at her insistence the little prince was made to watch, despite the protests of his nurse.

'He is so young.'

'He is young,' said the queen.

'Your majesty –'

'There are those in this country who do not think he should be heir to the throne, that he is not the king's son. Now they are saying he is not my son either, but a changeling. He will need to know how to deal with such men.'

And so the little prince sat at her side while the apprentice John Helton was drawn on a hurdle towards them, then made to stand on a cart.

The mood of the crowd was by no means certain. It strained and roared like a great beast, some calling out curses, others singing 'Deo Gracias', as the cries of this man became less and less human.

Partway through she felt a certain light-headedness, as though the top of her head had lifted and she was spiralling up, outwards and upwards, towards the grey-white sky. There was a bitter fluid in her throat.

The little prince seemed to be straining forward, though in reality he had not moved. They both remained very still before the eyes of the crowd, as the man was cut down by the executioner, who made several incisions in the spine, then severed the legs at the hips. Finally he held the head aloft, and men came with buckets to wash away the blood.

At last there was nothing left of John Helton but a putrid smell that clung in the air.

Only then did the queen permit herself to hold a scented cloth to her face.

Afterwards the little prince became very excited. His face was flushed and he ran about his rooms, jabbing his tiny sword first at one person then another.

'*You* shall die – and *you* – and *you*!'

Until his nurse took it from his hand and picked him up to restrain him.

'I shall put him to bed,' she said.

She did not look at the queen, but there was reproof in every lineament. And the queen sat back, very pale.

'Yes,' she said. 'He should rest.'

The queen with such as were of her affinity [now] ruled the realm as she liked gathering riches innumerable. The officers of the realm . . . peeled the poor people and disinherited many heirs and did many wrongs . . . [and] the queen was defamed and slandered that he that was called prince was not the king's son but a bastard born of adultery, wherefore she, dreading that he should not succeed his father in the crown of England, allied unto her the knights and squires of Cheshire . . . and made her son give a livery of swans to all the gentlemen of the county and to many other gentlemen of the land, trusting through her strength to make her son king . . . and making privy means to some of the lords of England to stir the king that he should resign the crown to her son, but she could not bring that purpose about.

An English Chronicle

The Hanged Man

Early in 1458 a great council met at Westminster, and despite the king's absence, the council strove for peace between the lords, for there was a great quarrel between the Duke of Somerset and the Earl of Northumberland on one side and the Earls of Warwick and Salisbury on the other. All these lords brought many men with them, the former lodged outside London and the latter inside.

In March the king and queen came to London [where, on the 25th day of March] the king, with great difficulty, engineered an agreement between the lords. Thereafter, as a sign of their amity, the king, queen and all the lords went in procession to St Paul's . . . [and this was called the Loveday].

John Benet's Chronicle

This same year the Earl of Warwick was at a council in Westminster and all the king's household gathered them together for to have slain the said earl . . .

Brut Chronicle

34

The Earl of Warwick

It delighted him, the sudden descent into confusion and chaos. While the faces of those around him congested with rage or fear, his mind became as cold and clear as ice. He stripped off his cloak as one man seized it, struck another in the leg as he leaped upon a bench and pulled a tapestry down on a third. His men fought to clear a path for him to the door; he backed towards it, calculating that he would be able to slam it in the face of his opponent.

All the time, with one fragment of his mind, he was watching the queen, her avid face, the way she held herself as if it were agony for her not to join in.

No one was killed, and he regretted that. He would have liked to have cut some man's throat in the council chamber and left him there – a blood offering to the queen. Instead he ran with his men down the steps to the river, where a barge awaited them.

They stood together on the barge, panting, laughing and congratulating one another, as a sharp hail of arrows followed them into the water, and that fragment of his mind that always operated separately went over his actions to see whether there was anything more he could have done. At the same time he noticed that one of his men was bleeding.

'Are you all right?' he asked, and the man replied that he was quite well – it was nothing more than a scratch – but the earl noticed that he seemed shaken. 'You should have it seen to,' he said, already considering whether or not to replace him. There was no substitute for the ability to respond in the moment to the unexpected challenge.

He himself was in a fine mood. He felt vividly and keenly alive, as he always felt after fighting, especially if he had killed. It was as if with each life he took he became more alive. In the middle of a fight he had, on occasion, lifted a man's visor to see the moment when his eyes became suddenly vacant and still. Because it was this that most convinced him of the presence of God.

Now he issued instructions to the boatman, having changed his mind about their destination. They would go where it would most annoy the queen.

It had become a kind of game between the earl and the queen. She dismissed him from his post in Calais; he ignored her, building relations instead with Duke Philip of Burgundy. She cut off the supply of money to Calais; he took to piracy to pay his men. She introduced conscription in the French style to swell her army, sending out commissions of array to every town, village and hamlet; he sent out letters and bills to be pasted on the doors of every church and inn:

Woe to that region where the king is unwise or innocent.
Our king is stupid and out of his mind. He does not rule but is ruled.
The government is in the hands of the queen and her paramours.

When the French raided Sandwich he had spread the news that their attack was instigated by the queen, and led by her paramour, Pierre de Breze.

And, of course, he continually questioned the paternity of the prince: *She would have you fight for her bastard child, the false heir to the throne.*

Now, however, he had to concede that it was something more than a game. He remembered the queen's face as her men attacked him; he had no doubt that she had given the order that he should be killed. It was not safe for him to stay in the country. The queen had demanded that he give up Calais to Somerset's son and so he would return to Calais and continue his campaign there.

. . . and he went soon after to Calais, of which he had been made Captain . . . Soon afterwards the young Duke of Somerset, by canvassing those who hated the Earl of Warwick, became Captain of Calais, and a privy seal was directed to the earl to discharge him of the captainship: however, the earl, forasmuch as he had been made captain by authority of parliament, would not obey the privy seal but continued exercising the office for many years after . . .

An English Chronicle

After 24th June [1459] the king held a great council at Coventry, which was attended by the queen and the prince. However the Archbishop of Canterbury, the Duke of York, the Earls of Salisbury and Warwick . . . were absent. Because of this, on the advice of the queen, all the absent lords were indicted by the council at Coventry.

John Benet's Chronicle

When they heard this news, the Duke of York, the Earl of Warwick, and the Earl of Salisbury resolved to go to the king . . . *John Benet's Chronicle*

35

Cat and Mouse

'We must intercept them,' the queen said. 'We must prevent them from meeting.'

Her scouts and spies had determined that the Earl of Warwick had already returned to London from Calais, and had entered the city unopposed with a well-armed force. The Earl of Salisbury, his father, was still in the north, at Middleham, and the Duke of York was at Ludlow. But they had indicated that they would come together to the king. So at some point they would have to meet. The queen had consulted several maps.

It was anyone's guess where they might converge, as the Duke of Buckingham pointed out to her.

'It does not matter,' she said. 'We will be ready for them.'

So the king had been sent to Nottingham, while the queen and prince stayed at Chester, and Henry Beaufort, the new Duke of Somerset, patrolled the West Midlands.

The queen had ordered three thousand bows for the royal army, without issuing any money for them, and had commanded the sheriffs to demand that every village, township and hamlet should provide the king with able-bodied men at its own expense.

The Duke of Buckingham did not like this French custom of compulsory conscription. It led to the gathering of a mob, rather than a trained army. However, day after day the queen continued to raise support for the prince, riding through all the towns and villages of Cheshire. Everywhere the little prince was greeted with joy, though the Duke of Buckingham surmised that the joy would fade rapidly when bills were posted on every inn and church door, and bailiffs arrived to round up the reluctant men.

They would not be paid, of course, so they had been told they could plunder and loot.

The queen persisted in touring well into the evening, riding along all the roads, lanes and country tracks carrying the little prince with her on her horse. Only once did the boy complain.

'I'm tired, *maman, je suis fatigué.* And my legs hurt.'

'Sit up, *mon petit*, hold your head like so. If the head is held up the legs do not hurt. It is all in the position of the head.'

And she carried on, her own head held high, although the Duke of Buckingham noticed it trembling a little, like a wind-shaken flower.

When she heard that Warwick had managed somehow to evade the Duke of Somerset's men, she did not falter.

'We must change direction,' she said. 'We will occupy all the roads through Staffordshire. The Earl of Salisbury is most likely to come through Staffordshire.'

She issued further commissions to Lord Stanley and other local magnates to muster their armies and meet the king near Birmingham.

The Duke of Buckingham suggested that this cat-and-mouse game would wear them all out. The king and queen should come together, he said, and summon all the lords to them.

'They have been summoned before,' she said. 'Does the cat summon the mouse?'

The Duke of Buckingham permitted himself a small smile. The queen was not noted for her sense of humour.

'Perhaps now they will be prepared to negotiate,' he said. 'I do not think they want open war.'

'They will tire first,' said the queen.

The Duke of Buckingham was used to not being listened to. Nearly forty years of marriage to the Duchess Anne had taught him that on most occasions women would do what they wanted in the end. Even so, he gave it one more try.

'I hear his majesty the king is unwell,' he said. 'If we could regroup our forces at a central point – Chester, perhaps – it would give him a chance to recover and us a chance to gauge the size and strength of our recruits. And the rebel lords would also see them,' he added.

Now the queen did appear to be listening. She tilted her head towards him as though actually considering what he had said.

'I will go to Eccleshall Castle,' she said.

When the king joined them the duke could see how ill he was. He looked blighted, as though by an old wound, or by some fatal flaw inherent at his birth. He chewed slowly and could barely sit up.

The queen seemed unmoved by this.

'My lord, we must send out a great force,' she said. When the king said nothing, she knelt before him.

'You must send Lord Audley and Lord Dudley – with as many men as you can spare – to intercept the Earl of Salisbury.'

Slowly, infinitely slowly, the king lifted his head.

'I have received letters,' he said at last. 'The earls and the duke say they will come to me – to promise their allegiance.'

The queen looked up sharply.

'How many times, my lord? They promised their allegiance after Dartford, then St Albans and after the so-called *Loveday* at St Paul's. No,' she said, 'we are done with negotiations. Now is the time for a show of strength.'

The Duke of Buckingham could almost see the king thinking that with the queen it was always time for a show of strength. But he reached out his hand – it was frail and withered, like the hand of a very old man – and touched her cheek.

'Marguerite,' he said.

The queen managed not to shy away.

'We must *act*, my lord,' she said.

And the king could not withstand her, the duke could see that. The Lords Audley and Dudley were sent for and commanded to intercept the Earl of Salisbury and bring him to the queen, dead or alive.

The Battle of Blore Heath: 23 September 1459

On the following Sunday, the Earl of Salisbury, intent on approaching the king, was confronted near Newcastle-under-Lyme, by eight thousand men of the queen's affinity. When they refused him passage, the earl, accompanied by three thousand men, engaged in battle with them [at Blore Heath] . . .

John Benet's Chronicle

And there was Lord Audley slain, and many of the notable knights and squires of Cheshire that had received the livery of swans [from the queen].

An English Chronicle

[The Earl of Salisbury] killed or captured in all two thousand of [the queen's army], and forced the rest to flee . . . *John Benet's Chronicle*

The battle lasted all the afternoon from one of the clock, and the chase lasted until seven in the morning . . . *Gregory's Chronicle*

For three days the Hempmill Brook ran red with blood . . . *Brut Chronicle*

36

The Queen's Pledge

She would not stop interrogating the messenger.

How could they have lost the battle? So many against so few? Had they taken no prisoners? Why had they not tried to find out at least where Salisbury was heading now?

It was as though by asking him the same questions over and over she would make him give her different news. The messenger remained on his knees, looking downwards. If he did not have a stammer when he started, he had one now. 'Y-your majesty,' he said, 'it w-was all we could d-do to flee.'

He repeated all the information that he had already given them: the expected reinforcements from Stanley had not arrived; many of the queen's men had been killed in the battle or in the rout that followed. Salisbury's men had pursued them through the night, all the way to the River Tern, hacking down every man they found. The earl had tricked them all. After the battle he had moved by night. He had paid a friar to fire off his cannon at various points in the woods so that no one would know where to find them.

The king said little throughout all this, except to weep at Audley's death.

'He is so young,' he said.

The messenger looked as miserable as if he were awaiting his own death.

The queen stopped abruptly, mid interrogation. Her face was very pale. Everyone who saw her thought that she would, in fact, order the messenger to be put to death. But then suddenly, without warning, she left the room.

Her steps were quickened by memory. Warwick declaring her

adulteress at St Paul's Cross, her son a bastard. York confining her to her rooms at Windsor Castle, curtailing her household, her expenses. York again leading the attack against the king at St Albans, his men murdering the Duke of Somerset, her dearest friend.

Rapidly the memories flickered like tiny fires until, by the time she reached her room, her whole mind was lit to a sheet of flame.

She fell to her knees and tried to pray, but her grievances burned in her like holy fire.

She closed her eyes, and her fists.

Before God she pledged that she would not rest until her enemies were brought so low they would never look up again. They would all die, either in battle or as traitors, their steaming bowels dragged out before her, in full sight of all the people of the land.

'The men I have recruited will now be gathered,' she said to the king. 'We will go to them together.'

Despite the king's evident frailty she insisted that his new army needed to see him; he must ride with them, at their head.

'I will ride with you,' she said.

She would not be persuaded by any arguments. She had grown tired, she said, of waiting in rooms. If she had to she would put on armour herself, like Joan of Arc.

So together they rode through the wet fields to the place where all the men of all the shires were waiting with such weapons as they had. And when they came upon them the queen let out an exultant cry, for the army she had recruited was indeed vast. It seemed as though half the men of England would be setting out for Ludlow with the king and queen.

The Battle of Ludford Bridge: 12 October 1459

Soon after [the Battle of Blore Heath], the Duke of York, and the Earls of Warwick and Salisbury, assembled an army of 25,000 near Worcester. The king and his lords, with 40,000 men arrayed for war and banner unfurled, advanced towards them.

John Benet's Chronicle

The Duke of York made a great deep ditch and fortified it with guns, carts and stakes, but his party was weaker for the king had 30,000 harnessed men, and others not armed but compelled to come with the king.

Gregory's Chronicle

My Lord of Warwick drew up his forces putting Andrew Trollope to lead the vanguard, because he trusted him more than he trusted anyone else. [But] this Andrew had received news by a secret message from the Duke of Somerset, which rebuked him because he was coming to wage war against the king his sovereign lord, saying as well that the king had proclaimed among his host that all who were adherents to the opposing party but wished to return to serve the king would receive both great rewards and a pardon for everything. Then Andrew Trollope secretly went to the members of the Calais garrison . . .

Jean de Waurin

At Ludlow Field Andrew Trollope with many of the old soldiers of Calais departed secretly from the Duke of York's party to the king's party and there showed the secret plans of the duke his lord . . . *London Chronicle*

Then the Duke of York and the other lords, seeing themselves so deceived, took counsel briefly the same night and departed from the field, leaving behind most of their people . . . *Brut Chronicle*

The king's gallants at Ludlow when they had drunk enough of wine in the taverns full ungodly smote off the pipes and hogsheads of wine, so that men went wetshod in wine and then robbed the town bare, carrying away bedding, clothes and other stuff, and they defouled many women . . . *Gregory's Chronicle*

The duke fled to Wales breaking down the bridges after him that the king's men should not come after. *Gregory's Chronicle*

. . . then the Duke of York, with his second son, departed through Wales towards Ireland, leaving his eldest son, the Earl of March, with the Earls of Warwick and Salisbury, who, together with three or four men, rode straight to Devonshire. There, by the help and aid of one Dinham, a squire, who secured a ship for them, they sailed to Guernsey, where they refreshed themselves, and thereafter to Calais. *Brut Chronicle*

The king, in response . . . ravaged all the Duke of York's lands between Worcester and Ludlow . . . *John Benet's Chronicle*

37

Duchess Cecily

He was almost in tears, this messenger.

There had been no battle, he said, and her husband was gone, with her sons, taken ship and gone, and most of his men had submitted to the king. But the king's men had run through the town and robbed it to the bare walls, destroying the houses, setting fire to barns and slaughtering cattle and pigs in the street, running to their knees in wine and blood. And they were heading for the castle now.

'You must leave at once, my lady,' he said.

There were not enough men left in the castle to fight. Many had already abandoned her, riding away on horses they had no business to ride. And she was left here, with her two youngest sons and her daughter, Margaret.

'How should I leave?' she said.

'You must leave any way you can,' he said. Already the outskirts of the town were blazing. There would be nothing left.

She nodded once, as if to herself. The king's men, keyed up for battle and cheated of it, were running wild with the mindlessness of collective force. She could hear them already, like the roar of a distant sea. But behind this mindlessness was a deadly intent: that the people of Ludlow would never again place faith in the lord who had abandoned them. When the enemy came to the castle they would destroy it. She turned to her remaining servants.

'You must leave now,' she said, and her elderly steward started to protest but she interrupted him.

'Take what you can and go.'

She turned to the messenger. 'You also,' she said.

There were many different exits from the castle, tunnels and hidden gateways.

'See to it that everyone leaves,' she said to her steward.

'My lady – what will you do?' her steward said.

'Don't think about me,' she said. Then, in her most imperious tones, she added, 'What are you waiting for? Go.'

No one disobeyed the duchess when she spoke in that way. The messenger was already leaving. The steward and one or two other servants began to remonstrate with her, but she said, 'Look to yourselves. If anything remains afterwards you may return. Someone will be needed to repair the damage.'

And when they protested again she said, 'Go. I will not leave until every last one of you is gone.'

And then at last they started to obey.

The duchess turned to her children, George, aged ten, Richard, seven, and Margaret, white-faced, a girl of thirteen.

'Come with me,' she said.

And Duchess Cecily took the hands of her two younger children and left the castle by the main gate, with her daughter following behind, to face the oncoming mob.

38

The Market Square

We ran like the berserkers of old, through fire and rivers of blood, floating carcasses and wreckage. No damage too great, no desecration left undone, and all the town behind us was a smoking ruin. It was as though a great jagged rift had appeared in our souls, unleashing monsters and demons. We drank and we ran, forgetting everything, including ourselves. And so we came to the marketplace.

And there she stood, a woman in her middle years, of middle height, bearing all the insignia of the House of York.

She stood by the market cross, holding the hands of two young boys, a fair and pretty girl clinging on behind. Flakes of soot and sparks flew all around them, but her voice rang out as we surged forward.

'Take me to the Duke of Buckingham,' she cried.

Three times she cried it, and all of us stopped short.

She could feel her daughter's ragged breath on her neck, her youngest son quivering like a dog. Her elder son did not want to be seen holding his mother's hand, but she held it nonetheless, tightly enough to stop the blood.

She fixed the foremost man with a piercing glare.

'Where is the duke, your leader?' she said. 'Take me to him.'

'We'll take them all right,' someone shouted, 'one piece at a time,' and there was a murmuring roar of approval. But she hooked her fierce gaze on to the man who instinct told her was a leader.

'Take me to my brother the duke,' she said. He understood, she knew, the rules of war. And they knew who she was, of course. The Rose of Raby, sister-in-law to the Duke of Buckingham. And perhaps they knew they would be rewarded for taking her hostage. At any rate, as she continued to glare at their leader, they fell into a grudging silence. And the man turned to his fellows and raised his arms.

'We have hostages,' he said. And then he turned back. 'You are our prisoner,' he said.

'Then you will provide me with an escort,' she replied.

There was a flicker of appreciation in the man's eyes. Then he turned to the crowd, holding up his sword, and said, 'Stand back – all of you. You there – send word to the duke – we have hostages for him. You, you and you, stand guard – the rest of you fall back.'

Grumbling and reluctant, the crowd made way. Then Cecily Neville and her children stepped forward and men raised their swords to clear a path, yet the crowd still jostled them as they passed.

The Duchess of York with her children was sent to the Lady of Buckingham, her sister, where she was kept long after . . . *Brut Chronicle*

39

Margaret Beaufort Visits Her Mother-in-law

It seemed a long time since she had seen her son.

Sometimes she woke feeling the imprint of a small body near her heart; the pressure of his feet near her ribcage. She would lie awake for several moments worrying about him, wondering whether he was warm enough in the great castle, whether his stomach ached, whether he was awake now – if he had a bad dream, who would go to him?

Then she would get up quickly, even before it was light, and immerse herself in the affairs of her day.

She had set about her new estate zealously, seeing to it that walls were repaired, the marshy land on the border reclaimed and drained, the bridge moved further downstream and broadened and strengthened so that trade could pass.

And her husband, Henry, thought there should be a new mill. He had made a working model and drawn extensive, meticulous plans.

While she worked she was able to fend off thoughts about her son and everything she was missing: his first tooth, his first steps, his first words.

But sometimes, as now, it caught her so that she could do nothing at all. She could only stand still, as though she had forgotten how to move.

She stood by the window of her room. The late-autumn sunlight, though golden, had no heat in it. It flitted over the surfaces of leaves, turning them to a sharp green that was almost yellow then returning them to dullness, or changing the bare twigs from a blackish brown to a soft grey. She watched the play of colours as they came and went, came and went.

She didn't hear her husband knock; only gradually became aware of him standing behind her, not quite close enough to touch.

'My lady mother,' he said, 'has invited us to visit her.'

She moved her head a little. They had not visited the duchess since she had taken her sister Cecily into custody.

Her first impulse was to say that she did not want to go back into that household, but Henry continued to speak.

'It occurred to me,' he said, 'that my father might also be there. If he is not with the king.'

She said nothing. She did not want to see the duke.

'It is not impossible,' he said, 'that Pembroke would also come.'

Jasper. Who had not responded to any of her letters about her son. She turned slowly towards her husband.

'Or at least,' he continued, 'that there would be news of him; that we would find out where he is.'

Hope flared in her, she couldn't help it. 'You think so?' she said.

'I cannot say for sure.'

'But – if we found out where he was – would you come with me?'

He knew she was talking about her son. 'I would,' he said.

Her heart began to pound quite painfully.

'We should set off soon, before the weather turns,' he said, then paused. 'Will you come to eat now?'

She hadn't eaten at all that day. 'But there is so much to do,' she said, looking round her room as if she would like to pack up everything right away. He nodded.

'Even so, you must eat,' he said.

They set out the following week, while the weather was still mild, though the rivers were running high and they were delayed more than once by a bridge that was broken and unsafe. Margaret sat impatiently in their carriage, thinking what a difference it would make if people were only made to maintain their property. How many battles might have ended differently if more people repaired their bridges and the roads?

She did not say this to Henry, who read most of the way. He

did not seem to want to discuss the forthcoming visit, or speculate about the presence of Duchess Cecily. He would only say that it was right to go now, while the war was going in the king's favour, for once. He did not say that the opportunity might not come again.

She had realized that he was doing this for her sake; he had no especial desire to return home ('I am not the son they wanted to survive,' he had once said), so she was grateful to him, and tried not to disturb him with her impatience. Still, she could not help but envisage their arrival, and how the duke might be there, and Jasper with him, and what she would say.

But when they got there it was immediately obvious that they were the only guests. The duchess stood in the entrance, looking somewhat dishevelled, with a small group of servants behind her. There was no sign of Cecily, or the duke.

'Is my father not here?' Henry said as soon as they had greeted her.

'Your father?' said the duchess. 'Who knows where he is? With the king, I expect. And likely to remain so for the foreseeable future.'

Margaret followed Henry into the house, feeling the full weight of disappointment.

The duchess ordered a servant to show them to their room, then immediately forgetting that she had done so, began to take them herself. She walked heavily, unevenly, complaining of the pain in her hip.

'It's the damp – it never lets up,' she said over her shoulder.

Margaret would not look at Henry. It seemed to her that the whole trip was likely to be a complete waste of time.

'. . . leaves me here in charge of my sister, of course,' the duchess continued. 'Expects me to keep her under lock and key. "Treat her well," he tells me, "but keep her in close confinement. Do not let her leave. See to it that she has no visitors, and sends no messages to anyone." As if anyone could ever tell Cecily what to do! Even as a little girl she was quite intractable – always has been.'

The duchess paused a little, out of breath, then rapped on a door.

'Cecily,' she called. 'We will be eating soon.'

Silence. But Margaret thought she could hear movements from inside the room.

'Did you hear me?' said the duchess. 'I said we will be eating shortly.'

'I am pleased to hear it,' came the response.

'You will join us, of course.'

'I do not think so.'

'We have guests,' said the duchess. 'Your nephew and his wife. They are anxious to see you.'

'This is not a zoo,' the voice said, distinctly.

'Well, suit yourself,' said her sister, continuing along the corridor. 'It might as well be a zoo,' she said, turning to Margaret and Henry. 'I feel as if I have been put in charge of a wild and stubborn beast . . . Here we are.'

She opened a door and stood beside it breathlessly as two servants struggled in with their trunks.

'I will leave you to prepare for dinner, but don't take too long – the cook gets in a fearful temper if we keep him waiting.'

They entered the room. It was pleasant enough, low-ceilinged with small windows. And in the centre there was a double bed.

At home she did not sleep with Henry. As soon as they had moved in she had claimed a separate room, and Henry had made no objection. Now he stood awkwardly beside the bed. 'I'm sorry,' he said.

He was referring, of course, to the absence of his father, of Jasper. She didn't look at him. 'You weren't to know,' she said.

But you could have found out, she thought, unfairly, perhaps. But now they were stuck here, perhaps for weeks if the weather changed. She turned to the first of their boxes and began unfastening it. She remembered the very first time she had met Jasper, when she had felt a crushing disappointment that he was there and not Edmund. And now she felt the same bitterness about his absence.

But there was no help for it; no help for anything at all.

'I could write to him,' Henry was saying.

'It doesn't matter,' she said, tugging roughly at the strap.

Less than an hour later they sat at the table with the Duchess Anne, while a steward served them a watery chicken soup.

'It will be a very modest affair, I'm afraid,' the duchess said in a low voice as though the steward could not hear her. 'We have had such trouble getting supplies. Of course, you are near a market,' she said to Margaret. 'That makes all the difference.'

Margaret smiled wanly. The soup looked slightly viscous; there were globules of oil on its surface.

'Are you all right?' the duchess said suddenly. 'You look very pale.'

Margaret glanced at Henry.

'I think we were hoping,' he said, 'to hear some news of the little boy.'

'Your son?' said the duchess in surprise. 'He is with his uncle, is he not?'

Margaret bowed her head. 'We – do not get much news,' she said. 'And because of all the – disturbances – I have not been able to visit.'

'But you may be sure that he is well taken care of,' the duchess said, and then she added, almost slyly, 'What you need is another little one, eh? Take your mind off the first.'

And to Margaret's horror she leaned over and patted her stomach, which was almost concave; she could see her mother-in-law registering the fact that there was no child there.

But she was saved from responding by the arrival of the Duchess Cecily, whose wry tones preceded her down the stairs.

'Am I too late for the feast?'

'My lady sister,' said the duchess with the same irony. 'We are indeed honoured.'

The Duchess of York did not look like a prisoner, or like a woman whose husband would be indicted. She looked considerably more regal than her sister, though she wore a severe gown of grey and black. Turquoise stones glittered on her fingers and in her uncovered hair, of which, it was said, she was excessively proud.

Proud Cis – that was what they called her. The whole nation knew she had stopped a rampaging army in its tracks.

Henry rose to greet his aunt and Margaret rose too. Unsure of the etiquette – how did one behave before an imprisoned duchess? – she sank into a deep curtsy. Duchess Cecily barely acknowledged either of them. Margaret could feel her eyes assessing her dismissively, as people were wont to do, before sitting at the table to the left of her sister.

They looked alike; Margaret could see that now they were in such close proximity. They had a similar prettiness, though Henry's mother looked much older than her sister when in fact there were not many years between them. And Cecily seemed somehow more composed. Duchess Anne was greying and unravelled, whereas Duchess Cecily looked as though none of the hairs on her head or the threads of her gown would ever dare to unravel.

The first thing she did was to send the soup back.

'If I had wanted warm water I would have asked for it,' she said.

Duchess Anne raised her eyes towards heaven. 'My lady sister,' she said, 'imagines she is running this establishment.'

'Whereas my lady sister,' Cecily said, tasting the wine, 'is rehearsing for a role as keeper of his majesty's prisons. So, Henry,' she added, abruptly changing the subject, 'how have you been? Not too busy fighting battles, I hope.'

Henry flushed darkly, looking down.

'He has been ill,' Margaret said.

'And do his illnesses coincide with the battles?' Cecily enquired. 'How inconvenient.'

'At least,' Henry's mother said, 'he did not desert his wife.'

'No indeed,' said Cecily. 'Merely his king.'

In that moment Margaret conceived a strong dislike for the Duchess of York. She glanced at Henry, who was still staring in consternation at his plate, then back at the duchess, who was smiling faintly, enjoying the exchange. She took a breath.

'My husband cannot help his illness,' she said. 'But my lady is right to suppose that even if he were well he would not see the point in engaging in fruitless warfare. And if more people thought like him, the land would not be torn apart – father pitted against son, brother against brother and –' she glanced quickly at them both – 'sister against sister.'

They were silent; surprised perhaps, reappraising her.

'I stand rebuked,' Duchess Cecily said, giving her a narrow stare. Henry was now smiling at his soup.

More courses arrived and the atmosphere began to thaw. The food, though modest as Duchess Anne had said, was good and the wine flowed freely. Henry's mother became voluble and told anecdotes of her childhood with Cecily, so that even her sister began to smile. She talked about their father, who had such a passion for hunting, despite his failing eyesight, that few people were willing to accompany him.

On one occasion, she said, he had heard there was a great white stag in the forest, and he was determined to shoot it. Their mother had said that he should not go; he would surely put an arrow in one of the servants.

'I don't care if I shoot all the servants!' Anne cried in a deep voice. 'I will bring home that stag!'

The Duchess Cecily joined in, imitating their mother. 'If you shoot all the servants, Ralph, then the two of us will be alone. And then I will certainly have to shoot you!'

And they laughed together, the two sisters, briefly and gleefully, as if there were no differences between them at all.

Later, Margaret and Henry returned to their room. And to the bed they were to share, which seemed suddenly enormous. She stood and looked at it and did not know what to do. Henry stood also, equally embarrassed.

'I shall go out, if you like,' he said. 'While you get ready.'

And so he left the room, and she stripped to her chemise, and got quickly into bed, occupying the least space she could manage on the furthermost edge.

And in a little while he joined her; she felt the weight of him on the mattress. He turned away from her so that they lay back to back, and in a relatively short time she heard his breathing change.

She had assumed, at first, that it was the difference in their ages that bothered him, or respect for her widowhood, and then that it was her manifest unattractiveness that kept him from her room.

At least he was not surprised that she had not conceived. There had been no necessity for awkward explanations.

And at first she had been relieved, of course; she still felt mainly relieved. But here, in this strange bed in the household that was not hers, she felt suddenly hollow with longing for the love she had lost, or never had.

He was not Edmund, she thought.

In the parliament held at Coventry they that were chosen . . . were enemies to the foresaid lords who were out of this realm. In the which parliament the said Duke of York and the three earls and other were attaint of treason and their goods, lordships, and possessions escheated to the king's hands and they and their heirs disinherited to the ninth degree, and by the king's commission in every city, borough, and town cried openly and proclaimed rebels and traitors and their tenants and their men spoiled of their goods, maimed, beaten and slain without any pity.

An English Chronicle

Around 24th June [1460], the Earls of March, Warwick and Salisbury and Lord Falconbridge landed in England from Calais. And on 2nd July, which was a Monday, they entered London with a vast band of armed men.

John Benet's Chronicle

They sent a herald to London to ask if the city would stand with them in their just quarrel and grant them leave to pass through the city. Those that were not friendly to the earls counselled the mayor to place guns at the bridge to keep them out, and so there was division among the citizens . . . but 12 discreet aldermen allowed the earls to enter in the name of the city. And so on the 2nd day of July they entered into London . . . then was a convocation of clergy held at St Paul's and the said earls came and the Earl of Warwick spoke to them about the causes of their coming to this land . . . the misrule and mischiefs thereof and how with great violence they had been repelled and put from the king's presence . . . and they made an oath upon the cross that they . . . willed no harm to the king.

Margaret Beaufort Visits Her Mother-in-law

The king, who was with his council at Coventry, rode to Northampton.

Then the Earl of Salisbury by common assent of the city was made ruler and governor of London, and the Earl of Warwick [and many other lords] went forth to the king at Northampton . . .

The earls came to Northampton with 40,000 men and sent certain bishops to the king beseeching him to allow them into his presence, but the Duke of Buckingham, standing beside the king said, 'you come not as bishops but as armed men', and he said that if the Earl of Warwick came into the king's presence, he would die. The messengers returned with this message to the earls. Then the Earl of Warwick sent a herald to the king offering hostages to him and saying that he would come unarmed, but the king would not hear him.

Then on the 10th day of July at two hours after noon, the Earls of March and Warwick let cry throughout the field that no man should lay a hand upon the king or on the common people, but only on the lords, knights and squires, and the trumpets blew . . .

An English Chronicle

The Battle of Northampton: 10 July 1460

That day was such great rain that the king's guns sank deep in water and could not be used . . . both hosts fought together for half an hour. Then Lord Grey who led the king's vanguard . . . went over to the earls which saved many a man's life. Many were slain and many fled and many were drowned in the river . . .

An English Chronicle

40

Rain and Treachery

At midday the rain began, turning both camps to a quagmire.

Warwick's men advanced with the hard rain blowing in their faces, and were met with a deadly barrage of arrows.

When he looked behind he could see York's son, the Earl of March, leading his men over the Nene marshes, which had turned to a viscous mud. Many were forced to dismount and struggle on foot through the swamp. It looked as though they would die there, sinking slowly into the sodden ground.

Until, as promised, Lord Grey's men laid down their weapons and began to help Warwick's men through the barricades.

Warwick could see the hands reaching down, hauling men up the slippery slopes, and felt the first pangs of conquest, tinged with disappointment. For he knew that the fighting was over now, almost before it had begun.

Yet not all was over, for the king's men, seeing this treachery, began to panic, and a great fear broke out amongst them. There was a backwards movement in the lines, a kind of chaotic pulse as they attempted to flee across the River Nene, which was already swollen and bursting its banks after some days of rain.

What followed had its own deadly beauty. Men ran tumbling one over the other, with a kind of clumsy grace, as the banks of the river collapsed. Several were trampled, or borne down beneath the water by the weight of their armour. From his vantage point, the Earl of Warwick could see their faces twisted with fear, stretching like the faces of demons. Fat bubbles of mud escaped from their lips.

He was reminded, inevitably, of Dante, for *The Inferno* was a book he held in the utmost reverence. He thought of the fifth circle, where the angry men strike and mangle each other on the banks of the River Styx. Those who 'swallow the filth of the loathsome swamp', or who are 'fixed in its slime'. And the sullen men, gurgling beneath the water:

> 'We were sullen in the sweet air that is gladdened by the sun, bearing indolent smoke in our hearts: now we lie here, sullen in the black mire.'
>
> This measure they gurgle in their throats, because they cannot utter it in full speech . . .

These words had always struck him – he, who was known for his persuasive powers, his fluent speech. He could not read them without a sense of anxiety, almost constriction, in his own throat. And so, after a little while of mesmerized watching, he turned his horse, to give his orders to his men: that no nobles should be taken prisoner, but all killed, except for those bearing Lord Grey's badge of the black, ragged staff; and that no man should harm the king.

When the battle was over and the earls had the victory, they came to the king in his tent and assured him that they had come not to hurt him but to be his true liegemen . . . *An English Chronicle*

The victorious earls paid all honours of royalty to King Henry and conducted him to London in solemn procession, Richard Neville, Earl of Warwick, bareheaded, carrying a sword before the king in all humility and respect.

Crowland Chronicle

[Warwick] put to death the Duke of Buckingham . . . and the Lords Beaumont, Egremont and Shrewsbury, all great lords . . .

Milanese State Papers: newsletter from Bruges, July 1460

Rain and Treachery

The queen, hearing this, went away into Wales, but one of her own servants, whom she had [created] an officer of her son the prince, plundered and robbed her, and put her in doubt of her life and her son's life also . . . and she rode [away] behind a poor young man of fourteen years called John Coombe, born at Amesbury in Wiltshire. *Gregory's Chronicle*

41

John Coombe of Amesbury

All I could hear were the shouts of the men as they set about one another, and all I could think was *I wish I knew this horse better* – for it was a new one, new broken in. Then I saw her face – white, then dark, then white again – she was running, dragging the little prince with one hand and holding her skirts with the other, but she couldn't see where she was going in the dark and the rain. So I shouted – 'Here, majesty, here!' – and she turned towards me, near slipping over in the mud.

I scoop the prince off her while she tries to clamber on to the horse, but her skirts are weighed down with mud and the horse skitters, and all I can think is, *We're dead!* So I put out a hand and haul her up, by the scruff of the neck almost – she kicks herself over somehow and we're off.

Which way though? Haven't a clue. Seems like the horse is deciding, for the forest is thick all around us and there's only one or two ways it *can* go. Once or twice it buckles and I grip tight with my knees, expecting it to go down any moment – rolling over and crushing us all. But somehow it doesn't happen – the horse gets a trot on gamely, even with the three of us on its back, its breath steaming in the rain.

The little prince says nothing, nothing at all, but I can feel him clinging to my back, and I can feel his mother's breath on my neck. I remember thinking, *That's a queen's breath, that is!* and when we stumble I can feel her heart banging, and I think, *That's a queen's heart, near mine!* She says nothing either. Until the road opens up a bit and I turn partway round and ask her, 'Where to, ma'am?' shouting through the rain, and she says, 'Harlech,' without a pause.

Well, I can't argue with her, can I? Even though Chester's nearest, and to get to Harlech you have to pass right through Wales and a lot of Yorkist terrain. Not to mention I don't know the way.

All I can do is urge the horse forward in the direction that the sun set, and hope it doesn't stumble and break all our necks, and hope no one's following and we're not set upon suddenly and taken in ambush.

And hope – more than hope – that I don't fail her – I don't let her down.

And for once Hope seems to be listening, for at last we come to the old road that runs by Chester and then we can gallop.

It was a good horse, that one – faster than I could hope for, fording streams and jumping hedges, like it knew what it had to do. And carrying three of us all the time!

Only when morning comes, grey and drizzled, do we get off and walk a little way just to see if we still can.

The little prince you'd think'd be half dead with weariness, but he stares at me right sternly as his mother hands him down, then totters to a hillock. She bends over him, taking his boots off, combing her fingers through his hair, taking him to where he can pass water. I fill my flagon at the stream and we all drink. And I can't help glancing at her curiously – I never thought I'd be this close to a queen!

All her skirts are well muddied so you can't tell the colour of them. Even her face is spattered and her hair escaping from its hood. She hands the flagon to her son, wiping it first, like any mother, but somehow – I can't explain it – like a queen.

'When will we get there?' the little prince wants to know, but all she says is, 'You must be very brave.'

'I am!' he says, and she smiles.

She looks so different when she smiles!

'We will see your Uncle Jasper,' she says. 'He will take care of us.'

Pembroke! I think. So that's the reason for Harlech. I didn't know he was there – but I did know he'd come into a right rich inheritance of lands after the rebel lords were attainted.

I manage to find some berries and I hand them to her and she hands them to her son.

'Can I have goose?' he says.

'Yes, my darling,' she tells him, 'and pheasant and boar – but we must be patient for a while.'

I'm clemmed too, but there's nothing else to eat, and no money and nothing to sell. Anyway, we can't be seen in the town.

When she stands up straight she isn't any taller than me. We walk a little way to give our legs and the horse a break, but she hardly looks at me at all, she's too busy watching the little prince, who runs ahead of us waving his tiny sword.

'He's a fighter, ma'am,' I say, and her face, though melancholy, breaks into that smile again – still without looking at me.

All her store of tenderness was for that child.

Then it's time to mount the horse again and ride on most of that day; no food, little to drink, and the rain falling steadily all around – dripping from leaves and boughs, collecting in rivulets in the stone walls, running in little streams down the hills and gathering in pools in the brown fields.

Until at last we can hear the cry of seagulls and soon after we can see the tower, rising grey out of a grey sea. And we're all exhausted, but still there's a little voice singing inside me, because I've done it – we've made it, and I haven't let her down.

There are guards at the castle gates and we ride almost all the way up to them, then I dismount and tell them – unlikely as it is that the queen's here. But even in the state we're in, sodden and wrecked, she still manages to look like a queen – both her and the little prince sitting up straight as arrows – and I watch the suspicion in the guards' faces turn to confusion, and someone sends a message back inside the walls.

I help the queen and the little prince to dismount, and she looks at me then properly, for the first time, wiping hair and rain from her face.

'What is your name?' she says with that lovely quiver in her voice.

'John Coombe of Amesbury, ma'am,' I tell her.

'Well, John Coombe of Amesbury,' she says, 'I can give you nothing, for I have nothing to give.' And for a moment she looks vexed enough to cry, and I remember how they stripped the jewels from her, and I start to protest – I didn't do it for reward – but she says, 'Today you have saved the crown of England.'

And she leans forward and kisses me, once, twice, on either cheek, and our eyes meet and I can see the little golden lights in hers.

Then the gates open and the earl himself is hurrying out – a tall, gaunt man with a beak of a nose – and she rushes forward, and I'm left with the horse.

'Wildfire I name you,' I murmur, and she snickers and whickers into my hand.

That was years ago now – I've told my children and my children's children the story of that poor, proud queen. Tragic she was, like a queen in a storybook.

Nothing in my life ever matched up to it, before or since.

My wife knew it, I think, though only once did she let on that she knew, years later, nursing our third little girl that died. I was telling my story to some guests at the inn we kept.

'John is a man who gives his heart only once,' she said, right sourly. I denied it, of course, but over the years I've thought about it and it's true. I've been the queen's man all my life – even after all that happened. Especially after all that happened. In that time with her I gave her everything – all I had – without thinking about it. Maybe you can only do that when you're very young.

And if that isn't love, then what is?

[The queen] moved very secretly to Jasper, Earl of Pembroke, in Wales . . . where she received many great gifts and was greatly comforted, of which she had need . . . [but] she dared not stay in any place that was open, but only secretly.

Gregory's Chronicle

And soon after she went to Scotland. *An English Chronicle*

The king of Scotland with a great army laid siege to Roxburgh Castle and took control of it, but on 3rd August [1460] he was killed there. Then the Scots quarrelled among themselves as to who should be the guardian of their new king, who was only eight years of age. So they abandoned Roxburgh Castle and returned to Scotland. *John Benet's Chronicle*

Around 8th September, the Duke of York returned from Ireland to England.
John Benet's Chronicle

42

Two Sisters

As soon as the news reached her that her brother-in-law, the Duke of Buckingham, was dead, the king's army scattered and lost, Cecily knew her sister had no more authority to keep her there.

She gave the messenger a purse of silver, and told him to order a carriage, and then she put on her finest clothes. Her lady dressed her hair once, then again, to make sure that all the threads of grey were hidden in the gold, for her husband was coming back from Ireland.

No one disturbed them; the whole household was in mourning. She herself wore a dark blue gown out of respect to her brother-in-law, but the sleeves were lined with silver, because blue and silver were the colours of her house, and the feathers in her cap were peacock blue. There was no doubt that she looked younger than her forty-five years; her cheeks were pink again, her eyes shining.

Then she went to find her sister.

Anne was sitting in the garden in the rain. She looked suddenly old, entirely drained of colour, her hair and skin and eyes all of the same greyish-yellow hue. She was leaning to one side, as if the blow had knocked her sideways, or as if she were no longer capable of supporting herself. Cecily remembered that her hip was probably paining her.

She did not move or look up as Cecily approached, but remained staring at the grass with a perplexed look, as if in its complicated network of blades she might find a solution to the mysteries of life; or see in it a different world, one in which her husband still lived.

Everything that Cecily had been going to say – that she was grateful for the hospitality her sister had shown her and regretted that it must come to an end, and hoped that one day she might return the favour – died on her lips, as she took in the baffled emptiness of her sister's gaze.

She thought of the duke's drinking, his sudden rages and excessive sentiment, his overly physical demonstrations towards any other women who were near – surely her sister would be better off without that? She might marry again, after all.

These words, too, died on her lips. In the end all she said was, 'Well, sister – I am leaving now.'

I am going to meet my husband, she did not say. Her sister, like herself, had been married all her life. And now her husband had been killed by their nephew, Warwick.

Anne did not look up. 'Go, then,' she replied, as though from a great distance.

Cecily hesitated, made a movement towards her, then stopped. She would not embrace her – that was not something they did, and too much had happened between them. But after a moment she sat beside her on the seat.

They did not touch or hold hands or look at one another. Above them the rain collected in the leaves in tiny trembling pools before spilling in little waterfalls to the earth.

43

Richard of York is Reunited With His Wife

And the same year the Duke of York came out of Ireland and landed at the Red Cliff in Lancashire . . . and thus he came towards London in white and blue livery embroidered with fetterlocks, and then his lady the duchess met with him, in a chariot covered in blue velvet drawn by four pure coursers . . .

Gregory's Chronicle

He loved her for dressing like a queen, after spending the best part of the year in imprisonment. She got out of her chariot and looked at him, and he looked at her, but they did not embrace – they would not embrace in public.

Later, he clung to her, sinking to his knees and holding her round the hips. She raised him up and kissed him. 'Richard,' she said, and kissed him again. She cupped his face in her hands. 'There is only one way forward now,' she said.

He knew it. They both did. The alternative was dispossession, and death. But he did not know if the others would stand with him, if he should go to them first.

'Warwick –' he said, and, 'Salisbury –'

'No,' she said, keeping that gentle pressure on his face. 'You must go straight to parliament. Make your intentions clear.'

There was no time for discussion and, anyway, there was nothing to discuss. 'I will go,' he said.

Almost at the beginning of parliament the Duke of York suddenly arrived with great pomp and splendour and in no small exaltation of mood, for he came with trumpets and horns, men-at-arms and a very large retinue . . . When he arrived, he made directly for the king's throne, where he laid his hand on the drape or cushion as if about to take possession of what was his by right and held his hand there for a brief time. At last, withdrawing it, he turned towards the people and . . . looked eagerly at the assembly waiting for their acclamation . . .

Whethamsted's Register

The duke took the king's place claiming it for his right and inheritance and saying he would keep it to live or die, wherewith all the lords were sore dismayed . . .

Great Chronicle of London

44

Richard of York Claims the Throne

The silence was so much more eloquent than words. He saw at once that they would never accept him; had never intended to. Almost without his consent his fingers left the throne.

Some had turned their faces from him, some could not hide their dismay, while others regarded him with a stony reproach. He, who had given his life to this land.

A look of incredulity entered his eyes. It was true, then. They would stand with their existing king, however mad and feeble. Even though that king's claim was in no way superior to his own.

Disbelief turned to anger. He had fought for this country, bailed it out of debt, governed it in lieu of the king while he lay like a larva in his cocoon. He closed his eyes. And in that moment he envisaged clearly all the ways in which he could end this dispute once and for all. For his soldiers surrounded the palace and the king was in his power.

Had not the king's own grandfather had the reigning king murdered?

Someone was speaking to him. He opened his eyes. Thomas Bourchier, the archbishop, was asking him a question.

'Do you wish to speak to his majesty?' he said. 'I can take you to his rooms.'

'His majesty should come to me,' the duke replied. The abrupt tone betrayed his sense of injury. Several more lords dropped their gazes. With some difficulty he mastered himself.

'No one is to leave this assembly,' he said to them all, then he looked the archbishop in the eye. 'I will go to the king,' he said.

When the archbishop heard this reply he quickly withdrew and told the king of the duke's response. After the archbishop had left, the duke also withdrew, went to the principal chamber of the palace [the king being in the queen's apartments], smashed the locks and threw open the doors, in a regal rather than a ducal manner, and remained there for some time.

Whethamsted's Register

[The duke] claimed the crown as his proper inheritance and right, putting in writing his title and claim to be rightful heir. *Brut Chronicle*

This disturbance continued, albeit without killing or bloodshed, for about three weeks, during which time the whole parliament was occupied with discussion of the duke's lineage and rights . . . *Crowland Chronicle*

After much debate, it was decreed and concluded that King Henry should reign and be king during his natural life . . . after his death the Duke of York should be king and his heirs after him and immediately he should be proclaimed heir apparent and also protector of England during the king's life . . . While the commons of the realm were assembled in the common house, debating the title of the Duke of York, the crown hanging in the midst of their house suddenly fell down; this was taken as an omen that the reign of King Henry was ended.

Brut Chronicle

On Saturday, the 9th day of November, the Duke of York was proclaimed through the city heir apparent to the crown and all his progeny after him . . .

Great Chronicle of London

At this time Queen Margaret, with Prince Edward, the only son of the king and herself, was staying in the north. *Crowland Chronicle*

45

Margaret of Anjou Receives the News

She could hear her own heart banging; she could hardly see. They had dispossessed her son, for whom she had worked so tirelessly. They had annulled, by act of parliament, his right to inherit the throne.

Somehow she contained herself, gazing blindly at the wall in front of her. When she closed her eyes the words of her own pledge came to her. She had promised before God that she would not rest until her enemies were brought so low that they would never look up again.

She thought she had spoken or shouted aloud, but when she opened her eyes again the Earl of Angus was looking at her quizzically.

'We must summon an army,' she said.

The Duke of York, well knowing that the queen would spurn and impugn the conclusions agreed in parliament, caused her and her son to be sent for by the king, but she being a manly woman, used only to rule and not be ruled, not only refused to come but also assembled together a great army . . .

Hall's Chronicle

The Duke of Somerset and the Earl of Devon, with many knights and gentlemen of the west parts, fully armed, came through Bath, Gloucester, Evesham and Coventry to York . . . *Annales Rerum Anglicarum*

All these people were gathered and conveyed so secretly that they were assembled to the number of 15,000 before any man would believe it . . .

Gregory's Chronicle

46

The Queen's Speech

By the time she reached York the numbers had swelled to twenty thousand. They had massed together in a great field outside the city and the queen stood on a raised platform to speak to them.

She was not used to addressing so many people and all that morning she had felt as though her nerves were strained to breaking point; not because of the size of the crowd but because she might fail to move them – say the words wrong, or not loudly enough to be heard, fail to communicate the urgency and desperate nature of their cause.

Yet once she stood on the wooden platform and saw the great sea of armed men stretching in all directions, she felt a sudden, fierce exultation. She opened her mouth, trusting the wind to carry her words.

'My loyal men,' she cried. 'True subjects of your king. You have gathered here today to fight for a true cause – the greatest cause there could be – to save this realm. Which has for so long been divided, and brought to ruin and decay by the premeditated and malicious actions of certain traitors.'

She could hear a low growling murmur from the crowd.

'Yes,' she said, nodding. 'You know well who those traitors are. As you know – all of you – what damage they have done – what crimes they have perpetrated – what murders and robberies – what cruel slaughter of the king's own people. Ask yourselves,' she said, gazing round the wide arc of the field, 'what is the true cause of the poverty and misery of this land? Why has it been brought so low?

Because of the greed, malice and *impious savagery* of the Duke of York and his associates.'

The growling murmur rose to a low roar.

'Who have gathered together large numbers of the king's people and stirred them to unlawful rebellion. Contrary –'

She had to pause as the roar increased in volume.

'Contrary to the many oaths of allegiance freely sworn by them to their most merciful king, who of his great clemency has freely and repeatedly forgiven them and offered them pardon. And they – as freely and repeatedly – have *broken their oaths.* The Duke of York has repeatedly and without conscience broken his many oaths!'

Now she had to pause for several moments as a great cry went up against the perjured Duke of York.

'These men – these rebels and traitors – have plotted against their king and against you. They have taken your king into their custody!'

Cries of 'Shame!'

'And this is the true cause of the destruction and decline of this land. For no Christian land may long endure where the prince is robbed of his rule – his laws overthrown and all justice exiled out of it! I say to you that this treacherous usurping of power is more harmful to this nation than any foreign war, famine or sickness. I say to you that by their cruel and unpardonable actions these, your enemies, work irreparable harm upon you, your children and your land. Therefore, I command and beg you, as you have any pride or love left in you for your country and your king, to exercise all rigour against them – and against the Duke of York – before *he destroys you all!*'

Once again she could not be heard.

'You do not stand alone. You follow a queen. And I will either conquer or be conquered with you. I have often broken their battle line. I have mowed down ranks far more stubborn than theirs are now, and by God's grace, and with your help, I will do so again. I will do anything in my power to prevent them. I will not rest until they are utterly destroyed. Because now they pursue their intent to its most damnable conclusion – to promote the false claim of the Duke of York to the *realm and crown of England.*'

More cries of 'Shame! Shame!'

'And to this end they have drawn up an heretical act – a so-called *Act of Accord* – proposing to utterly disinherit and dispossess my son the prince – your prince – of his birthright and inheritance.'

Here she picked up the little prince and held him before them all, so that the roars of enmity changed to acclamation.

'You see before you my son – who is the king's son – and your prince. *Who will be KING!*'

This last word came out in a kind of howl, which was drowned by the cries of 'God Save the Prince! God save Prince Edward!' She stared round at them all shaken, exhausted, but ecstatic, as thundering waves of approval broke from the sea of the crowd.

She had agreed, reluctantly, that she would proceed no further than York, but return to the Scottish queen who had invited her to stay at Edinburgh Castle for the Christmas season. She would rather have stayed with her men. But now at least she knew she could go. For this vast army would march south in her son's name, against the Duke of York.

All marvelled at such boldness in a woman, at a man's courage in a woman's breast, and at her reasonable arguments. They said that the spirit of the Maid [of Orleans] who had raised Charles VII of France to the throne was renewed in the queen.

Commentaries of Pope Pius II

Eventually the lords in London learned the truth and, on 9th December, the Duke of York, the Earl of Salisbury, the Earl of Rutland [who was the Duke of York's second son, one of the best disposed lords in this land] and many more knights, squires and numerous people with them, set off from London towards York.

Gregory's Chronicle

On 21st December the Duke of York and the Earl of Salisbury, with 6,000 fighting men, came to Sandal Castle, where they spent Christmas, while the Duke of Somerset and the Earl of Northumberland with the opposite party lay at Pontefract.

Annales Rerum Anglicarum

The Battle of Wakefield: 30 December 1460

At Wakefield, while the Duke of York's men were roaming about the countryside in search of victuals, a fierce battle was fought between the Duke of Somerset, the Earl of Northumberland and Lord Neville with a great army and the other party . . .

Annales Rerum Anglicarum

When [the Duke of York] was on the plain between his castle and the town of Wakefield, he was surrounded on every side like a fish in a net.

Hall's Chronicle

47

The Duke of York is Surrounded

He fought on, of course, with the methodical, dogged power for which he was justly famous: hips braced, left arm raised to parry the thrusts, right arm swinging rhythmically back and forth. His feet knew where to place themselves, as though the knowledge was etched into their calloused soles. His trained eye remained focussed even when there were too many opponents for him to see. It sought out undefended flesh, the moment of imbalance. The men who surrounded him were grunting with the heft of their blows. And despite the cold and the thin needles of freezing rain, sweat ran into his eyes, blinding them.

Yet there was something in his peripheral vision, winking out of sight; something he did not wish to see. The shutter of his eye flickered once, then something dark occluded it and there was a glancing blow to the side of his skull.

And then he saw them, standing in a group, both on and not on the battlefield.

He faltered long enough to receive a further blow between his shoulder and neck, and then another to his thigh. He swung round, driving his axe into a man's arm, and received in turn a blow that drove his helmet into his skull.

He could see them clearly now, though his eyes were full of blood. He tried to speak to them through his broken teeth, but there were no words for what he had to say. And then he was on his knees, the blade of an axe swinging towards him; blotting out his view.

There fell in the field the Duke of York, Thomas Neville, son of the Earl of Salisbury, Thomas Harrington, many other knights and squires and 2,000 of the common people. And in the flight after the battle Lord Clifford killed Edmund, Earl of Rutland, son of the Duke of York, on the bridge at Wakefield. And the same night the Earl of Salisbury was taken by a servant of Andrew Trollope. And the next day the Bastard of Exeter slew the Earl of Salisbury at Pontefract . . .

By the counsel of the lords they beheaded the dead bodies of the Duke of York, the Earls of Salisbury and Rutland, Thomas Neville, Thomas Harrington [and four others] and placed their heads on various gateways at York.

And in contempt they crowned the head of the Duke of York with a paper crown.

Annales Rerum Anglicarum

48

The Paper Crown

There is no silence like the silence of a battlefield when the battle is over. Nothing equals that deadly calm. Rain falls on abandoned flesh, on contorted limbs and broken armour. And on the three heads over the Micklegate, plastering wet hair into sightless eyes, causing the paper crown to slip then cling to one ear. In the shimmer of rain the lips appear to move . . .

My first child was called Joan. I held her when she was born, red and angry, and wondered if she looked like my mother. And then I held her again when she was pale and still, her little fingers stiffened, and marvelled at the thing that life is; delicate enough to be drawn in on a breath, powerful enough to shape the world.

And so for my first son Henry, and later William, then John, then Thomas, then Ursula.

Ursula, who would break your heart, with her moon-face, her wobbling limbs.

And now Edmund, of course.

They follow you, these dead children. They never left, like the living ones. They sat with us at table or stood with us at church. They were there at the wedding of my eldest living daughter, Anne. And they had grown quite tall.

When your children die part of you dies with them; you join them, piece by piece. Each time I went into battle I knew I might be returning to them, rejoining the pieces of myself. And so it wasn't hard, not really.

I recognized the moment just before it came, because they were there. I felt the hard embrace of the ground, the swift kiss of the axe, and knew that the moment had come, and it was time. I was father, at last, to my dead children.

When the death of these lords was known, there was great sorrow for them.

An English Chronicle

EPITAPH FOR RICHARD DUKE OF YORK

Let it be remembered by all noble hearts that here lies the flower of all gentility, the mighty Duke of York, Richard by name, Prince royal, gentleman of renown. Wise, valiant, virtuous in his life, who loved well, loyally without envy; the right heir proved in many lands of the crowns of England and France. Normandy he guarded from danger; in Ireland he established such government that he ruled all the country peaceably. Of England he was long protector – he loved the people and was their defender . . . This noble duke died at Wakefield while treating of sweet peace, forces overcame him – the year '60, the 30th day of December, he was fifty years old as people remember. Pray to God and to the most fair Lady that his soul may repose in Paradise, Amen.

49

The Queen Hears the News

She felt an intense, frightening joy.

It threatened to rip her open, burst her apart.

She walked to the window and stood with her hands clasped as though praying, but she was not praying. Her heart was pounding quite irregularly, pummelling the inside of her chest. But by the time she turned back to the messenger and to Mary of Gueldres, widow of the Scottish king, she had established a degree of control.

'God has done this,' she said, nodding, and there was only a small catch in her voice. 'God would not permit my son to be disinherited and dispossessed.' She advanced towards them, still nodding. 'He would not have my line destroyed – my son murdered in his bed. He has granted me this victory.'

Mary of Gueldres, who had learned to be more circumspect about the will of God, did not say that to her knowledge no one had threatened to murder the prince.

'You will be leaving us then,' she said as a beatific smile spread over the Queen of England's face.

York, she was thinking. *York is dead*. Tears came into her eyes.

'Yes,' she said faintly, 'I must rejoin my men.' She wiped her eyes quickly, surreptitiously. 'I will need more men,' she said. 'And horses – and supplies.'

Mary of Gueldres was one of those women who did not need to say much. Slight shifts of her face conveyed what she meant. Now she did not say that the Queen of England had no money.

'We must come to some agreement,' Queen Margaret said, beginning to pace. 'I owe you a great deal already, and I will pay – everything – once my kingdom is restored. But I must go to London – I must rescue my husband the king from the hands of his enemies and have that monstrous act revoked and destroyed!'

Queen Mary's eyelids drooped as though in acknowledgement that she understood Queen Margaret's position – she herself would be doing the same. Still, there was the little matter of funding so great a journey.

'I have no money,' Queen Margaret said, 'but when all England is restored to me I promise you will not regret your kindness and generosity.'

Queen Mary did not say that promises did not feed an army. Queen Margaret had half turned away from her, and it was clear that she was thinking.

'My son, the prince,' she said, 'will marry one of your daughters – we have discussed it already.'

One of Queen Mary's eyebrows moved fractionally.

'And – Berwick,' Queen Margaret said, as if to herself. Then she turned back to the other queen. 'You may have the town and fortress of Berwick for Scotland,' she said.

Queen Mary's smile was full and broad. 'We must draw up the agreements,' she said.

And so Queen Margaret travelled south that January in some style, wearing clothes given to her by Queen Mary – a long black gown and a black bonnet with a silver plume, accompanied by a handsome retinue. She rode hard through the bald landscape, impatient of all delays caused by the weather or by ice, so that the Scottish lords were impressed with her stamina and zeal. And her English companions could hardly get her to pause to listen to them.

When they reminded her, for instance, that there was not enough money to pay her troops, or to supply so great an army with food all the way to London, she replied that they could plunder and loot – that was what armies were for. And since they would be travelling through territory that belonged to her enemies, that was a good thing – they should know they were destroyed.

And when they suggested that perhaps she should not have given up Berwick, that contested territory which had for so long belonged to the English crown, she replied that it did not signify – her son was going to marry a Scottish princess and all the territories of England and France would one day revert to him.

The little prince rode with her, or on his own horse when he was able, or in a small carriage, his pale face looking out on to the frozen land that would be his with eyes as bright and unblinking as a bird's.

I have heard it said that the northern lords will be here sooner than men expected, I have heard within three weeks . . . in this southern country every man is very willing to go with the lords here and I hope God will help them, for the people in the north rob and steal and be agreed to pillage all this country . . .

Paston Letters

50

Duchess Cecily Hears the News

Something odd had happened to her breathing, something that disturbed the action of her lungs, so that each breath was quite different and distinct from the next: this one retaining the air too long; the next one interrupted on the in-breath, shaky on the out.

It was as though she had forgotten how to breathe.

Or as though she were attempting to breathe in a place where no air was; at any rate, she was peculiarly aware of the labouring of her lungs. And her heart – her heart was struggling like some wild thing that had been buried alive.

In the days after hearing the news she felt as if she were warding off some terrible thing, some vast danger or calamity – as though there could be a worse calamity, as though her life were not already in a state of collapse. She could not see or think or plan ahead more than a few moments into the future. Because now that future seemed to her like a wall with no point of entry, or a blankness in her mind.

Her husband, whom she had loved . . . but she couldn't finish the thought. It was as though there was nothing left to think.

She could not remember a time when she had not loved him. Before him, there was nothing; after him, that nothingness was threatening to engulf her.

In the moments when she was not thinking, he was with her. She thought she heard him once reciting the names of all their children who had died.

They'd had together thirteen children.

In other moments she thought that she felt something – almost intangible, but still a feeling – as though her second son, Edmund, had slipped his hand into hers, the way he used to as a child, sucking the thumb of his other hand. He was always more affectionate, more companionable, than her other sons; always a little overshadowed by his older brother. And then it threatened to undo her: she could feel a trembling inside, could not release the muscles of her jaw for such trembling, or rise for the weakness in her legs.

And so she remained in her room, awaiting news of her eldest son.

The Earl of March [when he heard the news of] the death of his father and loving brother was wonderfully amazed with grief, but he removed to Shrewsbury and other towns on the River Severn, declaring to them the murder of his father and his own jeopardy and the ruin of the realm. The people on the Marches of Wales, which above measure favoured the lineage of Mortimer, gladly offered him their assistance, so that he had a puissant army of 23,000 ready to fight against the queen. But when he was setting off news was brought to him that Jasper, Earl of Pembroke, and James Butler, Earl of Wiltshire, had assembled a great number of Welsh and Irish people to take him captive to the queen . . .

Hall's Chronicle

The Earl of March desired assistance of the town for to avenge his father's death, and from thence went towards Wales, where at Candlemas he had a battle at Mortimer's Cross against the Earls of Pembroke and Wiltshire . . .

Brut Chronicle

[And so] the Earl of March met with his enemies on a fair plain near to Mortimer's Cross on Candlemas day in the morning, at which time there appeared three suns and suddenly all joined together in one.

Hall's Chronicle

The noble Earl of March fought the Welshmen beside Wigmore in Wales, whose captains were the Earl of Pembroke and the Earl of Wiltshire . . . and before the battle, about ten o'clock before noon, were seen three suns in the firmament, shining full clear, whereof the people had great marvel and thereof were aghast.

The noble Earl Edward them comforted and said, 'Be of good comfort and dread not – this is a good sign, for these three suns betoken the Father, the Son and the Holy Ghost, and therefore let us have good hearts and in the name of Almighty God go against our enemies.' *An English Chronicle*

51

The Three Suns of York

It was so beautiful that for several moments he could hardly breathe or speak.

Two lesser suns accompanied the main one on either side, connected by a luminous ring or halo. As though the sky were so pure, a crystalline blue, that it had become mirror-like in its purity, reflecting the sun to either side.

His father, he thought, and his uncle, and his brother, translated into a triptych of celestial light. Tears stung his eyes as he contemplated the burning sky; its fierce, cold beauty.

But he was aware of a rising moan from his men, almost a wail of distress, and several of them bowed over, hiding their eyes. They could not see what he saw.

In a moment he had spurred on his horse and was riding among them.

'Good people,' he called. 'Brave men and warriors – don't be afraid. This is a good sign – a great sign of God's favour.'

He did not stop until they had all turned towards him; and he stationed himself so that the light of three suns shone on his armour.

'These three suns – come this day, before this battle – are the three sons remaining to the House of York.' He beat his hand against his breastplate. 'Myself and my two brothers will carry on the cause and the name of York, and we will, all three, be gloriously reunited before long. Like the Father, the Son and the Holy Ghost.'

He did not mention his murdered father, his uncle or his brother. They did not need a vision of the dead, but of the living.

'So be heartened by this vision God has sent you,' he cried, 'and let us go before our enemies in God's name!'

There was a short, absolute silence, then a wave-like movement began through the ranks of men, and in one line after another they sank to their knees in prayer, until the whole army was kneeling on the frosted earth.

Edward, Earl of March, sat on his horse and watched over them, thinking about his father, that dour and dogged man, whose mission he would now fulfil. The light of three suns was reflected in his narrowed eyes.

[Edward of York] was very tall of personage, exceeding the stature of almost all others, of comely visage, pleasant look and broad-breasted . . . [in the field he was] earnest and horrible to the enemy, and fortunate in all his wars.

Polydore Vergil

The Battle of Mortimer's Cross: 2 February 1461

On 2nd February 1461, Edward, Earl of March, the Duke of York's son and heir, won a great victory at Mortimer's Cross in Wales, where he put to flight the Earls of Pembroke and Wiltshire and took and slew knights, squires and others to the number of 3,000. In that conflict Owen Tudor was taken and brought to Hereford . . . this Owen Tudor was father to the Earl of Pembroke and had wedded Queen Katherine, mother of King Henry VI. Believing and trusting all the way to the scaffold that he should not be beheaded until he saw the axe and the block and the collar of his red velvet doublet was ripped off. Then he said, 'That head shall lie on the block that used to lie in Queen Katherine's lap.' And he gave his mind and heart wholly to God and full meekly he took his death . . .

He was beheaded in the marketplace and his head set upon the market cross and a mad woman combed his hair and washed away the blood of his face and she got candles and set more than a hundred of them around him burning.

Gregory's Chronicle

52

One Hundred Candles

It was happening, it was happening & I didn't want to know it. All those people out there watching, including the priest, so I ran into the church & I beat my hands on the statue of the Virgin, till she spoke to me like sometimes.

What are you doing that for? she says, and *Get off my robe.*

'Holy Mary, Mother of God,' I say, only I'm stammering so bad I can hardly say anything, & so I bury my face in the folds of her gown & weep.

Have you been a bad girl again, Mary? she says.

'No!' I say. 'I haven't – I haven't!'

But she knew all the same.

Mary, Mary, she sighs. But I wasn't bad – I wasn't. What would she know about such things – being who she is?

'Th-they're k-k-killing him, M-m-m–'

Mother, she prompts me. *Now you know I can't do anything about that, don't you?*

I did know it. The times I've asked for things she couldn't give. But this was different. They were killing him & his poor soul'd go to purgatory, which is a terrible place, full of owls & horseshit.

I tell you what, she says, when she can see I'm getting worked up. *Why don't you tell me all about it?*

That's her all over, hungry for news. She knows I have trouble telling my stories, but she likes to hear them anyway. She knows all the stories of the village. Everybody's business stored up in that cool stone head.

So I did. I calmed down & told her. How I was hanging round the alehouses again. And she tutted at me & said, *Mary,* in that tone of hers, but it's warm in the alehouse & sometimes they don't drive me away, but let me in for a bit of a dance in return for a drink or some pie. But this night they were in a mean mood & pricked my legs with their daggers to make me dance higher. And that's when he spoke.

'Gentlemen,' he says, 'that's no way to treat a lady.'

No one ever called me lady before.

'Tell her to get her great flat feet off the table then,' someone said.

He wasn't pleased. He shook his head. Then he turned to me & held out his hand, just like a knight in one of them stories.

'Madam,' he said, & there's that much catcalling & jeering I can hardly hear.

'If you would care to allow me to escort you away from this *uncouth* company,' he said.

I could've said, *Where to? To one of them barns where the hay's frozen like needles and the rats chew your hair all night? Or back to your room, with you?*

But there he was, holding his hand out like a knight to his lady, so I took it & leaped down, landing with a great thump at his side.

And he wrapped his cloak round me & we left, all that room staring after us!

Then all the laughter & jeers broke out again & someone slammed the door behind us, but I didn't care, with his fine soft cloak wrapped all round me.

He asked me where I was staying & I said nowhere, & he seemed content with that. I wondered where he was staying & if he would take me to his rooms, for we passed another inn. But he led me round the back, to an outhouse, & a dog barked at us from behind a gate.

Then he looked at me & said, 'If you spend the night here you will be safe enough, so long as you leave early in the morning.'

I understood by this that he was leaving, but I didn't want him to go, so I caught his hand & kissed it, then I pressed it up against my chest where my heart was knocking like a prisoner, & the look in his eyes changed, becoming wary. Then he smiled & tucked my hair behind my ear & then he shook his head & sighed.

And then he spread his cloak out, lovely, on the floor.

At this the Virgin whistles through her teeth, the way she does when she's displeased. But what does she know, being, as I've said before, a virgin?

And when he'd finished his business with me he rose & said that he would like to keep me company more, but there was to be a battle in the morning, & he had to lead his men.

That was a new one to me – not the usual reason they give, but I could see he wasn't joking. So I said, 'Will you come back to me after?'

What I meant was, *Will you stay alive?* But it came out wrong.

He smiled quite sadly & said no one could tell. Then he thanked me for my company & said he couldn't wish for a more pleasant way of spending the night before a battle. And still I didn't want him to go. So he took the ring off his finger & pressed it into my palm & told me to say a prayer to the Virgin for him.

And he was gone then, slipped away into the shadows, like a cat or a fox.

Or like all the other men you've ever known, the Virgin says. But I shake my head. 'He was kind to me,' I say, & she gives that little snort of laughter.

Yes, very kind, she says, meaning he used my body.

But I know men & she doesn't, & that *is* the kindness they give.

I can feel her withdrawing from me, very stern, because she always sees what's in my heart. So I clutch at her stone robes & beg her to help, beg her to intercede for him like she's supposed to. But she doesn't answer for a long time. Then she says, *See them candles?*

I look round. The church is full of candles, it having been Candlemas.

Go into the chancel, she says, *& there you'll find a bowl of water & a cloth. Take them & clean his head up for me – I don't want to see it all gore when he stands before me. Take it & clean him up & light all the candles you can see around him, so that I know which one you're talking about – & I'll see what I can do.*

At first I think she might be joking. She's played tricks on me before, just to see the priest beat me. And sometimes I've played tricks on myself, thinking it's her that's talking when it's only the voices in my head. But I go into the chancel & there sure enough is the bowl of water & the cloth & a taper for lighting with.

So I gather up all the burnt ends of candles into my gown & hold it above my knees with one hand & hold the basin & cloth with the other hand, & go out to the market cross to find him. Hoping I won't find the priest instead, but then it comes to me that if he strikes me I can offer him the ring. It seems the right price to pay.

All the people are scattering now in twos & threes, looking disappointed the way they do after an execution, like they expected something more – the Lord God, maybe, in a fiery chariot with a lot of fiery souls – & the bodies are being cleared away on a cart.

At first I don't recognize his among all the other heads – it looks different all drained of blood & the poor stump of its neck. Then I look to his hair, short grey stubble & the scar that stood out on his temple & see the pouches under the eyes. I don't want to look, but then I tell myself that this is for him, this head lay on my breast & I kissed it, & I mop away the smears of blood & the dribble from his lips.

'Holy Mary, Mother of God,' I murmur, 'look after him like you said. Take this man to you & spare him the pains of purgatory, for he is a good man.'

And I had a brief image of him being kind to her as he was to me, but I stopped it sharpish & I lit the candles so that she would know.

And no one stopped me so long as I kept her name on my lips all the time while I was bathing his head & lighting the candles, & no one laughed at all.

Not long after [the Battle of Mortimer's Cross] Queen Margaret, with the prince, the Dukes of Exeter and Somerset, the Earls of Northumberland, Devon and Shrewsbury, several barons and many others to the number of 80,000 fighting men, came towards St Albans. *Annales Rerum Anglicarum*

The northern men, with the queen and prince, made their way towards the southern parts and advanced without interruption until they came to the town and monastery of the English martyr Alban. In every place through which they came on both sides of the Trent but especially on this side, they robbed, plundered and devastated, and carried off with them whatever they could find or discover, whether clothing or money, herds of cattle or single animals, or any other thing whatsoever, sparing neither churches nor clergy, monasteries nor monks, chapels nor chaplains . . .

Whethamsted's Register

The northern men . . . swept onwards like a whirlwind from the north, and in the impulse of their fury attempted to overrun the whole of England. At this time too . . . paupers and beggars flocked from those quarters in infinite numbers, just like so many mice rushing from their holes, and everywhere devoted themselves to pillage and plunder, regardless of place or person . . . they also irreverently rushed . . . into churches and other sanctuaries of God, and most wickedly plundered them of their chalices, books and vestments . . . When priests and others of Christ's faithful in any way sought to resist . . . they cruelly slaughtered them in the very churches or churchyards. Thus did they proceed with impunity, spreading in vast crowds over a region of thirty miles in breadth, and covering the whole surface of the earth like so many locusts, made their way towards London . . .

Crowland Chronicle

The queen came south with a great fellowship to defeat the articles and conclusions taken by the authority of the parliament beforesaid. Against whose coming the Duke of Norfolk and the Earl of Warwick with a great people went to St Albans taking King Henry with them . . . *Great Chronicle of London*

On 12th February the king left London accompanied by the Duke of Norfolk, and went to Barnet. That same day the Earl of Warwick left London with a great ordnance to meet the king at St Albans. Meanwhile the Duke of Somerset and the Earl of Northumberland came from the north as far as St Albans, laying waste all the towns and villages that stood along their way. *John Benet's Chronicle*

53

A Great and Strong-laboured Woman

Oddly enough, it was not the news of the failure at Mortimer's Cross that troubled her, or even the loss of Jasper Tudor, who had fled and, some said, left the country, but the news that the Earl of Warwick had John de la Pole on his side, as one of the generals in his army.

John de la Pole, son of her great friend the Duke of Suffolk, for whom she had never ceased to mourn, and Lady Alice, his wife.

That little boy. She could see his small, pointed features even now. And the little girl, Margaret Beaufort, to whom he had been briefly married.

He was not a little boy any more, of course – what was he – eighteen? And married now to one of the Duke of York's daughters. The Earl of Warwick's right-hand man.

Even so, she did not know, she was not certain, that when the time came she could easily see him executed. She felt something quivering inside her at the thought of it; almost a sickness.

It was Lady Alice who had given her the advice that had helped her to conceive.

My own son is such a comfort to me, she had said. *And the thought that he is already married is also a comfort.*

But it was not in the queen to concede that Lady Alice might also feel injured. Such concessions were a form of weakness. She could only feel her own injury, the betrayal. When the time came – and it would, if God granted them the victory as He must – she would show no weakness. She would execute everyone it was necessary to execute.

She turned back to her advisors at the table.

She had surrounded herself with those young men – the new Duke of Somerset, the Earl of Northumberland, Lord Clifford – whose fathers had been killed at the first Battle of St Albans, and told them Warwick was their prey. After they had taken Dunstable, where a mere two hundred men had fought against them under a local butcher, she had sent out more than double the usual number of scouts. And they had come back with reports of Warwick's position. He was north of the town, they said, setting all his men to dig up the roads or block them with great nets full of nails and ditches filled with spikes, so that no man or horse could pass. He had brought the king with him, as hostage.

And while they took in this information, Warwick's own scouts arrived – or those sent out for him by his steward, Lovelace. Sir Henry Lovelace, Warwick's most trusted steward and leader of his Kentish troops, was working for her. Had she not spared his life after the Battle of Wakefield on condition that he would never take up arms against her again? And she had offered him money and an earldom for his pains.

Warwick had no idea that the queen was so close, the scouts said. And they swore that they would tell him she was more than nine miles away, to the north. All his attention was to the north, they said.

The queen rose and walked a little way from them. Her fingernails dug fiercely into her palms. Somewhere in her head a bird was singing. When she spoke, her voice was so soft they could hardly hear.

'Why then, we have him,' she said.

The Second Battle of St Albans: 17 February 1461

On 17th February the lords in King Harry's party pitched a field and fortified it very strongly, but . . . before they were prepared for the battle the queen's party was at hand with them in the town of St Albans, and then everything was out of order, for their scouts did not come back to tell them how close the queen was . . .

Gregory's Chronicle

The northern men . . . were forced to turn back by a few archers who met them near the Great Cross, and to flee to the west end of the town where, entering a lane which leads from that end northwards as far as St Peter's Street, they had a great fight with a certain band of men of the other army. Then, after not a few had been killed on both sides, going out to the heath called Barnet Heath, they fought a great battle with certain large forces, perhaps four to five thousand, of the vanguard of the king's army . . . The southern men who were fiercer at the beginning were broken very quickly afterwards, and the more quickly because, looking back, they saw no one coming from the main body of the king's army or preparing to bring them help, whereupon they turned their backs on the northern men and fled . . . The northern men, seeing this, pursued them very swiftly on horseback and, catching a good many, ran them through with their lances.

Whethamsted's Register

And so [as night fell] the Duke of Norfolk and the Earl of Warwick fled and lost the field . . . *Brut Chronicle*

They abandoned the king, who was then captured by the other lords.

John Benet's Chronicle

Succession

The queen and her party had the victory and caused the Earl of Warwick and his men to flee, and King Henry was taken and brought to the queen his wife, with whom was the king's only son, Prince Edward, a child of about seven years, and his father dubbed him knight . . . *Great Chronicle of London*

54

The Little Prince

After the king had knighted him, the young prince himself knighted thirty men, including Andrew Trollope, who knelt before him and said, 'My lord, I have not deserved it, for I slew but fifteen men, and they came to me while I stood still in one place,' and everyone laughed. Except for the prince, who stared solemnly forward with eyes fierce and bright as a kestrel's.

Only once or twice the direction of his gaze wavered, seeking reassurance in his mother's eyes. And she never took her gaze from him.

Then, after the ceremony of knighting, the prisoners were led forward. First came Lord Bonville and Sir Thomas Kyriell who had looked after the king during the fighting and had sworn that he would come to no harm. Everyone looked to the king, knowing that he had promised them mercy, and he smiled back feebly at them all.

So it was a surprise when the queen spoke. 'Fair son,' she said, 'what deaths shall these knights die?'

He walked forward then, conscious of everyone's eyes on him, on his soldier's brigandine of purple velvet, his jewelled sword which he thrust before him, first at one man then another.

'Let them have their heads taken off,' he said.

There was a small ripple of unease, quickly suppressed. Everyone present expected the king to speak, but he remained sitting with two fingers pressed to his lips, while the queen glared triumphantly at the two astonished knights. As they were led roughly away, Lord Bonville could not prevent himself; he said, 'May God destroy those who have taught thee this manner of speech!'

And the queen's eyes flickered for a moment, but her virulent smile did not fade.

The Lord Bonville that came with King Harry would have withdrawn as other lords did and saved himself, but the king assured him that he should have no bodily harm. Nonetheless, notwithstanding that surety, at the insistence of the queen . . . he was beheaded at St Albans and with him a worthy knight called Sir Thomas Kyriell, by judgement of him that was called the prince – a child.

An English Chronicle

This battle was done on Shrove Tuesday in which were slain 9,000 persons.

An English Chronicle

And on Ash Wednesday the queen and her party sent to London for supplies . . .

Brut Chronicle

She sent a chaplain and a squire to the mayor of London, requesting money, but they came back empty-handed . . . *John Benet's Chronicle*

And great watch was made in the city of London for it was reported that the queen with the northern men would come down to the city and rob and destroy it utterly . . . *Great Chronicle of London*

When the news was known here, the mayor sent to the king and queen, it is supposed to offer obedience, provided they were assured that they would not be plundered or suffer violence. In the mean time they keep a good guard at the gates, which they keep closed, and . . . the shops are closed and nothing is done either by the tradespeople or by the merchants, and men do not stand in the streets or go far away from home . . .

Newsletter from London, 19 February 1461

The queen and her party sent [once again] to London for supplies which the mayor ordained, but when the carts came to Cripplegate the commons of the city would not let them pass . . . *Brut Chronicle*

The mayor ordered bread and supplies to be sent to the queen and a certain sum of money. But the men of London took the carts and parted the bread among the commons . . . and as for the money I know not. I think the purse stole the money. *Gregory's Chronicle*

Then the northern men being foreriders of the queen's host came to the gates of London and would have entered the city. But the mayor and the commons fearing they would fall to pillage . . . held them out. *Great Chronicle of London*

The Duchess of York, being at London [then] sent over the sea her two youngest sons, George and Richard, which went to Utrecht. *Brut Chronicle*

This same time the two brothers of the Earl of March, George and Richard, were sent to Philip Duke of Burgundy for safeguard of their persons, which were of the said duke notably received, cherished and honoured . . .
An English Chronicle

[Then the city of London] dreading the manners and malice of the queen, the Duke of Somerset and others, lest they would have plundered the city, sent the Duchess of Buckingham and knowledgeable men with her, to negotiate with them to show benevolence and goodwill to the city . . . *An English Chronicle*

55

Duchess Anne Petitions the Queen

The night before she left the city the duchess had a dream, in which her dead husband was playing with their grandson. He had an elaborate toy, not unlike a convoluted abacus – although the beads were gold and silver and precious jewels – which he held out to the little boy, Henry, who pushed the beads carefully along one twisted pathway after another. There was hardly any light in the room and the beads shone.

They both seemed very absorbed in their task and didn't look up as she entered. She had to say, 'Humphrey – *there* you are!' just as if she had mislaid him and had been looking for him all this time, before her husband saw her. And there appeared on his face an expression of infantile naughtiness, which was the expression he wore whenever he played with their grandson, egging him on to all kinds of mischief. 'Sssh, don't tell your grandmother,' he would say, loud enough for her to hear, and the little boy, understanding that there was a conspiracy, would press his finger to his lips.

But the little boy didn't look up, he just went back to his game.

She didn't notice at first, so intent was she on her missing husband.

'Humphrey, where have you *been*?' she said, but the playfulness of his expression only intensified. He looked at the boy. And for the first time she noticed that their grandson was sitting on a throne; a small throne, adapted to his size. It gleamed dully in the gloom.

Also she saw that he didn't resemble their grandson at all. He was smaller, for one thing, with reddish hair.

But the duchess was not going to be distracted, not after so many months of mourning.

'Humphrey, I do wish you would tell me how these wars will end. And what should we do about the queen?'

But her husband only shook his head. His long nose seemed even longer in the half-light. He turned to their grandson. 'Don't tell your grandmother,' he said.

At this the little boy finally looked up. He had a pale, thin face, not at all like her grandson's, and he spoke to the duke clearly, in precise tones: 'She is not my grandmother,' he said.

The duchess turned back to her husband to ask who the little boy was, and what the duke was doing with him, but he had gone.

And the duchess woke, as she had done for many mornings, on the verge of tears. In the not quite light before dawn she lay in her bed, feeling weighed down, somehow, as if all the tears she had not cried had altered the composition of her body, making it heavier, and damp.

Certainly it was more prone to aches and pains.

She did not know why she was still grieving. She did not know that she had loved her husband so very much, only that he was a fact of her life, had been there for as long as she could remember, and was now gone.

She had to draw again the parameters of her life, and did not know how; that was it. Or maybe she was mourning the fact of mortality itself. And there was no cure for that, apart from the obvious.

The duchess shifted in her bed, then – feeling a certain resistance from her hip – lay still again, pondering the strangeness of her dream: the little boy, who was not her grandson, who had sat on a throne.

It was nonsense, of course. They had only the one grandson, after all these years, who was now Duke of Buckingham in his grandfather's stead, at the tender age of five. Her second son, Henry, had as yet produced no children from his marriage to Margaret Beaufort. She had meant to speak to her daughter-in-law about it on their last visit, but something had held her back. Perhaps the suspicion that it might be the fault of her son, a thought which she did not want to investigate. Her daughter-in-law Margaret already had a son, after all.

If the little boy in her dream was not her grandson, then who was he? It must have been her grandson. People often did not look like themselves in dreams. What was her husband trying to tell her – that their grandson would be king?

It was only a dream, and it was just as well. As if there were not enough contenders for the throne in this land.

The duchess made a more concentrated effort to move from her bed, tentatively testing her hip; whether it would stand if she got out of bed on the usual side, or whether she had better try the other leg first.

He had left her to old age and rheumatism, that was it.

But she would have to get up somehow, for that day she had to travel to the queen. Who seemed likely to besiege the city, and whose men were ravaging all the countryside about. The mayor and aldermen had pleaded with her to go, to exercise what influence she had, which was little enough, God knew, as she had told them. But they had said that the queen would listen to her, because both her husband and her eldest son had died fighting for the king. *Only you can save the city*, they had said.

What would she say to the queen? *Your majesty, you must moderate your men.* As if that would work. She was as likely to influence the weather.

Which had been atrocious lately. Freezing rain and snow falling in equal amounts, turning all the roads to slush. Even on the main road from London there would be cracks and great pools, and all the rivers were in flood. Why could people not wage war after Easter, as the Irish were said to do? Even if they were not attacked by the queen's men, who were running riot, it was said, they might not reach St Albans that day.

Still, she had promised to try. She would travel in a carriage bearing the queen's insignia, together with the Duchess of Bedford (who had been married to the king's uncle) and four of the aldermen. To ask the queen to be *pitiful and clement* in her dealings with the city.

Four anxious aldermen, her husband's voice said, *accompanying Duchess Anne.*

How he had loved his word games.

She hoped the queen would understand that she could not curtsy as well as she used to.

Making a concentrated effort, she managed to reach her bell and summon her maid, who helped her to get out of her bed and dress in her warmest clothes, her winter ermine, gathering up her grey hair into a hood. The maid held up a copper plate to her as a mirror, but the duchess barely glanced at it. She looked old, old before her time, but that did not matter, so long as she looked respectable. Because who knew the outcome of that day? If her husband knew, she thought, sitting down again with a grimace, he had not told her.

Which was just like him, she thought.

The journey was as bad as anticipated, though at least they were not attacked. And the queen's humour was, if anything, worse.

'The city of London has turned traitor,' she said. 'It has stolen our food and locked its gates. Against me, its queen.'

The two duchesses and the four aldermen remained on their knees; the queen had not given them permission to rise. The queen, on the other hand, was pacing about.

'How dare they?' she demanded. 'By what licence or law do they act in this way?'

Behind the duchess, one of the oldest aldermen began a quavering speech.

'Your majesty,' he said, 'it is only that the people are afraid.'

The queen whipped round at once.

'They *should* be afraid,' she said, 'but they are not. If they were truly afraid they would open the gates. They are defiant. Do they want my men to lay siege to the city?'

Duchess Anne did not know how much longer she could cope with the pain in her knees, her hip.

'Your majesty would have the right,' she said faintly. 'No one could blame you.' Her voice seemed to be getting fainter. The queen looked at her.

'Are you not well?' she asked, rather sharply.

'It is nothing, your majesty. Only my hip. And old age, I suppose. And – widowhood.' She managed a brave smile. And could sense a change in the queen's mood as she looked at her.

'Be seated, all of you,' she said peremptorily, and with a series of minor groans and creaking movements, the four aldermen and the other duchess rose gratefully from their knees and took seats at the table. Duchess Anne tried and failed to move, and the queen held out her hand. 'My lady,' she said.

The duchess took the queen's hand. Very small and frail it looked, quite belying her character. The duchess hoped profoundly that her weight would not pull the queen over, but pushing at a pillar with her other hand, she somehow struggled to her feet.

'You are in pain,' said the queen.

'My hip,' the duchess replied with a little gasp. 'It does not like the weather, your majesty.'

The queen nodded once. 'None of us like the weather,' she said. 'My men have travelled from the far north of this country, through drenching rain and snow. They have fought a great battle to save you all from murderous rebels and traitors. They are exhausted and starving, and how are they paid? By being locked out of the city they have defended with their lives.'

She was addressing them all, but none of them replied.

'You have travelled this day only from London,' she went on, 'and already you are tired and hungry, no doubt. I would offer you refreshments, but as you see,' she held out her hands, 'I have nothing to offer.'

Various appeasing noises came from the aldermen – it did not matter – they did not expect – it was too good of her majesty – but abruptly the queen's mood seemed to shift again.

'Come, my lady,' she said, 'let us sit together.'

Ignoring a glare from the Duchess of Bedford, who, as widow of the king's uncle, should have taken precedence, Duchess

Anne manoeuvred herself into a chair that was next to the queen and a little way from the rest of the group, so that when the queen spoke it seemed as though she were speaking to the duchess alone.

'I feel your loss very deeply,' she said, fixing her great dark eyes on the duchess's face. 'Your husband was one of our greatest friends.'

Unexpectedly, the duchess felt almost tearful. 'Ah, my lady,' she said.

'He gave his life to our cause.'

And my son, the duchess thought. Her eldest son – the light of her eyes. He, too, had died in these unending wars.

'We have both suffered,' the queen said. 'We both know what it is to be alone.'

She spoke as if she too had lost her husband, the duchess thought.

'We are women alone,' repeated the queen. 'Who is there to help us? Who will take our hand in our hour of darkness, or accompany us into the valley of the shadow of death?'

Well, about half of England in your case, the duchess thought, yet at the same time she was strangely moved by the queen's words, as if they had found a corresponding echo in her own heart.

Also she was aware of a sense of pressure from the aldermen and the other duchess. *Speak*, they were saying to her silently.

'Your majesty has many loyal subjects in the city,' she began.

'It does not seem like it,' said the queen.

'Oh, your majesty – they are as loyal to you as they have ever been – but they are afraid.'

'You said that before,' said the queen. 'Why should they be afraid?'

Of the great mob you have let loose across the countryside, no one said, *cutting a swathe of destruction thirty miles wide.*

'They seek your assurance,' the Duchess of Bedford said, evidently tired of being left out, 'that if you come to the city there will be no plunder or looting.'

And one of the aldermen said, 'If we have your solemn assurance, majesty, we will open the gates.'

'Do you bargain with me?' the queen demanded.

'No, no,' said Duchess Anne, almost laughing. 'We are begging for your grace.'

The queen looked at her and her sudden anger seemed to drain away again.

'What do you think I should do?' she said.

Aware of the full force of the Duchess of Bedford's glare upon her, Duchess Anne spoke almost timidly.

'If they could have some reassurance from you, your majesty – some words of comfort and hope – that we could take back to them, saying that you pardon them for their crimes against you, perhaps – and that they will not be harmed.'

'That your men will comport themselves with discipline and respect,' put in one of the aldermen.

'That people will not lose their livelihoods or their homes,' said another.

'And there will be no riots or burnings,' added a third.

The queen looked from one to the other. 'They have listened to rumours and lies,' she said.

Duchess Anne said, 'Then tell them, your majesty – tell them in your own words, that you, their beloved queen, will protect them like a mother.'

For a long moment the queen was silent. Then she said, 'They should take it for granted that I will protect them. Why do they doubt me – and not my enemies?'

'They have not heard you, my lady,' said Duchess Anne. 'They must hear your own words.'

The queen rose and walked to the back of the room, gazing at the tall windows. The four aldermen looked at one another, and towards the Duchess Anne. The Duchess of Bedford also seemed to be trying to catch her eye, but Duchess Anne gazed downwards, at the fine-grained wood of the table. Finally the queen spoke.

'They should not need my assurance,' she said, without turning. 'They should obey me, without requiring any proof.'

No one spoke.

'But I will write a letter,' she said.

LETTER FROM MARGARET OF ANJOU TO THE CITIZENS OF LONDON: FEBRUARY 1461

The late Duke of York, of extreme malice long hid under colours . . . has on an untrue pretence feigned a title to my lord's crown, royal estate and pre-eminence, contrary to his allegiance and several solemn oaths freely sworn by him, and fully proposed to have deposed him of his regality . . . [his associates] have promulgated several untrue [rumours] that we intend to . . . rob and despoil you of your goods and property [but] we desire that you know for certain that none of you shall be robbed, despoiled nor wronged by any person [in our company].

[The aldermen] . . . promised a certain sum of money to the queen and the Duke of Somerset, suggesting that he should come to the city with only limited numbers. Consequently certain spearmen and men-at-arms were sent by the duke to enter the city before he came: of these some were slain, some sore hurt and the rest put to flight. Immediately after, the commons, for the salvation of the city, took the keys of the gates where they should have entered, and courageously kept and defended it from their enemies . . .

Thereafter King Harry, with Margaret his queen and the northern men returned homeward towards the north, against which northern men as they went homeward, did harms innumerable, taking men's carts, horses and beasts, and robbing the people [so that] men in the shires through which they passed had almost no beasts left to till their land . . . *An English Chronicle*

And this was the downfall of King Henry and his queen, for if they had entered London they would have had all at their mercy. *Annales Rerum Anglicarum*

Less than an hour [after the king and queen left] . . . reports circulated that the Earl of March with 40,000 Welsh [was on his way] . . .

Newsletter from London, 22 February 1461

The Earl of Warwick met with the Earl of March beside Oxford . . . and he sorrowed sore for his father and for his brother the Earl of Rutland, and for the two battles which had been so costly. But then the Earl of Warwick informed him of the love and favour that the commons had for him, and that they wanted him to take the crown of England, and so his heart was somewhat made glad and comforted. But he was sorry that he was so poor, for he had no money.

So on the 26th day of February Edward Earl of March came to London out of Wales and the Earl of Warwick with him and 40,000 men with them both, and they entered the city of London . . .

Then came tidings of the coming of the Earl of March to London and all the city thanked God and said: Let us walk in a new vineyard and make a gay garden in the month of March with the fair white rose of the Earl of March.

Gregory's Chronicle

On Thursday 26th February the Earl of March and the Earl of Warwick came to London with a great power and on the Sunday afterwards all the host mustered in St John's field . . . Then it was demanded of the people whether Harry were worthy to reign still and the people cried 'Nay! Nay! Nay!' Then they were asked if they would have the Earl of March as king and they cried 'Yea! Yea! Yea!' Certain captains then went to the Earl of March's place at Baynard's Castle and told him that the people had chosen him as king. He thanked them and by the advice of the Archbishop of Canterbury, the Bishop of Exeter and the Earl of Warwick . . . he consented to take it upon him. On Tuesday 3rd March he caused it to be proclaimed that all manner of people should meet him on the morrow at St Paul's at 9 o'clock and this they did. Thither came the Earl of March with the lords in goodly array and there went on procession through the town singing the litany. After the procession the Bishop of Exeter delivered a sermon, declared the Earl of March's right and title to the crown and demanded of the people whether they would have him as their king as their right demanded, and the people cried 'Yea! Yea! Yea!' Then all the people were asked to go with him to Westminster to see him take his oath.

London Chronicle

When he came to Westminster Hall he alighted and went in and so up to the Chancery, where he was sworn before the Archbishop of Canterbury, the chancellor of England and the lords, that he should truly and justly keep the realm and maintain its laws as a true and just king. Then they put royal robes on him and the cap of estate, and he went and sat in the chair as king.

London Chronicle

Edward of York was at that time nineteen years old. *John Benet's Chronicle*

56

The New King

I could see the throne, a light coating of dust on the crest, a cold gleam on one corner.

This is it, I thought, *this is it, for which my father lived and died.* It seemed to grow luminous and shimmer in my eyes. A trick of the light, surely; great curtains of light were coming through the windows, streaming with dust.

It was not to be, Father, it was not to be, I told him, as if his dust too were streaming in with the light. Less than five months ago he had lain his hand on this same throne and turned to face the assembled lords. Less than nine weeks ago, he was killed.

Now, when I put my fingers lightly on the rounded edge, before taking firmer hold, I swear I felt his fingers descend with mine. And the hard surface grew warm.

And so I sat on it, as he never sat. And was deafened by the roar of approval from the crowd, as he must have been deafened by the silence.

To all the people which there in great number were assembled were declared his title and claim to the crown of England, whereupon it was again demanded of the commons if they would admit and take the said earl as their prince and sovereign lord, which all with one voice cried 'Yea! Yea!' Which agreement concluded he entered into Westminster church in solemn procession and there as king offered and after took homages of all the nobles there present.

Hall's Chronicle

Thereafter he went through the palace to Westminster church, where the abbot and a procession awaited him in the church porch with St Edward's sceptre, which he grasped, and so he went into the church, offered with great solemnity at the high altar and at St Edward's shrine, before coming down into the chair where he sat in the seat while 'Te Deum' was solemnly sung . . .

London Chronicle

[Then] he returned by water to London and was lodged in the bishop's palace . . . and on the morrow he was proclaimed king by the name of King Edward IV throughout the city. *Hall's Chronicle*

And so Edward, oldest son of the Duke of York, took possession of the realm of England at Westminster. *Brut Chronicle*

It remains to be seen how King Henry, his son, the queen and other lords will bear this, as it is said that the new king will shortly leave here to go after them.

Newsletter from London, 4 March 1461

And after the king rode north with all his lords to subdue his subjects and avenge his father's death. *Brut Chronicle*

57

Henry Stafford Receives a Summons

'I do not want you to go,' Margaret said. There was a tight feeling in her chest and throat because of all the words she could not say. Henry said nothing, but made a slight adjustment to the timepiece he had been devising from a series of weights and measures.

They had covered this ground before. The new king had immediately begun to send out commissions everywhere in the land. It was said that he would muster the biggest army that had ever been raised. He had promised to stamp out the threat from the north, the false king and his traitorous queen, who had sold Berwick to the Scots and allied themselves with that nation and with the French; both of them ancient enemies of England. He had promised that this would be the last battle: no more would the land be torn apart by war. Everyone who supported King Edward was promised rich rewards in the new Golden Age that would begin; everyone who didn't would be automatically attainted.

It was no longer possible to avoid this war

The people loved their new king. He was nineteen and had never lost a battle. He looked like their image of what a king should be: a towering giant with tawny hair; a great laugh that sounded most frequently on the battlefield.

But her husband was not going to fight for him. His father and brother had died fighting for King Henry; he could hardly fight for the opposing side now.

They had discussed this, and come as close to an argument as they had ever been. What would happen if King Henry lost? No one seriously seemed to think that he could win – even with the Scots behind him. And then what?

What about me? she wanted to say. *What happens to me if you are killed or attainted? How will I ever get my son back then?*

She had already lost so many people in this conflict. Her father, for one, if you went back that far. Her husband Edmund – still she could hardly say his name. Her uncle, the Duke of Somerset. And two fathers-in-law. She had cried, suddenly and fiercely, for Owen Tudor, as she had not cried for the Duke of Buckingham.

And also, of course, she had lost her son.

No one knew what had happened to Jasper, who still had custody of him. He had fled after the battle in which his father had been executed. It was impossible to get news, unsafe to travel or to send messengers anywhere in the country.

She wanted to say all of this, promising herself that she would not cry, but she could not trust herself. All she could manage to say was, 'I don't want you to go.'

And Henry listened attentively, just as if she had not said it before, moving tiny weights along a wire, saying nothing. He was not considering her. No one ever considered her.

Then he said, 'It is in Euclid, you know, the balance of equilibrium, the relationship between weight and force.'

She did not understand him. He said, 'I can no longer weigh my own life against this conflict. It will not balance.'

That was it, then. She was defeated by geometry. She turned sharply and left the room.

Later she realized that what she should have said was that she did not want to lose him. It was true, in fact: she had grown accustomed to his patient, conscientious presence; even to the silences between them. She had discovered that she liked being married.

She would miss him.

But she didn't say any of this. He concentrated on his plans for the new mill, she on the draining of a dyke.

She was inclined to blame her mother, who had taken it upon

herself to visit. Her own husband had joined King Henry and fought at the Battle of St Albans, despite his age. She had made many pointed comments, about *those who sat on the fence*, or who *kept themselves safe at the expense of others.*

Margaret had managed somehow to bite her tongue. There was so much that she could say to her mother, even though it was not strictly relevant: about why she had given her up, for instance, when she had kept all her other children, why she had not fought harder to keep her. Had she ever longed to see her, to hold her, as she herself longed to see her own son?

But she knew the answers, of course. She was the only one of her mother's children to be the daughter of a duke; her mother had not given her up entirely, they had continued to spend time together, and so on.

She knew the answers, and so there was no point asking the questions. But there was so much she did not know. Had her mother ever loved her father? How and why did her father die?

She could have asked, of course, but she would not get any answers. She thought of all the words that went unspoken in the world, throughout time: what happened to them, where did they go? What would happen if they were all spoken? How different would the world be then?

In private she prayed earnestly as usual, yet always with a hollow sensation – had she not prayed earnestly for Edmund, and for their son? She had discovered in herself a dull resentment against this God who never listened to her; who had allowed Edmund to be killed, her son to be taken away.

She discovered this in herself and it dismayed her – what God would listen to her now? Still, she went through the form of prayer, increasing her devotions if anything, and the frequency of her fasts. Her eyes reddened, her skin grew papery and dry.

She prepared a balm for Henry, because armour would surely set off the virulent outbreaks in his skin. In the bottom of the phial she dropped a tiny charm – a St Christopher – and she stitched a cross to his shirt. The night before he left she lay awake, wondering if he would come to her finally, actually hungering for him; she would cling to him through the night.

She could hear him moving restlessly around his room, but he did not come into hers. It was like a small death.

She fell asleep just before dawn, but on waking with a cold sickness in her, reflected that he would not come, of course. He would not run the risk of leaving her with child when he might not return. He would not put her through what she had been through with Edmund.

It came to her that no one had ever considered her in that way before, put her first or even taken her into account. Not since Betsy. But that was a thought she couldn't think. She made herself get up, though her limbs felt heavy.

It was a still, frozen day. Though it was March, winter still had its bone-hard grip on the land. The clouds were banked heavily, full of snow.

She gave him his gifts, which he received gravely, and said he was sure he would be invincible now. Then uncharacteristically he made a little joke, about how he had put on so much weight he might not fit into his armour, and she tried to smile. Then she was watching at the window as he set off with a few attendants, just as she had watched Edmund so many times. He turned to wave and smile at her, his face illuminated by the snow.

On the 13th day of March our new king, Edward, took his journey north and the Duke of Norfolk with him and the Earl of Warwick and Lord Fauconberg with many knights, squires and commons to the number of 200,000 men.

Gregory's Chronicle

58

The Baggage Train

Because they did not want to be accused of plunder, like the queen, they asked the city to provide them with a baggage train, to keep them well supplied all the way to York. And so many thousands of carts were provided, each drawn by horses, containing large quantities of: mutton, bacon, salted fish, dried beef, peas, beans, salt, flour, barley, oatmeal, butter, cheese, ale, wine, kettles, hooks, tripods, pans, cauldrons, ladles, dishes, forks, knives, spoons, pestles, shovels, axes, scythes, sickles, crossbows, arrows, guns, gunpowder, pellets of lead, spears, hammers, mallets, flails, staves, shields, breastplates, maces, caltraps, saddles, bridles, nets, tents, blankets, banners, dressings, heralds, trumpeters, singing boys, carpenters, fletchers, blacksmiths, servants, grooms, physicians, chaplains, cooks, bakers, armourers, wheelwrights, labourers, and followed by merchant victuallers, pedlars, prostitutes, beggars, mummers and minstrels. The sound of it rumbled across the land as it lumbered into motion, like a great beast . . .

And by easy journey came to the castle of Pontefract. *Hall's Chronicle*

59

Recruit

We felt it first before we saw anything, the grumbling & quaking of the earth. But then we saw it: mile after mile of men & horses, wagons & carts, all moving as to the beat of a giant heart.

We watched & could not stop watching. I did not know there were so many people in this land, all joined by one heart & mind, one purpose.

It was one of those moments that rarely comes, when you have to seize the chance to change your life & everything in it.

So I left my home & everything I knew, & went to join the king.

In March [1461] Edward IV marched towards York and, when he came about eleven miles from the city, he camped at a village called Towton. When King Henry knew that his enemies were at hand, he did not at once issue out of his tents since the solemn feast of Palm Sunday was at hand, on which he was rather minded to have prayed rather than fought, so next day he might have better success in the field. But it came to pass by means of the soldiers who, as their manner is, dislike lingering, that very same day, by daybreak, he was forced to sound the alarm. His adversaries were as ready as he . . .

Polydore Vergil

I stood in line, in the massed ranks, my breath coming out in the cold air & mingling with the breath of men & horses until it was one breath & us all one giant breathing animal. I thought then, *This is it.* This was the reason I left my home & set off with all the others on that great northward march. But I didn't say anything. I stood in line, breathing with all the others. Hoping to keep on breathing if we could.

Then I looked up & there was the first snowflake falling from a yellow sky, carelessly like, not knowing whether to land here or there, hovering over us before dancing downwards to its death.

And then there were more, thicker & faster than you could count them. When you looked ahead it was into a swirling whiteness, but when you looked upwards it was different, hurtling downwards like great black flakes of soot. Looking likely to bury us all.

The Battle of Towton: 29 March 1461

There was great slaughter that day at Towton and for a long time no one could see which side would gain the victory so furious was the fighting . . .

Jean de Waurin

The archers began the battle, but when their arrows were spent, the matter was dealt with by hand strokes with so great slaughter that the dead carcasses hindered them as they fought. Thus did the fight continue more than ten hours in equal balance . . . *Polydore Vergil*

A great number, eleven thousand armed men came against King Edward, all which with God's favour he killed manfully and put to flight. And then the king fought on foot, and many knights fled . . . *John Benet's Chronicle*

60

The Bloody Meadow

He lost his sword at one point, but fought on with an axe, which he drove down through the helmets of his opponents into their skulls. No one withstood him. Those who saw his gigantic figure looming suddenly out of the snow knew that their moment had come. He cut through them all easily as through blades of wheat. They collapsed or tumbled, some teetering sideways, others throwing out their arms in a series of awkward gestures, most dying with some kind of prayer on their lips. Like leaves in a forest, or blossom in an orchard, they fell, or like the whirling flakes of snow, dropping back into the earth from which they came. Until the new king felt like Aeneas in the underworld, walking among the dead.

Shortly it was difficult to move for all the bodies; the carcasses hindered them as they fought; and no one could see who was winning. Yet hour after hour the king raised his arm and drove it downwards; while the blood pumped in it he would not pause. And the weather was on his side, driving the enemy's arrows back into their own faces.

Then, when the fading light was utterly extinguished, and in certain places the corpses were piled almost to the height of a man, a great shout rose up from his lines. 'Norfolk! Norfolk!'

For the Duke of Norfolk, though mortally ill himself, had sent a strong force of soldiers who had finally arrived and attacked the left flank of the Lancastrian army.

And their lines broke, and panic seized them like the panic of wild animals in a forest fire.

Their ranks being broken and scattered in flight King Edward's army eagerly pursued them, cutting down the fugitives with their swords like so many sheep for the slaughter, and made immense havoc among them for a distance of ten miles, as far as the city of York. *Crowland Chronicle*

Of the enemy who fled, great numbers were drowned in the river near the town of Tadcaster, eight miles from York, because they themselves had broken the bridge to cut our passage that way, so none could pass . . .

Letter from George Neville to Francesco Coppini

So many were drenched and drowned . . . that the common people there affirm that men alive passed the river upon dead carcasses . . . *Hall's Chronicle*

After a sore, long and unkindly fight – for there was the son against the father, the brother against brother, nephew against nephew – the victory fell to King Edward, to the great loss of people on both sides. Of King Henry's party there were slain above 20,000 commons besides lords and men of name . . .

Great Chronicle of London

When Edward Duke of York had won the day at Towton he gave thanks to God for his glorious victory. Then many knights, earls and barons came into his presence, bowed to him and asked what they ought now to do for the best: he replied that he would never rest until he had killed or captured King Henry and his wife, or driven them from the country as he had promised and sworn to do. The princes and barons of his company said: My lord, then we must make for York, for we are told that Queen Margaret and some of her supporters have gone there for safety.

Jean de Waurin

61

Flight From York

Moments before the messenger arrived Margaret of Anjou looked up and caught sight of her husband's face. His expression was so bleak and stricken that it caused a qualm of terror to pass through her, so that when the messenger burst in and prostrated himself on the floor she was on her feet crying *No!* before he had even spoken.

The messenger sobbed out his desperate news, but before he could finish the door opened again and several men came in – Exeter, Somerset, Roos – all talking at once. They were saying that she would have to leave, now, without delay. The enemy army was even now approaching the city gates.

She could not understand this.

'Where is my army?' she said. 'Where is Northumberland? Dacre? Scrope?'

'Your majesty, there is no time,' said the Duke of Exeter. 'They are approaching from the south – we will leave by the north and head for the forest of Galtres. In the darkness they may not pick up our trail.'

Still she was more bewildered than frightened. It was midnight and the snow was still falling. She could not accept what Exeter was telling her. He was a man of few words and usually grim.

'My son – is asleep,' she said.

'Where is his nurse?' he asked.

Without waiting for an answer, he turned and began giving orders to one of his men to wake up the prince. Then he left the room abruptly, his men following, and she could hear him barking more orders at the servants. 'Get the pack horses ready,' he was saying.

Now a sick fear clamoured in her stomach. She swayed slightly and a hand grasped her elbow. But it was not Exeter, no – nor her husband, who sat by the fire with a look of desperate mourning on his face; no one was speaking to him. It was the young Duke of Somerset, pressing close, looking so much like his father that for a moment she was transported back to an earlier room.

She looked at him in blank bewilderment. 'Where will we go?' she whispered.

'We must return to Scotland,' he said, his voice equally low. 'By God's grace they will still support us there.'

'So we must fly – like thieves in the night?'

'And live to fight another day,' he said. 'While I live I will fight for you, my lady.'

But she could not take his ardour now; she could not cope with the pressure of his closeness. She moved away, pressing her fingers to her face. 'We must prepare ourselves,' she said, as though trying to convince herself of something she could not believe. 'Check that no one is still sleeping – summon them to the hall.' There was no volume to her voice; it was as though her throat were swallowing the words.

Somerset hesitated for a moment, but then he bowed and left the room. She was alone, with the king.

She stood facing away from him, clenching and unclenching her fists.

How could it happen? After all her victories – Ludlow, Wakefield, St Albans? Her great march south, gathering half the country to her cause? How could it be that everything was so swiftly lost?

The king spoke, surprising her; she had almost forgotten he was there.

'The land of Israel lies empty and broken,' he said.

She turned round to him. 'What?'

'He displays His power in the whirlwind and the storm.'

'What power?' she said. 'What – power – has allowed this – this catastrophe to fall upon us?'

The king lifted his hands, and let them fall. 'There is only the will of God,' he said.

'How is this God's will?' she said, her voice rising now. 'What

God would give you a kingdom and then take it from you – and destroy it?'

The king's face was full of grief, but he held out a hand towards her and it was hardly shaking at all. 'Marguerite,' he said tenderly, and then he smiled. It was that same smile, unique in its kindness, that he had given her at their first meeting, when she had been so foolishly reassured by it. She was not reassured now. She moved away from his touch as though he might contaminate her.

The king let his hand fall. 'The will of God,' he said, in a strained, breaking voice, 'is greater than any man – or king. It cannot be comprehended or imagined.'

He was asking her, it seemed, to comprehend him, to imagine him in the fullness of his misfortune, making the great effort – as only one so thoroughly acquainted with misfortune can – of acceptance. But it repelled her, this acquiescence, this passive acceptance of a disaster so great that she could not begin to understand it.

'We have lost everything,' she said, staring at him. 'What do we have? You are king of nothing – I am queen – of nothing . . .' She gave an incredulous laugh.

The king bowed his head. 'Naked I came from my mother's womb, and naked I will return,' he said.

'Stop it!' she cried. 'Do not give me your counsel of despair. It sickens me – you –'

She stopped herself saying it, but she knew from the look on his face that he understood exactly what she had been going to say.

But she would not take it back. They stared at one another, each of them wounded in a different way.

If you had been a different man, she was thinking, *a different king. If you had not deserted me when I most needed you . . .*

'I'm sorry,' the king whispered, as if he had heard her, and he began to weep soundlessly, tears spilling from his eyes.

She was appalled by him, by his grief, and by the magnitude of his acceptance. It was as though he had already known. She remembered his face before the messenger arrived – how had he known? It was this fey quality he had, this instinct for misfortune. He knew because it was in his nature to know certain things and not others. He was differently attuned, like the strings of an Aeolian harp that vibrate before any sentient being can detect the wind.

It repelled and fascinated her, this eerie knowledge that brought with it not power, but submission. She felt as though if he reached out to her now, or she to him, she would fall into an abyss. She turned quickly away.

'We must get ready,' she said. 'We have to pack up everything we have and go. Fortunately we do not have very much . . .' Her voice trailed away and she closed her eyes, because for a moment her mind would not think any further. She had the sensation of the ground giving way beneath her. There was only the abyss, and the king on the other side of it. Then she remembered herself: she was the queen, and mother to the prince.

'I must go to my son,' she said. Quickly, she left the room, and the king, and stepped into the corridor. Already servants were dragging boxes and trunks along it, and when she reached her son's room he was dressed and blinking in the torchlight, waiting for her to tell him what to do.

She sank to her knees before him and buried her face in his hair. This at least was real, he was real; the smell of him, the fine curling hair. She wanted to weep into his neck.

'We are going on a journey,' she said, and he did not protest, or ask why she was crying, but allowed her to take his hand and lead him out of the room and towards the great hall, where hundreds of others would be gathered, waiting for her to tell them what to do.

As soon as the queen heard the news, she and her people packed up everything they could carry and left York in great haste for Scotland. *Jean de Waurin*

King Henry, the queen, the prince, the Duke of Somerset, the Duke of Exeter, Lord Roos, be fled into Scotland and they be chased and followed.

Paston Letters

62

The Reckoning

The blood of the slain mingling with the snow which at this time covered the whole surface of the earth, afterwards ran down in the furrows and ditches along with the melted snow for a distance of two or three miles.

Crowland Chronicle

He could smell blood on himself.

The wind was blowing his own stench back to him, which was the stench of blood and mud and sweat. He had scrubbed the blood from his face, but it still stained his arms, his clothing. And he felt bruised, as though he had been kicked all over. His ribs hurt, and his sternum, though to the best of his knowledge he had not been injured there. But he could feel each breath he drew; it was slow and painful.

But it was his breath. He was alive.

The battle was over. He was king.

'I am king,' he said quietly, to himself or to his father, he was not sure.

Forty years of King Henry's hapless reign were over. The House of Lancaster was crushed. A new England could begin.

It began like this, with death.

He had sent his men out to gain some idea of the numbers of the fallen, and to cut the throats of any of those still living. He had commanded that no quarter was to be given, nor any prisoners taken; even the common soldiers would be killed.

Then he had walked out to see the battlefield for himself.

After yesterday's whirling storm and frenzied fighting it seemed preternaturally calm. A light breeze blew with only a few flakes of snow caught up in it, but many of the bodies were partially covered by the snow that had already fallen, and he was glad of this; he did not want to see the expressions on the faces of the dead, the way they looked up with their emptied eyes; and he did not want to find anyone who was not yet dead, whose sufferings he would be forced to end.

A powerful sense of strangeness afflicted him, as though he walked with both the living and the dead.

It was commonplace after battle, an eerie feeling, as though you were in some way still bound to those you had killed. But there was another sensation that was new to him, like a vast solemnity. As though only now had he seen what it meant to be king.

He had been proclaimed king already, of course, but nothing had brought it home to him like this, the battlefield thick with corpses, the air that reeked of death.

Warwick came towards him, limping badly but cheerful as he ever was, following great slaughter.

'Well, cousin,' he said. 'You have made your mark.'

The new king smiled affably enough, though he felt as though his face had stiffened. When he said nothing, Warwick indicated the bloodied snow. 'Red flowers on white,' he said, and the king nodded, and they embraced.

'This is the greatest battle ever fought on English soil,' Warwick said. 'In centuries to come soldiers will sing of it – they will teach warfare by the lessons of this day.'

He went on to talk about Norfolk's men, and the rout, and the other glories of that day. He did not mention his own achievement, though it was great. He had been wounded in the first battle, when his troops had been ambushed by Lord Clifford's men and seemed likely to flee. Undaunted, he had got down from his horse, hacking off its head before all his men in order to rally them to him. *I will live or die with you this day!* he had cried.

'You are very quiet, cousin,' he said. 'Are you thinking about the old king? He is as good as dead. Our men will find him, never fear.'

The new king smiled. 'I was thinking about my mother,' he said.

'Ah, she should have been here,' his cousin said.

The first herald returned to say that it was not possible to count all the dead – they were strewn all the way along the road to York, in a broad pathway some nine miles long and three miles across. The new king nodded slowly, and prodded a corpse with his foot.

'And we have the problem of burying them all,' he said.

'Is that all?' said Warwick. 'There are men enough left for that. That is a happy problem for a victorious king.'

King Edward ordered the herald to find enough men to dig the graves.

'Pay them extra,' he said, for many great pits would have to be dug.

Then he turned to his cousin. 'We should go to York,' he said, but Warwick replied that it might be as well to wait. For there was no one in that city who would not have lost a father, brother or a son, and the usual cries and lamentations would have to be got over with.

But the new king clasped his cousin's shoulders as if he would embrace him again, forcing the older man, who was at least half a foot shorter than the king, to look up at him.

'I will write to my mother,' he said, 'then I must go to York. I must take the heads down from the gate.'

Warwick did not ask which heads, or say that that task could be done by one of the king's lieutenants; he could see that this was a matter on which the king would not be moved.

And so they set off that day, riding along the corpse road to York.

And King Edward tarried in the north a great while and made great inquiry of the rebellion against his father and took down his father's head from the wall of York, and made all the county swear allegiance to him and to his laws . . .

Gregory's Chronicle

63

4 April 1461: Duchess Cecily Receives a Letter

She had to sit down to read it; her steward guided her to a chair.

She sat in the great hall of Baynard's Castle while all her household gathered round her.

She broke the seal on the letter awkwardly, her hands trembling. The trembling was new. It was as though, in the weeks since her husband's death, she had grown suddenly old.

And then she couldn't read it; her eyes blurred, then cleared, then blurred again.

But it was her son's writing. He was alive at least on 30 March, when the letter had been written.

Desperately she focussed her vision on the first line of his writing.

The field is won. England is won.

The paper drooped over her hand. She looked around at all the faces waiting anxiously, fearful, expectant. For a moment she couldn't catch her breath. Then she said, 'The Lord be praised,' and a great shout went up from the assembled crowd. For several moments she could not have been heard even if she had been able to speak.

Her steward leaned over her, asking her if she would take a little wine. Mutely she shook her head, then handed the letter to him. As the noise subsided he read aloud for her; all the details of her son's victory, how long he had fought, how many men had been killed.

She listened but could not take in the words; she could not believe it was true.

It *was* true. Everything they had believed in, had fought for, everything her husband and son and brother had died fighting for, had come true.

She had thought they had lost, but they had won. Her son had won. Tears started to her eyes. She closed them quickly. And then she felt it, her husband's kiss on her forehead. She moved her lips soundlessly.

'Thank you,' she said.

64

The World Turned Upside Down

Those who helped to inter the bodies, piled up in pits and trenches prepared for the purpose, bare witness that 8 and 30,000 warriors fell on that day, besides those who drowned in the river . . . *Crowland Chronicle*

The burying of the dead went on for many weeks, well into the sowing season. Then the corpses had to be left as they were, rotting in the fields, because there would be no harvest unless the fields were tilled.

There were fewer, far fewer men to till the fields.

And so much damage had been done.

After a summer of rains and an autumn of floods, then snow that went on into spring and slowly melted, the land was drenched. Fields turned into marshland, rivers burst their banks, streams flowed where there had been no streams before. Then there was the damage done by man; one great army after another trampling the roads to mire, destroying bridges, hacking down woodland, burning or plundering the crops.

It was hard to recognize the land. Those parts of it that had not been destroyed stood barren. Brown pools stippled the fields and reflected a sullen sky.

So many men who might have worked the land for last year's harvests had been conscripted into the queen's army or had joined the great train of men following the king. So few of them had returned. Small hamlets stood deserted, farms abandoned, doors hanging from their hinges and clattering in the wind. Crops had rotted in the soaked earth, diseases spread among cattle and sheep, so that famine seemed likely to follow war.

Corpses were left in open pits, staring sightlessly at the sky, while men returned to do what they could: digging ditches to drain the land, repairing bridges and roads sunk under the weight of wagons, mending fences, tending the sick beasts and the wounded men.

Those who still had homes repaired them and battened down the doors against those who had not, who grew feral in their homelessness. Those who had to travel on deserted roads armed themselves as well as they could. The homeless crept into abandoned barns or cottages for shelter, or banded together into armed groups, attacking anyone who passed.

Then one or two of the markets reopened. People gathered to sell what they could, to lament the weather and the rising prices, or to talk about the new king. As though by common consent, no one mentioned the old king, or the numbers of the dead. Like a wife well beaten, teeth knocked out, ribs broken, who will pick herself up as soon as she can, adjusting her headdress to cover the bald patches where her hair has been torn out or to shade the bruised eye, the people did not discuss their injuries or the possibility of it happening again, but focussed as though with shortened vision on the task at hand; the journey on broken roads, the difficulty of finding a carpenter or a blacksmith.

Still, there was a new king, and the people turned their faces towards him as though towards the sun. And put away despair and nursed what hope there was, for a new England had begun.

65

Fair and of a Good Favour

Later she would be called the most beautiful woman in all England, though this was difficult to ascertain, and not everyone agreed. However, they did agree that Elizabeth Woodville had the capacity to make people believe she was beautiful, with a smile or a sidelong glance. She had gilt-blonde hair that fell almost to her knees, and heavy-lidded eyes of an indeterminate colour. Those who disliked her said that they were dragon's eyes; but at a certain angle and in a certain light, they looked languorous rather than snake-like.

She had met the new king on several occasions before he was king. She remembered him before all the wars began, as a young boy at court, when she had been in the service of Queen Margaret. He had been perhaps ten or eleven years old, she seventeen, but she had seen the look in the eyes of that great overgrown boy even then. It was on that look that she was pinning her hopes now.

For her husband had died a few weeks ago, at St Albans, leading a cavalry charge against the Earl of Warwick. Her brother, Anthony, was in the Tower, and her entire family under the shadow of attainder, having fought for generations on the Lancastrian side. All the lands that had been given to her on her marriage were in dispute, her sharkish mother-in-law having put in a claim for them as soon as her son had died. And then, in that month of May, the new king had ordered the confiscation of all the property and possessions belonging to her father, Earl Rivers.

Deprived, that was how she felt in the wake of her husband's death; a response more primitive, more atavistic, than simple grief.

She had taken her two young sons and moved back to her father's manor at Grafton, where she had grown up.

She knew that King Edward had left York after the feast of Easter and was now progressing towards London to prepare for his coronation. She knew that he was stopping at several stages along the way to celebrate his great victory. She knew, this well-informed young woman, that he would be passing within a mile of her father's manor, and would stay at the hunting lodge at Stony Stratford, where he would take advantage of the vast parks and forest to ride out on the chase.

Her father had told her that she was wasting her time, and treading on dangerous ground. He had encountered the new king before. A little more than a year ago, he and her brother had been captured by Warwick and taken to Calais, where they had been roundly insulted by the earl and by his father, Salisbury (who was dead now), and by the young man who was now king. She could expect nothing from him, he told her. It would be better to lie low until the worst of the storm had passed. *Don't tempt fate*, he had said.

Her mother had told her to show a little bosom but not too much, and had given her an emerald necklace that brought out the greenish lights in her eyes. She had adjusted her daughter's hood so that some of the flaxen hair could be seen.

Be proud, she had said, *but not too proud*.

Elizabeth Woodville had promised that she would not be too proud. If necessary she would remind the new king that both their fathers had been knighted at the same time by the infant King Henry VI; that her mother was the daughter of the counts of Luxembourg, and King Edward was anxious to secure friendly relations with that country. However, it was on the look that he had given her so long ago that she was counting.

Accordingly she had dressed herself with particular care. Even as a child she had taken meticulous care of her clothing and possessions, only flying into one of her rare rages if one of her younger siblings had interfered with them in any way.

She made sure that her two flaxen-haired sons were as handsomely dressed as she before getting into her carriage. She knew the course that the hunt would take, the grassy plots where a feast could be laid out, and it was to one of these that she directed her driver now.

Her little boys wanted to know where they were going and when they would get there, but she ignored them, preoccupied as she was with the nature of her plea.

Soon the carriage drew to a halt and she dismounted, telling the driver to wait. She walked a little way from it with her sons, looking for a likely spot. The older one, Thomas, slashed at the grass with his short sword; the younger one, Richard, stopped to pick up pebbles. And both of them wanted to know when they would eat.

'This is no picnic,' she told them, taking hold of their hands. 'Keep your peace and wait.'

They went on complaining, of course, but being well acquainted with the resistant wall of their mother's will, the outward composure that only rarely flickered into rage, they did not press her too far.

The oak tree stood to one side of a clearing, spreading its great boughs more than halfway across. Its leaves stippled the ground with light and shade.

Here, she thought, pulling her sons towards it.

'Why?' said one, and 'I want to go home,' said the other, but their mother told them sternly that they were there to wait. It would not be long, she said.

And, in fact, it was not long. Her sense of timing, one of the gifts of the orderly, did not let her down. After a short while they could sense tiny tremors in the earth through the soles of their feet, then hear the drumming of horses' hooves.

Swiftly she adjusted her hood with jewelled fingers before taking hold of Thomas's hand again, in order to appear maternal, and also to prevent him from running away.

Then she stood still, outwardly languorous, inwardly coiled like a spring. Something of her tension must have communicated itself to her sons for they stopped their squirming protests and the three of them stood silent and watchful, staring out from the dappled shade with identical blue-green eyes.

The ground trembled as the noise from the hunt grew louder, and laughter and shouting could be heard.

Then the first riders appeared.

Still she did not move. She had admirably calculated both the distance and the angle of their approach, and they could not see her at first. Only when several riders had already passed did she step forward from the shade of the tree, putting back her hood at the last moment so that when he turned he would see her hair and her eyes. Then she called out in a clear voice, 'Your majesty!'

Several riders turned.

If the king did not turn round she would not call out again.

She lowered her eyes, sank in a deep curtsy to the ground, then raised her eyes again.

And the young king checked his horse, and turned.

This poor lady made humble suit unto the king that she might be restored unto such small lands as her late husband had given her in jointure. Whom the king beheld and heard her speak, as she was both fair and of a good favour, moderate of stature and very wise, he not only pitied her but also waxed enamoured of her. And taking her afterward secretly aside, began to enter into talking more familiarly . . .

Thomas More

And certainly, whatever conversation they had, it worked in spectacular fashion, for that June the king in his great clemency allowed all Elizabeth Woodville's lands and property to revert to her by writ of the Privy Seal. Her brother was released from the Tower, her father's offences were pardoned, and all the property confiscated from her family was officially restored, so that people wondered what charms and persuasions she could possibly have used.

Fair and of a Good Favour

When the king first fell in love with her beauty of person and charm of manner he could not corrupt her virtue by [either] gifts or menaces. Whose appetite when she perceived she virtuously denied him. But yet did she so wisely and with so good manner that she rather kindled his desire than quenched it.

Dominic Mancini

66

Consequences

[And King Edward] returned to London again and there he was crowned the 28th day of June in the year of Our Lord 1461. Blessed be God.

Gregory's Chronicle

Margaret Beaufort was certain in her own mind that her husband was dead. Henry was no warrior, she knew he would not return. She saw him stumbling around the battlefield in his ill-fitting armour. Mentally she prepared herself for the role of widow again; made plans to resist being married off once more.

She could not weep for him in the way she had wept for Edmund, but she did feel a crushing weight of sorrow. She was surprised at how much sorrow she felt. She hoped he had not suffered much, that he had not lain awake and wounded through the night, waiting for his throat to be cut in the morning.

Above all, she worried for her son, who was still at Pembroke Castle, as far as she knew, though nobody knew where Jasper was. Jasper who had taken her son *into safekeeping*, he had said.

She could not sleep. She could only lie in bed going over her anxieties as though probing a sore tooth with her tongue. Had her son's nurse stayed with him? Who was left to defend the castle? What would the new king do to those who had opposed him?

There was the sourness of anxiety in her mouth; her stomach was tight like a knotted rope.

Gradually the snow melted and there came news of the dead. So many lords were killed and their line ended. Her stepfather Lionel,

Lord Welles, was dead. She went to Maxey Castle to comfort her mother, who would not be comforted.

All the time she was waiting for her turn; preparing for her role as widow.

Then he returned.

She was so surprised to hear from him that she had to read the message twice, and felt a rush of blood to her head. She was not a widow. And she was glad. She had not known she would be so glad.

She ran to meet him when he arrived, to help him from his horse, and saw immediately that he was ill; not wounded, his squire told her, but ill. His eyes were entirely glazed. The affliction he intermittently suffered from had flared in him just as she had thought it would: great red welts had appeared on his face and body; he shook convulsively and cried out in his sleep; he thought he was being roasted in eternal fires.

She attributed the rash to the armour that had chafed his skin. But his breathing was laboured and his teeth chattered so that he could hardly speak. She sat with him and pressed damp cloths to the top of his head, which was sweating, and made compresses and cooling potions for his flesh. She believed herself to have healing hands. Sometimes when she passed her fingers lightly over a broken limb or a diseased organ she could tell where the problem was, as though her fingers were her eyes. There was a sense of trapped heat here, an absence of heat there. In another life she might have been a surgeon.

But she couldn't seem to heal Henry, though he had no physical wounds. When the fever passed he sank into an exhausted melancholy. Sometimes, while being fed or bathed, he would turn his face away and weep. His skin was still too painful for him to be held.

She stayed with him, hoping that when he recovered he would accompany her to find her son. Gradually he got better, but still he would say nothing about the battle itself, except that the wind had turned against them, blowing all their arrows back. 'The wind,' he said wonderingly. And the snow, through which they could hardly see.

Once he said he had been stumbling over dead bodies for what seemed like hours. The snow had filled their open mouths, covered their exposed eyeballs. Gradually it had covered the corpses themselves, and still he had gone on, slipping and stumbling over them, trampling on their faces and hands, without knowing which way to go.

That was what he dreamed about, when he cried out in his dreams.

The king and queen had escaped, he believed, but he had fallen behind and got lost. All he could think about was home. He had spent several days in hiding in woodland, or begging for bread from local farms, always doggedly returning home.

She rested her hand on his. 'You are home now,' she said, but she could see in his eyes that he was not home; he did not know what home was any more.

In May the king returned to London and received a hero's welcome. He made a proclamation promising good and just government, an end to the oppression of the people, the manslaughter, extortion and robbery of the old regime. But it was said that there would be further executions, that all those who had fought against him would be attainted and dispossessed.

In June the queen led an army of Scotsmen into England and attacked Carlisle, but they were driven back by the Earl of Warwick's brother, John Neville. Then King Henry rode south with an army to Durham, but they were driven back by Warwick himself.

King Edward promised pardons for all those who had fought with King Henry, who would now submit to him, and at last Margaret's husband roused himself.

'I should go,' he said.

Margaret wanted to go with him, but he said it was too dangerous. Everywhere there were uprisings and rebellions. For all they knew it was a trap.

In the end she accompanied him as far as London, and then he set off alone, with the pink welts still fading on his face, and begged on his knees for pardon, while she waited fearfully in their lodgings – without telling him she had written in advance, expressing her hopes and good wishes for the new king's future reign, that they could all live in peace now, as his loyal subjects, and that she would soon be reunited with her son.

When Henry returned he seemed surprised by the reception he'd had. The king had been most conciliatory, he said. They were invited to the celebrations following his coronation.

He sat down, still looking surprised.

'We must go,' she said.

'I suppose we must.'

'I want to speak to the king about my son.'

He looked at her.

'I do not think we can ask for any more favours.'

'I have to ask.'

The great hall was packed. Hundreds of burning torches were reflected in the golden ceiling, the polished floor. There were many ladies dancing for the king, in vivid colours, peacock blues, violets and saffron yellow. The king danced with some and watched several others from a long chair draped in velvet.

He looked magnificent, and at ease.

She did not dance, because Henry said, quite accurately, that he couldn't, but she watched the king closely, waiting for a moment to approach. He spoke to one courtier after another. His attention was caught by two of the ladies in particular, she noticed, one of them very young and dressed in a modest, peach-coloured robe, the other older and married, wearing a low-cut gown.

She edged closer, ignoring her husband's warnings. By the time she had pushed through the press of people, the king had moved, and was standing with a group of friends. She located him without difficulty – he was nearly a head taller than everyone else – and she manoeuvred herself towards him like a small, burrowing animal until she was standing quite close, but not in his line of vision. The king did not turn towards her. He continued to watch the dancing, making occasional comments to his companions, at which everyone laughed.

At last she stood by his side, feeling shorter than ever next to his great height, and waited for him to finish his conversation.

His hands, she thought, were very red.

Finally he looked at her, as a man looks and does not look at a woman who is not attractive to him, and she sank into a curtsy.

'The Countess of Richmond,' he said.

She made all the proper replies, and then rose. She had to angle herself backwards to look at him. If she looked downwards in proper humility he would not hear what she was saying because of all the noise. Conscious of this difficulty, she asked if he had received her letter.

'I have received many letters,' he said.

'I was writing about my son.'

'Your son . . .' he said vaguely.

'My little boy, Henry. I was hoping for your permission to see him again.'

'The young Earl of Richmond,' the king said, holding out his goblet to be filled.

'I have not seen him for some time.'

'He is with his uncle, is he not?' said the king blandly.

'I do not know where he is.'

'Do you know where his uncle is?'

'I have not heard, your majesty.'

'If you did hear I am sure you would tell me. I am almost certain of it.'

'I don't know where his uncle is – that is the problem –'

'It is a problem for me too. But I am hoping to remedy it soon.'

Before he could turn away again, she said, 'I was hoping that my son could be returned to me.'

'To you?' said the king, as if surprised. 'That is one possibility.' He looked at her consideringly, then said, 'How old is your son?'

'He is just four years old.'

'Just four. And heir to so many estates.'

'I have not seen him for so long – I do not know who is looking after him, or where he is . . .'

'He is in Wales, is he not?'

'When I last saw him he was at Pembroke.'

'We are having a little difficulty in Wales. Some dispute about the rightful lordship of the land. But I intend to resolve that as quickly as possible.'

'He – it is just that – I do not know what has happened to him.'

'We will find that out when we have reclaimed our castles there.'

She tried again. 'Your majesty, I would dearly like to see him again. I pray for him daily – that he will be returned to me.'

'Or to some suitable guardian.'

'I think that I would be his most suitable guardian – while he is so young.'

The king did not answer immediately and she was afraid that she had said too much, but then he smiled at her, that charming smile that did not charm her.

'You can be sure that I will give it my full consideration,' he said. And she knew she had been dismissed, that there was nothing more to say.

10th August 1461: Commission to William Herbert, knight, to take into the king's hands the country and lordship of Wales and all castles, lordships, manors and possessions late of Jasper, Earl of Pembroke, a rebel . . .

Calendar of Patent Rolls

4th October 1461: All the castles and strongholds in north Wales and south Wales are given and yielded up to the king's hands. And the Duke of Exeter and the Earl of Pembroke are flown and taken to the mountains and several lords with great power after them. *Paston Letters*

12th February [1462]: Grant to William Herbert, king's knight, for £1,000 in hand, paid for the custody and marriage of Henry [Tudor], son and heir of Edmund Earl of Richmond, tenant in chief of Henry VI, in the king's hands by reason of his minority. *Calendar of Patent Rolls*

She sat by the window of her room with her eyes closed as though she were praying, but she was not praying. She had used up every prayer she had. In her hands she held the book of hours given to her by Margaret of Anjou, so long ago. She remembered, even now, feeling disappointed by the gift.

When you write in it, think of me, the queen had said. But she had not written in it. And now she wanted to write, but she did not know what, or how. So much had happened, she did not know where to begin.

They had not been able to travel to Wales, because of the fighting there. Jasper had fought a battle near Caernarvon and lost, and not been heard of again. Then, in the king's first parliament that November, her mother's husband, Lord Welles, had been attainted posthumously and all his lands and possessions had reverted to the king. But Margaret's own possessions had been protected.

The parliament had dragged on, and it was not until February that the blow fell. That 'cruel man, prepared for any crime' now had possession of her son.

When she closed her eyes she could see an image of a little boy wandering along the corridors of a great house, alone and frightened. He was about the same age as she had been when she had met the Duke of Suffolk. But she could not bear to think of him in that way. She of all people knew what it was to be alone, without a mother, at that tender age.

The hiss of rain at the windows reminded her of that earlier room that she could not quite remember. Where the duke had shown her his map of the world.

And now that world had changed. England had changed. So many of the ruling dynasties of the land had been wiped out, the relationship between the north and south of the country permanently altered – the border with Scotland had changed. And all the territories in France were lost.

She ran her fingers round the edges of the book. They were not quite steady, her fingers.

Her lips pressed together in an uneven line. She opened the book at the last page, which was blank, feeling the texture of the paper, which was not quite smooth. She picked up the quill and dipped it into the pot of ink. Because her hand was not steady, a small scatter of droplets flew across the page. She looked at them with a pang of self-reproof as they sank into the paper, then wiped her eyes and pressed the quill down a little harder than was necessary.

EXTRACT FROM THE SECRET CHRONICLE OF MARGARET BEAUFORT

In this year, being the first year of the reign of King Edward IV, Henry Tudor, only son and heir of Edmund, late Earl of Richmond, and Margaret, Countess of Richmond, was taken from the custody of his uncle, Jasper Earl of Pembroke, and given to one who had caused the deaths of his father, Edmund, and grandfather, Owen, for the duration of his minority, he being at that time four years old, and the right of his marriage awarded to the same.

She paused to press the heel of her hand to her eyes.

Contrary to the will and expectation of his mother, who was wonderfully grieved by this judgement, cast down utterly and brought so low that she could not see how she might once again begin to rise.

About the Chronicles

chron-i-cle: A factual written account of important or historical events in the order of their occurrence.

England has a rich and varied tradition of chronicle writing. Most early chronicles were written by monks and associated with the great monastic houses, which often had a designated chronicler. The most famous example of this was the monastery of St Albans, a great Benedictine house one day's journey from London, and thus well placed to receive important guests – monarchs and aristocrats, papal nuncios, etc. – and to record contemporary events in the capital and all over Europe. John Whethamsted, abbot of St Albans from 1420–40, and then from 1452–65, encouraged the compilation of Registers, recording local history (including the accounts of the two battles of St Albans), and may have written some of these himself.

The monastery of Crowland provided a chronicle with continuations that conclude in 1486, and seem not to have been written by a monk, but by a bishop or lawyer who was staying in the monastery.

By the fifteenth century the monastic tradition of chronicle writing was in decline. The Lancastrian kings, however, from Henry IV onwards, were great patrons of literature. Humphrey, Duke of Gloucester, fourth son of Henry IV, effectively created the university library at Oxford by his great gifts of books. In the reign of Henry VI, various colleges at both Oxford and Cambridge were founded, including King's College, Cambridge, and Eton College, Windsor, and in the reign of Edward IV, William Caxton brought his printing press to England.

As a result there was a greater variety of chronicle writing than ever before. The *Brut* – a French history of England which begins in legendary pre-history and concludes (in continuation) in 1461 – was widely popular in the fifteenth century and printed by Caxton in 1480. A further continuation, usually ascribed to John Warkworth, Master of Peterhouse, Cambridge, covers the first thirteen years of the reign of Edward IV.

Latin was still widely used as the language of chronicle writing. The chronicle attributed to John Benet, vicar of Harlington, was written in Latin. John Rous, an antiquary from Warwick, wrote his histories in both English and Latin, and John Blacman wrote his memoir of Henry VI after the death of the monarch also in Latin. The *Chronicon Angliae*, sometimes known as *Giles' Chronicle* after its nineteenth-century editor, is an anonymous Latin chronicle written by a cleric at the end of the 1450s containing an account of the reign of Henry VI, and the *Annales Rerum Anglicarum* is a Latin compilation of short, disconnected narratives. However, in this period the English language finally replaced Norman French and Latin as the language of literature. This seems to have opened the field to popular readership and a number of freelance writers of chronicles in English. John Hardyng, a north country squire who fought at Agincourt, presented a verse chronicle to Henry VI in 1437, which was critical of the lawlessness of the reign. William Gregory, a London skinner, sheriff and mayor, wrote his *Historical Collections of a Citizen of London* in English, though since the chronicle finishes three years after his death in 1467 it is assumed that there is an anonymous continuator.

A new group of chronicles came from the towns. These civic narratives were all written in the vernacular, and most were centred on London – *The Great Chronicle of London*, *Chronicles of London* and *The Short English Chronicle* were all written at this time. The author of *The English Chronicle* is unknown, but it seems to have been written soon after Edward IV came to the throne in 1461, and like the *Brut* is strongly Yorkist in sympathies. These chronicles were described by their editor C. L. Kingsford as 'rude and artless' but they are a great source of information about English history in the fifteenth century.

Other accounts of the period are written by foreign emissaries. These include Jean de Waurin, a soldier who fought for the French at Agincourt, and Philippe de Commynes, who wrote his memoirs at the court of Louis XI of France. Domenic Mancini, an Italian poet, was sent from the court of Louis XI to report on English affairs. He provides a particularly valuable account of the usurpation of Richard III.

Polydore Vergil, Italian cleric and Renaissance humanist historian, came to England in 1502 and was encouraged by Henry VII to write a comprehensive history of England, an Anglica Historia, which was not finished until 1531. He has sometimes been called the 'father of English history', and his epic work marks a shift in historical writing towards the 'authorized version' that could be printed and widely distributed throughout the known world.

None of these chronicles, however, can be said to be definitive. They are partisan, contradictory, unreliable in certain respects, but also vivid and readable accounts of a tumultuous period of English history. Their approach to writing and to history is very different from that of the contemporary historical novel; they convey the spirit of the age without resorting to interior perspective or reflection. It seemed to me that the different approaches were complementary, and might usefully be brought together.

Acknowledgements

The author is especially indebted to the Royal Literary Fund, for financial support and employment throughout this project.

Several people were helpful to me while I was writing this novel. Especial thanks are due to Fergus Wilde and Josie Christou for help with the Latin translations; to the librarians of the Chetham's and John Rylands libraries; to Liz and Tom McIlroy for taking me to Pembroke Castle, and to Dave and Jackie Lamb for their hospitality while I was there. Ian Pople supplied me with books and Ian Hunton helped me through several computing crises. Ben Pople and Alan Parry also rendered a similar service with patience and goodwill. I owe a big thank you to my readers, Anna Pollard, Anthony Taylor and Paul Andrews, for supportive and discerning comments. I am especially grateful to Anna for her unstinting support, optimism and help with the family tree. And last (but not least) thank you to my agent and editor for more helpful comments, and for taking me on!

read more

LIVI MICHAEL

REBELLION

This second book of Livi Michael's Wars of the Roses trilogy continues the story of Margaret Beaufort and Margaret of Anjou – two women who will stop at nothing to place their sons on the English throne . . .

In exile in France with her young son Prince Edward, Margaret of Anjou at last gives up on promises of aid from King Louis and sets sail for England. There, she will return her husband Henry to the throne – and ensure young Edward will be its heir.

Meanwhile, Margaret Beaufort, separated from her son Henry of Richmond when he was an infant, sees the unrest surrounding the Lancastrian defeat as her chance to finally get him back. But the steps she takes to return her son imperil the kingdom and the throne's current occupant – King Edward IV.

With rebellions tearing the country apart, how far will each woman go to further the interests of their sons? And who can stand in their way?

'Has the colour and power of the best of the chronicles she uses' *Sunday Times* on *Succession*
'Her writing is superb, her sense of time and place immaculate.' Berlie Doherty, author of *Treason*